PRAISE FOR OLESYA LYUZNA & GLITTER IN THE DARK

"Lyuzna will leave you gasping with her twists. *Glitter in the Dark* is not to be missed."
NEKESA AFIA, author of the Harlem Renaissance Mystery series

"A sparkling debut, more fun and sexy than a bathtub full of gin."
LEV AC ROSEN, author of the Evander Mills mysteries

"An utterly alluring dance through Jazz Age New York City . . . Lyuzna weaves a gold-threaded tale of glamour and danger. A striking debut."
MEGAN ABBOTT, *New York Times* bestselling author of *Beware the Woman*

"Lyuzna lays on the period detail and springs surprises just where you don't expect them. A colorful period debut that's clearly laying the groundwork for a series."
KIRKUS

"*Glitter in the Dark* is first-rate noir fiction that shimmers brighter than the sequins on a chorus girl's costume, and its mystery will leave you breathless."
TESSA WEGERT, author of *The Coldest Case*

T0356241

"Lyuzna's prose is razor-sharp, and she immerses the reader in Roaring '20s New York, full of hot jazz, Ziegfeld stunners, and murder most foul. I can't remember the last time I was this excited about a debut!"

HALLEY SUTTON, *USA Today* bestselling author of *The Hurricane Blonde*

"This debut turns back the clock with authentic detail and sharply drawn characters and a strong sense of violence and lawlessness."

FIRSTCLUE

"Ginny sits comfortably among the ranks of classic private eyes, with all the moral ambiguity and world-weariness noir fans could want—plus a welcome dash of queerness, courtesy of a sapphic romance subplot."

PUBLISHERS WEEKLY

"Quick-paced and action-packed . . . Historical fiction fans will enjoy the cultural references, while mystery fans will relish the intricate and dangerous web Ginny and her loved ones must navigate."

BOOKLIST

"Unlikely detective Ginny Dugan shines as she tracks a killer through the glamorous and gin-soaked speakeasies, parties, and bedrooms of Jazz Age Manhattan. *Glitter in the Dark* is a stunning, sexy, and sparkling debut!"

JENNY ADAMS, author of the Deadly Twenties Mystery series

GLITTER IN THE DARK

OLESYA LYUZNA

THE MYSTERIOUS PRESS
NEW YORK

To all my lovers—
If I could live my life again, I'd make the same mistakes, only sooner.

◆

GLITTER IN THE DARK

Mysterious Press
An Imprint of Penzler Publishers
58 Warren Street
New York, N.Y. 10007

First Mysterious Press edition

Interior design by Maria Fernandez

Library of Congress Control Number: 2024941954

Paperback ISBN: 978-1-61316-597-3
eBook ISBN: 978-1-61316-598-0

10 9 8 7 6 5 4 3 2 1

Printed in the United States of America
Distributed by W. W. Norton & Company

CHAPTER ONE

I t's long past midnight, but Ginny Dugan is wide awake as she jumps out of the cab on Lenox Avenue, stretching her arms toward the sky, the lights of Harlem's finest nightclubs bouncing off the blue scales of her dress. Tonight, these swank joints will draw big crowds with their velvet cords and gleaming silverware, promising polite waiters and dancers who never stop smiling. Ginny's been around long enough to know better. The best thrills in this city are hidden in the shadows, and you can catch some real sparkle if you don't mind getting your hands dirty.

Mary has to hurry in double time to catch up with Ginny's quick steps. A few stray curls come undone from her barrette, the scarab beetle in its center winking in the low light.

"You sure this is the place?"

The dull yellow streetlamp flickers against an old brownstone with no distinguishing marks except a crooked bronze eighty-three. As the summer breeze rattles a discarded newspaper past the entrance, Ginny wonders if they made a wrong turn. But the rhythmic hum beneath their feet is unmistakable, and her painted lips stretch wide as she pulls her friend toward the door.

"There's no doubt about it. This is our night, Mary, just you wait."

A panel in the steel door slides sideways, revealing a pair of skeptical eyes. Ginny rises to the challenge, the words leaping off her tongue as hard and fast as she can manage.

"Mayday, honey, and make it snappy."

The passcode works, even if the charm rings off-key.

The door swings open to a short flight of steps down to the basement, with tiny windows fogged by the heat of dancing bodies. As her eyes adjust to the dim, Ginny soaks up the view. Every vice is served up in style. Showgirls cuddle close to the picture executives who pay their bills, their bright eyes wide-open for bigger prizes. College boys gather by the bar, trading vials of white powder to soar higher than Daddy's skyscrapers. Con men from all walks of life dart through the shadows, pawning easy smiles for padded wallets, their fake diamond cuff links distracting from the dirt beneath their fingernails.

Before long, Ginny and Mary are in the thick of it, knocking limbs on the crowded dance floor, with the full-throated bass notes of a tuba echoing through their bones. The band pounds through the song at breakneck speed, the musicians locking eyes with each other, barely looking at their rapid-fire fingers dancing across the keys.

"And now," the presenter slides into center stage as the music breaks, white teeth flashing, "it's ladies only!"

Ginny grabs two glasses filled with silver-green liquid from a nearby waiter, passes one of them to Mary, and the juniper prickle shoots a new idea into her mind. Through the haze, Mary's blue eyes are dark as wishing wells.

"What about it?"

Mary's up to the task, so Ginny grabs her by the arms and soon they're spinning into dance, the crowd roaring louder as they cut across the floor, narrowly avoiding two women in matching suits locked in a passionate embrace. The blue fringe on Ginny's dress mixes with Mary's silver sequins until they're blurred together, crashing through the club like a tidal wave. Ginny's face hurts from smiling, but she can't stop, the smoke and the sweet perfumes driving her to dizzying new heights as they spin, faster and faster until the song ends and they collapse against the bar.

It doesn't take long for the admirers to swarm to their side, flashy college boys raising their arms for another round. Ginny checks her wristwatch. Only took five minutes to get some suckers to buy them drinks. She throws a triumphant wink at Mary, who sits with her legs swinging against the bar, swiping the sweat from her forehead with the back of her hand. But Mary's attention is elsewhere as the glittering drinks are served, so Ginny nudges her in the side, ignoring the dark-haired guy going on about his daddy's investment company.

"You really think we'll see her tonight?" Mary says with a sigh. "This doesn't look like the place—"

"My sources never lie." Ginny gets her tips from a handful of coat-check girls and powder-room attendants, and this time, it took her much longer to get them to spill. Even her chattiest sources are getting nervous, whispering about heart attacks in Harlem, their friends dropping dead in the middle of the dance floor. Out loud, they blame the heat wave, but suspicions linger between the lines, something more sinister lurking just out of sight. She can't blame them for giving her a hard time.

Still, her sources finally gave up the goods, and they've never been wrong before. Josephine Hurston is a tough act to catch, but if she's singing anywhere tonight, it should be here. Ginny's nerves hum like electric wires, but Mary doesn't seem to share her enthusiasm. She keeps flicking looks at the dance floor, eyes brimming with sorrow. "You've got your front desk face on. What's the deal?"

"Oh, nothing," says Mary, shrugging around a half-hearted sip of gin. "Got any friendly advice for a secretary on the far side of her twenties still chasing hopeless dreams?"

Ginny drops her glass and turns toward Mary. It's an old joke between the two of them, pretending Ginny's dead-end advice column is more than an afterthought, stuck in the back of each issue of *Photoplay* with all the ads. Mary's eyes crinkle with amusement, but there's a sad note in her voice that makes Ginny wonder what's bothering her friend.

Ginny takes another look at the careful rouge spread across Mary's cheeks, the brand-new dress that must've cost her half a month's wages. She's expecting someone. "Who's the guy?"

Mary's mouth falls open. "How did you guess?"

"That's why they pay me the big bucks." Ginny downs the rest of her drink, trying not to cough up the fumes. "Honestly, I don't know why I bother anymore. Quirk always wants me to write the same damn things. Be patient with your man, and maybe he'll put a big old handcuff round your finger. Be a good girl, and if you're lucky, you can look forward to thirty-odd years of dull petting with the lights off."

This statement draws a raucous wave of laughter from the college boys, and Ginny's drink fills before her eyes. Mary's silent at her side, running circles around her glass with her fingers. The dark-haired guy digs an elbow into the bar, watching Ginny through narrowed eyes.

"You play it tough, but I bet you're all talk." His words come in a careless drawl, and Ginny feels heat prickling her cheeks. The alcohol thrums through her veins, and she turns toward the guy, chin hiked into the air.

"What are you saying?"

"When it comes down to it, I bet you'd give up all the dancing and drinking for a handcuff of your own. Just like any other woman."

Now he's just asking for trouble. With his buddies flanking him on both sides, the guy flips a long lock of hair from his forehead with a satisfied smirk, flicking a silver lighter open so the flame dances high above the bar.

"I'll be right back." Mary's candy-scented breath is soft on her neck.

Ginny waves her away, her attention flush on the guy in front of her. "I bet I could drink any of you guys under the table."

As she reaches for her gin glass, his expression changes, and he shakes his head. "Gin's too easy. Let's say we raise the stakes?"

He motions to the bartender, who bends down for a moment before returning with a fat black bottle, the label peeling with age. There's no telling what's inside. Ginny unscrews the cap and takes a sniff. The smell hits her hard, like rubbing alcohol mixed with burnt sugar, and she recoils, fighting the urge to gag. This feels like one of Dottie's cautionary tales, the ones about clueless little girls getting poisoned with dirty bootleg, about iodine-based Yak bourbon, Panther whiskey mixed with fusel oil, the kind of stuff that puts murderous thoughts in your mind before you go blind. The bottle feels hot beneath her fingers, and a shiver at the base of her skull makes her wonder if she's making the worst mistake in her life.

But then the guy pulls the bottle away, quirking an eyebrow at his friends. "Thought so. Told you guys she didn't have the stomach—"

Ginny heaves a deep breath, pressing her palms against the bar. She knows his type, these overfed rich boys with the insolent stares skimming right past you. She's entertained guys like these at every party hosted by her social-climbing mother back in Kansas, watched her sister Dottie spinning in their arms at every dance, listened to their overbearing stories as they looked down their noses with those patronizing smiles glued to their lips.

If anyone should be taught a lesson, it's guys like these—and with her liquor tolerance, she's just the woman for the job. Call it community service. She'll be doing the world a favor by knocking that inflated ego down a couple notches.

"Winner gets the lighter," she says, pointing at the solid silver box between his fingers.

"That's hardly fair. What do I get if I win?"

"Whatever you like," she says. "Doesn't matter, 'cause you've already lost."

He sure likes that, and wastes no time whispering exactly what kind of prize he wants in her ear. Licking his lips, he pours equal drinks into their empty glasses, the dark brown liquid thick as molasses. His friends are already taking bets. Ginny catches the silver blur of Mary's dress on the other side of the room, looking up at some older guy with his back to the bar, square shoulders straining against a midnight blue suit. She feels a pang of irritation. Mary sure has rotten timing, but luckily Ginny's had plenty of experience fending for herself.

When the time comes, she tips the glass down her throat, hoping this isn't the way her life ends, on the wrong side of a stupid dare in a speakeasy where no one will ever find her body.

The liquor is sticky sweet in her throat, burning like a bad cold. She coughs into her elbow. The other guy finishes his glass with some effort, his eyes unfocused as he wipes his lips. His friends pour another round, they're yelling words of encouragement, but it's like she's underwater, the voices drowned out by the dull thud of her own heartbeat.

Ginny throws back another glass. The world goes dim. Pinpricks of male laughter break through the fog, and then she sees the silhouette of the dark-haired guy dropping his glass in defeat.

"She makes you look like a real daisy, Hart." One of the guys claps him on the back, and Ginny resurfaces, her smile spreading slow and warm across her face.

"What's in this?" she says, dragging her fingertips against the bottle. Tastes like whiskey mixed with sugar and something else, a medical twist like cough syrup. Either the guys don't hear her, or they just don't care, because the silver lighter is the only answer she gets.

Her eyelids grow heavy, and she slumps against the bar, fingers curling around her prize. Dark thoughts trickle through her mind as she remembers the day at the office, banging out her answers to all those letters until she couldn't take another word. Those small-town girls with their celluloid dreams, looking to *Photoplay* to catapult them to success. It's getting harder to keep her cool as she types out the same words, flipping her color wheel to find the right shades for their complexions, pushing Pond's cold cream and Elinor Glyn's new book and whatever else the ad men are selling that day. All that work for a lousy monthly wage that barely covers cab fare, which means crashing at her sister's apartment until she figures out her life. Dottie might be more subtle than their parents, but Ginny can still feel the full weight of her disapproval whenever their eyes meet over the dinner table. Even now, with her brain gone to cotton from the liquor, Ginny can't stop thinking about her life, wondering how the hell she made it to the most electric city in the world, only to get stuck in one hell of a dead end.

Suddenly, the band stops playing. Ginny peels away from the bar, trying to steady herself as the crowd goes still, all faces turning toward the stage. The presenter's smile is two shades brighter, his walk a little bouncier as he brings his lips against the microphone, almost like a lover, "Ladies and gentlemen, put those hands together for the woman of the hour. Count your lucky stars, because here comes the one and only . . . Josephine Hurston!"

Ginny sucks in her breath, craning her neck above the spellbound crowd. Mary's nowhere to be found. She'll be heartbroken if she misses this performance, but there's no point in trying to find her now, with the bodies surging closer to the stage, everybody aching for a look at the star. Josephine is this month's hot ticket to a good night out in Harlem. Catching her show is like a row of identical hearts in a ringing slot machine, but if Mary can't be bothered to hang around, then let her waste the night on some man instead.

The band members shuffle into a new formation, and the presenter is introducing them as Billy Calloway and his Rippling Rhythm, but all eyes are turned toward the velvet curtain. A spotlight swings toward the stage, and she appears at last, sliding slowly to take her rightful place by the microphone. An elegant Black woman dressed in ghostly silver, from the heavy veil descending over her coiled curls to the sharp tips of her dancing shoes. She's careful at first, feeling through the notes with a soft rasp blurring the edges of her words, but then the torch song builds in power until it's pulsing through the room, her voice going down smooth as whiskey only to burn you from inside.

"Trouble, trouble, I've had it all my days . . ."

The audience pushes Ginny into dance. She can't feel her feet anymore. She might as well be floating above the ground, loose-limbed and smiling under the hot glare of the stage lights. Soon she's so full of the music, the rhythmic thrum purring through her entire body, that she feels her eyes glossing over with bright joyful tears. This is heaven, she thinks. She's finally high enough to feel it.

But something's off, a dark note ringing in her ears no matter how hard she tries to lose herself in the torch song. Ginny catches a movement up front, three wiry figures pushing through the crowd. They disappear behind the backstage curtain with their hands on their waistbands. Twisting her head toward the exit, Ginny watches the crowd already parting in the back, harsh voices growing louder behind the steel door.

The electric lights sputter once, then fade to black.

The band tapers off into silence. Ginny's breath sticks to the back of her throat.

"Police!"

And just like that, the spell is broken.

She's caught up by the crowd, elbows banging against her ribs, rough sequins rubbing her skin raw. As she's carried farther away from the stage, she realizes with a jolt that they're bringing her straight toward the exit, where the steel door is swinging open, half a dozen cops pushing past the bouncer with batons raised, the buttons on their coats gleaming like monstrous eyes.

Ginny can barely breathe. There's no way she's falling into this trap. She's already been at the station twice this summer. Three strikes and she's out of the apartment, those were Dottie's terms, and without a place to stay for free, she'll have to go back to Kansas, all her big-city dreams scratched out like a sloppy first draft.

So Ginny heaves a deeper breath and pushes against the crowd, joining a current rushing in the opposite direction. The liquor blurs her vision, and all she can see is a tiny electric light glowing through the backstage curtain. She shouts out Mary's name a couple times, but there's no silver in the crowd, so she keeps pushing forward until she's at the curtain, flinging herself at the red velvet with all she's got.

The concrete walls echo the shouts in the club, the sound of bottles smashing at the bar. The backstage hall is empty except for a group of dark figures at the far end, three roughnecks with bandanas up to their eyes, a woman in a cloak who must've fainted into their arms. Ginny squints through the shadows, but she can't make out their faces, just the irritated hiss of their voices.

"Cutting it pretty damn close, don't you th—"

"—will *kill* you for messing up the plan—"

The woman is limp between two of them, her arms drooping over their shoulders. It might be the liquor or the rattle of her heart, but something makes Ginny take a few steps closer. She's been around long enough to know what this looks like. The night won't end well for this woman.

"You," she says, trying to bring her hoarse voice to a louder pitch, "what the hell are you doing?"

The taller one, clearly the leader, snaps his head toward her. Ginny catches a glint of amber eyes beneath his wide-brimmed hat, jagged scars rucking up the side of his face. He motions to the others, and they lift the woman's body between them. As the cloak slips sideways, there's a flash of silver, and she sure recognizes those pointy shoes.

It's Josephine Hurston.

"You're drunk," says the taller man, his voice slippery smooth, hypnotic. "You're seeing things. For your own good, I hope your memory fails you tomorrow, and this night fades away like a bad dream."

The others are already rounding a corner. Ginny takes off in a sprint, her nerves buzzing through her body, her heartbeat loud in her head. She can't let them get away with this, can't let them take Josephine. But the floor slips beneath her feet, and the tall man catches her by the elbow. She's close enough to smell him, the acrid smoke and sharp cologne covering up a third, animal scent, sending a rash of goosebumps up Ginny's arms.

Before she can do anything, he pulls a gun from his waist, metal flashing in the red light.

Then he slams it into the side of her head, and the world goes dark.

CHAPTER TWO

When she wakes up, the first thing she sees is the side of a crate. Wood on all ends, barely any light coming through the slats. Ginny slams a fist against the wood above her, splintering her knuckles. Her pulse pounds out a painful rhythm against the side of her head. When she touches her temple, her fingers come away slick with blood.

Damn. They've buried her alive. She bangs harder against the wood on all sides, her fist going as bloody as her head. That's what she gets for cheating death with the bootleg liquor. Maybe party girls don't get a second chance.

The world comes into sharper focus, and she can hear two sets of footsteps coming closer, the smell of smoke and car exhaust filtering through the slats. Voices break through the heavy silence, and she holds back her fist, listening hard.

"What do we do with her, boss?" The speaker can't be much older than her, wobbling through faux bravado. Ginny's blood chills as the boss responds, the slippery slide of his voice cutting straight through her core.

"It's time you proved yourself, kid." He drums his fingers against the lid. "Take care of the bitch and let's get out of here. By the time they find her, she'll be somebody else's problem."

One last startled breath rips through her body before the lid swings open and a quick round of bullets shreds through the air, stinging her shoulder before plunging her into darkness.

The rest of the night comes in wild flashes. She fades in and out of consciousness for hours before the lid comes off the crate, and her vision focuses on two Black guys in fashionable felt hats peering down at her, their surprise turning to shock when they see the blood gushing from her shoulder to her chest.

"Billy," one of them puffs out a breath. "She's fading fast. We gotta—"

Billy tears a strip of fabric from his shirt and wraps her shoulder, and then she resurfaces in a hospital bed, the two men replaced by a middle-aged nurse in starched white.

"How—" Ginny props herself up on her elbows. Her shoulder smarts with the movement, but it's dulled by some kind of pain-killer this time. "What happened?"

The nurse makes sure to shake her head in a show of disapproval before giving up the goods. "You caught more than a good time last night, young lady. Maybe that will teach you to stay out of Harlem."

"You can skip the judgment." Ginny lowers her legs off the bed. Every movement takes twice the usual effort, but she keeps going, finding her dancing shoes, wincing at the way they pinch her toes. "Will I live?"

The nurse hesitates. "You got lucky. The bullet only grazed your shoulder. Skip the dancing and the bad company, and you might live long enough to become something respectable."

Ginny slips off the bed and grabs her evening bag, tossing a bitter smile over her shoulder. Her words blur around the edges, the drugs dulling their usual bite. "I wouldn't bank on that."

Before she can make her escape, she knocks straight into a couple cops in the hospital hallway, and her heart picks up a frantic rhythm before she remembers they must be here for her bullet wound, not her bad decisions at last night's party.

"A few words, Miss Dugan," says the older one, flicking a toothpick sideways between his teeth. "Looks like you caught a bit of lead last night, and we'd like to know exactly how."

"Yeah, what kind of night puts a nice girl like you in the cross fire?"

She hasn't crossed paths with these two cops in the past, but it would only take them a moment to pull her records, and she knows exactly what kind of picture that will give them. Even if they forgive her for all her past antics, dancing half-naked on the grand piano at the Radium Club, bruising an officer's nose with her faux diamond rings when he tried to cuff her—even then, there's no chance they will take her side in this story. They'll call her jazz baby to her face and drunk slut behind her back, and she'll be just where she started, except worse, a fugitive from last night's sudden police raid who got exactly what she deserved.

"I hardly remember a thing," she says, leaning against the wall. "You know how it is. One moment, I'm getting out of a cab to see a friend, and the next I'm falling to the ground with a bullet in my shoulder. You gotta love this city."

"Says here you were out in Harlem," the younger guy squints at a stack of papers. "Two guys checked you into the hospital. Did they do this to you?"

The hot hospital air presses hard against her face, and suddenly an even darker thought emerges in her mind. If she's not careful, she'll send these cops chasing the guys who saved her, playing straight into her attackers' hands. Whatever is happening here, she needs to kill this angle and get away from these cops as quickly as possible, before she brings trouble to the only people who bothered to help.

"All right, I'll give you the goods." Ginny motions for the cops to come closer, lifting her voice with a suggestive tone. "I was foolin' with a real special friend of mine, if you catch my meaning. Thought we'd spice things up for once, so he pulled out his gun and we had a real hot time—except the goof must've lost his head completely, because the gun was loaded, and it went off just when things were getting interesting." She forces out a devastated sigh, fluttering her lashes like Clara Bow. "Those boys found me bleeding just when dear Hart went running for help. I promised to keep his name out of the papers. You can imagine the scandal."

It's a ludicrous story. Still, she knows they've bought it even before she's done, and she gets a kick out of these cops looking for the guy she beat in last night's drinking contest, feeling around for fetishes while he suffers through a pounding hangover. Even if they find him in the messy aftermath of last night's revelry, they'll chalk up his evasions to embarrassment at his ungentlemanly behavior, and the case will be closed for good.

After a change of clothes at the apartment, Ginny's back on the city streets, her heart drumming a wild tempo against her ribs. Fear numbs the pain enough to keep her going. Each passing stranger might be one of the guys who left her for dead, and she keeps her eyes on the ground, hoping to hell they aren't following her to finish the job.

Ginny joins the throng outside the *Photoplay* office, sticking a hand against the stitch in her side. The wall clock chimes a cheerful eight inside the entrance hall, but her headache says back to bed, and skip the bootleg liquor next time. A bony elbow knocks her sideways, and the pain from the bullet wound ricochets through her entire body. Ginny catches Caroline's razor-sharp bob whipping through the air beneath a Jeanne Lanvin cloche fresh off the pages of this month's *Vogue*.

"Watch it," Caroline says, not bothering to say Ginny's name, hardly aware she exists. Ginny doesn't have the energy for a snappy comeback, so she shuts her eyes against the jab, wishing for this day to end as soon as possible.

Once she's through the revolving doors, she sees Mary rubbing the sleeve of her cardigan against her eyes. Her buttons are done up wrong, last night's makeup flaking off beneath her cornflower blue eyes, but Ginny's never been happier to see her. The fear curling in the pit of her stomach unspools.

As the *Photoplay* crowd floods into the building, Ginny breaks away, following Mary to the front desk. Mary sways into her chair with an exaggerated flourish, like Olive Thomas fainting into the crowd in *The Flapper*. She snaps back with a smile, but exhaustion still crackles through the faint lines around her mouth, the slow-shutter movements of her limbs as she rattles through the drawers. Ginny bites back the urge to spill the whole story. If too many people find out about her brush with death, those guys might soon learn she's still alive, and she'd hate to give them a chance to change that.

"You look like hell, kid," Ginny says. "But I'm sure happy to see you're okay. Cops get you last night?"

"This bad girl still walks free." Mary lifts a bare wrist in the air. She flings a small cardboard box onto the desk, eyes shining triumphant. "Which calls for a celebration. Since you look about as good as I feel, what do you say to some chemical relief to start your day?"

Ginny pulls one of the sugar packet–shaped tubes labeled *Starks' Headache Powders*, shaking it in front of her eyes.

"Are they any good? Or did the ad men finally put you on their payroll?"

Mary pops a packet onto her tongue and swallows without any water.

"Good enough for me, and hey—if we die, we die together, right?"

Ginny rips the packet down the middle, tipping it into her mouth. A medicinal tingle means this is some strong stuff. You never know what's in these things, these patent meds Mary gets for free from eager ad men, but Ginny mentally crosses her fingers for some fun side effects that won't put her in a hospital.

"Where'd you go last night, anyway? I lost you in the crowd." Ginny crumples the empty packet between her fingers.

"I was gonna ask you the same thing. I waited outside for an hour, but you never showed. Thought they might've taken you to the station. I was damn worried."

It takes her a moment to catch Mary's meaning, how an arrest would've meant one last strike, and shipped straight back to her parents' place in Kansas. Last night has given her a new set of fears, and she almost wishes she could go back to a time before she witnessed the kidnapping—but then she remembers Josephine, dealt a much more dangerous hand than hers.

"Listen," Ginny lowers her voice, flicking her eyes at a laughing group of staff writers passing the desk, "I ended up backstage, and you wouldn't believe what I saw. Josephine Hurston—and a group of guys carrying her away. Looked like they'd drugged her."

Mary's mouth falls open, her eyes going wide. "You're messing with me."

"All above board, I promise." Ginny lets out a sharp sigh. "I wish it wasn't true. No idea where they took her, but it's not looking good."

There's a new emotion swimming in Mary's eyes, beyond her initial surprise. Like she's figuring something out, and she's not sure if she's ready to share. "Did you get a good look at the guys?"

Ginny shakes her head. "It was dark as hell, and they were all wearing bandanas." But she'd recognize the tall one anywhere, that much she knows for sure.

Mary presses her lips together, running her fingers along the surface of her desk. "Listen, Ginny—"

Then a door opens behind the front desk, and one of the telephone girls swings a beckoning arm in the air, clay bracelets clicking.

"You available?"

"Yeah, just a minute—" Mary's curls zip through the air as she turns back to Ginny, all business. "Oh, before I forget. Afraid I'll have to skip tonight's party."

Ginny gives her friend a good stare. Nobody ever skips out on a Gloria Gardner party. Her guest lists skim the foamy cream off New York high society, each party bringing opulent delights, from exotic cocktails in thin-stemmed glasses to showgirls swinging from crystal chandeliers to Gloria's dramatic entrance halfway through the night, high cheekbones swept with the latest rouge, looking every bit a queen in a handsewn gown from Erté or Poiret or Chanel.

And that's what she is, really, the reigning queen of the Ziegfeld Follies. Any other night, Mary's words might've kept Ginny at home, but a chance to spend some time with Gloria is too sweet to pass up. Even last night's attack can't dull her anticipation. Every moment in Gloria's company is like gold dust sprinkled all over, their nights together blurring into the highlight reel of Ginny's life in New York. Swimming in private pools dressed in nothing but borrowed diamonds, jetting around town in Gloria's gleaming Rolls Royce, sneaking into the New Amsterdam Theater after hours with a speakeasy's worth of champagne. Ginny wouldn't give up a chance to feel Gloria's warm magic for anything in the world.

When she looks back at Mary, her words are only half-hearted. Mary's a good friend, but it's not like she needs her to have a good time when Gloria's involved. "What, your new meds can't handle two hangovers in a row?"

"Not tonight. Sorry to bail on you, Gin, but you see—" Mary's already turning away, but she throws a quick wink over her shoulder. "I've got big plans."

"Last night's mystery man wants an encore?"

"Maybe." Mary gives Ginny's knuckles a squeeze. "I'll tell you everything tomorrow, all right?"

The wall clock stutters to five past eight, and Ginny hurries through the hallway with blood pounding through her ears. She's not late, not by any normal standards, but there's no way she's giving those boys the satisfaction of seeing her out of shape. A two-year streak of early arrivals is easy to break, but once lost, her reputation for teeth-gritting hard work would be impossible to recover, so Ginny picks up the pace, knocking past rows of identical doors until she reaches the end of the hall.

She catches her breath outside the newsroom. The place is already surging with activity, sharply dressed folks tapping out complex patterns on rows of typewriters. Ginny marvels at the flashes of violet scarves and sharply darted suits, mauve lipsticks from Paris and dress hems bursting with feathers. All these years in the same office, but the view still takes her breath away every time.

Ginny slumps into her chair, ignoring the dark spots around the edges of her vision. A peal of laughter from the opposite end of the room draws her attention. The staff writers are huddled over a page on Caroline's desk, and she's reading out the article in her clipped Boston accent.

Ginny knows everything about that trio, those untouchable senior writers who get all the best stories, front row seats to opening nights, intimate interviews with the brightest stars. There's Prescott Folmsbee, looking relaxed in a baby blue blazer that matches his eyes, a fresh white orchid blooming from his buttonhole. He looks like Gary Cooper and writes like Scott Fitzgerald, so he gets dibs on every star interview thrown at the magazine. Paul Winstead is the opposite, all sharp edges and sober suits, an unlit cigarette dangling from his lips as he shakes his head at Caroline's article. They say he pens editorials for *The Times* in his free time, and the brass keep doubling his paycheck to stop him from seeking out greener pastures.

In most circles, Caroline is known only as the daughter of Richard Van Allen, an oil man with a yen for buying movie studios. But that blaring truth fades to silence at the doors to the *Photoplay* office, because anybody who doubts her creative merits earns an icy stare and a swift change of topic. Ginny should know, she's been on the receiving end of Caroline's cold scorn way too many times.

She could spend the entire day watching the trio moving through their charmed lives, whisking one another away to expensive meals at French restaurants, brushing invisible specks of dust from their suits as they debate their work for the latest issue. One day, she'll be part of that circle, popping open her checkbook for another round at Chez Georges. That dream has sustained her for two years, but her patience is wearing thin, and there's no telling how many more depressing letters she can handle—especially with the real world beckoning from last night's encounter, her shoulder smarting with each movement, Josephine's stage costume flashing silver at the edges of Ginny's vision.

She shakes off the memory and returns to the letter on her desk, peering down at the cursive letters running with dried tears. Cathy from Oklahoma needs help with her crooked nose and knock-knees. She's desperate for a boyfriend, but how can anybody love a girl like that?

Ginny pushes a page into her typewriter and hesitates above the keys.

Nothing's wrong with you, Cathy. You've got a pushy mother and a bad case of self-doubt. Chin up, old girl. Get out of town and keep moving until you no longer care.

The message dies in the back of her mind. Slamming down the return lever, Ginny types out her real answer.

Consult a bone specialist about remedying knock-knees. Plastic surgeons can sometimes improve a misshapen nose, but make sure to go to a reliable one. Moping about your looks will get you nowhere. It's time to take matters into your own hands and decide what kind of woman you'd like to be—before the rest of the world decides for you.

The slow crawl of the morning speeds up as Ginny settles into her usual rhythm. By lunchtime, the newsroom is mostly empty, and her pile of envelopes is replaced with a fresh stack of answers. Despite the familiarity of the routine, her mind keeps skipping to the previous night, stuttering through the sequence of events like a broken movie reel. She gets to her feet in her corner of the newsroom, wincing when her shoulder bumps against the wall, the pain drowning out her surroundings in a blinding haze. But the meds are doing their job, because her head is light and clear as the sky.

Josephine's disappearance won't go unnoticed for long. On stage, she's an enigma, always hidden behind elaborate veils and stage costumes, only her rich, throaty alto unmistakable no matter what she's wearing. But surely the great Josephine Hurston has a family, same as any girl on this island. Won't be long until somebody starts asking questions, but by then, it might be too late.

A door slams in the distance, sending a gust of hot wind through the hallway, carrying the smell of cigarette smoke, car fumes, and a hint of expensive woodsy cologne. Heavy steps creak across the old parquet boards. Not the hurried tread of your average over-caffeinated newsroom worker, not the showy clatter of a telephone girl's new heels. This person walks like he owns the place.

"Mr. Quirk!"

The large figure blocks out the doorway, his broad profile silhouetted like a face on a Roman coin. The editor-in-chief gives Ginny a quick absent nod before continuing his walk to the end of the hall. A flicker of an idea bursts into wild flames in Ginny's mind. Josephine's disappearance will be front-page news soon enough, but with the August issue of *Photoplay* coming out in a few weeks, this is her chance for a head start on the story. There's an angle here, right at the crossroads of Josephine's star power and her sudden disappearance. While those guys from last night still think Ginny's dead, she's in the perfect spot to chase down the story, find Josephine, and finally catch a break from her dead-end advice column.

Pulling the last page out of her typewriter with a snag, she adds it to her stack and rushes out of the newsroom, skidding through the empty hallway until she reaches the door at the end.

Mr. Quirk is hunched behind the pebbled glass window, his imposing figure blurred over the desk telephone.

"Let 'em sue us over the Valentino piece, Lord knows we've sold enough copies to afford it."

Ginny's fist freezes in front of the door. The glass is supposed to make the editor more approachable, but it only speeds up the tempo of her stammering heart.

"I said what I said—it was a funny article and you know it, the people liked it and we meant no harm. What else can he expect— Well, let his agent call me, then! Fine. Sure, talk later."

His shadow slams down the receiver. Ginny swings her fist against the door, knocking harder than she intended to overcompensate for her fluttering nerves. The voice answers after the first knock.

"Come in."

The office paints an imposing picture. Wide walnut desk with polished brass fixtures, mahogany armchairs smelling of expensive leather, wall of framed *Photoplay* covers behind Mr. Quirk's back like his own personal army of well-coiffed starlets. A wall that says, "Hey, you might be a big shot, but I've got all the stars from Betty Bronson to Constance Talmadge on my side." Many celebrated studio execs have sat in these armchairs, but Ginny's attention lingers on the girls on the wall, exactly where it's supposed to be.

"I've finished my column for the August issue," she says, lifting the stack of pages.

Mr. Quirk's pale eyes seem to look right through her. Ginny clears her throat, squaring her shoulders against the uncaring force of his gaze.

"Anyway, since you're always asking us to show initiative, I'm here to pitch you a story."

Mr. Quirk folds his arms. His feet tap a staccato rhythm beneath the desk.

"Have a seat."

Ginny drops into the armchair. The speech that came so easily in the newsroom sticks in the bottom of her throat. It takes her a second to remember how to spin her drunk night in Harlem into the smash hit it needs to be to sell magazines.

"You've heard of Josephine Hurston, sir?"

He tips his chin forward. "The singer. Of course. We ran a piece on her in April."

"She was a hit," Ginny says, "I got so many letters about her stage costumes, her makeup, everything. So, I think we could run another story on her, especially since there are some new developments."

Mr. Quirk's hand hovers above a jade cigar box, but he decides against it at the last moment, shoving the box with a scrape to the edge of the table.

"I don't see how you'd fit her into your column. Unless her agent is looking for exposure? Any word?"

"No, that's not it. You see—" Ginny heaves a breath, steadying herself. "Last night, the club where Josephine was performing got raided. And then she was kidnapped."

Quirk's pale brows rise into perfect half-moons. "Oh?"

"I was backstage, I saw it happen, and I think I know how to find the men who took her." That's not strictly true, but a little confidence goes a long way in this business. "Just imagine—this could be the breakthrough we need to take the magazine to another level. Real serious journalism about a woman admired on both sides of the Hudson. Think about the difference we could make."

With each word, his eyebrows droop lower and lower. When she's finished, he looks like he's just seen a damn ghost.

"I see," he says, straightening in his seat. "Is everything all right at home? How's Dorothy?"

Ginny blinks at the sudden change of topic. This might be the most important conversation in her life, and still Dottie finds her way into the room, as though her feather-clad shadow is right behind Ginny, smiling as wide as the starlets on the wall.

"She's fine."

"Happy to hear," says Mr. Quirk with a rare twinkle in his eye. A twinkle for Dottie. "I do hope she's still dancing for Florenz."

"Sure is. So about that article, Mr. Quirk—"

"Yes?"

"Do I get the green light to get started? We have to move fast if we want to catch the guys who took her. I'll start by retracing my steps to the speakeasy, maybe interviewing the guys in her band—"

The twinkle fades from Mr. Quirk's eyes, and his face goes blank as a wide slab of stone.

"Absolutely not."

It comes so quickly that Ginny barely manages to regroup, her heart sinking.

"But—I don't understand—"

"How long have you been with *Photoplay*, Ginny?"

"Two years, sir."

"And what exactly is your job description?"

"I'm the *Friendly Advice* girl. I deliver modest but uplifting tips on fashion, makeup, and comportment."

She rattles off the points in a mechanical drone, painfully aware of what's coming next.

"That's right. And you're wonderful at your job, Ginny. We've seen a promising rise in the number of fan letters. These young girls look up to you like an older sister, don't they? Sounds like you're making a real difference already."

"Sure I am," she says quickly, squeezing the sides of the armchair. He's smiling again, his face softening around the eyes, and for a moment she wonders if there might still be a way to change his mind. "But I can do so much more, sir. Caroline moved on from the column in half a year, and now she's chasing bigger stories—"

"That's another matter entirely. Caroline earned her promotion."

Ginny grinds her teeth together. The room suddenly feels very hot.

"I can earn mine," she says. "Please, just let me—"

"Impossible," says Mr. Quirk with a shake of his head. "And even if I thought this was the right time for you, there's no way I would approve this—this outrageous idea. We're a celebrity magazine, Ginny. Our readers are looking for distractions from their difficult lives. They want glamour, not this dirt you're so set on digging up."

"But she could be in real danger," Ginny says. "And I can help—"

Mr. Quirk spreads his hands across the table, his look hard enough to crush. "Then go to the police. Let them do their job, and you'd best remember to do yours." He shifts in his seat, his eyes lingering on the abandoned cigar box at the edge of the desk. The silence in the room has a real weight to it, and Ginny can feel it pressing down from every direction. Mr. Quirk flings a colorless look her way, and the muscles around his jaw relax after a moment. "Here's an idea. I need somebody to cover the Follies premiere. I was going to give it to Prescott, but since Dorothy is in the chorus line, perhaps you could give it a try?"

Her heart lifts at the suggestion, but it's not enough to brighten her mood. Typical Quirk, swooping in with a consolation prize right after turning down the only idea that really matters to her. But a story's a story, and she'd be a little fool to turn her back on this one.

"I'd like that, sir."

"Wonderful." He pats her palm with a fatherly smile, the kind you reserve for a spoiled child who's finally learned her lesson.

The *Photoplay* girls on the wall reflect Mr. Quirk's patronizing scorn in their frozen grins. The message is clear. If you're pretty, you get pinned up on somebody's wall, immortalized in your prime like a rare butterfly. If you're plain, skipped over on nature's great Max Factor assembly line, you can spend the rest of your life fighting your boss for a promotion—or be a good girl and get out of sight. Any way you put it, the world's stacked up against you.

Out in the hallway, Ginny inhales the smell of ink and dust, paper fresh off the press, and trails of perfume in the air. The smell of opportunity. Two years of keeping her head down, working her ass off for a shot at something big. If Quirk wants another puff piece about the Follies, she'll give him that—but not until she gets to the bottom of whatever happened to Josephine. *Photoplay* runs on pure glitter, but real careers are made in the dirt.

CHAPTER THREE

E leven hours later, in a penthouse high above the dark rustle of the park, Ginny digs her heels into the carpet with a sharp sigh. She raises her second glass of corky champagne at nobody in particular, inspecting the bubbles drifting to the top. Another terrible day, liquored out of existence.

The party is past its initial burst of excitement, and guests have settled into small groups around the parlor to rest their sore feet after many rounds of dancing. Whispers hum through the room, muffled behind glove-clad fingers over parlor games, the comfortable silence swelling with the warm crackle of a gramophone. Two male dancers are locked in a passionate embrace in the corner, but nobody pays them much attention except for a servant quietly removing their untouched champagne glasses. The crystal chandelier breaks through the darkness, casting a lunar shine across stuffed lemon armchairs and dull mahogany tables. The lull breaks for only a moment when one of the showgirls faints all over the carpet, clutching her chest, but a glass of water and the jumping beat of a new record brings her back to the dance floor, spinning circles in her faded yellow dress.

Ginny drums her fingers to the song, some Eddie Cantor ditty about the moon shining on the moonshine. Another silly show tune. That's what you get when you party with the Ziegfeld Follies. All froth, no substance, like the champagne in her glass. She throws back the last of it and shuts her eyes, jagged little stars prickling her tongue back to life.

No such thing as a boring party, so long as the booze keeps flowing.

Besides, there's an opportunity here, with the guests wilting sedately into stuffed armchairs, flicking heavy-lidded eyes away from their games in search of new diversions. Showgirls don't like to be bored. They get restless, and before long, they'll tell you anything for the promise of a good time.

Crossing the oriental carpet with a smile stretching across her face, trying to ignore the ache still piercing her shoulder, she joins a group of showgirls in bright dresses in the corner, shaking her empty glass in mock dismay.

"I'm out of giggle water, that should be one of the cardinal sins."

"Here, take mine." A girl with a smoky voice and a rose behind her ear pours some golden liquid into Ginny's glass. "I'm not feelin' too bubbly anyway, no point wasting good booze just to fall asleep."

"Who sleeps in July?" Ginny nudges the girl in the side. She has to play it cool for the showgirls to take the bait. Although she can't say what exactly she's looking for, these girls are her best bet when it comes to show business, and one of them might unwittingly give her a clue about Josephine. There are some familiar faces in the crowd, girls in Dottie's chorus line, but thankfully her sister is deep in conversation with the stage manager on the other end of the room. "The city's wide awake, baby. Close your eyes, and you'll lose the chance to make your dreams come true."

"All right, let's hear it." The girl wedges her hands into her hips, and five stacked bronze bracelets slide down her tanned arms. "What's your story?"

Ginny takes a long swig of champagne. "Ever heard of the Eighty-Three? I caught a surprise concert last night, and you won't believe who it was. Josephine *Hurston*."

"No!" Excited murmurs shuffle through the group. A girl in a turban widens her kohl-rimmed eyes and shifts closer. A knobby wedding ring pokes through her gloves, and Ginny vaguely remembers her as the stage manager's wife. Is it Zita? All their names sound the same after a while, blurring exotic syllables together to jazz up their humble origins. Whatever looks better on a marquee. "Harlem has the best music. I sure wish we could get some singers like Josephine to join the revue, we'd be a million times better off."

The smoky-voiced girl pulls a cigarette from her pocket and shrugs. She still looks unimpressed, although Ginny can't tell if that's just her natural expression. "Not a chance. Remember what happened in May?"

"What do you mean, Anita?"

"Josephine?" Anita blows smoke through her nose, shaking her head at the memory. "She auditioned for the Follies, but they turned her down."

Ginny catches her breath against the glass and takes another sip to steady herself. There it is. The world of show business is even smaller than she'd imagined. "How's that possible? She's a legend."

"Beats me. I only caught the end of the audition when I was getting ready to leave. Gloria was there. You'll probably have more luck asking her."

As if on cue, the double doors swing open, revealing the hostess in a drop-waisted raspberry gown. Gloria Gardner flashes smiles all around, the diamonds around her neck reflecting the light from the chandelier as she summons a waiter with a fresh batch of drinks on a silver tray. Her presence draws appreciative murmurs from all corners of the room, the showgirls snapping to attention, twisting their bodies to catch some of her light.

Gloria's smile brightens as she glides over in a mist of vanilla and peaches, flinging her arms around Ginny. The hug lasts only a moment, but Ginny can feel her heart lifting at the gesture, the promise of a good time drumming up the tempo of her pulse.

"Are you talking about me?" she says in a breathless murmur. "Good things?"

Ginny smiles back despite herself. A familiar heat prickles her cheeks. There's a kind of magic to being in Gloria's spotlight. "Anita was just bringing me up to speed, Glo. Did you hear anything about Josephine Hurston auditioning for the Follies?"

A natural pink flush mixes with Gloria's coral rouge. For a moment, she drops deep into thought, running a manicured finger over her sharp chin, pursing her bow lips like a film star. Then the smile is back, and she lowers her voice in a way that forces the other girls to lean closer.

"You got me there, Gin darling. Sweetest voice I've ever heard, but she didn't agree to Sharp's terms. He can be such a brute."

Zita twists a napkin between her fingers, but if she's upset by Gloria's comment about her husband, she doesn't mention it.

"How did she look that night? Did she seem upset?" says Ginny.

"Hard to say, with that veil covering her entire face. You know I respect a woman with an act, but if you ask me, she's got something to hide."

"Some kind of deformity?" Zita lowers her voice to a stage whisper.

"Don't be simple." Gloria tucks a platinum wave behind her ear. "It's just strange, that's all. Could be anyone behind that veil. What does fame even mean to someone like that?"

The previous night's memory pricks through the champagne haze. Gloria's got a point. Nobody's ever seen Josephine without her veil, although many tabloids have speculated about her reasons for wearing it. There's been talk about a childhood accident that took out both her eyes. A jealous lover desperate to keep her to himself. An off-stage identity she's scared of revealing, with guesses ranging from a foreign diplomat's daughter to an image-conscious Hollywood starlet to a plain old recluse. The mystery has only made her more popular, proving her voice alone can carry her act to the heights of Harlem's nightclub scene. Ginny remembers Josephine's silver veil shimmering in the stage lights, the intricate netting catching on her microphone as she plunged deeper into the torch song. The lyrics echo through her head, and she can feel her skin quilling at their dark meaning.

It seems that trouble's going to follow me to my grave.

"Ginny caught her show last night," Anita is saying, her voice accelerating with excitement. "Can you believe it, Glo? Can't think of anything better than that. Maybe the Hall of Mirrors—"

"*Where fortunes are reversed in style.* Right, like that place is even real." Zita adjusts her turban. The nerves in her temples are jumping. "I'm sick and tired of people coming up with new speak-easies every day, like a joint is somehow better 'cause it's a secret—"

"You're just mad 'cause you're not in the loop." Anita grinds her cigarette into a nearby ashtray. Zita watches the gesture with longing. "My sister's a coat-check girl in Harlem, and she says all the rumors are true. The Hall of Mirrors, Moonglow, everything."

The sound of heavy feet breaks through the music, and soon Otto Sharp joins their circle, his dark suit standing out against the bright dresses of the girls. He looks just like the man in the Arrow Collar ads above Times Square, but his good looks are marred by a deep-seated fatigue, the lines around his eyes growing deeper when he faces Zita.

"It's time for us to leave."

"Oh, but honey—"

"Come on." He flicks a look back to the exit. "Early rehearsals tomorrow, and that goes for the rest of you as well. Don't go too hard on the champagne with a week until the premiere; you remember what happened last time."

"We had too much fun, that's what happened," Gloria whispers into Ginny's ear, her warm breath tickling her neck. Ginny lets out a laugh, and Otto Sharp snaps his attention toward Gloria. One look from her seems to soften his demeanor, and the smile makes him look younger.

"You're all fun, all the time, aren't you?" He squeezes Gloria's arm, then takes a few steps toward the door. "Come on, Zita, darling. Don't fall for it. We both know you don't have Gloria's tolerance for liquor."

"I'm staying a while longer."

"Now, don't you—"

"Oh, let her stay," says Gloria with an easy laugh. "We'll take real good care of her."

Otto seems to falter for a minute, eyes locked with Gloria's, but then she wins their silent battle and he leaves without another word. In the far corner, Dottie follows his departure with an empty expression, her drink untouched on the table beside her.

A dark cloud lingers above the group for a few moments. When another waiter brings a fresh tray of drinks, Gloria leans closer to Ginny with a smile.

"Dottie's looking sore for a girl who just got promoted."

"What do you mean?"

"You haven't heard?" Gloria tilts her head sideways, following Ginny's gaze. Dottie keeps staring into the distance. "She got invited to Sharp's party last night, and this morning he announced she'll be doing the fan dance. Your sister's on the rise."

A fan dance is a solo number, a huge deal for any Follies chorus girl. But Ginny knows her sister well, and the one thing that's constant is that she's never satisfied with what she's got. Ginny turns back to the girls, trying hard to settle the jealousy rising in the pit of her stomach.

"What were we talking about?"

"Secret clubs," says Zita, taking a large swallow from her glass. Her skin has gone pale at the edges of her greasepaint, and she looks like she'd like something stronger. "I bet Anita thinks Ace is real too—"

"Oh, you'd love Ace, Ginny." Anita's features crackle with excitement. "My sister says that's where you go to see the real stars. Louis Armstrong, Bessie Smith—even Billy and his Rippling Rhythm are playing there tomorrow, loved their sound back when they still played for the Cotton Club—"

Ginny almost drops her glass. Billy Calloway and his Rippling Rhythm. The band that played last night's show with Josephine. She remembers the guys who helped her out of the crate this morning and feels the disappointment throbbing down the side of her head as she realizes she missed her shot to question them about the singer. But there's still a chance, so long as she can get into Ace tomorrow.

"Sounds like my kind of joint," she says. "Maybe I'll check it out."

"If you're lucky," says Anita. "It's Harlem's best-kept secret. Nobody knows where to find it, and even if you do, I hear you need a key to get in—"

"Listen to her," Zita mutters under her breath. "Don't bother, Ginny. Save yourself the hassle and stick to the clubs that actually exist."

As the women launch into a fresh argument and Gloria breaks away to mingle with some other guests, Ginny sinks into an armchair, alone with her thoughts. Ace sounds like a challenge, but she's got enough contacts of her own to figure out how to get there, and she can't help thinking she might get to the bottom of the story much sooner than she expected. She pictures herself holding a fresh copy of *The Times*, her byline printed proudly below the headline. Quirk will be forced to give her a raise to keep her on the masthead. She'll finally get her own place in the city, and the people who doubted her along the way will crawl back, begging for forgiveness.

Moments later, she hears the measured clop of her sister's dancing shoes on the carpet. When she looks up, the fringe on

Dottie's dress is swinging in her eyes, blurry through the dimly lit room.

"Are you ready to go?" Dottie tilts her head sideways, cranberry red lips turning down symmetrically to show her impatience. There's something artificial about her stance: fingers knitting together in front of her body, toes straining into first position, spine stretched toward the heavens. Dottie operates like clockwork, every movement coordinated with calculated poise for her life's performance.

"Hey, you." Ginny lifts her empty glass in greeting. "Did you hear? I caught a Josephine Hurston show last night. Now I can finally die happy."

"I could hear you from across the room." Dottie looks down at her toes, as though checking to make sure they're in the right position. "You were asking a lot of questions. Don't tell me you're chasing another story."

"And what if I am?" Ginny peels away from the back of her armchair, so she's close enough to whisper. She should be careful with what she shares with her sister, after all the dreams Dottie has shot down over the years, but this story is too big, and she just can't resist. "Josephine's missing. I saw it with my own eyes. Backstage at the Eighty-Three, a group of guys grabbed her, and then—"

"You've been drinking again, haven't you." Faint frown lines crease her face. "I can't deal with this right now. Come on, we'd better get going if we want to beat the traffic."

Ginny tries to ignore the comment, but it wedges deep into her stomach, and she shrinks back against the armchair. "It's still early. What's with the rush?"

"You know I've got rehearsals tomorrow, and with the premiere coming up—"

"Oh, please. Look around. These girls are in the same chorus line as you. It's too early to even look at the clock, let alone ankle out of here with the party still going."

"Not like you'd understand," says Dottie under her breath. "Maybe if you spent more time working than drinking, you'd be in a hurry to leave too."

Heat crawls into Ginny's cheeks, and she wonders if it's a felony to smack her sister on the head with her glass.

"That's not fair, and you damn well know it. I *am* working, even now, and my column—"

"*Friendly Advice*? Seriously? Please don't tell me you still think it's a respectable job for someone—well, someone from our circle—"

"Like dancing for Mr. Ziegfeld is so damn respectable? I heard about the fan dance. Congratulations, Dot. You used to be a real dancer, and now you're just a glorified decoration."

Dottie stiffens, nostrils flaring. It's a low blow, reminding her sister of her hopeful start touring the country with the Denishawn Company. When she left home at fifteen, everybody thought she'd be the next Isadora Duncan, but then she came to New York and got snapped up by Mr. Ziegfeld's talent scout on her first night out. Mother didn't like that much, but still Dottie could do no wrong, even when she sold out to Broadway like any other girl. The rest is history.

The heavy smell of Dottie's rose perfume hits Ginny in the nose as her sister leans closer. "Mr. Ziegfeld pays all your bills and more. You don't get to take his money and denounce him in the same damn breath."

The empty glass grows heavy in Ginny's hand. She's racked up one hell of a debt to her sister over the years, coming up short for rent each time with her advice columnist's salary, borrowing petty cash and pin money and whatever it takes to survive in this city. And Dottie never goes too long without reminding Ginny exactly where she stands.

"I'm just *saying*," Ginny goes on, swinging her leg against the armchair. No way she's shutting up now, whatever Dottie might think. "Of all the girls, you're the only one who takes it so damn seriously. You might have the sense to be ironic about it like Gloria—"

"Keep your voice down." Dottie twists her neck to the side to see if anyone's listening, but the other guests have the sense to feign indifference. "Never mind. We can talk in the car. You've left it with the valet, haven't you?"

It's all about the car, the same story as always. Her glossy Buick, the only good thing carried over from her Kansas past. Of course Dottie wants to leave together. Too busy dancing to learn to drive. Why bother, when she's got her kid sister acting as personal chauffeur at all hours of the day?

After a few moments of strained silence, Dottie's wet brown eyes harden into resignation, and she wraps her shawl tighter round her shoulders.

"Fine, have it your way." Dottie turns away, searching the room for her fiancé, the next target on her list. Charlie is playing poker with the fainting showgirl, Mazie something. Dottie comes over and places a proprietary hand on his shoulder, forcing his attention away from the game. "Would you drive me home, dear?"

He pitches his golden head into a profile shot, the corners of his lips already twisting into an apologetic smile. Ginny's breath catches against the back of her throat. Her finger traces his profile into the sweating champagne glass. If she shuts her eyes, she can pretend she's touching him, warm skin instead of cool glass, his mouth curving up for her alone.

The illusion shatters when she opens her eyes. Still talking to Dottie. The light bounces off her engagement ring as she squeezes his shoulder with an impatient palm.

"Sorry, darling—I'm still seeing double from all these drinks. Strong stuff. Would you wait an hour longer?"

"Oh, surely—"

He lifts a palm to stop her.

"Don't you start. With the way this city is turning, accidents on every corner—not to mention all those deaths in Harlem. The streets are filled with madmen—"

Dottie darts one last look around the room, but nobody is awake to her personal crisis. She leans in for a quick kiss, then turns to the door with a swoop of her shawl.

"All right, then," she says. "I'll get a cab."

Ginny shoots daggers at her sister's retreating back until the parlor door clicks shut. There she goes again, ruining a perfectly passable night. Dottie acts like she's the lead performer in everybody's lives, so you'd better play along if you want a taste of the limelight. Mother's favorite daughter, the only one who was going places. The one who got all those ritzy dance classes in Wichita, the custom spangled costumes inspired by the Ballets Russes, the expensive wartime debut with Cherryvale's most eligible bachelor on her arm.

The one who got Charlie.

She watches the glossy back of his head as he gives an agreeable nod to his partner. Mazie sticks her tongue through a row of seed pearl teeth, slapping a ten of hearts on the table. Her entire hand is reflected in a gilded mirror on the wall. She pretends not to notice, instead tilting her head at a flattering angle to catch the light against her marcelled waves. Wouldn't be the first girl to accept defeat to please him—but Charlie's a gentleman, more likely to lose than take an easy win like that. And yet his posture is tense tonight, shoulders straining at the seams of his dinner jacket.

There's a ruthless fizzle in the air. Something's coming.

Ginny clasps her wrist, feeling the drum of her heart beneath her fingers. It's just the champagne. Makes her sentimental in all the wrong ways, raising long-buried memories from the dead. Like a stain across the embroidered peacocks on Gloria's carpet, something raw and primal, a slap in the face of good taste and social niceties. Ginny turns away from her sister's fiancé, a slash of pink across her wrist from squeezing too hard.

Distraction comes with Gloria, swinging her way toward Ginny, hooking an effortless arm beneath her elbow. "Let's say we finally get lit now that the old fire extinguisher is out of the way?"

Gloria claps her hands together in a shiver of crystals. A handful of sleepy guests peel away from their armchairs, blinking up at her with the light from the chandelier bouncing off their beaded lashes.

"Listen up, my darlings." Gloria's voice jingles up and down an octave before settling into a breathless contralto, drawing the people in the room closer with every note. "We've got a special guest with us tonight. Some of you are lucky to know her, but for our newcomers, meet the one and only Ginny Dugan of *Photoplay*—only member of the press who's welcome here, don't worry about *The Enquirer*, Zita—and she's got a special talent for finding out the truth about people."

"Dugan?" says Mazie, reluctantly tearing her eyes off Charlie. "You're Dottie's sister?"

Ginny pulls a glass of champagne from a nearby tray and swallows it whole. Zita seems to brighten at the gesture, cracking a painted smile in Ginny's direction.

"Sure they're related? It's like Dottie before Prohibition."

"Damn right. Any takers?"

Zita shoots a gloved hand into the air.

"Do your worst. I should warn you, those reporters like taking their stabs at my private life, but none of them ever got a lick of truth out of me."

The guests move their armchairs into a semicircle around Ginny. Even Charlie drags his chair across the room, his movement sending a pleasant ripple over her skin even though he's barely looking her way. He places the chair with its back to the group and straddles it with his feet wide, resting his chin on folded arms. The light leaps against his class ring as he turns it around, boredom glossing over his handsome features.

Gloria summons light to half a dozen candles from a passing waiter. Soon the parlor is submerged in a crimson glow, casting haunting shadows across the haughty faces of the guests. Whispers die out as they turn their attention to Ginny, who brings herself to her full height with her eyes on Zita.

Kohl swoops around her lashes in Egyptian flicks, with dusky Max Factor greasepaint to complete the exotic look. Whiff of sandalwood sharpened by bergamot and lime, like the latest Guerlain from last month's issue. And yet her irises are washed out blue, with a defiant smattering of freckles poking through the paint. Farm girl, Ginny thinks, comes to the big city to transform her life into one big Valentino set. Her voice grasps for a Boston accent, but the Texas twang still slips through every vowel. And then those gloves, turned inside out. A smile lightens Ginny's face, that a-ha moment she recognizes so well as the puzzle comes into place.

"Your husband is a man with big-time charm, but we all know that," she says, setting the words like jewels before her audience. "Kind of guy who sells fantasies, and you're his biggest one. Except he goes traditional behind closed doors, and he doesn't like his wife smoking—so you've dialed up that Shalimar and turned out your gloves so he won't notice. Might want to take 'em off before he sees through your act."

The air settles into deadly silence. For a pure, painful moment Ginny wonders if she's missed her mark, shot out in the wrong direction in the shadows—then Zita peels off her gloves without a word, revealing the dirty ash stains round her fingertips.

"How did you—" Her painted eyebrows rise into startled half-moons.

"Seams," says Ginny. "And some of the label's still showing where you cut it off. Doesn't take a medium to figure it out."

"I've worn them like this all night. No one noticed."

Gloria turns toward Ginny with a smile warming her entire face.

"You are a marvel," she says. "Remind me never to get on your bad side."

"Impossible," says Ginny. She can feel all eyes on her, but the only one who matters is Charlie, leaning so far ahead that she catches the pale line of his clavicles beneath the starched collar. There's an intensity charging through his entire body so palpable that Ginny's face heats up just looking at him.

Gloria brings her hands together, and on cue the others clap along. Ginny catches a fearful glance from Zita, no doubt wondering what other things she's left undisclosed. *Your secrets are safe with me,* Ginny wants to say above the indifferent glare of the crowd. Everyone comes to this city to become somebody else. If knock-kneed Virginia Kathleen from Kansas can transform into glamorous advice columnist Ginny Dugan, there's no use in disturbing the muddy waters of other people's pasts.

She goes through several other guests before the thrill of her performance fades, and the party moves on to the next round of drinks, chattering politely as guests clink glasses together with renewed vigor. Ginny keeps herself busy with champagne until someone's hand covers her bare shoulder. She knows it's him before he says a word.

"You've changed since Cherryvale."

The glass slips from her fingers and falls to the carpet with a dull thud, spattering shards in all directions. A year's worth of sophistication peels away beneath the familiar pressure of his cool gray eyes.

"Charlie Darby," she says, rolling the name round her mouth. She's prickled by the foreign feel of it, even though he's been with her sister since last summer. Not the kind of name she can say lightly, that's for sure. The drumbeat of her heart picks up again, but the champagne softens the blow, so she faces him head-on in the flickering candlelight.

He's close enough to touch, closer than ever before. The blunt edges of his face have sharpened, cheekbones jutting like shark fins. A blue silk scarf is tucked into his collar instead of a tie. Everything new and expensive, like a coin fresh off the mint.

Heat rolls off his body in waves. She can't tell if she wants to press up against him or run away.

"I've got a confession," he says. "Promise not to laugh."

"All bets are off," she says, heart pounding. "Let's hear it."

"I don't know. Something about seeing you tonight is bringing up all these old memories. Remember the old brick factory?" he says. "Didn't think we'd ever make it out alive. You were such a little troublemaker."

Ginny remembers. Bruised knees, ripped skirts, running through the wreckage with this confident older boy while her sister played with dolls on the edge of the field. Always the clean one, Dottie, with her dance recitals and tea parties, skimming across the bright, uncomplicated surface of things. But it was Dottie who caught Charlie's eye when they grew older, and it was Dottie on his arm at the town debutante ball. Since then, his eyes have slipped over Ginny like the surface of a mirror.

But that part of her life is ancient history, and not even Charlie can undo the progress she's made in the big city.

"I'm not that girl anymore."

A waiter with a dustpan kneels to pick up the glass from the carpet. Ginny spots a chip in the rim and a pool of crushed glass around the embroidered peacock's tail.

"You might get hurt," says the waiter.

Ginny blinks into his earnest face, wondering if the champagne is messing with her perception.

"The carpet," he continues, pointing downward. "We will vacuum, yes? Then you come back."

Before she can process these words, Charlie pulls her away from the damage and out of the parlor. The door shuts on a chorus of curious murmurs. Onward through the dim hallway, watched from the golden wallpaper by the sharp-chinned oil portraits of Gloria's ancestors, Charlie's confident strides followed by the unsteady patter of Ginny's heels. She tries to remember the number of turns they take, but nothing feels real except for the weight of his fingers on her elbow. The warmth spreads through her entire body until she might be floating through the hall, beyond the bronze flicker from the wall sconces, scuffing the paneled ceiling with her patent leather shoes.

They pass through double doors into a cream silk room hung with several tapestries of Versailles. A hunting party towers above the four-poster bed, dogs biting into a straining deer. Curtains closed over tall windows, dust covers sliding off alabaster armchairs. A guest room, Ginny decides with a shiver. Not in use.

No one will find them here.

Charlie lifts his chin toward the tapestry. The light from the wall sconce plays tricks on his face, magnifying a curious smile into a grimace.

"Unusual choice for a city suite," he says. "Do you hunt?"

Something in his tone pushes her into a lie, even as she searches for the words to ask about her sister.

"Sure I do. Listen, Charlie—"

He cuts her off with a lifted arm. "Please, there's something I need to say, and it might be a while before I can get you alone again."

Ginny slides into an armchair, dust cover be damned. She'd rather take what's coming sitting down. Charlie pulls a flask from the lining of his jacket and swallows without looking at her. He releases a heavy breath, like a terminal patient finally relieved of his pain.

"I couldn't take my eyes off you all night. You're really something special."

Ginny pulls at a loose blue sequin on her dress, a hand-me-down from Dottie. *You should've noticed me sooner,* she wants to say. *I've been here all along.* All these years in her sister's shadow, watching from the window as Charlie took her away in his blue Packard, hearing their laughter in the hall when he surprised her with flowers in the morning, feeling the full heat of his attention dialed up for Dottie alone. Not a word for Ginny, not once, like their shared history meant nothing to him.

She's got plenty of words for him now, but she won't give him that satisfaction. Instead, she thrusts her jaw into the air and gives him a defiant look.

"Should've saved some liquor for me, then. Don't leave me hanging."

He shakes the flask, keeping his eyes locked with hers. "Still some left if you want it. Even though we both know you're not that kind of girl."

There's a quickening inside her, blood pounding through her skull.

"What's that supposed to mean?"

"I know your game. It's always the good girls who try so hard to be bad."

"Who says I'm trying?"

"Call it experience. You'll know it when you're older. Still a kid, aren't you?"

"I'm twenty-three," she says, eyes narrowed. "And if you knew me at all, you'd be singing a different tune."

"Oh yeah?"

Ginny rises from her armchair, closing the distance between them in three gliding steps. She covers his hand on the flask and tilts it down her throat, catching every drop of whiskey until she is on fire. A new record sputters to life in the distance, and a muffled wave of laughter echoes through the halls. The parlor could be on another planet, it feels so far from them now.

"How's that for proof?" she says.

His smile is gone, and now his golden features are still, with a single curl resting in a question mark on his forehead. He pulls the flask away, carefully returns it to his inside pocket. There's a finality to his actions that inspires a protest in Ginny, and she takes a step back, knocking into a table. Retreat is not an option, but still she struggles for one final attempt, even as the ragged pounding in her chest tells her there's no going back.

"You're engaged to Dottie. If that's the kind of girl you like, I don't see what we might have in common."

He moves closer, leaning forward to place both hands on the table behind her. The edges of his shirt graze her bare arms, sending shivers all over her body. Dashes of blue swirl through his gray eyes like waves in an ocean. His spicy cologne pierces the still air.

"Dottie's a nice girl," he whispers. "But she's nothing compared to you."

Her breath catches as he leans closer. The force of the kiss pulls her under, and before she knows it she is drowning.

CHAPTER FOUR

S he can still feel him the next morning.

Rubbed into her skin, his cologne seeping all the way into her pores. Rib cage blooming with the ghost of a bruise, her neck tender from the force of his kisses. She remembers something slippery and violent, gnash of teeth and knuckles breaking through those leading-man looks. A flicker of darkness as he flung her down on the bed, down, down, deeper than she's ever gone before.

Deeper still than all the others before him, and she's no stranger to a bit of rough with the lights off. She's known ragged highs in powder rooms after nightfall, college boys popping Arrow collars in the backseats of their shiny coupes. Jazz men with long musician's fingers, playing her curves like a mean sax through a haze of reefer smoke and whiskey. Even one sailor with a husky baritone, whose faded tattoos she traced to the thrum of a rowdy sea shanty in her ears.

Point is, she's no tight-lipped virgin. Not like her to keep shaking like this, with the sun already slapping through the curtains. But it's like he's still here, digging a hand into her neck with that smug grin, whispering terrible things that send her body temperature shooting up into oblivion.

You're mine now, Ginny Dugan. I'm gonna make sure you never forget it.

He's there, sure enough, even as she pushes through the canopy. Last night blurs around the edges, and she can barely remember how she ended up in her own bedroom. Stumbling past a pair of silver dancing shoes, she knocks into the Japanese screen that cuts the room down the middle, cursing out an embroidered crane for its frozen indifference.

"What are you looking at?" she whispers to the bird, giving it a kick for good measure. Anything, anything to break the silence.

Her room hasn't changed overnight, but there's something sordid in the disarray all the same. Scuffed oak desk, trail of cigarette ashes through the rug, a creased copy of *The Times* shouting about heart attacks in Harlem. Mismatched furniture dragged from far ends of the apartment when she first moved in. She's been here for years, but her digs still feel temporary, like some hotel room waiting to be cleaned. Her life could be swept away in a single stroke.

And maybe it should be, after last night. Not for her sister's sake. She's too far gone for loyalty after that look in his eyes over the shattered glass. It's something else. Something broken beyond repair, now that he's shown her what she really is, the kind of girl who keeps on taking until there's nothing left.

Kind of girl who reaches rock bottom and just keeps sinking.

Murmurs rise across the hall, followed by the cheerful clang of silverware on china. Ginny brings a hand to her forehead, plucks her emerald silk kimono from the floor with the other, and pushes through the door with her lips set in a tight line.

The hallway sways around her and for a moment she feels like a sailor trapped inside a sinking ship. Champagne hangovers are the worst, she decides, steadying herself against the wall. Should've stuck to whiskey last night, but Gloria loves her bubbly.

Out of the gray light of the hall and into the dining room, Ginny inhales the welcome smell of dark coffee sloshing in the maid's pitcher. Dottie sits with her ankles crossed beneath the oak table, her straight back inclined over a platter of uneaten fruits. Her dressing robe is tied over a leotard, curls pinned away from her face, cheeks already flushed from exertion. Knowing Dottie, she's been up since the crack of dawn, tapping out dance routines in her bedroom.

Ginny grabs a firm young apple from her sister's plate and falls into a chair at the shady end of the table. This act of petty theft catches her sister's attention, and she twists toward Ginny, arms crossed.

"How was Charlie last night?"

Ginny jolts in her chair, her elbow colliding with the maid's tray. Scalding drops of coffee prickle her fingers.

"Beg pardon, miss." It's one of the new girls, hired by Dottie on a whim to keep up appearances for Charlie's frequent visits. Twenty-five years old, and Dottie's already the spitting image of their mother, her head stuffed to the brim with silverware and seating charts.

"No, no, it's—" *Keep it together, Dugan. Better play it cool.* "It's all right. What about him?"

"He was awfully distant last night." Dottie picks at the fruits in her plate, clicking her fork against the china.

Ginny looks down at the violent red skin of the apple. This one is no good. A wormhole cuts through its core like a bullet wound. She sticks her finger inside.

"Was he? I hadn't noticed."

"I'm worried about him. Some of the girls stayed late, and it just makes me wonder— Well, they're not all like us, you know?" Dottie blinks her eyes open and shut several times like a doll before she gathers her thoughts. "Some of them come from bad families. Did you see how Mazie kept looking at him all night?"

"The girl in the yellow dress?"

"That *awful* yellow dress," Dottie pushes the words through her teeth like a curse. "You saw him after I left. How was he?"

"Charlie? Damn boring." Ginny's heartbeat quickens at the lie. She tightens her grip around the apple to hide the tremor in her fingers. "Sat in a corner all night while we got lit. So quiet we had to check for a pulse to make sure he was still breathing."

Dottie heaves a sigh and puts down her fork. Stealing a side-glance, Ginny notices a slackening around her sister's jaw. No sign of suspicion yet. She wonders if any of the other showgirls saw her leaving the parlor with Charlie, but there's still time. Still a chance to keep the secret in the dark where it belongs.

In the morning light, Dottie looks exactly like an illustration in a magazine. Dusty brown curls quiver around the soft heart of her face, as big blue tears threaten to pierce the surface of her eyes. Typical Dottie, gorgeous even in distress.

"I was too hard on you last night, Gin." She sniffs into the back of her hand. "I'm sorry about that. I didn't mean to snap, it's just— Well, with Charlie's late nights at the office and the premiere coming so soon—"

The sincerity hits Ginny like a sucker punch. Dottie takes a shaky sip of coffee, looking innocent as Mary Pickford, the poster girl for manners and propriety. The dining room spins out of focus, and Ginny feels the heat pressing down on all ends.

"Sharp's working you extra hard, huh?" She tries to keep her voice level, but it wobbles and dips in the end.

"It's not just that. We've had to learn a whole new set for the after-party. He's calling it the Midnight Frolic." Dottie's lips curve down at the edges. She stares at a spot just beyond the table, and for a moment her cool expression threatens to break under the strain. "It's a disgrace to the show, if you ask me. He's got us dancing on a transparent bridge above the guests, and Mazie walking around in a balloon dress so they can pop it with their cigars."

"Can't you skip?" Ginny brushes her damp hair away from her ears. This Midnight Frolic sounds like the exact opposite of Dottie's idea of a good time. Always so proper and good, even with Charlie. Ginny doubts her sister has ever gone beyond a few dry kisses in the back seat of his coupe.

"That's out of the question, unfortunately. I guess we all have our dues to pay." Her voice falls in the end with a dull thud. Something is troubling her, but knowing Dottie, she'll take it to her damn grave. As she squints in Ginny's direction, a fine wrinkle emerges between her brows. "What's that on your neck?"

Ginny doesn't need a mirror for an answer. She slaps a hand over the right side of her neck, and the pain shooting through her head is enough to tell her Charlie must've left her a souvenir last night. Damn him.

Her tongue feels inflexible in her mouth as she struggles to come up with a good lie. "One of Gloria's bright ideas. She pulled out some greasepaint, and before we knew it, we were painting each other silly. You didn't miss much."

"Huh," Dottie traces circles on the table. "Well, you'd better be right about Charlie. He's been good to me. I just hope my luck doesn't run out."

Luck is for suckers. That's what she'd say after a couple gin rickeys at any of her usual haunts, but it won't fly in the innocent morning light of the dining room. Maybe some things are best left unsaid. Last night was an accident, the kind of thing that happens when you mix champagne and old memories, the stars aligning once in a lifetime for a single shattering explosion. Like a brick to the head when you walk too close to a construction site. An accident. Charlie won't say a thing to her sister, and Ginny might as well play along. She's lived long enough to know there's no real glory in honesty.

So Ginny forces a bite of the rotten apple and kisses her sister on the cheek with a wet smack.

"No chance of that, baby," she says. "Everyone knows you're the star of his show."

Two packets of Starks' carry Ginny through another day at work. By noon, there's sweat pooling at the edges of her silk scarf. She doesn't dare to check the dull throb underneath. One glimpse in the privacy of her bedroom was enough, those raw bite marks gone purple as a vampire's kiss.

Ginny wastes no time on goodbyes at the end of the day. Last night's party lingers in her mind, and not just because of Charlie.

She can't stop thinking about Ace, the secret club tucked away somewhere in Harlem, and Josephine's band set to perform there tonight. This could be her chance to confirm that she's on the right track, that Josephine is really missing—and if she's lucky, she'll talk to Billy and his Rippling Rhythm and find out what really happened.

Beaded purse slamming into her thigh with a tinny jingle, she races through the hallway, flying into the reception area at full speed—but there's one person she can't sidestep on her way to freedom.

Mary sits with her back to the maze of offices, wrapped in a plush cardigan the color of strawberries. Her right leg thuds against the wood of the desk like a metronome, chin resting on the heels of her hands. She turns toward the noise from Ginny's rushed getaway with a finger on her lower lip. Red nails to match the cardigan, chewed to a pulp into ragged half-moons.

Right in front of her, there's an enormous bouquet of pure white roses.

"Looks like last night was a success," says Ginny.

Mary's doll mouth twists into a smile. "Actually, these are for you."

Ginny throws her purse onto the desk and takes a seat in the stiff wooden visitor's chair. Up close, the roses are large as snowballs, tied together with a slim scarlet ribbon. The crisp card nestled in the blooms is unmistakable—and so is her name, carefully written in a familiar elegant hand.

"What does it say?" Mary leans across the desk.

Can't stop thinking about you. C

His cologne is all over the card. And just like that, she's back in Gloria's guest room, tangled in the damp golden sheets with Charlie's fingers dipping beneath her rolled stockings, her breath shuddering against his cheek as he drove her over the edge, pushing her beyond anything she'd ever imagined. The purple spot on her neck goes tender beneath the scarf, and Ginny runs her fingers against it, grazing the ghost of his kiss.

"Ginny?"

She blinks up at Mary, then fumbles to fold the card into her palm. It's unbelievable, how little it takes for him to get under her skin. Ginny forces a nonchalant smile and flicks one of the rosebuds to the side.

"Just another sucker," she breathes, trying to ignore the thump of her heart. "White roses are for girls who spend their nights in bed with a cup of chamomile and a Mary Baker Eddy book. The guy doesn't know me at all."

"Who is it?" Mary leans closer. "Somebody from last night?"

"Yeah. You missed a lot, by the way." Ginny looks away from the roses, and a sudden thought crackles through her mind. "Ever heard of a place called Ace?"

To her surprise, Mary gives her a solid nod.

"I've been there just once, but I'll never forget it. It's in the back of this diner in Harlem, place called Grill King. Top secret, and you need an invitation to get in—a playing card."

"What kind of card?"

"An ace of clubs. Funny, isn't it?" Mary looks down, suddenly bashful. "My fella says it took him months to get on the guest list. It's very exclusive. I think I saw Natacha Rambova in the audience, but I can't be sure." She runs a hand down one of the roses. "Are you taking 'em home?"

Ginny thinks of Dottie and shakes her head hard enough to knock a pin out of her hair. "They're all yours. Unless your man would get jealous?"

"Oh, it's nothing like that. He's very understanding, and our relationship is really more of a business deal—with strings attached."

The bright flush in her cheeks tells Ginny those strings aren't too bad either. The double doors from the street swing open, and a pair of telephone girls stride in with their arms linked. Ginny lowers her voice under their curious stares.

"Come on, spill. What happened last night?"

Mary pretends to tidy her desk, waiting for the girls to pass. There's a wicked glint in her eyes when she finally looks up.

"I'll tell you everything, but I need a favor from you first. It's a big one, so decide carefully."

"If you just want to mess with me—"

"Nothing shady. I promise."

Pinky lifted in the air, earnest face extended into a shy smile. Ginny settles against the back of her chair.

"Oh, all right. You know I can never resist you."

Mary claps her hands together and leans even closer. Despite the deep circles beneath her blue eyes, her features crackle with a new energy, each movement brimming with excitement. "I snagged an audition to be a showgirl. With the Ziegfeld Follies!"

Ginny leans back in her chair, trying to form her face into a look of encouragement. The whole world is showgirl crazy, and now even Mary's fallen under that spell, no doubt dreaming of feathers and sequins while she sorts papers for the boss. Mary's always been a dreamer, but this news feels sudden as snow in July. They've spent many days and nights together over the past two years, from coffee breaks at *Photoplay* to crashing speakeasies all over town, and she certainly should've known about her friend's plans to conquer the stage of the New Amsterdam.

"That's real sweet," she says, busying herself with a peppermint from Mary's candy jar. It swirls before her eyes in endless green. "Does seem kind of sudden, though. I thought you wanted to be in the pictures. What happened to that?"

Mary puffs out a breath. "Of course that's still the dream, but the Follies is the first step to take me there. So many showgirls have gone on to the big screen. Mae Murray, even Marion Davies—"

Marion Davies had Hearst behind her the entire time, with his dollars and his big-shot connections. Ginny remembers the man in the blue suit at the Eighty-Three, Mary craning her neck with eyes wide open, nodding along to his every word. Things can go south real fast when you trust the wrong people with your dreams.

Ginny's silence hits Mary hard, her smile slipping by a few degrees. Slowly, she rattles through the drawers of her desk and pulls out a small covered container smelling of cinnamon and sugar. It's a Polish cake she's brought in before, and now she lifts the lid with a defeated sigh.

"I made kolacz," she says in a smaller voice. "Would you like some? We don't have to talk about—"

Ginny grabs her friend's small hand. Josephine's disappearance is playing tricks on her, and now she's seeing shadows everywhere she looks. The gnawing in her stomach is probably a heavy dose of jealousy at Mary's success, and she'd be a petty fool to listen to it now, especially when Mary is the kindest, most giving person she's ever known.

"Marion Davies, who? It's high time somebody knocked her off her throne." She reaches for a slice of kolacz, picking a few sugared almonds from the surface and popping them in her mouth. "You're a triple threat, Mary Gliszinszky. Hell of a chef, dancer, and—"

"—maybe an actress too?" Mary brushes away a curl, self-conscious. "I don't know. I did a couple impressions last night, and my fella says I got the range. Look—"

Mary's face goes suddenly blank, and then it rearranges into a look of pure, blinding horror. Brows shooting high on her forehead, gaping mouth with her fingers pressed into her skin. There's a sense of lost innocence in the sag of Mary's soft cheeks, reminding Ginny of the first time she saw a dead sparrow in the field outside Cherryvale. It takes all she's got not to turn away.

She drops the last piece of kolacz into her mouth, chewing slowly.

"Wow. That's—really something."

"He liked that one the most. He's real sweet with me, always full of compliments, but he's dead serious when we talk about the business. But the thing is—" Mary shoots a look at the wall clock. "Well, my audition is two hours from now, and I still don't have anyone to replace me. I'd sneak out, but I don't want to get into trouble in case the gig flops. And it's Advertising Day too, so the boss will blow a fuse if I pull this number on him."

"You want me to fill in?"

A quick succession of nods. "Yes, yes, it's really easy—just sit here and take in the ads. I've got a list of companies we've already approved, you can accept their ads right away. Any new ones come in, just send them to Betty and she'll take their information. And don't let anyone give you grief—they're a mean crowd, but I know you're tough enough to keep 'em in their place."

The prospect of spending the rest of the day greeting advertisers feels like one hell of a drag. But one look at the glimmer in Mary's eyes kills the excuses bubbling up on the tip of Ginny's tongue.

Might as well keep someone else's dream alive, at least for a while. It might also give her time to come up with a plan to crash Ace tonight, since there's no way she'll get her hands on an invitation by nightfall.

"All right, count me in, showstopper."

"You'll do it?"

"Only if you promise to stay in touch when you make it big."

Mary's smile is wide enough to dimple her cheeks. "What would I do without you, Gin?"

It must be a slow day for advertising, because Ginny spends the first couple hours of her new gig flipping through magazines. When no one's looking, she folds down the corner of the *Friendly Advice* section, so it flips out on its own whenever the magazine is opened.

She shuffles through today's issue of *The New York Times*, looking for some mention of Josephine's disappearance. She goes through the paper from front to back, but she doesn't find a single word about the singer. It's already been two days since that night at the Eighty-Three, and there's no way a star of that caliber could go missing for long without someone reporting it. If she could get into that secret club tonight to see Billy and his Rippling Rhythm, she'd be one step closer to finding the missing singer—even if the whole world keeps on pretending that nothing's wrong.

She flips through the paper, lingering on a bold article about people dying in nightclubs in Harlem. A doctor chronicles the perils of drinking in this ungodly heat wave, while a preacher chimes in on the destructive effect of jazz on young people's immortal souls. So far, seven people have met their deaths on the dance floors of Harlem's finest nightclubs, clutching at their chests for moments before going still as stone. All of them under thirty. Somehow, Ginny doubts that dirty jazz or hard liquor are to blame. *The Times* can do better than that. She crumples up the paper and returns to her pile of magazines, drawing mustaches on silent film stars until they all look the same.

After a while, the first customer knocks through the doors, reeking of smoke and cheap whiskey. Fear jabs cold needles into her stomach before she realizes he's shorter than any of those guys at the Eighty-Three, but the thought lingers as he hobbles up the steps, puffing through round red cheeks with enormous effort. At last, he hoists himself to the top, slamming the bottom of a soiled briefcase right into the glossy stack of magazines.

"Ain't fair to put in so many steps just so I can shake your hand, doll." He glowers at Ginny, like she's personally responsible for this architectural flaw.

"Why? Is there some affliction that's ailing you, sir?"

He rubs the bristles on his chin with a meaty hand.

"See, I gotta drink sometimes for the nerves—got a prescription, don't you look at me like that—and it makes it damn near impossible to go uphill at all."

"There's plenty of offices with an elevator." Ginny leans forward on her elbows. "Could try one of those next time."

Another man passes through the double doors, eyeballing the entrance hall like he's on a very expensive field trip.

"The other girl was nicer," the fellow in front of her continues, pulling a tattered piece of paper from his case. "Asked me about my condition and the like."

"Mary's a saint, mister. Now what's your—"

"Miss Evergreen's Reducing Pills."

She finds the company in the middle of Mary's list, marked with an asterisk as a top-paying advertiser. Ginny's about to change her tune when her attention slips back to the other guy, who's staring at her intently as he comes closer, like he's trying to figure her out with each step. Ginny takes the first guy's money without counting, and he makes his labored escape down the stairs, muttering something about poor manners.

The next customer is dressed like a cop on a shoestring budget, his suit crumpled beneath a thin trench the color of dust. He looks like a private dick, and he stares down at her beneath his hat brim like she's his prime suspect. There's something appealing about the full weight of his attention settling on her alone, but Ginny remembers her close call with the cops at the Eighty-Three, and the intrigue of this encounter quickly turns sour.

She meets his glare with crossed arms, trying to remember what the hell she's done this time.

"Guilty conscience?" He sets his palms on the desk. Up close, he smells of sun and train stations.

"Depends on who's asking."

"Detective Jack Crawford." He leans closer, and Ginny notices his eyes for the first time, a startling shade of green that stands out against his pale skin. "If you've done nothing wrong, you've got nothing to worry about."

He's playing hardball, but Ginny's no fresh-faced kid. It takes more than a few sharp words to get under her skin. She lifts her wrists in the air.

"I hope you brought your handcuffs, detective. I've been a bad, bad girl."

His expression doesn't change, but a pink flush crawls into his cheeks. He clears his throat and pulls a small leather notebook from his pocket. "Why don't you tell me all about that."

"Wouldn't want to make it too easy. At least take me out to dinner first."

He steps away from the desk. "Been going to dinner with a lot of men, have you? Married men?"

Ginny's caught between a laugh and a gasp as she tries to figure out the guy's game.

"I'm a modern girl, detective. And I don't see any ring on *your* finger, although," she lowers her voice, "you never know, do you? It's always the quiet ones you gotta worry about."

He writes something in his notebook, and Ginny wonders if he's taking down this piece of wisdom for future reference.

"Listen, let's cut the small talk, shall we? My client knows her husband has been seeing some other woman behind her back, and my investigation has brought me straight to you, Miss Gliszinszky—"

The confusion clears, and Ginny claps her hands together, unsure if she should be glad he mistook her for Mary, or dismayed at the imminent loss of attention when he inevitably leaves the office. No wonder Mary's mystery man is so big on secrets, if his wife has already hired a private dick to track down his mistress. Ginny shuffles the papers on the desk, making sure to conceal Mary's nameplate behind the bouquet. She makes a mental note to tell Mary that her guy might not be telling her the full story. Fooling around with married men is no walk in the park. Ginny should know.

"You've got the wrong girl. There's no Miss Gliszinszky around here."

"But surely—"

"Looks like you came all this way for nothing, detective."

Jack keeps his green eyes fixed on hers for a moment that stretches into eternity. He can't be much older than she is, but his face already bears all the marks of a hard life. Frown lines trailing down the edges of his mouth, a poorly healed scar glowing white on his right cheekbone. He'd be pretty with a good night's sleep and a smile, but it looks like both those things are out of the question.

He's the first to give up, dropping his gaze to his notebook. As he pulls a business card from its pages, Ginny notices another card sticking out above the cover, and she snatches it from him before he can stop her.

One side bears a red crosshatch pattern with an ornate border. The other shows an ace of clubs.

Ginny can feel her knees going weak, heat prickling her entire body. "Hot damn."

Jack pulls it out of her grip and stuffs it in his pocket, shaking his head at his own blunder. "That's confidential—"

"You bet it is." Ginny lets out a low whistle. "Guess I misjudged you, detective. Where the hell did you get that?"

He hoists himself up, stretching his spine toward the ceiling, grasping for the authority he gave up the moment he blushed at her joke. "I'm not at liberty to discuss my clients' business with strangers."

Ginny rises from her chair, flinging a look at the wall clock. Her shift's almost over. She slips into her jacket and places her red cloche on her head, coming around to the other side of the desk to face Jack. It's hard to hide her excitement, the frantic beat of her heart pounding loud in her ears.

He doesn't move. Questions swim beneath the surface of his eyes.

"You don't know what this is," Ginny says slowly. "Do you?"

"It's just a playing card."

With crossed arms and his mouth in a hard line, he's looking at her like she's some Coney Island medium trying to con him out of another fiver—but there's a reason why he's been carrying that card around in his notebook instead of tossing it. He got it from a client, and he knows it's important, even if he refuses to admit that to her face.

"Is that what your client wants to hear?" She reaches to swipe a fleck of dust off his trench coat, and he stiffens at her touch. "You don't have to play hardball with me, detective. I bet you're dying to find out what this card means, you just don't know where to start."

"And you do?" He brings the notebook to his chest, but he's already relaxing, a cautious spark of humor flicking over his features as he looks at her.

"Like I said, detective, I'm a modern girl." Ginny hooks an arm under his elbow and pulls him toward the exit. "And you're damn lucky you met me."

CHAPTER FIVE

I t's past the dinner hour when Jack meets her at Grill King, and the place is packed despite its shabby décor. Ginny takes in the red and white checkered tiles, a dozen booths with paint chipping off the tabletops, and a frowning waitress who refuses to play along with their game.

"Ace? What are you on about?" She swings a tray loaded with dirty dishes to the counter, shaking her head. A skewed nameplate says her name is Bertha. "This is a respectable establishment, we don't have any gambling here, so you'd better get going."

Jack nudges Ginny in the side, and his smile is a touch too triumphant for the occasion. He's already tipping his hat, half-turned toward the door, but Ginny doesn't give up so easily. One thing she's learned from years of conning her way into clubs is that confidence goes a long way. So when the waitress tightens the strings on her apron a third time with a sharp whipping sound, Ginny steps in front of Jack with the look of a girl who's never lost a single battle.

"Ever heard of the Ziegfeld Follies, Bertha?"

Bertha nods yes, sure she's heard of them.

"Well, that's what I am. A Follies girl." She leans close, giving her a smile like solid gold. "I'm Dottie Dugan, and I got the invite from Mr. Sharp himself. He'll be mighty mad if I'm not in there by the time he comes around, you got that?"

"You don't look like a showgirl." Bertha inclines her head forward, squinting down at Ginny as though the right angle and lighting might make a difference. "Too scrawny."

"You really need to get with the times. This is the look." Ginny feels a pang of irritation at the woman's scrutiny. What does she know? Gray under-eye circles in a pasty face the shade of curdled milk, box-dyed red curls drooping to her shoulders. Still, the comment calls back many embarrassing sessions in the gym at Cherryvale high, girls pointing at her concave chest with cruel mirth. Hours staring at Dottie's perfect curves, a miniature mirror image of their mother, wondering if she might've been adopted. Almost a decade later, fashion has shifted in her favor, and now it's Dottie's turn to bind her chest and run herself ragged with calisthenics every morning. She wonders who decides these things, and if she'll be back to undesirable in a few short years, when fashion inevitably veers back to Gibson girl shapes and pouty lips like her sister's. Better enjoy her heyday while it lasts.

"Who's the guy?" Bertha traces Jack's disheveled suit with her eyes. "He looks like a cop."

Jack clears his throat. "Actually, I'm an— associate of Miss Dugan's, a patron of the, uh, theatrical arts—"

Before he can dig himself a fresh grave with that awkward lie, Ginny swings an arm around him, hiking her chin higher in the air. A real star doesn't tolerate any second-guessing. "The *guy* is our little secret, Bertha, and I'd like to keep him that way. Now would you let us in?"

She flashes the card in the waitress's face once again, and finally Bertha relents, beckoning them to follow her through the kitchen, past rows of gleaming pots and pans until they reach a small door in the back. With one last disdainful look at Jack, the woman unlocks the door and lets them inside.

The setup is similar to many other joints on this side of town. A curtained stage in the far end with the band running through a few smooth numbers, no headliners or jazzy tunes so early in the night. Steps lead to a higher level, crowded with round tables draped in snowy linens, candles shimmering behind small bouquets of roses. It's a classy joint, painted silver and white, with gilded stars shining from the ceiling.

There's hardly anyone on the dance floor save a few liveried waiters, so Ginny pulls Jack toward the bar, the best place for a couple early guests to look completely at ease.

"How the hell did you find out about this place?" says Jack, craning his neck toward the ceiling.

Ginny keeps her eyes on the band, trying to find the guys who pulled her out of the crate that night at the Eighty-Three. The people on stage are second-rate compared to Josephine's band, a little slow with the transitions, stumbling over the keys as the tempo picks up. Now, they're launching into a rowdy rendition of "Charlie My Boy," and Ginny hates that she knows all the words. Even worse that the damn song brings her back to last night, making her wonder what's next for her and Charlie. She can picture their next encounter, him picking up Dottie after work with only a polite nod for Ginny, clearing up any doubts as to what happened between them. That's how it goes for these Princeton guys—they'll love you to death in the night, but once daylight rolls around, their fiancée is back in the picture and you're back to being invisible. Charlie's no exception, and it suits her just fine, except for the fact that his name keeps playing dirty tricks on her when she least expects it, and there's no telling how much time it will take her to forget the feeling of his hands around her neck.

A passing waiter warbles along, "You thrill me, you kill me, with shivers of joy. . . . Oh, Charlie, my boy."

Ginny turns back to Jack, trying to slow down her jumping heartbeat.

"That's a boring question." It was a lucky shot, she has to admit that. Mary could've given her the wrong address, and hell, who knows how many Grill Kings there are this side of town. But she doesn't want to go into details with Jack. Let him think she's a damn genius who's better at his job than he is. She stretches her legs under the bar and flings a look over at Jack. "What's a guy like you doing chasing down cheating husbands, anyway?"

She offers him a drink of her gin, but he shakes his head. "Pays the bills. What made you decide to become a secretary?"

"Actually, I'm a writer." She straightens her back. "You could be chasing bigger stories too, you know. Aren't detectives supposed to care about getting the bad guy?"

His expression is unreadable in the blue light. He gives her a long, hard look, with a casual touch of disdain. "That's the stuff of cheap paperbacks, kid. You'll see my point when you get older. It's a rough world out there, and there's no chance of getting all the bad guys—but there's always a steady supply of cheating husbands."

That's the second time someone's called her a kid, and it's getting old real fast. Who does he think he is, talking down to her like his terrible sense of style and jaded view of the world make him superior? This self-righteous prick who earns a living trying to bring down bright girls like Mary, just for messing with guys who should know better. He's just like the cops who come in to raid her favorite speakeasies, arresting the flappers on the dance floor instead of the gangsters who own the joints. In this damned man's world, it's always the women who have to shoulder the blame, and it takes all she's got to calm the anger bubbling deep inside. Oh, how she'd love to wipe that self-satisfied smirk off his face.

"Come *on.*" Ginny gives him a prod in the arm that makes him recoil. She tries to keep her tone steady, unbothered. "Keep up that kind of thinking, and soon enough you'll be a sad old man with a drinking problem. You gotta have bigger dreams, detective."

"I don't drink." His voice is stiff, his eyes averted. "Anyway, I don't see you living the high life either, if you spend your Friday afternoons watching the front desk at some second-rate gossip rag—"

"*Photoplay* is the nation's leading celebrity magazine." She swivels toward him on her stool, gin glass forgotten. "And my story will make a real difference. Unlike your petty, meddling, ridiculous investigation—"

He lets out a dry laugh. "Let me guess, is your story about the most fashionable hat shapes for the summer of 1925? I bet you're investigating as we speak—"

"You're not even a real detective." She takes a sloppy sip of gin, inhaling the juniper fumes like medicine. Smug Jack Crawford, damn him. She hates how wrong he is about everything, how right he is about the hats. *Photoplay* ran a piece on them just last month, but it's not like he'd understand that there's room for both puff pieces and serious journalism between the pages of a single magazine. "I could do your job with my eyes closed, and I'd look better doing it too."

He gives her a slight eye roll, but she can tell that her words are getting under his skin. "You have no idea what you're talking about. The skills it takes to do my job—"

"Bet you can't teach me anything I don't know already." Ginny wedges her elbows against the bar, feeling the alcohol loosening her sore muscles. The band continues its warm-up routine on stage, with no sign of Billy or his band. She might not need to hang around the bar with Jack, but teasing him is giving her too much satisfaction to quit now. He flips open his slim leather notebook and pulls out a pen.

"Fine. Watch and learn." She stares at him sideways as he writes, the concentration pushing his brows together. "When you've got a suspect, you need to start with the three basic tenets. Motive, means, opportunity."

He maps them out in a pyramid and keeps on talking, adding points and subpoints, his eyes glowing with enthusiasm as he gets into it. Ginny's never met anyone quite as obsessive about something so dry. Instead of listening, she watches his face, drowning out the lecture with her own thoughts.

"—and Clendenen's Detective Manual is the absolute authority on this. That's why profiling is the most important skill for any detective."

"Cheers to that." Ginny downs her drink and drops the glass on the bar. "Still, that's all theory. You got the wrong girl today, and something tells me that wasn't a one-time thing—"

"You were acting suspicious—"

"What, like a *home-wrecker*?" She stretches out that last word, keeping her eyes on his. The irony of the moment isn't lost on her, and she can't help wondering if there's some sense to Jack's fixation on profiling, because he got at least part of the truth about her dead right.

The moment snaps as the bartender comes over with a fresh bottle. Ginny gives him a nod, and he leans in.

"Hey, any idea when Billy Calloway and his Rippling Rhythm are up?"

"They've got an eight o'clock slot. You want anything else? We got a new shipment of gin, top-shelf stuff—"

Ginny nods *yes* and watches him pouring the liquid into her glass. The familiarity of the motion calls back too many nights in her past, and she relaxes at the bar. Everything's under control. Billy Calloway will be here tonight, and then she'll have all the answers.

Jack gives her a lingering look, then follows the bartender to the other end of the bar, opening his notebook once again. It's obvious he wants her out of earshot, but it's doubtful that his investigation warrants that level of secrecy. Ginny leans in over her drink, trying to imagine the conversation. *A teetotaler walks into a speakeasy.* God, the jokes just write themselves; he's making it too damn easy.

Ginny swallows her drink and leaves her place at the bar, enjoying the heat of the lights on her skin, the soft undercurrent of alcohol running through her veins. For a secret club, this place seems pretty tame. A few dancers are shuffling around the center of the room, their arms hanging limply over each other's bodies. The band slides through a few more popular classics, mostly jazzed up show tunes. It's not the best time, but still she sways to the beat, closing her eyes to enjoy the feeling of the music thrumming through her body.

Something forces her eyes open, and then she's looking straight at the tall man with the scars from the Eighty-Three.

He's deep in conversation with a bored blonde woman in a sharp men's suit, but there's no mistaking those cold amber eyes, the scars tracking all the way down his jaw. He seems to feel her attention, because he breaks away from the conversation and meets her gaze with a look that sends her stumbling back to the bar, her mission forgotten.

The man takes a faltering step forward, but he seems to change his mind when he sees Jack and the bartender. Ginny digs her elbows into the bar, breathing hard. She doesn't want to think of what this means for her, what this man will do after learning his guy botched her execution, so she turns her attention to Jack's conversation instead.

"—right next door, and you're saying you don't have a clue?" Jack is saying, his shoulders tensing at the seams of his suit. "I'm not asking for much, just give me a timeline. You know I'd only ask if it was important—"

The bartender leans forward and lowers his voice. "I know who you are. I'm willing to let that slide, but if you start making trouble—"

"A name, then. If you've heard of me, then you know I've still got the connections to make things difficult for you."

The bartender's face clouds over. He polishes the same glass again. When he looks back at Jack, there's a note of fear in the lines around his eyes. "Vivian Templeton. But I can't promise she'll give you anything more than a good time."

The bartender points across the room, a white cloth swaying in his fist like a flag. Ginny recognizes the gorgeous blonde, but her tall companion is long gone, and she leans against the railing of the staircase, taking intermittent drags from her cigarette holder. Her lazy demeanor snaps into action when she catches Jack's eyes on her, and she stubs out the smoke against the railing and cuts across the floor, disappearing inside the powder room before Jack can catch up.

Ginny pulls on a smile to hide the desperate tremor of her heart, the tall man's shadow flickering in her side vision.

"Guess that's a dead end for you, gentleman Jack. Who's gonna give you all the dirt now?"

She expects him to brush her off, fall back into their bantering rhythm at the bar, but instead he slams a hand against the wall and curses under his breath. Strike one for gent Jack. Maybe there's a temper in there, beneath all the dusty detective manuals.

"She'll come out eventually." He leans against the bar. His knuckles are white around the edges. "It'll be fine."

"She might." Ginny slows down her voice. The case means something to Jack, that much is obvious. Maybe he's too cash-strapped to go long without delivering. His conversation with the bartender made it sound like a matter of life or death, but one thing rings clear—if the client who gave him the playing card is looking for dirt on Mary, then Ginny had better get ahead of him before it's too late. Besides, the blonde didn't look too happy to see the man, so she probably doesn't dream of finishing his dirty work. "Unless there's another way out of that powder room. You know, a secret exit in a secret club—"

Jack turns toward her with a frantic look. "You can go in there. Talk to her."

"What would I even say?" Ginny rolls her eyes, turning to leave. "I'm just a *Photoplay* girl, writing about hats and other silly things. I don't know a thing about big, bad, *serious* detective work—"

His arms shoot out and grab her shoulders. She would never admit it out loud, but she kind of likes to see him desperate. "All right! I get your point. Just talk to her, okay? It's about Miss Gliszinszky. Ask if she's been in here recently. That's all."

There it is. Her chance to throw him off Mary's trail for good, and he'll even thank her for it. Ginny shakes out of his grip and turns on her heel, enjoying the power surging through her body at this subtle exchange.

The powder room is made up in style: dove-gray seats and high mirrors scrubbed to a gleam, pink tiles and soft silver braziers on the walls. The blonde is already there when Ginny arrives, dabbing flame-red rouge into the apples of her cheeks with her lips pursed. Her hair is cut into a daring Eton crop that would look ghastly on any other woman, but she's got the bone structure to pull it off, and Ginny feels a genuine surge of admiration.

"I absolutely adore that shade," says Ginny as she settles into an adjacent chair. "Wish I had your complexion to pull it off."

The woman's twin diamond earrings sparkle as she acknowledges the compliment.

"Aren't you sweet as punch. I'd trade my faded mop for yours any day, like that." She snaps her manicured fingers. "Put Theda Bara to shame with that color. Is it natural?"

Ginny faces herself in the mirror, pulls out a powder compact for decency. There's nothing special about her dark brown bob, the woman's just indulging in compliment ping-pong as the occasion requires. This one knows how to play by the rules—now Ginny just needs to find out if she can break them too.

"My friend says I should grow it longer," she sighs with mock resignation.

"No!" The woman swabs right off center. The rouge looks blurry on her face.

"Always telling me what to do. I'm sick and tired." Ginny shakes her head, hoping Mary will forgive her for all these lies. She doesn't have to work so hard to get Jack his answers, but part of her is curious about Mary's secret life without her. If Mary was in here with her fella, then this Vivian woman will probably know what happened—and the truth might help Ginny come up with the perfect lie for Jack. "Can you believe it, she sent me in here to find an earring she'd lost. Said a woman named Vivian would know where to find it. That wouldn't happen to be you, would it?"

"Depends on who's asking." Done with her makeup, the woman slides her chair closer, so the spicy tang of her perfume hits Ginny right in the nose.

"She might've been wasted that night, so who knows if she was even in here. Her name is Mary, she's about this tall—" Ginny swoops her arm five feet above the ground. "Said she came here with some big shot. Do you remember her?"

"Mary, Mary . . ." Vivian cups her chin in her hands, leaning against the dressing table. There's a flicker of recognition on her face, but when she turns back to Ginny, it's gone. "Sorry, honey. Doesn't ring any bells."

"Are you sure?" Ginny leans closer. Her interest in Mary's affairs burns brighter with Vivian's lie. Whatever she's covering up must be bigger than a wild night on the town, and Ginny can't shake the feeling that Mary's hiding more than the identity of her mystery man. "Any way I can jog your memory?"

The woman lets out a snort of laughter and pulls away from Ginny, rising with the crinkle of her silk suit. "You're a real sweetheart, looking out for your friend like that. But this isn't the kind of place that deals in secrets, and if you're any sort of friend, you'll lay off the questions."

Ginny swallows her words, leaning away from the force of the woman's stare. There's something dark and heavy there, behind the casual tone, like she's seen things. Done things. The kind of past you can't laugh off.

Noticing Ginny's discomfort, Vivian spreads her made-up face into a smile and pulls a satin drawstring pouch from her inside pocket.

"I can't give you answers, but I got something else if you're looking for fun."

"What do you—"

"A good time." She squeezes the pouch between her fingers. "Help you forget all your troubles."

Vivian's smile barely falters, but Ginny catches a warning buried deep beneath the sales pitch. "What are you saying?"

The woman leans closer, her whisper tickling Ginny's cheek, "You didn't hear it from me, but word's out that you've messed with some bad joes. Your time's running out, Ginny Dugan."

The moment stretches endlessly as Vivian pulls away, examining her face with calculated interest. Ginny's questions fade to nothing as the awful truth echoes through her skull.

They know her name.

"I saw you with him," she manages through her pounding heart, "the man with all those scars. Who is he?"

"None of them have any names." Vivian worries the edges of her pouch with her nails. "But they all work for the Eagle, and if you're on his hit list, then don't waste your time making long-term plans."

She should've known that she wouldn't get away so easy. Ginny rises from her chair, but Vivian pulls her down by the wrist, shooting tense looks around the empty powder room. When she speaks again, her voice is back to its normal pitch, and it's like she never shared anything at all.

"Anyway, I got the remedy for any kind of trouble, so help yourself. Might help you get your mind off that friend of yours."

Even if her days are numbered, it might still be a good idea. The gin is already wearing off, and she can feel her nerves rattling through her body again, guilt jabbing its cold needles through her stomach as every wasted moment takes her further away from finding Josephine, closer to her own untimely death. Ginny thinks of rolling a thick reefer cigarette between her fingers, then lighting up and holding that bitter herbal smoke in her mouth until her worries dissolve to nothing.

"You got any reefer?"

Vivian scoffs like she's personally wounded. "Get with the big leagues, honey. Grass is yesterday's news. This stuff, on the other hand—"

She pulls a shiny cylinder from her pouch and holds it up to the light. It looks just like a lipstick tube, and Ginny can't tell if this woman's messing with her. Before she can ask what the hell's going on, the door to the powder room swings open, and a waiter pokes his head inside, catching Vivian's eye with a significant nod.

"That's my cue." She draws the pouch shut and saunters out the door, saving one last lingering look for Ginny. Unspoken warnings in her kohl-rimmed eyes. "Think about it. You know where to find me if you change your mind. I've got a good discount for pretty girls."

Back at the bar, Jack sits with his fingers drumming against the surface, restless eyes roving through the crowd. When he spots Ginny, he jumps off his stool and closes the distance in a few quick steps. His notebook is already popped open in his hands. *Please, how desperate can you get?*

"Well?"

"No luck." Ginny looks around the club, watching the floor filling with dancing bodies as the band revs up for a Charleston. No sign of the tall man, but there's no telling who else might be working for the Eagle. From this point forward, she can't trust anybody, not the waiter with the gleaming tray piled high with drinks, not the bartender winking at her empty glass. She probably shouldn't trust Jack either, but something about his hopeless sense of style and stubborn commitment to his case endears him to her. This guy might be annoying as hell, but he's clearly no gangster, and that should be enough for now. "She knows something, but she made it clear she'd never spill."

Jack curses under his breath. It's a minor setback, but he seems to be taking it hard. She really doesn't get the big deal.

"I'm sure you'll find some other way."

"Yeah, or my client will find some other detective." He stares down at his shoes, then flicks his gaze back to Ginny, like he's figuring something out, calculating his next move.

Ginny turns her attention to the stage, trying to distract herself from the frustration gnawing at her insides. The warm-up musicians have disappeared behind the curtain, and now a new band is setting up onstage. And there he is. There he is.

Ginny comes up to the stage, close enough so she has to crane her neck to see the band, and in the very center, that same suave-looking Black sax player meets her gaze. It's Billy. His eyes widen, and she can't tell if it's with surprise or recognition. Twisting side to side to check on his bandmates, he jumps off the stage and closes the distance between them. The guitarist looks up from tuning his instrument and raises an arm in half greeting. A memory flashes through her mind. He was the other guy with Billy that night. Ginny waves back.

"You remember," she says.

"Good to see you," he says. "Got some more crates backstage if you want to take another nap."

Jack slants a sideways look at Ginny, but she ignores him. Let him think what he wants.

"What are you doing here?" Billy's low voice crackles with nervous energy. His face shares none of the guitarist's enthusiasm, but at least he recognizes her.

"I know Josephine is missing," Ginny says. "I want to talk—"

"You should leave. This doesn't concern you."

Although his tone is dismissive, Ginny can feel her excitement brimming. Billy isn't denying anything. That means Josephine must really be missing. As he turns to leave, Ginny grabs him by the sleeve. She won't let him slip away so easily, not after everything she's done to get here.

"Aren't you going to do anything about it?"

Billy's arm stiffens under her fingers. She can see the melancholy swimming in his eyes. He shifts his weight, and the neon lights glint blue-gold across his sax. He nods at a point just behind her shoulder.

"That guy's with you?"

Ginny turns toward Jack, standing silently with his hands folded over his body. He looks like one hell of a square in that ash-gray suit, his notebook sticking out of his pocket, the dismay from his dead-end case still all over his face. There's nothing shady about him, except for his hopeless lack of ambition and unfortunate taste in fashion. Still, Ginny can't see any use for him beyond gaining entry into Ace—if she needs someone to shoot down her life choices, she can always talk to Dottie.

"It's just me." She pulls Billy away, but he keeps darting suspicious looks around the club. Up close, she can see his eyes are rimmed with red, evidence of little sleep since that night at the Eighty-Three, and the skin is drawn taut over the bones of his face.

"And who's to say I can trust *you*?"

"That's your call." She can feel him slipping away, ready to escape her grip at any point, so she scrambles for one final argument. "I'm the last person to see her alive, and I'm going to keep looking—with or without your help. But I'm your best bet to find Josephine, so if you want answers, you'd better help me out."

Billy lowers his eyes, staring at the polished tips of his shoes. The moment stretches into eternity, but he finally lets out a heavy breath and beckons for her to follow. "Fine. There's eyes and ears all over this place. Let's get the hell out of here, and we'll talk."

CHAPTER SIX

Billy leads her past the stage, maneuvering with ease through the blue velvet curtain. The backstage area is paved in utilitarian cement, one long dimly lit hallway with rows of doors on either side. They walk so quickly that it begins to feel like a drive through intriguing but foreign territory: a flash of stocking here, a puff of powder there, with murmurs of girlish laughter filling the hallway in sudden uproarious bursts.

Footsteps clatter behind them, and Ginny turns to catch a glimpse of Jack rushing to catch up. Something about the hard set of his jaw feels like trouble. Once they're in the alley outside the club, Ginny pulls him to the side, conscious of Billy casting suspicious looks in their direction.

"What the hell are you doing?"

"Are you okay?" He's out of breath, adjusting the tip of his felt hat. "Sounded like you were arguing, and then you just left with this guy—"

"No kidding, ever heard of something called privacy? I guess that's not something you need to know as a detective—"

Billy leans in to light up his cigarette, shading the flame against the wind. "You done? Maybe this was a bad idea—"

"No, no." Ginny curses under her breath. Jack leans against the wall, staring resolutely into the dusty windows of an abandoned pharmacy. The stubborn set of his shoulders tells her there's no chance of getting rid of him. Fine, let him win this time. "I know this guy, he's harmless. Just ignore him, all right?"

Billy gives her a dubious look, but he doesn't move. Heaving a breath, Ginny looks out into the depths of the alley. If it weren't for the rush of cars in the distance and the small fire on the edge of the musician's lighter, the place would be drenched in the kind of darkness that swallows you whole.

"You play a mean sax," Ginny offers, mostly to break the silence.

"Aw, that was nothing." Cigarette waving through the air, trail of smoke behind it. "I've been off my game. Should've seen us performing with Josie. Really performing, not like that night at the Eighty-Three. Filled every seat in the Cotton Club, even the standing ones. Wasn't room enough to move, they loved us so much."

In the background, Jack peels open his jacket and pulls out his notebook. "Did your band always play with Miss Hurston, Mr. Calloway?"

Ginny flings him an irritated look. If this is his way of thanking her for that talk with Vivian in the powder room, it's a strange way of showing his gratitude. It's her damn story. She doesn't need his help.

Billy pulls on his cigarette. "It was more than that. We're soulmates, and I don't say that lightly. We haven't been apart for more than a day, not until she disappeared. Feels like someone ripped out half my heart."

Ginny lets out a breath. For the first time since that night at the Eighty-Three, her suspicions are confirmed—Josephine's disappearance was more than a side effect from tainted bootleg liquor. She catches Jack scribbling furiously in his notebook, and she edges into the conversation before he can snatch the next question away from her.

"That night at the Eighty-Three. You were with her the entire time?"

"Right on. It was a risky gig from the start, and I'd like to think I warned her, but I jumped on it like any old fool. They said the Eighty-Three would be different. Our territory. None of those big guys strutting in like they owned the place, like they owned us. Not like the Cotton Club, where they'd put a paper bag against your face and kick you off the stage if you were any darker." His eyes cloud over. "Turns out the night was rigged against us from the start. You remember the raid."

Ginny steps closer to get a drift of his smoke, the nicotine tasting delicious on her tongue. "The cops came running pretty quickly. Bastards won't stop till they close down every last speak in the neighborhood, will they?"

"It's not that simple. Whatever's happening is bigger than Harlem, bigger than the cops. And it all starts and ends with Josie."

Jack keeps scribbling in his notebook. His chin swings up and down with the motion. Ginny has to fight the urge to rip the book out of his hands, but he just keeps moving forward with his questions, like she's not even there. "Could you describe everything you remember from that night?"

"That night was different from the others, all right. The band got there early to get warmed up. They wanted us up at midnight, so we were jamming from ten. It was a good crowd, kind of folks who cheer no matter what you play. I didn't do much talking with the other guys, most of them were new players Josie had hired a few weeks ago, I didn't know them too well. So we're playing, see, and then comes our cue: one o'clock, Josie's surprise entrance. She comes in, hitting all the beats, but something's off about her. Might've been nervous, but now I wonder if she suspected how the night might play out."

A barely perceptible flicker passes across his face, and Ginny wonders if there's more to the story than Billy is letting on. She can't remember Josephine's posture that night, the glare of the lights against her silver dress was too distracting. There was a faltering start, time slowing down as Josephine pushed her voice to hit the high notes. But it was her first time seeing Josephine in concert, so there's no telling if anything was out of the ordinary at all.

"Still, we keep playing. Get through the first number, and suddenly there's a bang on the door. I look at the other guys and they're thinking the same thing, we gotta get out of here, fast. They kill the lights. It's a mob out there, everybody screaming and stomping on each other. Somehow, I get my sax into the case and pull myself together. Through the stage exit, there's a fire escape, and I get out of there and run a few blocks away in case the cops come rounding people up. There's a drugstore the guys know, Josie too, it's like our safe spot in case anything goes wrong."

"Did the others join you there?"

"Sure did. Except Josie never showed. We came back for a second look closer to four, five in the morning, but we only found you."

He nods toward Ginny, and Jack looks at her for the first time. His eyes are serious, appraising her with detachment. She can feel something shifting between them in that moment. She wishes he'd stop asking questions, but calling him out in the middle of the interrogation might scare off her witness. "Was Miss Hurston known for any unusual behavior?"

"Josie was straight as a ruler, most of the time. Didn't smoke, didn't drink. Said that was what they wanted, to keep us sedated while the white folks took over Harlem. Josie dreamed of owning her own club someday, launching her own revues to rival the ones on Broadway. She's truly one of a kind."

The back door slams open with a metallic clang, and Ginny jumps away, flattening herself against the wall. The man's face is drenched in shadows, and she scrambles for some kind of weapon, her throat already ripping around a scream—but then he lifts his chin, and it's only the guitarist.

"We're on in five," he says with a look around the group. "Everything all right?"

He leaves after an affirmative nod from Billy, but Ginny can't stop shaking, her vision swelling with the image of the nameless tall man. Only Jack's attention forces her to pull herself together. There's no way she's falling apart in front of this gumshoe. He takes a weighted pause, then continues with his questioning.

"Any way she might've planned it? Has she ever disappeared for long periods of time?"

Really, Jack? Ginny wonders how long he's been living under a rock, because no Harlem superstar on Josephine's level would ever dream of leaving behind that kind of stardom. It's a special kind of fame that elevates beyond the tabloids. Cultivated in kitchens and smoking lounges, passed on by word of mouth through the entire city overnight. Nothing like those studio stars with their overwritten biographies planted in magazines by their agents. Josephine's the real deal.

Still, the question gives Billy pause. "There was one time. Maybe in the spring, can't be sure now. Late April, I guess, or May? She didn't perform for a week. But that was different, Ruby told us she had a cold, something real serious. And she came back good as new."

Josephine auditioned for the Follies in May, and now it sounds like whatever happened then was enough to put her out of action for a solid week.

"Who's Ruby?" says Ginny.

"Her sister. She's a big deal around Harlem. Publishes her poems under the name Rose Red. Anyway, you'd better talk to her first, she's the one with the dough—their father was the late Marcus Hurston, the property developer? I can give you her address if you're interested. She won't be in until late, probably at one of her readings, but you can catch her after nine tomorrow morning." He tugs on the cigarette. "Tell her I sent you. She's keeping a low profile in case somebody from the press comes to bother her."

It happens in a split second. Ginny turns toward Jack, and somehow she knows he's going to betray her. His words fall like heavy coins on the ground between them. "Those reporters are out for blood, right?"

"Damn straight." Billy flashes a dangerous look. "Predators, all of them. You can't be too careful these days. But you must know all about that, right?"

Ginny can feel her heart tumbling over itself in her rib cage, and she braces herself for the final blow. "What do you mean?"

"Figured you were a society girl or something. Bet you know how to keep a low profile—even when it comes to hiding out in a crate of stage equipment with a bullet wound. That takes something special, you know."

She gives him a nod, feeling faint. Jack looks as though he might blow her cover right there, but instead he extends an arm for a handshake.

"Don't worry about discretion. We've got it covered."

Billy doesn't ask about Jack's line of business, but then his look says private dick all over, so it's no big mystery. Looking between the two of them with an exhausted glint in his eyes, Billy dictates Ruby's address, a place up in Sugar Hill. And then he's gone with the creak of the stage door, leaving behind only a blue-gray cloud of smoke.

"A bullet wound?" Jack leans back for a better look at her. "What's this really about?"

"None of your business," Ginny says. She doesn't give a damn what he thinks of her, but whether he gives her pity or contempt, she doesn't have the energy to deal with that right now. "What's with the 'we' anyway? This is my story, and I don't know what makes you think—"

Jack snaps his notebook shut. "You're having fun, playing pretend?"

The outburst knocks the wind out of her. He's peeled away from the wall, and the hard set of his clenched jaw tells her he's angrier than he's letting on. It doesn't make sense—until it does, and Ginny wants to slap herself for being so stupid. Of course he was never here to help her out. That weak act of chivalry was just a way to get closer to a client with real cash, and now he's hoping to get her off the case so he can claim it for himself.

"What's your problem?" A summer breeze shivers down her bare arms, but her anger compensates for lost heat. "I don't see any cheating husbands around here. Doesn't look like your kind of case at all."

"Ridiculous. If you really wanted to help, you'd leave the case to somebody with some real experience. Maybe I should've told him the truth about you."

She stares up at his face, wishing her heels were a little higher, and she didn't feel like a damn child craning her neck. "Don't pretend you care about helping anyone either. You're just in it for the money. I bet you'll drag out the investigation long enough to cover your bills, and then you'll drop the case like it's nothing."

"That's not—" He catches his breath, shakes his head. She's caught him off-balance, but he's too stubborn to back off now. "You think you'll do any better? You're just looking for a good story for your gossip rag, so you can get famous off someone else's misfortune."

Ginny can feel her cheeks burning. He thinks he's got her number, but he doesn't know a thing. He has no idea what it was like that night at the Eighty-Three. The way the scene has been playing in her head like a skipping movie reel with no breaks, how she can't stop thinking about the implications of Josephine slumping between those men. She was drugged. She can't be sure yet, but Ginny knows what that might mean. Jack wouldn't understand. How many times she's found herself in the same situation as Josephine, fading out of consciousness from too many drinks while some cad tried to drag her to his coupe. How many forced petting sessions she's stumbled away from, all alone, with her friends whispering about her ruined reputation the next day. A guy like him can't know how the toughest girls can be brought low with a dose of something extra in their drinks, and how many times she's cheated assault through sheer dumb luck.

Josephine's story might be her key to a promotion, but solving the case is the only way to her own peace of mind, because in some other world, it's Ginny's body dripping silver between those three men, Ginny's body missing without a trace, with all the headlines drowned in silence until it's too late.

She doesn't tell him any of this. If he sees her as another hungry reporter, so be it.

"I don't care what you think of me," she says, stepping away until she's halfway through the dark alley. "Either way, I'm going to Ruby's place tomorrow, and you'd better not follow."

On her way home in the streetcar, Ginny presses her forehead against the glass. Pushing eight or nine in the evening, the sky flushes blue velvet, and the streets fill with polished cars carrying glittering men and women along the nightclub circuit.

Any other week, she'd be among them. Puffing smoke rings into the night with Dottie in the seat beside her, her sister's soft voice humming out show tunes above the car horns. Nightlife always hits a peak on Fridays and drags out until the end of the weekend, but not tonight, and maybe never again. She's already done the odds in her head, and there are only two possible ways this sordid story can end: either she saves Josephine and brings the Eagle to justice, or she knocks out her last breath in some dirty alley.

Ginny traces a stick figure in the fogged-up glass, pretending it's Jack Crawford with those crossed arms and creased felt hat.

She rubs him out with the heel of her hand as the streetcar stops a block away from home.

The city is a bright blur. Pushing past crowds of tired clerks headed toward the station, ignoring the revelers in their crunchy jewels and swishing silks, Ginny shuffles along the pavement to her building, trying hard to silence the frustration building inside her.

But there's someone waiting under the gold and cream awning, warm light glossing over his handsome face. There's no mistaking the easy slouchy posture, that back-patting way he's talking to the doorman, their laughs drumming through the night air. That same fair-haired boy she knew in the cornfields, with a smile for her alone. Ginny's heart skips over itself, her feet speeding up against the pavement, until she's close enough to touch him.

"This is a surprise," she says, suddenly conscious of the crumpled folds of her skirt suit, the lopsided angle of her red cloche. Charlie turns on his heel. The fond sparkle in his gray eyes is enough to make her knees buckle.

"Hello there." He leans in, and Ginny freezes—could he be reckless enough to kiss her in front of the doorman?—but then his lips skim her cheek in polite greeting and he pulls away, taking in the view from a distance. "I was on my way back from the office, thought I'd stop by. Harry was telling me about the latest Yankees game. Lost out to the Sox, didn't they?"

And Harry, oblivious to Charlie's great yawning disinterest in baseball, rocks back on his heels, nodding fast enough to send his doorman's cap slipping down his forehead. "Babe Ruth is sitting this one out, that's why. Mark my words, they can't win without him, and it's a damn shame."

They go on in this manner for a while, a spectacle of small talk with Ginny as the captive audience of one. She tunes out and watches Charlie, so at ease with anyone he's ever met. He was always like this, from the first moment she set eyes on him in Cherryvale. A pretty boy with a trust fund the size of Kansas would be hard to like if it wasn't for this charm, the warmth in his eyes that made you feel like the most important person in the world whenever he spoke to you. Like a moment in the sun, the kind of attention you want to wrap around your body forever.

He pats Harry on the back and turns his attention back to Ginny. "Shall we go?"

She blinks at him. "Go?"

"Yes, your sister must be so impatient already, upstairs. Wouldn't want to disappoint her, would we?"

With a week until the premiere, Dottie won't be back from rehearsals until late, and Charlie knows it. The full weight of his words comes down hard. It's a risky game, a gauntlet flung to her feet, a dare that could get them both in deep, dark trouble. If Dottie comes back early—if Harry talks—

Then Charlie swoops closer, and his whisper drips into her ear like dark honey.

"Unless there's something else you'd rather be doing?"

His fingers linger on the back of her suit, and she can feel his heat through all the layers. She doesn't have to say anything. The answer is all over her face.

No, there's nothing else, nothing in the entire world.

They go up to the top floor, an inch of air cooling the space between them as the elevator boy pulls the levers and Charlie makes more small talk. She doesn't know how he does it. Her heart is in her throat, even if she tried to say something, it would come out all jumbled.

And then they're in the apartment, and it's empty, and he pulls her into her bedroom, leading the way like he belongs here. Like all that's hers is his—and it is, it is.

He shuts the door to her bedroom, then slams her against it, and the shock of the impact sends pain shooting through her shoulder. He mistakes her gasp for pleasure and keeps going, faster this time, running fingers down her rib cage, unbuttoning her jacket hard enough to rip the fabric. He smells of the sea, fresh cotton, and clean sweat, and Ginny sinks into his arms again, then onto her bed, with a strip of moonlight cutting against their bodies as they push against each other at last.

He tells her things, dark and devious and dirty, except this time she's sober enough, and they prick her like so many needles. She arches back into the sheets, staring at the butterflies on her canopy, whirling faster from the rhythm of their bodies. Before she knows it, she's coming, the butterflies blurring before her eyes, her breath shuddering against his skin, pulling him closer, so there's no telling where she ends and he begins.

Charlie, Charlie, he'll drive her half-mad at this rate, the things she'll do for him. The imprint of his hand lingers on her neck even when they're done, and she feels like a crime scene marked by many fingerprints.

He buckles his belt and pulls two cigarettes from the lining of his jacket, then searches for a light. Ginny wraps the sheet around her and grabs her beaded purse from the floor, taking out her silver lighter and flicking it open in front of him. He places both cigarettes between his lips and leans into the flame, then offers one to her.

Ginny pulls at her smoke as he turns the lighter over in his hands, lips curling at the edges, his expression hardening. He's not like other men, she decides. No sleeping after sex for Charlie, instead his leg is jumping beneath the sheets, fresh energy pumping through his veins.

"Way to put a fellow in his place, giving him another man's lighter."

Too late, she remembers the dare at the Eighty-Three, the monogrammed lighter a consolation prize for the hangover that followed. Ginny leans against his shoulder, puffing smoke into the air.

"Who says I got it from a guy?"

He circles an arm around her, squeezing a little too tight. "Like I wouldn't know the difference. Should I be worried?"

She leans into his shirt, inhaling him, closing her eyes. "Don't worry your pretty head about it. I won this a couple nights ago, but I couldn't pick the owner out of a lineup."

He taps a finger against the monogram, and the metallic sound tings through the night. "Now I'm really worried."

Ginny gives him a playful shove, and he surprises her with a deep kiss, pulling the smoke out of her mouth. It makes her head spin. She slumps against her pillow.

"Did you get the flowers?"

"Sure." Ginny rolls over to her side. "You should be careful. People at *Photoplay* saw me with them. Any of them could talk, and then—"

"So let them." He reaches for her neck, trailing kisses down to her collarbone. Ginny leans back on her pillow. The light from her cigarette glints against Dottie's pearl heart earrings on her bedside table. She borrowed them last week, but she keeps forgetting to return them, and now the sight of the ghostly beads makes her feel suddenly hollow, like she's only half herself. She pulls away from Charlie and flings them to the floor.

"I'm serious, Charlie. We have to be careful if we're going to keep doing this."

The faraway wail of a siren creeps through the open window. Charlie runs a hand up her thigh, going around in circles.

"Or maybe not," he says.

"What do you mean?" Ginny traces his jawline with her fingertips. God, he's so handsome, perfectly coiffed hair coming undone with sweat, those lips red as a girl's.

"Don't you get it?" Charlie leans down on his elbows, a lock of hair falling over his eyes. "I love you, Ginny. Only you."

Her mouth goes dry.

She's dreamed of those words for many nights, but not like this. Never like this. Two nights of thrilling, desperate sex aren't enough for love. Her heart might be a damn mess after all these years of chasing highs in the city, trusting the wrong men, chasing the right ones away, arming herself against future disappointments with a sharp word, a disdainful look. Men will say anything to bend you to their will, but Charlie looks so vulnerable in this moment, lips parted, eyes gleaming, that she can see he's being honest.

Still, the awful truth echoes through her brain. She doesn't love him back.

She bites down on her lower lip, tasting iron. "You hardly even know me."

"I've known you all my life." Charlie twists toward her, fumbling to relight his cigarette. "I think, deep down I always knew it was you, not Dottie. She could never understand me the way you do. We're the same, Ginny Dugan. We were always meant to be together."

The flame rises high on the edge of the lighter, dangerously close to the violet sheets.

"Have you told my sister?"

"Of course not. I think you should be the one to tell her, if you want. It's your call."

Ginny keeps staring up at the butterflies on the canopy, watching them quivering in the breeze. She keeps her eyes averted as she delivers the final chord.

"Look, I had no idea you felt this way. Thought we were just having fun. And I . . . Well, I don't think we should tell her. It's too soon."

The words feel right in her mouth, but when she tries to imagine a future where she will break up her sister's engagement for Charlie's sake, her mind goes blank. The night takes a sordid turn as she stares at her own naked flesh, at the angry fuchsia flush creeping into Charlie's face, all signs pointing to a wrong turn somewhere between the streetcar and the doorman, as though their tryst at Gloria's apartment should never have seen a repeat performance.

Charlie's breath whistles through his mouth like he's been punched in the lungs. He doesn't say anything, but she catches the nerve pulsing in his forehead. Ginny turns away, her bandaged shoulder smarting from the motion. Charlie never said a thing about the wound. He's looked past it like so many other things, but this moment makes her wonder how he could claim to love her without ever paying her any real attention. Ginny trails her fingers down a run in her stocking. She's torn in two, half wanting him like never before, half wanting to leave him forever and never look back.

"You should probably go," Ginny says, "I've got work to do. Quirk's got me on the Follies beat for the premiere—"

"I could help. There's a lot you don't know about the Follies." He twines fingers with hers and smiles, nice and easy, like the conversation is a slate wiped clean. She gives him a light smack on the back of his palm. His casual self-assurance is enough to fade out the earlier unpleasant moment, and she can't resist the opportunity to tease him.

"Right, of course you know everything, Charlie Darby—"

"I'm serious. I heard some things at the club today, though I'm not sure you can print everything. The things that happen behind the curtain . . ."

A dark shiver runs down the back of her neck. *Please don't mention Dottie,* she wants to say, but her dry throat keeps her silence.

"One fellow says some of the girls are taking pictures on the side. Nude pictures. Wearing even less than they do on stage, fancy that. I didn't believe him at first, but then he showed me a few from his collection—"

Ginny rises to her elbows. "Of Dottie?"

"No, no." He takes a long drag from his cigarette, his brow creasing. "Never mind. Just thought it was interesting. You never know what's really going on."

He's a serious guy, Charlie. Top of his class at Princeton, top dog at Winthrop, Wright, and Company, an investment bank with an office in a skyscraper on Wall Street. And yet here he is, falling for any old conspiracy theory like the next sucker. The Follies girls make mad dough, and there's no way they'd stoop to nudes to keep dinner on their tables. It's exactly the kind of salacious college boy story that would send Ginny into fits of laughter at her mother's parties back home, but she limits her reaction to an understanding smile, tracing the contours of his face with her fingers. There's something comforting about a man like that. Gives her the upper hand, and he doesn't even know it.

Jack Crawford, on the other hand, is nothing like Charlie. The thought of him sends her pulse into overdrive. No amount of sex can wipe out the memory of his dismissive smirk in the alleyway, those last words carelessly flung to her feet. God, how she hates him, from the teardrop crease in his dusty felt hat to his scuffed leather shoes. Guy who can't even afford a proper suit, lecturing her about right and wrong. He might ruin everything, if she's not careful. One word about her job to Ruby Hurston and she'll be out of the game for good, destined to live out the rest of her life in the shadows, running from invisible gangsters.

They sit in silence for some time, then Charlie turns to kiss the inside of her wrist. "Something's on your mind."

Ginny lets out a long, exhausted breath. "Life's been hell, Charlie. I can't catch a break anymore."

"It's Quirk, isn't it? Don't tell me he's giving you grief again. If you want, I can reach out to my contacts—ask around—"

"Stop." She knows what he'll say, something about his dinner club, that well-heeled spiderweb of connections around New York. Maybe he's right. It's a tough city if you want to get ahead on your own merits, and it would be easy for him to make a few calls so she can take her rightful place on the next rung of the career ladder. But there are always strings attached, a debt owed for any kind of favor, and Ginny's not in a hurry to get herself on the hook at twenty-three.

She sits up in bed and leans down, grinding her cigarette in the heart-shaped ashtray on the ground. "I can do it on my own, you know. I don't need your help."

Charlie kisses her lightly on the neck. "I know. That's what's so damn sexy about you. So what's the problem?"

His touch is soothing, but she can't stop thinking about Jack. She can already tell he won't give up too easy, especially with his latest case hitting a dead end. If only she could find a way to reclaim the story that's hers by right, get rid of that lanky accountant-looking guy whose long shadow seems to be cutting her bright future in half.

"It's just frustrating," she says. "There's something I want, Charlie, but this other guy is trying to take it away from me."

Charlie's teeth flash into a smile that's blinding even in the dark. He drops his cigarette into the ashtray, not bothering to put it out, so the smoke curls into the air.

"Poor guy. I feel sorry for anyone who gets in your way." He runs his hands down her skin, peeling away the sheets. "It's your party, Ginny. Just you remember that."

And then his head is between her legs, and Ginny has to bite down to keep her moans from rattling through the entire building. It doesn't take long until all her problems fade to nothing.

CHAPTER SEVEN

She doesn't sleep until sunrise, staring up at the butterfly canopy until her eyes are raw. Dottie's earrings glimmer in her side vision no matter where she looks. She falls asleep for a couple hours, shifting through restless nightmares until her alarm jerks her awake again.

She gets dressed in a hurry and grabs the earrings, the cool pearls sending shivers up her arms. Although it's barely morning, a classical record is already crackling in Dottie's room. Ginny knows the drill: pliés, relevés, and half a dozen other ballet moves with unpronounceable French names for a solid hour, until her sister is slick with sweat, her stomach muscles heaving in and out from the strain. She follows this morning routine religiously, to remind herself that she is still a real dancer. Sometimes, Ginny wishes Dottie would accept the truth—nobody comes to the Follies for professional dancing, and her self-delusions won't do her any good in the long run. But then, Dottie would only slam the door in her face and get back to her routine, so there's no point in saying anything at all.

This morning, the room is banging with activity, heavy thuds interspersed with labored breaths, then the scuff of leather on floorboards. Ginny lingers with her ear to the door for a moment, but her curiosity gets the best of her, and she enters without knocking.

Dottie's on the floor by the open wardrobe, surrounded by many pairs of dancing shoes, her pale pink journal flipped open to a blank page. She's still in her nightgown, a tattered robe flapping open at the sides. She looks like she hasn't slept all night.

"You should really learn to knock." Dottie aims for scathing, but her voice is soft, exhausted. A flush crawls into her cheeks, and Ginny notices her glancing back toward the wardrobe.

"Relax, I only wanted to drop these off." Ginny places the earrings on Dottie's bedside table, trying to keep the memory of last night out of her mind as she does it. Dottie can be oddly clairvoyant at times, and this would be the wrong moment for her dormant skills to kick in. Luckily, the general disarray around her seems to be the main issue of the day, and Dottie keeps her eyes on her journal.

There's a new addition on her bedside table. A sepia shot of Josephine Hurston, the glamour dialed up high, with a spiky signature in the bottom right corner.

"What's this?" She picks up the frame. "You never said you knew Josephine."

Quick as a flash, Dottie peels off the floor and snatches the frame out of Ginny's grasp. "I don't, okay? I caught part of her show back in May and she signed a picture, that's all—"

"So, you're a *fan*."

"It's only a silly photo. Are you done now? I've got work to do." Dottie returns to her spot on the floor, trying to cover the wardrobe with her body.

Ginny knows what she's hiding, of course. She discovered the secret spot last year, when she ran out of gin during a party she was throwing while Dottie was busy with rehearsals. There's a hidden cubby behind her wardrobe, stuffed to the brim with old journals, sweet mementoes from past crushes, and a few boxes of candied plums Dottie won't dare open until she gets downtime from the show and she can afford to gain some weight again. Nothing criminal. Ginny's flipped through those journals, but Dottie's darkest secrets would make a nun pity her lack of experience. Charlie this, Charlie that, ate too much birthday cake and now it's time to work it off. Sweet and bland, just like Dottie. She shuts the door without a second glance and heads downstairs to her car.

As she drives into the ritzy Sugar Hill neighborhood in Harlem, the unlit fronts of nightclubs are slowly replaced by rows of residential buildings, growing higher and prouder with each new block.

The dizzy spin of bodies she's grown to associate with Harlem, flash of lights and smoke seeping through the cracks, all that is washed away with the morning. Smartly dressed Black folks fill the streets, in three-piece suits and pressed dresses with their hats fashionably angled. The pavement is swept clean of the night's excesses, and the neighborhood yawns itself awake with fresh flowers in stalls and small dogs tugging on their owners' leashes.

Saint Nicholas Avenue is lined with bright townhouses stretching into the soft blue sky. Ginny can't tear her eyes away; the view is almost enough to make her forget about the target on her back. Every house tells its own story, as if each builder injected some of his own soul into the heavy bricks: an elegant bas-relief here, a rounded tower there. A kaleidoscope of colors sings through the street in peach, emerald green, candy-apple red. One of the houses is painted electric blue, and a quick check tells her it's the right address.

As she's parking her car, she notices a battered green Model-T Ford turning into the street, and she doesn't have to look hard to know who's behind the wheel.

"I told you to stay out of it."

Jack climbs out with his notebook under one arm, flinging her a neutral smile like they're two neighbors talking about the weather. It's not even nine yet, but it looks like they both had the same idea of trying to outrace the other to Ruby's doorstep.

"Good morning, Ginny. What a pleasant surprise."

He keeps on walking toward the door, but Ginny blocks his way at the steps, breathing hard. "What will it take to convince you to get off my back?"

Jack pretends to think, running a hand over his chin. He looks healthier in the daylight, the deep shadows beneath his eyes a few shades lighter. "A couple hundred might do it, but something tells me Miss Ruby Hurston will be more generous. Especially when I tell her about my credentials. Maybe we should just let her decide for herself, see who she trusts to take the case, what do you say?"

His tone is light, casual, but the look in his eyes is dead serious. He's not backing down. Probably thinks this is an easy win, a professional detective going up against a party girl with a chip on her shoulder.

If he knew her at all, he'd know she doesn't step away from a challenge. And this time, she's got it covered.

"Fine. I hope you've prepared a good speech, detective. Wouldn't want to embarrass you in front of a client."

His smile falters, but he doesn't show any sign of turning back. This is going to be harder than she expected.

The doorbell is shaped like a treble clef. Ringing it sends a strain of airy music through the house.

"Chopin," says Jack in a reverent whisper. But before she can question his unexpected musical knowledge, the door swings inward to reveal a Black middle-aged woman dressed in a maid's uniform.

"Good morning. Miss Hurston is indisposed, so you'll have to come back some other time." The words tumble out in mechanical succession, as though they've been rehearsed and repeated many times.

"Mr. Calloway sent us," says Ginny. "Any chance Miss Hurston would like to talk?"

The maid leans slightly out the door, looking both ways as though making sure they weren't followed. Billy's name seems to do the trick, and they're ushered inside without another word, the door closed behind them in a hurry. The narrow building feels like it's been squeezed in at the sides, but the walls are dappled with sunlight, smells of sharp spices floating through the air. Every piece has been selected with care, from the ocher rug embroidered with strands of gold to the dark mahogany shelves filled with books and sheet music.

The maid leads them through a hallway, lined with photographs from floor to ceiling. All of them feature the same graceful little girls, who grow older as they move toward the room at the end of the hall.

"Miss Hurston will see you in the parlor."

The thick burgundy curtains are drawn. The air is stale, hanging with dust, perfume, and the bitter tang of medications. A figure stirs on the sofa. Ginny can barely make out her features through the tangle of blankets, and Jack looks like his first impulse is to close the door and leave.

"Good morning," comes a surprisingly sharp voice from the mess. "Take a seat so I don't feel so damn uncomfortable for lying down."

They settle into twin armchairs a few feet away. Jack unfolds his notebook and poises his pen at the ready.

"Miss Hurston—"

"Call me Ruby. Miss Hurston's my anemic aunt who comes over once a year to tear down all my life choices. You'd think I'm out here giving coat hanger abortions instead of scratching pen on paper."

Ginny feels her chest opening up, laughter curling in the pit of her stomach. "Ruby, then." Jack scribbles something in his book. Ginny hopes he's taking down the joke for future reference. "We spoke with Mr. Calloway last night. He mentioned you'd be interested in finding your sister."

Ruby props herself up on a stack of pillows, folding her hands over the quilted coverlet. She's made up to the nines despite her sickbed, bronze skin flushing at the cheeks, with crimson lips and flicks of shadow giving her eyes a feline tilt. Even the mole at the end of her left eyebrow looks intentional, an emphatic punctuation mark that leaves no room for second-guessing.

"That's right. Billy tipped me off about last night. Said he met some people who might help me find Josie. Didn't say you were white. Do you even know your way around Harlem?"

"Sure," says Ginny. "I've been around—"

"Don't tell me, you've been to the Cotton Club a couple times with some guy named Chip or Chet, had a grand old time. And then it's back to Park Avenue in the morning, where you can show off your fine taste in entertainment for your girlfriends. I know the score. Your people are happy to swing through this part of town for a good time, but somehow you never make it to our bookshops."

Ginny's mind goes blank, and she feels a sudden unexpected wave of shame.

Jack clears his throat into a fist. "You're a writer, Miss Hurs—Ruby?"

Ruby coughs into an elbow, then points toward a stack of crumpled pages on the table beside the sofa. Ginny shuffles through the stack with a reporter's eye, skimming the jagged verses on newspaper cutouts and plain lined pages, each of them with the byline Rose Red. Doesn't take a genius to figure that one out—those crimson jewels flaming in Ruby's ears, her lips tinted a deeper shade, everything matching that same color. Romantic, passionate, intense red.

When she turns back to Ruby, she looks healthy as anything, her skin glowing even in the low light. But she keeps her hands pressed against her stomach, and she winces as she shifts in her seat.

"Writer, poet, all-around sweetheart. But let's cut the small talk. You two came all this way for nothing. I've got it handled, and I don't need to pay a couple good-time kids to find my sister."

Ginny exchanges a look with Jack. She can tell he's thinking the same thing: they're only a few words away from getting kicked out of Ruby's house for good, and then they'll both be screwed out of the case. Something shifts in the air between them, a silent agreement to hold their fire against each other until they can convince Ruby they can be trusted. Catching a small nod from Jack, Ginny leans closer.

"Did Billy tell you the whole story, though?"

"Sure. He and Clive found you backstage, coming down from some spectacular high in a crate of stage equipment. Just goes to prove my point—"

On impulse, Ginny unbuttons her collar and slides her blouse sideways, revealing the bandages over her healing bullet wound.

"I saw her, Ruby. I saw everything." Taking advantage of Ruby's momentary silence, Ginny continues. "Three guys in bandanas took her. She looked like she was out of it, like they'd drugged her with something. When I tried to stop them, they gave me the old bullet shower and left me for dead."

Something flickers through Ruby's eyes, but she shakes it away. "That doesn't mean anything. It's not like you have any kind of lead—"

"Oh, but I know more than you think. Your sister auditioned for the Ziegfeld Follies sometime in May, didn't she? Except they turned her down, and whatever happened at that audition was a big enough blow to put her out of action for a week."

Ruby looks down at her hands. Her nails are filed down to perfect ovals, each one a different shade of iridescent red. Despite the solid set of her shoulders, her fingers are quivering against the pale sheets.

"Fine," she says after a while. "That's one point for you. How did you know?"

"My sister dances in the Follies chorus line. Have you heard of Dottie Dugan?"

A change comes over Ruby. She sits up a little straighter, folding her arms over her lap. Although she's still grasping for the upper hand, she doesn't sound quite as confident anymore. "So what?"

Ginny crosses her arms. "So, I hear things. And when Billy mentioned Josephine's long absence in late spring, I put the two together. That's just the beginning, Ruby. Give me a couple days, and I'll make sure you're reunited with your sister in no time."

"And what's his part of the deal?"

"He's my assistant," Ginny points at the notebook before Jack can contradict her. "Takes notes so I can keep my hands free."

He kicks the leg of her chair, but she's too busy enjoying her victory to care. So much for his big pitch.

"All right." Ruby heaves a deep breath, wrapping the sheets around her. "Maybe I'll find her faster with your help. I don't even know how much I should pay for something like that. How much do you want? One or two grand, I guess?"

Ruby's expression is neutral, but Ginny can barely hold it together. Billy didn't lie when he said the Hurstons were loaded. Two grand is mad money, the kind of dough that can sustain a couple years of decent living. If she can get her hands on even half of that, she can finally move out of Dottie's place and start building her own life.

"Whatever you can spare," says Jack.

"Fine. Two grand it is. So how are we gonna do this?"

"Why don't we start with the day your sister went missing. Tell us everything that happened on Wednesday."

The loose muscles in Ruby's face tense up for a second, but then she shakes her head, lowering her smoky lids.

"I was supposed to be with her that night. Never missed a show before. Sometimes, I even joined her on stage—might not have Josie's pipes, but I'm still damn good. The best when it comes to harmonizing, none of the other backup singers could ever feel her the way I did. Some things come naturally when you grow up together."

Her eyes glimmer with tears, but she seems too proud to show them. She continues with renewed vigor to hide the trembling of her voice.

"I've been running myself ragged lately. Josie was out of a job when they closed the Cotton Club, so I asked around some other joints to keep us afloat. I was the one who got us the gig at the Eighty-Three. It was me—"

Ruby takes a moment to collect herself. The mellow notes of a tuba pulse against the window, and Ginny catches a man practicing in the house next door, his eyes closed with sorrow. Looking around the ornately decorated parlor, Ginny wonders why Ruby would care so much about getting gigs for Josephine, since the sisters clearly have more money than most people she knows.

"I got sick that day. My voice was gone, but I said I could still make it—Josie didn't approve, but it was an important night for us. . . . She made me stay home. Kept me company until the very end, kissed me goodnight, and went on her way. And I haven't seen her since."

"Was there anything unusual about Josephine that night? Was she acting strange?"

"Nothing big. She was nervous, but I chalked it up to a new venue. Always had to check the sound inside the place, she was hung up on acoustics."

Something about the story rings false, and Ginny struggles to summon her own memory of the night. Josephine, stumbling into the song with the veil swishing over her face, shifting into her stage costume with every note. Ginny doesn't know much about music, but she's seen enough outfits to know when a piece is tailored to the wrong fit.

"You remember what she was wearing?" Ginny asks.

Jack throws her a quick irritated look, pen hovering impatiently in the air.

"The most *divine* gown of silver faille," Ruby breathes with stars in her eyes. "Hand-embroidered with metallic beads that made it look like chainmail. And a matching veiled hat with mirrored panels. She was throwing light in all directions."

"She didn't look comfortable." It's just a hunch, but the way Ruby freezes reveals a layer of truth. "Looked like something borrowed to me."

"I— that's odd," says Ruby with a rapid intake of breath. "It was made for her. Must've been nervous. I don't know what else."

If Ginny had a notebook of her own, she'd sketch out Ruby's face in that moment, because there's nothing innocent about it.

A fat gray Persian cat pushes through the door. It climbs into Ruby's lap, and she runs an absentminded hand through the fur, cooing in a low, husky voice.

"What's that? You hungry, baby?"

As the cat settles against Ruby's stomach, she releases a sharp breath.

"Are you all right?" says Jack. "Do we need to call a doc—"

"It's all taken care of," she snaps. "I'm fine."

Ruby straightens a bit, and in the dim light, Ginny catches the edge of a bandage poking out of her sheets.

"Something happened last month that made Josephine fire most of her bandmates," says Jack. Ginny remembers Billy's words, about not knowing most of the guys in the band, and she has to hide a grudging respect toward Jack for catching that part. "Except you and Billy, I suppose?"

"That's right. This was after the Cotton Club closed. You see—" She hesitates, twisting the bedcovers around her. Always moving, those polished fingers jumping across the sheets. "I probably shouldn't share any of this with you, but it's important to give you an understanding of the situation. I think—at least, Josie thought—that whoever closed the Cotton Club was targeting her. It made her suspicious of the people around her."

"Who would wish her harm?"

"Who wouldn't?" Ruby's expression hardens. "She's the talk of the town. You know how fame can open all these closed doors. Get you in league with the big guys, the fast money. If you ask me, there was more to Josie's life than singing."

"You talking about crime?"

"No." The word is harsh on her tongue. "Josie was no criminal, but there were plenty of shifty types at her concerts. She never told me anything. Said knowledge could be dangerous, put a target on my back. I never really believed that until she disappeared. Damn." She rubs her face with a shaky hand. "She might've messed with the wrong guys."

"Do you know anyone else with something against her?"

"Lord," Ruby gives a dark laugh. "There were plenty of people who wanted to see her fail."

"What about Billy Calloway?"

"Billy's a sweetheart. They've been going steady since high school. He worships the ground she walks on. You know he first learned to play the sax to impress her? He's a class act. Any girl would be lucky to have a guy like Billy."

"He wasn't jealous of all that attention she was getting?"

"Oh, nothing like that. Sure, he might get a little snappy every once in a while, but you can see his point, when she spends every night putting herself on display for crowds of strangers. But at the end of the day, he's also a showman, and he gets his good share of attention too."

Ruby runs her hands through her hair, looking out into the distance. Her voice softens whenever she says Billy's name. Ruby sure seems fond of her sister's boyfriend.

"What about these strangers? Any of them ever get too friendly?" says Jack.

"It's strange, being up there on stage. I know what it's like from her point of view: with the lights in your eyes, you can barely see a thing. Like singing to God himself. But I've been in the audience too. The crowd sees everything. Some people begin to think they own you, all lit up like a mannequin in a shop window."

Ruby rubs her lips together, lost in the image.

"Sounds like Josephine liked the attention, though. She auditioned for the Follies, didn't she? That rejection must've been devastating to her," says Ginny.

"That was a dark time for Josie. She got—" Ruby hesitates. "Let's just say they lured her out there on false pretenses. When that guy called her aside after a show at the Cotton Club, she thought she'd hit the big time. Headlining on opening night, with all of Broadway at her feet. Turned out all they wanted was a female Bert Williams, and there was no way in hell Josie would paint her face and make a fool of herself for those people."

The way she says it pierces Ginny straight through the heart. She swallows around a lump in her throat and asks the question she's been putting off since they came through the door.

"You ever heard of somebody called the Eagle?"

Recognition flashes fast over Ruby's face, like a prickle of electricity charging through her whole body. She shifts against the sheets, and the way she digs her nails into her palms tells Ginny she's about to lie. "Doesn't ring any bells."

Jack closes his notebook. From the way he keeps parting his lips and flicking nervous looks at Ruby, it looks like something else is on his mind. There's a vulnerability about him that Ginny hasn't seen before, and it makes her like him a bit more than she wants to.

"There's something else." He stares down at his pen, twisting it between his fingers. "The Eighty-Three is right in the middle of the action. You've heard about the Harlem heart attacks?"

"What about them?" Ruby shrugs. "People get high, they get in trouble. Sometimes they die. It's damn tragic, but what can you do?"

"So you don't think your sister's disappearance has something to do with them? I mean—" He fumbles with his notebook. "I've charted them right here, see— All of them happening around Lenox, close to the Eighty-Three, you don't think she could be somehow involved?"

It's the first time he's mentioned anything like this, and the raw emotion behind his words makes Ginny turn toward him. A map of Harlem, torn around the edges, is pasted into the middle of Jack's notebook, with bright red crosses over several nightclubs. The opposite page is covered in lines of neat handwriting. Jack's spent many hours on this case, and Ginny can't think of a client who might pay him for his time charting deaths in Harlem. She wonders if there are exceptions to his rule of only working for money.

"That's impossible," Ruby snaps. She turns her face toward the shadows, but Ginny catches something behind the scenes, a flash of fear beneath the hard mask. The cat jumps off her lap and slinks back out the door. "My sister is nothing like those fools. She— She's going to be all right."

There's something there, Ginny thinks, as the maid returns to usher them into the hall, muttering about Miss Hurston's need for rest. Ruby's trying to convince herself it's not her fault. She's got a guilty conscience and a personal connection to the heart attacks, and Ginny makes a mental note to find out exactly what that might be.

Before they go, Ginny pulls one of the pictures off the wall while the maid isn't looking, tucking the small frame into her purse.

As they head to their cars, Ginny shows the photo to Jack. Josephine is an inch shorter and Ruby has that mole beside her left brow, but otherwise they look almost identical, the same mysterious smiles, even their curls twisted in the same direction.

"Twins?" Ginny says to Jack, and he nods in confirmation.

As she stares into Ruby's eyes in the photo, something stirs inside her. Must be tough, growing up in the shadow of Josephine's stardom. Everybody knowing her name, Rose Red relegated to the back pages of a couple local magazines. Wondering why she gets the short end of the deal when they look so alike, two different paths charted from the same spot, and yet only one of them gets the talent, the glory, the handsome man on her arm. Billy. The soft note in Ruby's voice couldn't hide her feelings no matter how hard she tried.

Ginny imagines that pressure building, year after year, until one day something breaks, and decades of pent-up rage come crashing to the surface. And then Josephine's out of the picture, and there's no going back.

CHAPTER EIGHT

G oing to Grill King is Jack's idea, and it's only when they're tucked into a booth in the back with the stained menus between their fingers that Ginny wonders if it's a good one. By the stunned look on Jack's face, she can tell that the visit to Ruby's place has cast the same spell on him, blurring the lines between them into some semblance of a friendly silence. After the waitress takes their order and they're alone again, she leans forward and asks the damn question.

"So are we pretending to be friends now?"

Jack folds his arms. "You tell me."

"You didn't sell me out to Ruby," Ginny says. "You going soft, or what?"

"Just dazzled by your charms," he says in a flat voice, leaning back against the booth. When the waitress brings over the coffee, Ginny spills a few drops on the table in her rush to get her fix. Her sleepless nights are adding up, and soon she'll need more than coffee to stay awake.

"I didn't realize you were at the scene of the crime," Jack says after a while. "Sounds like you took a bullet for Josephine. I'm guessing you've got some tough guys on your trail now."

Ginny crumples a napkin between her fingers. Keeping this story a secret made sense when those guys still thought she was dead, but the game has shifted since then, and with Jack's interest in the Harlem heart attacks, he might give her some tips about the local underworld.

"Ever heard of somebody called the Eagle?"

Jack shakes his head. "Why? Is he after you?"

"Looks like it. Vivian Templeton warned me about him, and then I saw their leader at Ace last night. Tall guy with a face full of scars. They know I'm alive, they know my name, so I'm guessing it's only a matter of time before they return to finish the job." Ginny tears the napkin clean in two. "I need to find Josephine before that happens."

"No wonder you're so hung up on the story."

"Yeah, more like I let them get away, and now it might be too late to save her." Saying these words out loud sends a jolt through her body, and she takes a huge gulp of coffee to hide her surprise. Something about Jack makes her want to confess everything, and that can only mean trouble.

"You shouldn't blame yourself. You were outnumbered. They were armed. Clearly, they'd planned this through in advance, and you were just a bystander." Jack hasn't touched his sandwich, and his expression is grave. "Can't change the past, but I can see why you'd want to make things right."

"Is that what the Harlem heart attacks mean to you?"

She's caught him off guard, and he blinks against the harsh lights of the diner, placing a protective palm over his notebook. "Something like that."

"And you're hoping this case will give you some answers?"

"Maybe." He pushes his plate to the side and leans in, so that his face is inches away from Ginny's, his voice breathless and hushed. "I've been working on this case since April, and my investigation is telling me Billy Calloway's involved in something more than music. Seven heart attacks since then, all of them happening at clubs in Harlem, and guess whose band is always playing?"

Jack's words have a foreign ring to them, like a story in a cheap paperback, and she can't believe he's right. Not Billy, with his smooth moves and pleasant smile, so talented with his sax, so sorrowful over Josephine's disappearance. But then she remembers the softness in Ruby's voice when she said his name, and she's no longer certain about anything. If he could cheat on Josephine, who says he couldn't do more damage?

"Could be a coincidence," she says. "And unless you're saying he's killing those people with his smooth jazz bars, I don't see the connection."

"I'm not saying he's directly involved, but there's something suspicious about him all the same. He's been seen talking to several known drug dealers, and I want to find out what he's been up to."

"So what, you think somebody's been dealing killer drugs in Harlem? I don't buy it," says Ginny. "We're living through the worst heat wave since 1895. Might as well add the damn sun to your list of suspects."

"I've been in this business long enough to know when something is off, and those deaths have mob involvement written all over. I'm guessing you've seen the articles in *The Times*. Someone's paying heavy sugar to hide the truth, but none of my connections know who, and—" Jack stops himself, looking away as though he's given up too much. When he continues, his voice is back to that calculated baritone, his face a cordial mask. "As for Josephine, folks in this part of town go quiet whenever I mention her name. Only ever talk about her singing, but I think there's more to the story—and if she was seeing Billy, maybe her kidnapping was no accident either."

Ginny stares down at the dark brown liquid swirling in her cup, bringing herself back to that night at the Eighty-Three. The bright glow of the spotlight kept all eyes on Josephine's silver costume, but she can't help wondering if it was only a disguise, a shimmering mirage designed to deflect attention from the dark truth. Despite the fervent note in Jack's voice, Ginny's not sold on the story. That kidnapping felt personal, and the way Ruby talked about Billy only confirms she could've had good reason to get her sister out of the way.

Jack clears his throat. He fixes Ginny with a look that means business, and she can tell he's finally getting to the most important part of his pitch. "I can work this case on my own, Ginny, but I think we could do a better job together."

So those are his terms. Jack might look like a sucker, but now she can see that every move was carefully planned from the beginning. Pretending to be concerned when he ran after her and Billy out into the alley, then following her to Ruby's place. There are layers to this guy, and Ginny isn't sure she likes what she sees.

"You want me to help you investigate the heart attacks? Why?"

"You can blend in with these people," he says. "When I walk into a speakeasy, all they see is—"

"A dry agent?" Jack looks like just the type to try and fail to bust an undercover joint, with his clothes screaming cop from a mile away. He frowns, but doesn't argue with her.

"I was going to say something else, but sure, let's go with that. I need someone who can walk through any door without raising alarms, and with your personal interest in finding Josephine, I'm guessing we'll be looking into the same suspects anyway."

"What's in it for me?"

He hesitates. "Well, I—"

"You thought it would be an easy sell, huh? I'm not some girl you picked up at the soda fountain. I can see straight through your act. I'm the one with the connections, and you wouldn't be sharing any of this with me if you didn't know I had the upper hand."

He puffs out a breath, and Ginny's pleased to see his unguarded surprise.

"You'll need backup," he says at last. "Connections will only get you so far. These guys tried to kill you the first time they saw you, but what happens next? Do you really think they'll miss an opportunity to finish the job?"

He's right. She hates to admit it, but he's right. Ginny's had plenty of practice fending off unwanted advances, and she knows exactly where to kick a guy to send him straight to hell, but this is different. Judging by his lanky build, Jack's no brawler, but there's power in numbers, and Ginny can't afford to let her pride prevail over common sense this time. And there's something else too—the fire in his eyes burning through the good guy facade, the inside knowledge about what happens in the dark, beyond the distracting glow of the Harlem nightclubs. He might be wrong about Billy Calloway, but one thing's certain: Jack knows more than he's letting on, and that knowledge might be her missing link to finding Josephine. She'll tag along with him to a couple speakeasies, let him chase ghosts through all Harlem if he likes—and in the meantime, she might catch some clues of her own.

"Fine," she says, chugging the last of her coffee. "You're in. Under one condition."

He flings her an easy smile. "Sure."

"My investigation takes top priority, on account of my days being numbered and all, so we're playing by my rules. And I know exactly where we're going next."

By eight o'clock, they're standing by the backstage exit of the New Amsterdam. It's the ugly part of the grand building, leading out into a dank gray alley. Ginny still can't believe she's spent most of the day with Jack. She nudges him in the ribs and he turns to face her, brows flying up on his forehead as he clicks his pen with a nervous thumb.

"This is my crowd. The Follies. So you keep quiet while I—"

"—while you interview the showgirls. I remember, Ginny." There's an amused twinkle in his eyes, and she can tell he isn't taking her seriously. Still, it feels good to have some kind of power back, with the Follies lead from Gloria's party and Quirk's assignment giving her a good excuse to talk to the girls. Jack's interest in the Harlem heart attacks means he needs her more than she needs him, and if she can't get rid of him yet, then she might as well get him to follow her lead.

Dottie opens the door, and a pool of light escapes onto the concrete. She's wearing a tight stage costume made of interwoven vines, and what looks like a large rosebush teeters on her head.

"Well, this is a surprise."

"Hello, sis. I got bored and thought I'd swing by with my friend to pay you a visit. He's a big fan. Practically got the Follies tattooed over his chest."

Jack clears his throat, flushing a delicate pink. "Well, that's not—strictly—"

"I'm kidding. Quirk assigned me a piece on the Follies, so here I am, ready to deliver."

Dottie squints through the darkness. "What's your friend's name?"

"Jack Crawford, miss." He tips his hat. "I'd love to take a look behind the scenes, if it's not too much trouble."

Dottie offers an apologetic smile. "You seem awfully polite for a friend of Ginny's. I don't have the faintest idea where she might've picked you up, but I'm glad. Come on."

They follow her through a labyrinth of dark backstage hallways, drawn toward the warm-up tunes of a cheerful piano. The great auditorium smells of greasepaint and dust, clean sweat and sweet perfume. A treasure trove of heavy gold and vivid green, carvings of roses and grapes dripping from curved balconies. Jack goes still at Ginny's side, craning his neck toward the ceiling with a look of hushed rapture.

On stage, a chorus line of girls dressed as flowers sway in tune, the corded muscles in their legs rippling beneath shimmering gossamer stockings. A sturdy young man holding a pair of oversized garden shears walks in front of them, wiggling his brows in a comical manner.

Gloria is sitting in the audience with her feet on the back of the seat in front of her, fiddling with a pearl necklace. Her costume glows like moonlight.

"Oh, I'd like to be a gardener," sings the man onstage, shaking the shears, "in a garden of girls."

Dottie falls in line, kicking her feet in tempo, a frozen smile glazing her face.

Ginny settles next to Gloria, who leans her platinum head against her shoulder. The orange silk lilies in her hair brush against Ginny's neck.

"Stop," says Otto Sharp, rising to face the chorus line. His wide shoulders are accentuated by a padded suit the color of a summer night sky. "I want to see flowers, not trees. Let's start from the top. More energy. You're blooming, blooming—"

"How come you're not up there in the garden?"

Gloria stifles a yawn. She stretches out one arm to the ceiling, and for one brief moment the flaming lilies around her wrists make her look like the Statue of Liberty.

"I've been around long enough to pick my own numbers, and this one just doesn't do it for me."

"I'll bet," says Jack. He's gone quiet, making a concerted effort to look anywhere but at the bare legs flapping on stage.

"Who's this?" Gloria leans back in her chair with her eyes tracing Jack all over.

"Jack Crawford, ma'am."

"What a pleasure, Jack darling. I sure hope there's more of you wherever you came from." She squeezes his hand, and Ginny feels a prick of irritation at the way he melts at the easy flirting, like she's found the key to him in seconds.

"Listen, Glo, I'm doing a piece on the Follies. Should be good publicity, with the premiere around the corner. Think the girls would object to an interview?"

"The girls will chew your ear off even if you don't ask." Gloria wraps the necklace around her wrist. "Just say *Photoplay*, and they'll be putty in your hands."

"And Mr. Sharp?"

Gloria pauses with the pearls between her nails. "I think he'll be amenable, if I get him warmed up first, of course."

"That sounds real jazzy, Glo. I knew you'd help."

"Like I said—anything at all, darling. Hang on a minute."

"Is she a chorus girl?" Jack follows Gloria's departure with glassy eyes. Ginny nudges him in the ribs.

"She's way out of your league, buddy. Last guy she married owned half the drugstores in New York."

It comes out despite her best intentions. Jack gives her a wild look.

As Gloria leans over Mr. Sharp's shoulder, her behind rounds out against the edges of her costume, completing a perfect hourglass. If you don't look closely, you'd peg her for a schoolgirl dressed up in mama's clothes, with those tight legs and rose-tinted cheeks. But the eyes betray her age, those hard diamonds scarred with the marks of a complicated life.

For Ginny, that makes her even more beautiful.

After a series of abortive starts and unsatisfying endings, Mr. Sharp declares the garden number passable, and the rehearsal comes to a close. Dozens of light feet scatter in the direction of the dressing room. Only Zita hangs back, staring out into the audience, her empty eyes bright like twin spotlights. She's laid on the greasepaint extra thick tonight, and bits of dusky paint are chipping off at her jawline. Ginny wonders if her marital troubles have been keeping her up at night—but then, she can't imagine marriage to

Mr. Sharp offering any kind of comfort, especially in the anxious days leading up to the premiere.

Gloria separates from the stage manager with a covert nod in Ginny's direction.

As Ginny rises to her feet, Jack lingers in the audience. He looks smaller than usual, sitting with folded hands in the red velvet chair. His eyes are lost in dark hollows, with a shadow creasing an early wrinkle between his brows. For all his fatigue, he jumps into a lively conversation with Gloria as soon as the star gets back to her seat.

The stage manager sits mopping his brow with a white cotton square, sweat rolling down his cheeks as if he's the one who spent hours kicking his legs into the air. Ginny extends a hand. He eyes it as if it's some foreign object.

"Ginny Dugan, reporter. I've seen you around some of Gloria's parties, thanks for taking the time to talk. I'm looking into some strange occurrences at this theater."

It was Jack's idea to start with something vague to see where Otto Sharp might take the conversation, and Ginny can see the man's mounting discomfort as his eyebrows shoot up to his hairline. "Excuse me?"

She keeps quiet, staring at a point just above his eyes. It's a tactic she's been dying to try ever since she read it in a spy story, supposed to get the suspect talking to fill the void. Sure enough, something cracks beneath the surface, and he lets out an oppressive sigh.

"If I have to hear one more story about the damn ghost—"

"What's that?"

"Isn't that your angle? The dead showgirl, come back to haunt the theater and terrorize the girls who've replaced her? Well," he snaps. "Don't look at me like that. You seem like a nice girl, but I know the game you tabloids play. You're all the same."

"Hold on there. That wasn't the angle at all, but you might change my mind. What's this about a death?"

The last word catches Jack's attention, and he goes quiet in the audience, turning away from Gloria.

"You've heard of Olive Thomas, of course. Ziegfeld Follies of 1915. Poisoned herself during the Paris run of the show in 1920, but this was before my time, so don't look so excited. If it's gossip you want, you'll be better off in the dressing room with the girls."

"Maybe you're right, let's leave the past and take a closer look at the present." She jots down a few random words just to grate his nerves a bit, then looks up. "Times are changing, Mr. Sharp. I've noticed all your girls are white, but everybody knows the best talent is in Harlem. Ever thought of showcasing the melting pot of our great nation?"

He shoots a quick look at Gloria, as if angling for a way out. She keeps her eyes on the long string of pearls around her neck. Zita is in the other seat next to Jack. She's waving her arms through the air, fluttering her lashes at double speed, while he nods in time to her every word. Ginny suppresses a sudden urge to step between them and force the conversation to a screeching halt.

"We've got plenty of variety here. Girls from almost all the states in our great nation. Great Plains to coal miner towns. That what you want to know? Anita Darling is half-Italian, and even Gloria here—"

"So you wouldn't object to a Black showgirl?"

He whips the handkerchief into his pocket. "I don't catch your meaning."

" 'Cause I know for a fact that you had an audition with a certain famous Black singer, and you turned her down, even though you won't find a more talented performer for miles. That doesn't sound like good business to me."

He stands with his hands in his pockets, breathing hard. The look on his face makes Ginny wonder if he's about to slap her.

"Your sources are no good, Miss Dugan. You want to hear the full story about Josephine Hurston, beloved Songbird of Harlem?"

Ginny's pen falters on the surface of her pad. Here it comes.

"I'll tell you about that one. We were going to hire her. I told her as much, we were branching out, and I wanted something fresh to spice up the show." In the audience, Gloria snaps her head toward them, as if this is big news to her. Otto continues, his expression hardening. "I wanted another audition to be sure, get her singing with the group, see how they mesh together. It's part of the casting process, and I wasn't going to make an exception for her. Seem fair to you?"

"Fair enough."

"She didn't like it. Snapped at me like I was asking something crazy. She had all these conditions, you'd think she was Marilyn Miller after *Sally* instead of some nightclub singer. Didn't want to do any plantation numbers, can you believe it?"

She sure can. Josephine sounds like a woman who knows her own mind, and Ginny can't picture her agreeing to play a slave on the stage of the New Amsterdam. She's got the kind of star power that goes beyond playing into tired racist stereotypes, and Ginny's surprised that Otto Sharp had the audacity to invite her for such a show.

126

"And then her man came to pick her up, and I thought, good riddance," the stage manager goes on, oblivious to Ginny's thoughts. "She'd be nothing but trouble, that's for sure."

"What about the man?"

His eyes cloud over at the memory. "Tall guy, dressed to the nines, with a low kind of voice. Real polite. But then he pulled her out of here by the arm so hard I thought she'd snap like a twig. Yelled at her in the hall, something about going behind his back. Threatened to rough her up if she did it again. Of course, I wasn't about to butt in between a man and his woman, but I didn't like the look of it."

"Do you remember anything else about him?"

"He was carrying a sax case, so I guess he was a musician, but you never know with guys like that. Might've been carrying a sawed-off shotgun instead."

Billy Calloway didn't mention seeing Josephine after her audition. And he didn't seem like a violent man. But with Jack's case against him combined with that fond sparkle in Ruby's eye when she mentioned his name, Ginny can bet he's a man who can keep a couple secrets.

CHAPTER NINE

"It's falling right into our laps. I don't know if that's a good thing."

Jack paces in the corner of the theater, hands locked behind his back. He's right. They've got the prime suspect right in front of them, and he's ticking all their boxes. Ginny leans against the wall, trying to fight off her exhaustion as Jack bends a finger for each new point. The day has left her bone-tired, and it's taking all her energy to remain upright.

"He's got the means—he could probably pick her up and carry her away on his own, or hire some guys to do it for him. No problem, check. Same goes for opportunity. He was right there on stage when the lights went out. He said he was keeping an eye on her, but he might've been watching to make sure she was in position for the kidnappers to take her away. Check."

"And now we got our motive. Jealousy." Ginny tries to picture the scene, Billy Calloway's handsome face curling in anger as he hires several guys to kidnap the woman who disobeyed him. Get her out of the picture so he can be with her sister.

"I don't know," says Jack. "It doesn't feel quite right. We're missing something here."

"She was trying out for the Follies behind his back. Maybe he was getting too possessive, and she wanted a fresh start." Ginny looks over to the stage and tries to picture Josephine's audition. The stage costume with the veil makes much more sense if she was trying to hide from more than just her fans—if the man she loved had suddenly turned violent. "You said it yourself, Jack. Billy Calloway got involved with some bad guys, and what if he was just as rough with his girl?"

"I'm not sure about that. The Follies would've given her a clean slate, but she would've been right there in the spotlight. New York might be a bit more tolerant than most spots in this country, but she'd have a hard time keeping a low profile. . . . If the plan was to get away from her boyfriend."

Jack bites down on the end of his pen and looks out at the theater. The main players are gone, and now the staff are coming out to clean up after the rehearsal. Guys in overalls with big buckets of dirty water, carting decorations out of view, scrubbing down the stage. Zita lingers out of Jack's sight, biting her nails as she stares intently at the back of his head. Ginny shifts so she doesn't have to face her, those round eyes gaping even wider like Jack is the only man in the entire world. *Damn showgirls with their crushes.* Ginny wonders if there's something in the paint at the New Am, or else Zita's gone out of her mind, risking her husband's wrath for Jack fucking Crawford, of all people.

"Maybe she didn't plan ahead," Ginny says.

"Josephine had her life together until the end. Remember the story about testing every new venue, making sure the sound was right? No, this was a woman who weighed the odds before taking a step." Jack pushes out a sigh. "Something's missing, Ginny. If this was a crime of passion, why would he send someone else to do his job? And why would he hire us to investigate her disappearance?"

"You've been following him since April," says Ginny. "You tell me. What kind of man is Billy Calloway?"

"He's careful, that's for sure. I never caught him doing anything underhanded, and he never lost his cool, except this one time. . . ." Jack taps his pen against his chin. "I saw him talking to some guy outside a club, and he looked about to murder him. They spoke for a couple minutes, then the other guy left, and Billy slammed his fist into the wall. It was terrifying to watch."

"Did you recognize the other guy?"

Jack shakes his head. "It was too dark. But I remember the way he moved, quick and furtive like he was always watching his back. I'd recognize that walk anywhere."

"Jack," Zita comes up to them, her painted eyebrows sloping like a sad clown's. "Sorry to interrupt, but— Well, could we talk in private?"

Her fingers hover over his arm. Jack's expression goes smooth, and he gives her a reassuring smile, the kind Ginny's never seen on his face. "One minute. I'll be right with you."

Zita hovers on the edges of the conversation a while longer, then retreats to the side of the stage, still watching them from afar.

"What was that?"

"Hmm?" Jack brushes his hair out of his face with an absent look. "Oh, nothing. We were talking earlier, she wanted to finish our conversation. Now where were we—"

"And on a first-name basis already. Damn, detective, you work fast."

A faint flush creeps into his cheeks, and he looks down, bashful. It's so easy to make him blush. She's never met a guy who gets so worked up about the smallest things, but then somehow folds back into a serious professional in a second if the occasion calls for it. Ginny tries to picture him growing up, the kind of boy he might have been. Top of his class, probably lived in the library, only breaking away from his books to help his mother bake a pie or mow the lawn. A good guy. If she knew him then, she probably would have teased the living daylights out of him—not out of real hatred, but from a secret insecurity that he's a much better person than she could ever hope to become.

The curtain parts in the middle, and Gloria pokes her head through the folds. From this vantage point, it looks like she's wearing nothing at all. The bare shoulder against the dark velvet sends a shiver down Ginny's back. It's unbelievable, how the sight of Gloria still has this effect on her, after all those late nights getting up to no good together.

Jack makes a big deal about studying a bas-relief of a bird of paradise on the wall behind him.

"Are you coming, Gin?"

"In a minute." Ginny looks at Jack's profile. "I'm going to check out the dressing room, see if I can get anything out of the girls. Think you can handle yourself out here?"

"I'll meet you at the backstage exit later. Try to stay out of trouble."

Ginny follows Gloria behind the curtains. Sure enough, her costume is hiked down her shoulders, but otherwise still covering up all unmentionables.

"You'll give that boy a heart attack if you keep that up." *And me.* Gloria smiles wide. "Can't help it, he's too delicious. Nice to see you've moved on since Charlie."

She says it so casually, without dipping the pitch of her voice by a single note. Ginny stops in her tracks. The moment drags out into eternity, anxious thoughts stumbling through her mind as she watches Gloria, the easy curve of her smile deepening as the silence stretches.

"You thought I wouldn't know?" Gloria places a warm hand on Ginny's back and gives her a gentle push in the direction of the dressing room. "The way you were looking at each other that night at my place. I thought the entire building might burn to the ground."

"Not here," Ginny says. They might be out of earshot, but the backstage walls are thin as paper. "Somebody might hear us—"

"I always wondered about that one," Gloria says, tucking a dark strand behind Ginny's ear. "So polite, like he'd stepped off the pages of Emily Post's manners guide. Never seemed like your type, not really."

"I don't have a type."

"Sure you do. Always going in for the hard boys, aren't you? The ones with a little too much liquor on their breath, with bad news written all over. I wonder why."

Ginny shrugs, feeling the heat building in her cheeks. "Used to think danger was exciting. I'm not so sure anymore."

"What happened after?"

After. The word has grown bitter in her mouth. She can't help thinking of Billy Calloway and all the ways he might be just like Charlie, except much worse.

"He says he's in love with me. Wants to break it off with Dottie."

Gloria's breath whistles through her teeth. "Now that's something. What are you gonna do about it?"

"Nothing. I don't know. I don't love him back, Glo. Does that make me a terrible person?"

Gloria leans against the wall. A shadow falls across her face. Lips pursed, she digs her fingers into her folded arms. "If anyone's terrible, it's Charlie. Nobody can fall in love that quick, unless he's been bricked in the head."

Ginny looks up, startled by the pitch of her voice. Like a hiss across the radio waves.

"What do you—"

"It's been what, a couple days? Read between the lines, Ginny. Sometimes love is just another word for control."

He does like to be in control, Charlie. Pinning her to the bed, smothering her with hard kisses until she can barely move. All the bruises he leaves behind, developing over time like photographs so she can never forget. It's part of what makes him so thrilling, this mean streak, but he's much too polite to be a real villain.

"You don't know him like I do. Charlie's always been a gent. He comes from one of the most respectable families in Kansas. Ask anyone, and they'll tell you Darby means God in their language."

"Not in mine. I'm serious, darling. I don't want to see you hurt, and I don't care how grand this guy is. In my eyes, he's a man who's trying to bend a woman to his will, and that's not something I can stand for."

"Wasn't it the same for you in Boston? Everyone tangled up in each other's pasts, unable to get out of the web?"

"Hm? Yes, I suppose. But I ran away as soon as I could, and now I make my own webs." Outside the dressing room, Gloria turns toward Ginny so they're nearly knocking foreheads. They're the same height. She's never noticed before, with Gloria always towering above the world like a golden idol. A warm thrill runs through her chest as they lock eyes. "I can help, you know."

"What do you mean?"

"You've got so much fire, darling. I know you can get reckless sometimes, but— Well, I can't stand by in silence if you're letting this guy mess up your life."

It's a mild comment, but suddenly Ginny feels like she's been slapped with a hand full of sharp rings.

"Stay out of it, Glo."

"But surely—"

"I got teeth and nails same as anyone. I can clean up my own damn mess."

Gloria regards her without a word, the surface of her face glossing over like a page in a magazine. "Whatever you say, darling. Come on."

The comment bites and claws like something nasty, and Ginny enters the dressing room in a foul mood. Everybody's always trying to tell her things. Jack Crawford with his droning lectures, Dottie shooting down her dreams, and now even Gloria, the one person she thought was on her side. They'd better get their facts straight. Reckless isn't stupid, and impulsive only means she can make decisions twice as fast as anyone else.

Inside the dressing room, the air hums with excitement. Sequins and feathers fly across the room, bare limbs tangling in gauze and silk. The girls swap their fancy plumage for sober street clothes, tossing banter like glittering batons to each other. It's like watching butterflies turn back into caterpillars.

As her anger recedes, Ginny feels a sudden crash of exhaustion, and she leans against a rack of costumes. She's been restless since that night at the Eighty-Three, and she wonders if she will ever get a solid night of sleep until they solve the case.

Ginny runs a hand over a beaded green dress. It makes her think of the sparkle in Mary's eyes when she talked about the Follies. None of the showgirls seem aware of a new girl joining the chorus line, and Ginny wonders what happened at Mary's audition.

"You like it?" says Gloria.

"Is it one of yours?"

Zita swings through the room behind them, her flushed cheeks bright even beneath the heavy greasepaint. "Oh, Gloria's too high and mighty to share. She's got her own room upstairs."

"Look who's talking." There's a touch of steel beneath Gloria's light smile. "Zita asked for her own room, first chance she got. Perks to being the stage manager's wife."

Although Zita's smile dims slightly as Gloria leaves, she doesn't seem too bothered, and she turns to Ginny with a new energy crackling through her body.

"I gotta ask. Are you and Jack together?"

A choked sound between a laugh and a cough claws at Ginny's throat. She must be joking. Tall, lanky, dead-serious Jack. Not exactly fit material for any kind of romance. There's no denying she's much closer to tolerating him now that they've found a way to work the case together, but there's no way in hell she'd ever picture herself with a guy like that.

Maybe Gloria has a point. She does like 'em dangerous. Jack's too much of a square for her taste, and she's pretty sure he'd prefer some sweet hometown blonde to Ginny's particular brand of woman.

"He's not my type, honey. I like my men with a little edge."

"Oh, good." Zita hugs herself for a moment, then turns to leave with her eyes still dancing. "He's a dream, that one. An absolute dream."

Ginny watches her climbing the stairs to her own dressing room, humming show tunes under her breath. Beside her, Anita shrugs out of a lavender costume, clicking her tongue in Zita's general direction.

"Don't worry, Zita's fantasies usually stay unfulfilled. Girl's got her head in the clouds, and I don't blame her, with what she's got at home."

"Guessing you're not a fan of Mr. Sharp."

"Eh, he's fine, but I don't like a man who bosses his girl around. Reminds me too much of my daddy. That's why I married Sal—not much of a looker, but he listens to me like I'm the damn pope." Her eyes brighten. "By the way, I got something for you. Help me with that zipper, sweetheart, and I'll tell you a story."

Ginny obliges, and Anita steps out of the beaded ensemble with a flourish. She's built for power with a sturdy torso and wide shoulders, tanned all over with a smattering of moles.

"Remember what you said about the Eighty-Three?" Anita admires herself in the mirror, then pulls out a drawer, fetching a pair of seamed stockings. "The cops, the raid, all that jazz. Well, looks like the owner's got bigger connections than Owney Madden, 'cause the Eighty-Three is back in business tomorrow night."

That can't be right. Not after what happened that night, bottles smashing, cops snapping cuffs on every guest they could catch. Josephine's kidnapping still unsolved.

"Are you sure? It looked final to me."

"Like I said, my sister's got her ear to the ground, and apparently it's all anyone can talk about. Big trucks hauling fancy food at all hours of the night. They're hiking the entrance fee to five bucks, can you believe it? Must be counting on some ritzy clientele after the raid."

Ginny knows what that means. The Eighty-Three is getting its fashionable makeover, and soon the Park Avenue crowd will flood into its basement room, leaving no space for locals to shake a leg in. She remembers Ruby's words and shivers despite the heat.

With her stockings rolled midway up her legs, Anita freezes. Her dark eyes widen as she turns to the mirror, looking like she's terrified of her own reflection. "It's happening."

"What—"

"Didn't you hear that?" She crosses herself with a muttered prayer, then returns to her stockings. "Happens almost every day, especially when we stay late rehearsing. The ghost can feel our energy zapped and knows we're at our lowest. Right here." She lowers her voice and points toward the mirror that covers the entire wall, floor to ceiling.

Ginny remembers Otto Sharp's story and pulls out her notepad. "You're saying this ghost lives in your mirror?"

"It's in the *walls*."

"You heard it too?" Mazie comes wandering over, already dressed in a sober black skirt suit that makes her look sick. Ginny wonders if she's had any more fainting spells since Gloria's party, because she's got the look of somebody with one foot in her own grave. And yet a charged expression crosses her face as she looks at Ginny, taking her in from head to toe before continuing her spiel. "Last time it happened, I thought there was gonna be an earthquake—I'm from California," she says by way of explanation. "So I know what that's like."

"I said three Hail Marys and it stopped." Anita crosses herself once more as she slips into a deep red dress. "Banging on the walls something crazy. Moaning."

Mazie nods. "I couldn't stop screaming. I had to curl up on the floor, yelling my head off, it was that bad."

"I told Mr. Sharp a couple times, but of course he didn't listen a minute. Said, *Anita, don't be silly. You women are always getting things into your heads,* something like that. But if he doesn't get rid of it soon, I swear I'm changing companies. George White has been after me since I was a teenager."

"You'd switch over to the *Scandals?*" Mazie's plain face widens at the notion.

"Better than losing my soul." Anita tucks her hair into a battered cloche. "You got that down, *Photoplay* girl?"

"Sure did." Ginny looks around the room, trying to find any sign of ghostly activity. It's a classy joint, the New Amsterdam. Even the dressing room is polished like a trophy. Racks of costumes for dress rehearsals, shoes stacked up against the opposite wall. Big wardrobe for the serious pieces. The best costumes are handsewn by Erté in Paris, with a price tag beyond a year's wages.

She settles into a chair in front of the mirror and tries to imagine what it's like to call this place your work. Sometimes, she catches a glimpse of a feather boa, breathes in the oily tang of greasepaint, and she gets it. Why Dottie spends her nights tapping out new numbers instead of doing the same in one of the many other joints in town. Why Mary would want to drop everything for a shot at the limelight on this particular stage. Why these girls keep fighting for a place in the chorus line, even if it means bowing to the capricious needs of the stage manager. There's an energy she can't shake, the old walls whispering sweet nothings in her ear. Ginny leans down on the dressing table and shuts her eyes. . . .

Something pokes between her shoulder blades. Jolting awake, Ginny turns to find herself uncomfortably close to Mazie's freckled face.

"You were sleeping." Reproach trickles through her colorless voice, but her hand lingers a beat too long on her back.

The other girls are gone. Even Dottie, probably running off to be with her beloved fiancé. Ginny slaps herself across the cheeks. There's no telling how long she's been out. With the ghost story swallowing her time, she forgot all about the investigation. Jack won't let her hear the end of it. Ginny Dugan, sleeping beauty.

Minus the beauty, she thinks as she studies her reflection.

"Do you need something to wake you up?"

"I'm fine." She rubs at the mascara stains beneath her eyes.

"It's our secret weapon." Mazie rattles around in her bag. "Only you can't write about it."

That wakes her up, all right. "Why not?"

"It's a Follies thing. That's why I waited for Anita to leave before saying anything. She's new, so I can't tell if she's loyal yet, and did you hear that whole thing about joining the *Scandals*? But I like you, Ginny. And I want to help."

There's something different about Mazie. Her wide eyes charged with intention, pale cheeks burning hot. And then Mazie is pulling her close, pressing her hot lips against Ginny's, trailing her fingertips down her neck. For one wild moment, Ginny relaxes into Mazie's arms, letting a wave of pleasure pull her under—

But then panic crashes through her whole body. She breaks away from the kiss, knocking a jar of rouge from the dressing room table.

"Oh," says Mazie after a minute, lowering her eyes. "I'm sorry. I thought—"

"No, no. It's not— I'm sorry, I'm just tired. I can't do this now." Ginny can feel her heart in her throat. An old feeling stirring deep in her chest, playground crushes at school, the softness of another girl in her arms in the changing room before gym. Feelings she's tried to suppress for many years, after learning the price you pay for loving another woman in any way that matters. Sure, she's had plenty of encounters after hours, drunk women falling into her arms on the dance floor, making out in public with a crowd of desperate men cheering them on. She's kissed women in secret too, and almost followed them home a few times—but something would always stop her at the very last moment, a voice awfully similar to her mother's saying she's a deviant, a freak, a waste of a perfectly good daughter.

She can't find the words to explain any of this to Mazie, but she doesn't need to. The girl is back to rifling through her purse, avoiding Ginny's eyes with all her might.

"Anyway. This doesn't change the fact that I really want to help, Ginny. It's heartless to keep you in the dark, with the way you've been going on—"

"I'm perfectly fine, Mazie."

"No, sure, sure you are. I just meant—" She clears her throat. It's clearly a speech she's gone through many times, but there's conviction burning through the rehearsed words. "I know what it's like, as a woman making it on her own in this world. You gotta put in twice the work to get half the recognition, if that. So you know what you gotta do?"

"What?"

"Level the playing field." She's pleased at this turn of phrase. "How do you think we stay so chipper after all those hours on stage?"

Mazie rolls a small gilded object across the dressing table. Ginny catches it between her fingers. A tube of lipstick. Cautious, she unscrews the lid, but the only thing inside is a shock of baby pink. Something familiar, but she doesn't get the point.

"Thanks, doll, but it's not my color."

"No, silly." Mazie's freckles dance as she laughs. She turns the tube around in Ginny's hands. "Other side."

She sees it now: a tiny gold button right by the edge. Ginny pushes down. A mist of white powder falls onto the table through a hole in the bottom.

"You have to breathe it in to feel the effect." Mazie crosses her arms on her chest, looking like a proud teacher. "You can keep this one if you like. I've got another."

She remembers now. Vivian Templeton at Ace, pulling a lipstick tube out of her satin pouch. She was pushing her own goods, like Mazie.

"Don't know if I can afford this." Ginny tries to return the tube, but Mazie only smiles as she gets up to leave.

"First time's always free. Come on, try it."

It's not like she's never gone beyond liquor. She's no fresh-faced kid, off the bus from some cow town with the stars in her eyes. There have been reefer cigarettes rolled on the spot, lying on some college boy's shoulder as the giggles rocketed through her body. Cocaine licked off strangers' fingers. She's never gone so far she couldn't backtrack from it, stayed away from the heroin syrup still sold on dirty street corners if you were desperate for a fix. She's always known when to stop before losing control, and it's not like one little fix will do her any harm. Maybe Mazie is right, and a pick-me-up is exactly what she needs right now.

So she arranges the loose powder into a line and leans down, breathing deep with her left nostril pushed shut.

It hits her like a mule kick, a fresh burst of adrenaline straight through the skull. She jolts back up, sparks dancing in front of her eyes.

"What the hell is this stuff?"

Mazie seems pleased with the results.

"It's kind of like medicine, I guess. The girls call it pep powder."

Pep powder. The kind of words that roll off magazine pages, shine from great big billboards. Like a one-step solution to some fundamental problem. Wash away fat with La-Mar Reducing Soap. Erase your wrinkles with Catherine McCune's Silk Muscle Lifting Mask. Fix your spine with a revolving hammock, find love with Elinor Glyn's new book, get laid by gargling with Listerine.

Pep powder. She's heard it before, but she can't tell if it's just one of those meaningless combinations, an amalgam of every ad she's ever seen. Whatever it is, it's working fast, and she doesn't have the patience to sit there remembering.

Time jumps along in bursts and crawls. She spends a good amount staring at the tube. The dressing room lights wink against its surface. Whoever came up with this nifty idea picked the right packaging. Gold, like money. Opportunity. Hope. Its promise of limitless value weighs heavy in her hand.

"Where'd you say you got this, Mazie?"

No answer.

"Mazie?"

The room is empty. The clock reads nine—no, past that, she's been here for over an hour. Ginny shoots out of her chair. *Jack*. He must be sick of waiting, if he's still there, of course. Waiting while she gets high in the Follies dressing room.

It's like whenever she tries to fix her life, she only digs herself a deeper hole.

She unscrews the lid and takes another look at the pale pink. Untouched, a perfect cylinder whittled to a sharp point, smelling of powder and rose oil. Not her shade by a long shot, but it's the kind of inoffensive hue that would delight her sister. Ginny draws a line across her mouth, rubs her lips together. The result is garish in the mirror, but it inspires an idea that makes her shake with laughter.

A twirl for her reflection, an affected little laugh, and the picture is complete.

"Why, it's a pleasure to meet you," she says in a soft, coquettish voice. "I'm Dottie Dugan, the greatest dancer alive!"

The mirror shakes with a sudden thud. Ginny's smile fades. She rubs away the lipstick with the back of her hand, shoots a wild look around the room.

"Hello?"

Nothing. The silence rings heavy in her ears.

The green dress sways in her direction, a faint tinkle of glass beads. Ginny falls into a chair. Was the door open before? Now it's cracked a sliver, with the darkness entering the room in harsh shadows. *Just a draft, that's all.* She doesn't know why her heart is suddenly racing over a bit of fresh air. Being alone in this room no longer feels like fun.

But is she alone?

Muffled screams echo through the room, a low, haunting sound that seems to be coming from everywhere at once. The dress keeps on dancing. Ginny jumps to her feet. Even with her heart beating in her throat, the drugs pumping through her veins, she still knows that ghosts aren't real. This is something else entirely.

"Cut it out." Her voice is a dying ember. She backs away from the mirror. "I'm not afraid—"

The room goes dark.

CHAPTER TEN

G inny trips over an abandoned slipper, then falls to the ground, bringing down something else with her. A cold steel bar pins her to the floor. Pain shoots through her shoulder. Silky fabrics cover her face, scratchy sequins cutting her skin. She remembers the green dress with horror.

This is how I die, she thinks. The Eagle caught up with her sooner than she expected, and now the last thing she'll see is green fabric. Then darkness, and nothing at all.

It might be minutes or hours later when the moans finally die out. Ginny keeps her eyes squeezed shut against the cloying perfume of the fabric. The pep powder in her veins tells her to get a move on, but the steel bar is too heavy, and she remains on the ground with her heart hammering loud in her ears until the electric lights sigh to life with a weary flicker.

"What the devil—"

Ginny pulls the fabric from her face. A pair of heavy utility boots advance into the room, their laces caked with white paint. She looks up at a ruddy young man with a prickle of ginger stubble across his jaw. A yellow plastic bucket hangs in his hand. A stagehand. The hammering tempo of her heart slows under his contemptuous gaze. She might yet live another day.

As her eyes adjust to the light, Ginny realizes she's trapped beneath a fallen clothing rack, and the stage costumes are now scattered around her like so many wilted flower petals.

"Hello there, old boy." She crawls out of the sequined heap with as much dignity as she can muster, given the circumstances.

"You shouldn't be here."

His restless eyes flick from the clothes on the floor to the messy vanity tables and back to Ginny.

"Maybe *you* shouldn't," she says, raising her chin in defiance. "It's a ladies' dressing room. Or were you spying on me? That's not nice, old—"

"Leave." He jerks his head toward the exit. The word leaves no room for negotiation.

Though she's not anxious to spend another minute in this room, she refuses to give this man the satisfaction of an easy victory. So she takes her time fixing her makeup in front of the mirror and retrieving her belongings, heart still battering in her chest. Plastering an innocent smile across her face, she walks out the door as slowly as possible, while his hand tightens on the doorframe.

Man or ghost, there's no one who can tell her what to do.

The power trip dies out in the maze of backstage corridors. Most of the lights are out, and even if she knew the complex path Dottie had taken to bring them inside, she wouldn't stand a chance after the pep powder. The cold electric lights snicker at her incompetence as she pushes blindly onward, trying to ignore the echoes that seem to follow no matter where she goes. Whispers collect in the corners. Her vision swims with fireflies.

Somehow, she makes it, and at last she pushes the bar of cool metal on the back exit. The theater spits her out into the alley, where a tiny light shows her that she's far from alone.

"There you are." Dottie stands with gloved hands clasped together, her figure casting an elegant shadow across the alley. The man behind her has his back turned to the exit, only a thin trail of smoke rising from the end of his cigarette. Might be the drugs or some twisted sixth sense she's gained in the past few days, but Ginny knows who it is before he turns. Before she's assaulted by his hard gray gaze.

Behind her sister's back, Charlie shoots Ginny a smile that tugs at the edges of his mouth like a mask.

Dottie steps closer. She looks younger without her stage makeup, radiant in the velvet dark. "We've been waiting and waiting—"

"Have you seen Jack?"

They were supposed to meet here, if she remembers right. But there are a lot of things she's starting to doubt, and it doesn't help that she's shaking like a dancer without the music.

"He was gone when I came out." Dottie casts a careful glance around the alley, as if he might be hiding behind a trash can or settling between the cracks in the brickwork. "I like Jack. He could be good for you."

"We're not together. Just a work thing. But I really need to find him."

"Charlie, have you seen Jack?" says Dottie.

He stamps out his cigarette and steps into the light. He smells of Ivory soap and clean smoke, with a heady undercurrent of marine cologne, like that night at Gloria's place. But then he swipes his bangs out of his face with a careless arm, and the light glints gold against his class ring. This man might say he loves her, but Gloria's words echo through her mind all the same.

Sometimes love is just another word for control.

"Which one's Jack?"

"The guy who came with Ginny. Oh, I suppose you don't know him. He's a tall fellow in a gray suit."

"Lost your man, now, have you?"

"I'll find him."

"Careful." Warnings flash through his eyes. "One wrong move, and there's no going back."

Dottie entwines her arms with his, snuggling her head on his shoulder. She's so soft around him, so relaxed, like a different woman entirely. Ginny feels a tug in the bottom of her stomach. "What could you possibly mean, dearest?"

He shakes his head with a smile. "Don't mind me. It's all this shoptalk at the office getting to me, I guess. Never marry a trader. Listen, you go on to the car, my darling—there's something I forgot inside the theater."

Goosebumps prickle Ginny's arms, and she tries her best to rub away the sudden chill. Dottie gives him a quick peck on the cheek, then leaves the alleyway with a swing in her step and a final carefree wave in Ginny's direction. She's glowing head to toe, like the rock on her finger has made her invincible.

As soon as Dottie is out of earshot, Charlie takes a step toward Ginny, hands in pockets.

"So," he says. "Jack, is it now? I knew there was someone else."

Ginny's nerves hum like electric wires. She's got no time for small talk, and the casual tone of his voice sets her teeth on edge. "Whatever you want to say, keep it snappy. I got better things to do."

Charlie slicks back his hair again, a gesture that once made her melt like summer snow, but now it only fuels her anger. This pep powder is playing tricks on her, but she wonders if it's showing her the truth at last, rubbing all the false shine off her old life.

"That's no way to talk to your *lover.*" He lingers on the last word, dragging it out with a flicker of a grin tugging at his lips. When he runs his hands down her arms, she takes an instinctive step away from him.

The truth shouts at her from every dark corner. He doesn't really love her. Never has. It's Dottie he wants, and all she's ever been is a welcome distraction.

"Is that what you are?" she says. The pep powder kicks at the back of her head, releasing words she's never dared to say aloud. "You're marrying my sister, Charlie. I think we both know that's not going to change. This was fun while it lasted."

"You're angry." He steps close, looking down on her almost fondly. "I don't understand. You're the one who didn't want to tell her—"

"Because I knew, okay? You're never going to break it off with her, Charlie. Just admit it."

He clicks his tongue. "I'm not a fortune teller. Who knows? Maybe I will marry your sister, maybe I won't, but in any case, nothing has to change between us. We don't have to give up our—"

"Our what?" She can feel her eyes burning when she looks at him. "You looking for a mistress in addition to your shiny bride? The full package?"

Charlie flinches at her words, his brow creasing with irritation. "Don't be crude. We've got something special going, don't deny that."

He looks like a spoiled little boy, tormenting his parents for a shinier toy. That's it, she thinks—charming Charlie, everybody's golden boy, getting everything he ever wanted in life. Of course he thinks he deserves to have it all. Buy one Dugan girl, get the second one free.

"You were never going to break off the engagement. Admit it." Her breath comes heavy through her nostrils, the pep powder keeping up its dark crackle inside her brain. "I should've seen it sooner. You might think you're all that, but you're just a cheap ad in the back of a magazine. Big words, pretty packaging, but inside you're nothing. Nothing—"

He grabs her by the arms, pushing her against the wall. The impact crashes through her skull, and she can already see blood where her bare arm collided with the brick. His fingers dig into her bullet wound, like he knows exactly how to hurt her, and the pain pushes a gasp from her lips.

"And what did you expect?" His smile is a grimace now, shadows cutting through his skin. "Thought I'd marry *you* instead? A big white wedding for Ginny Dugan?"

She tries to pull out of his grip, but he's stronger. He leans even closer, curling his fingers around her neck, the class ring digging into her skin.

"It's never going to happen." His breath is hot against her cheek, and there's nowhere she can turn, nothing she can do to block out his terrible words. "Nobody wants a girl who gets around as much as you do. Face it, you're broken beyond repair, and being my mistress is the best thing that could ever happen—"

Ginny kicks him in the knee. He trips backward. She can still feel his arms all over her, a ring of pressure around her neck so tight she can barely breathe. Charlie flexes his fingers, and she knows he's preparing for another round. "I'll tell her everything. Then the wedding will be off, and you'll be out of our lives forever."

His face breaks into a smile. Footsteps click across the concrete, getting louder by the minute.

"And who do you think she'll believe?" he whispers. "Her future husband—or her delinquent sister who can't keep her legs closed?"

Then he turns back to his bride-to-be, arms wide, leaving Ginny pressed against the wall with her heart drumming loud in her ears.

"Is everything all right?" Dottie says. "I thought I heard voices."

"I'm coming, dearest," says Charlie, hooking an arm under her elbow. "Looks like your sister is unwell. Perhaps we could offer her a ride home?"

"Wonderful idea—what do you say, Ginny?"

Dottie leans into Charlie's shoulder again, eyes glimmering in the low light. Ginny can feel the pain in her head, her neck, her shoulders. A raw ache where his fingers dug into her bullet wound. Her body is a collection of souvenirs from Charlie, and nobody knows. She's the only one who can stop him, but she's already failing on that count.

She shakes her head, trying to ignore the way the two of them look together.

Perfectly in love, that's how.

"I should find Jack," she says. "You two have a good night."

She keeps up a steady pace until she turns a corner. Their steps recede into the distance, and then the car door slams and they are gone. Ginny can already picture how it's gonna go. He'll take her sister home in his dark blue Packard. Dottie will raise her head skyward and marvel at the first stars peppering the night, thinking how lucky she is to have everything she's ever dreamed of. And then a few months will fly by in a haze of fast cars and parties, and they will be married, looking like a cake-topper couple in their brand-new Park Avenue apartment. They'll have a view above the treetops and a set of servants catering to every whim. A new start for Mr. and Mrs. Darby.

It makes her sick to even think of it.

The bricks are covered in grime, but it doesn't make any difference to Ginny. She presses her back into the wall. She can't help wondering if she's got it all wrong. Maybe she's the only one who can see the dark side of Charlie's personality, and he's perfectly charming with everybody else, including her sister. Maybe Dottie and Charlie are destined to rise to the surface, their lives an uncomplicated glitter under the sun, as Ginny sinks to the bottom under the weight of her secrets.

Her downward spiral lined with pep powder and hard liquor, until all that's left to do is drown.

It's that kind of night, full of anxious thoughts and self-pity. She could stay there forever, until the bruised darkness lightens into sunrise. Instead, her stream of misery is interrupted by a commotion at the far end of the alley. A shuffle of rough fabric, a dull thud, uneven steps clattering across the concrete. And then a single scream ringing through the night, before it's extinguished with the sound of fists on flesh and a sharp, choking breath.

"Stop! I don't know anything—"

Her heart drops a mile. *Jack.*

CHAPTER ELEVEN

She takes off on a run. The pep powder surges through her veins, pushing every muscle into overdrive. It's a jagged high, roughing up the edges of her vision, a feeling of sharp teeth gnashing at her heels that pushes her forward at breakneck speed. And then she's there, barely out of breath, blood pounding heavy in her head.

He's on the ground, circled by three wiry figures with bandanas around their mouths. There's a mean look to them, like underfed dogs with nothing to lose, darting eyes full of raw hunger. They turn on her as though she's the main course at a five-star restaurant, and they got in for free.

"Get the hell away from him."

The tall one steps aside, but it's only so they can trap her. She doesn't care. Kneeling next to Jack, she's careful to keep her back to the wall, facing the others. He's still breathing. Good sign. Blood spurts from his nose. His body folds in on itself, arms pressed into his stomach where he must've been punched. He's been hit in the side of the head with something heavy, and now his gray suit is caked with blood and grime. Ginny's heart plays a minor chord. A wet boot print glistens on his chest. Dirt, paint, and pebbles stick to the lapel. Those animals, they've stepped on him.

Jack curls his fingers around her wrist.

"It's okay," a bare whisper. "I'm fine. Leave while you can—"

A tug on her collar, and she's lifted to the wall, the tall one pinning her to the bricks with one hand. The pain in her shoulder is nearly blinding this time, and she bites her lip to suppress a scream. A wave of disgusting laughter rises behind him. Ginny pulls against his grip, aiming a kick for his kneecaps, but he's too quick. Her foot flails through the air. The smell of chewing tobacco and sweat fills her nose. A scar runs through his pale forehead like lightning. A flash of amber in his eyes, and the terrible picture clicks into place.

The Eagle is out for her blood, and he sent these guys to finish what they started.

Nausea hits her hard, and she wonders if he'll leave her alone if she vomits all over his boots.

"Like fishing. Good bait, better catch."

The others laugh like he's said something witty. Ginny spits in his face. He doesn't release her wrists to wipe it down, so a string of spittle slides down his forehead and settles in the folds of his bandana.

"I called the cops on you," she says. "Wanna waste your last moments of freedom on small talk?"

Nothing in those hard eyes. It's like looking into the void.

One of the others steps up. His bushy blond eyebrows grow together on his nose. A glint of a revolver on his waist.

"Didn't your mama teach you not to lie, little girl?"

"I live by my own rules."

Another crashing wave of laughter. A cough from the ground below. The situation closes in on her from all ends. This is worse than the Eighty-Three. Jack is out of action. She might as well be, with the white powder shaking her up like that. No one to hear her scream.

Her captor's grip slips from her wrists. The other guys come closer.

"Your boyfriend has been up to no good," says the tall man, his voice a soft, crawling rumble. He drags his dirty fingers down the side of her head, tracing the bruise he left behind several nights ago, the top half of his face crinkling with the coldest of smiles. "Almost as if you didn't tell him what we do to people who stick their noses in our business."

"That's right," pipes up the third guy, pulling a gun from his waistband. Ginny matches his voice to the kid who failed his job that night, his bullet only grazing her shoulder. He clicks the hammer and points the gun at Jack's slumped form on the ground. Ginny's heart skips a beat. Josephine's kidnapping already weighs heavy on her conscience, and there's no chance she'll let them kill Jack on her watch.

"He doesn't know a thing," her words rush together, "I'm the one you want."

"You?" The tall man quirks a brow. "We know all about you, Ginny Dugan. Turns out you're just a kid with an advice column and a history of making bad choices. This guy's a different story, so you can tell him to drop the case, or there's more to come."

Despite the drugs and the men crowding her on all ends, guns glinting, Ginny feels a pang of indignation at his words. "So, what, you don't want me dead anymore?"

The gun hits her in the jaw before she can move, the tall man clicking back the hammer like flicking a lighter switch. Her skull slams against the brick wall, and she regrets every dumb decision that brought her here.

"Not if you keep your mouth shut," he hisses. "And make sure your boy drops his case, or there's more to come."

"We got the dirt on him," says the one with the eyebrows. "He can't stay clean much longer if he messes with us."

The tall man rocks back on his heels, slipping the gun back into its holster. "We know all about his dealings at the Empire. Only takes one call, and Black Jack will be out of action for good."

"You got that, sweetheart?"

There's a pounding in her head, a tremor in her fingers. All she can do is nod. None of this makes sense. She feels distant from the scene, detached, like she's watching it unfold from above.

The kid flips his gun back into his pocket and leans down to pick up her beaded purse. She must've dropped it in the struggle.

"We're real nice guys," he says, rifling through the contents. "We'll leave the bag for you. Ladies love their bags. But we gotta take the money and things. Give us a head start."

She watches as he paws through her things with perverse fascination, shoving a few crumpled bills into his dirty pocket. He waves her handkerchief through the air, a little white ghost. Ginny catches a flash of a tattoo across his wrist, the ink gone blurry with time. If she squints just right, she can make out a large eagle spreading its wings.

Then he finds the lipstick, and even under the bandana, she can see him smiling.

"Someone's been bad." He shows the lipstick to the others. "Maybe we won't have to work too hard, eh?"

The tall man prods him in the side, and he goes silent, the smile fading from his eyes.

"You wouldn't take my lipstick too." She tries to sound like Dottie, sweet and unthreatening.

It's no good. He drops the shiny tube in his pocket, and that's when she knows the score.

These guys are in on the pep powder racket. She wonders if Josephine's kidnapping might have something to do with these drugs, but the painful throbbing in her head crowds out her capacity for critical thinking.

And then they leave, casting narrow shadows across the alley before disappearing around the corner. The echo of their footsteps on the pavement sounds like gunfire.

Her knees fold beneath her, and she crumples to the ground beside Jack. He's muttering something under his breath—*pain, pain,* over and over in hoarse gasps. She taps him on the cheek, trying to bring him back to reality. Her hand comes away slick with his blood.

"You here to rough me up too?" he manages. His eyes open just a crack.

"Oh, yeah, you know." Tears prickle at her eyelids, she sniffs to keep them at bay. "Just finishing up what those guys started. Keep you on your toes, partner."

"Don't you go soft on me, Dugan." He pushes up on his elbows, groaning from the effort. "Did they take all your things?"

"Left my bag, but it's not much." She presses her handkerchief against the side of his nose, stemming the gush of hot blood. "If we could get to my car—"

It takes them a while to get back around the corner, Jack's arm around Ginny's shoulders, stopping against the wall whenever he runs out of steam. She watches him closely, taking comfort in the even tempo of his breath, those long lashes fluttering shut against the pain. The pep powder is wearing off, slowing the thrumming energy in her veins so she struggles to gather her strength, trying to focus on Jack alone.

He's the job now, she decides. Keep him alive. Everything else can wait.

They finally make it to the Buick, and Ginny puffs out a sigh of relief when she sees that the tires haven't been slashed. She hauls him into the passenger seat, then climbs in on the other side.

"Listen," she says, twisting to face him. She doesn't know where to look, what to do, she's never been in a situation like this before, with someone else's life resting in her hands. Her reckless, incompetent hands. "Did they break anything? How many fingers am I holding up? I should take you to a hospital—"

Jack groans, pushes her hand away. "Jesus, Ginny. It's nothing. You'd think I was half dead, the way you're going on—"

"You might be. They could have killed you. They—" Deep breaths. Ginny rubs her face with her hands, staining it with Jack's blood. "They stepped on you, Jack. I can't believe—"

"That's how these guys operate. They wanted to send a message. For that, they needed me alive." He adjusts in his seat with a groan. "I recognized that tall guy. He was the one I saw talking to Billy Calloway a few months ago. The one with all the scars."

A noose of panic tightens around her throat, but she shakes it off, trying to think. If these guys are connected with Billy, then he might be the one calling the shots. Her theory takes hold in her mind, but the blood on Jack's face brings her back to the urgent intensity of the moment.

"How did it even happen?"

"I left the theater a while back, thought you'd be out here, but I guess you were busy with your own investigation. They followed me out. Must've seen me talking to Zita, maybe that's how they figured out I was on the case—"

Shame coils in the pit of her stomach. If she would've come out in time, maybe this never would've happened, and now she's got Jack's injuries weighing on her conscience. He studies her face, and suddenly the side of his mouth twists down in concern. His fingers graze the side of her head, absentmindedly tucking a strand behind her ear. The easy touch makes Ginny wonder if he's concussed, but she doesn't want him to stop. "Are you hurt?"

Ginny shakes her head, then presses his palm against her face, closing her eyes. It's cool and comforting, the callouses beneath his fingertips reassuringly rough.

"We're getting close to the truth, that's why they're putting the pressure on us. This is good, Ginny."

"They said they had dirt on you," she says.

His hand slips from her face. The silence in the car grows deeper, and he studies his bruised knuckles for some time before finally speaking.

"It's late. We should probably get going, start early tomorrow—"

She squints through the dim, but she can only make out his shadow. "They called you Black Jack. What were they talking about?"

"They were just messing with you, Ginny. Trying to get in your head. I know how these guys operate, they'll do anything to set you against me."

"Well it sounded damn real, and I'd like to be prepared for the next time we're ambushed in an alley. Come on," she softens her voice, reaching for his hand, but he slips out of her grip. "I can handle it."

Jack crumples his hat between his fingers, staining it crimson. "You don't know what you're asking me, Ginny. If I tell you— I've lost too much already, I can't—"

He looks like he might break down right there, but then he stops in his tracks, staring out into the distance. When he speaks again, there's a final note in his voice. "Some things should stay in the dark."

Even through her exhaustion, she can feel a spike of irritation at the base of her skull. Jack's face is blank as a stranger's.

"If we're going to be partners," she says, "we shouldn't have secrets from each other. If these guys find something to use against—"

"You want to go first?" His eyes flash dark. Dangerous territory. "I've noticed those bruises, the marks on your neck. I think we both know they're no accident."

Ginny bites down on her lower lip. The fight drains from her body until there's nothing left. Telling him the truth about Charlie would mean admitting her own weakness. Admitting she fell for her sister's fiancé like the worst cliché in the book. Admitting she was blinded by lust and nostalgia, so she surrendered the keys to her own destruction to the wrong man. He'd never respect her detective skills after that, never see her the way she wants to be seen by the world. Strong, sharp, independent. Not the kind of woman who falls prey to a man who never deserved her. Not a victim.

"You're right. I'm sorry." For a faltering instant, she tries to imagine a different life where they could be honest with each other. The idea is pure and painful at once, a fantasy that's never meant to be for someone like her. "Let's go, then."

She twists her key in the ignition.

As they shoot out into the night, Ginny keeps her eyes on the road. She drops Jack at his place in record time. It's only on her way home that she lets herself go, surrendering to the force of a single thought.

Those guys no longer see her as a threat.

If she were a man, she would've been shoulder to shoulder with her partner, and maybe they would have stood a chance. Instead, Jack took all the blows, while she was getting off her face on pep powder in the dressing room. She sees the truth staring back from her messed-up reflection in the window as she parks her car by the building, in the averted gaze of the elevator boy, in the hush of the sleepy apartment.

Maybe the worst parts of herself are true, and everything that's happened is her fault.

CHAPTER TWELVE

G inny starts the next day feeling like a sailor washed ashore, coming down hard after the previous night's drugs and battering, with her heart leaping at irregular intervals. One look in the mirror makes it worse. Bruises climb up her arms on both sides, a gash crusting over with blood above her elbow where she hit the brick wall. There's a ring of red around her neck. The right side is worse. That's where his class ring dug into her skin. She can still feel the cold metal on her neck, still see his face twisting inches from hers, his eyes dark as bottomless sinkholes.

Covered in greasepaint and her most modest dress, Ginny heads to *Photoplay* with her face shaded against the blinding sun. The office is mostly empty on a Sunday, but the upcoming release still has some people sitting at their typewriters to keep her company. Keep her busy, distracted from her thoughts. Ginny brings herself back to the previous night and begins to type. She remembers the sweet and dusty smell inside the theater, the gilded green whirl above their heads, the rush of stage lights against the flawless cast. Flowers and trees, picture-perfect stage manager and foul-mouthed stagehand, Anita's shameless banter and the saleswoman's smirk on Mazie's egg-shaped face. And then what happened after, blood and grime against the cold slab of brick, the thud of Jack's body against the ground.

Ginny squeezes her eyes shut, opens them again, and continues to type. That's not the kind of story that will get her in Quirk's good graces. Save the darkness for later, this piece is all about what happens in the spotlight.

Through the entire morning, she can't shake the feeling that something is off. Her hands are clumsy against the keys, weighed down by lead at the fingertips, her body behaving as though it no longer belongs to her. Her morning coffee wears out in a couple hours, and then she's back to a searing headache, a heartbeat that won't stop drumming against her rib cage, and a burning desire to shut her eyes against the world.

Strains of conversation follow her through the halls as she drops off the article on Quirk's desk. Caroline and Prescott walk past her with linked arms, looking like they've stepped off the pages of *Vogue* in their pastel suits, her with a Lalique brooch shaped like a dragonfly in flight, him with a smudge of brown shadow beneath his eyes like Valentino.

"—they're all coming, Scotty, I've booked us a table—"

"I don't know. I've never heard of this Eighty-Three until yesterday, and I don't trust any place named after its street number. Is it even safe—"

"Well, John Stuart just flew in from England and he says he wouldn't miss it for the world."

They go silent as they pass Ginny, but she's already heard enough to remember last night's conversation with Anita. The

Eighty-Three is reopening tonight, which means that they'll finally get a chance to check out the scene of the crime.

On her way out of the office, Ginny stops by the front desk. Mary is back, bright-eyed and friendly in a pale skirt suit and gloves. There's something different about her today. She might look like the same Mary who would greet you with a gumdrop at the front desk each day, but it's like she's been picked up and polished to a stylish sheen. Her lips are outlined like a fashion illustration, in a bright candy red that makes her blue eyes pop.

"Look at you." Ginny offers her hand, and Mary lets herself be pulled upright, spinning round with a soft laugh.

"You like it? I wasn't sure about the shade—"

"Damn right. You don't belong in this place anymore, Mary darling. Get yourself up on a stage already."

Mary drops into her chair and dips below the desk. She emerges with a small box tied with a blue ribbon.

"It's for you."

Ginny opens the box. Inside, there's a slim silver bracelet with a single star-shaped charm hanging from it, Mary and Ginny's names engraved on the back. It's so sweet, and so far out of Mary's budget, that Ginny falls into the guest chair with her knees going weak.

"This must've cost you a fortune." She looks up. Mary is smiling, cradling her chin in her hands. "It's beautiful, I just—"

"You like it? It's my way of saying thanks for filling in on Friday. You're a lifesaver. See the charm—it means we'll both be big stars someday soon, and then we can get lunch at the Waldorf-Astoria and remember our days at the magazine and laugh about it all."

Ginny takes another look at the bracelet, the tailored suit, the fresh shade of lipstick she's never seen on Mary. There's only one explanation for this sudden shift.

"Does this mean—"

"I got in." Mary claps her gloved hands together. "I promised not to tell anyone, but I could just burst if I keep it to myself. I'm going to be in the Follies!"

The words strike a different note after last night. The screams in the dressing room, the attack in the alley. Still, Ginny manages a smile for her friend, who's glowing like never before.

"Tell me everything, then. Are you quitting *Photoplay* for good?"

"Something like that." Mary brings a hand to her mouth, then remembers the glove and lowers it. No more nail-biting for this sophisticated new version of herself. Ginny feels a sudden twinge of melancholy, then shakes it off. This is good news. It's not like Mary's gone forever. So long as Ginny plays nice with Dottie and stays on the Follies guest lists, they'll be seeing plenty of each other at the New Am and beyond. "It's supposed to be a secret for now, but I'll make it official tomorrow. There's lots of hard work ahead, of course—I need to take dance classes and all that—but it's happening. And it's all thanks to you, Gin. I might've missed my shot."

"It's nothing." Ginny settles in the wooden guest chair, and the movement shoots painful static through her brain. She fastens the bracelet round her wrist. It's the perfect size, the star swinging side to side whenever she moves her arm. "Got any more headache powder? I'm all out."

Mary flings her another packet of Starks' without dropping her luminous smile for a second. As Ginny tips the powder onto her tongue, she remembers Friday afternoon, just a few days earlier, when Mary first told her about the Follies gig. There was something important she wanted to tell her, but last night has wiped it clean out of her mind, unless—

"I gotta tell you something." Ginny leans close enough to smell Mary's new perfume, a distinctly expensive blend of tuberose and jasmine. "A private eye came by the front desk when I was filling in for you. He mistook me for you, and—well, he accused me of sleeping with a married man. You know anything about that?"

Mary looks down and folds into herself, careful curls drooping around her face. "Would you be ashamed of me if it were true?"

"God, of course not. I'm the last person who would give a damn about something like that." Especially since she's been doing the same thing herself, give or take a wedding. Engaged isn't married, but still. *Still.* "Just thought I'd give you a heads up. He's not getting too far with his investigation—really, I think he's got the wrong girl—but you'd better be careful, you know."

"Yeah. Thanks, Gin." Mary tries to restore her previous smile, but some of the glow is gone. "You haven't told anyone about the audition, have you?"

"Lips are sealed."

"Good." Mary presses her hands together. "Listen, there's—well, something else."

"What is it?"

"I know you keep saying we gotta work extra hard to make our dreams come true. But I was wondering—" She lowers her eyes to the desk. There's a glimmer of doubt beneath the confidence. "I spoke to Mr. Sharp, and some of his terms sounded kind of strict."

"Sharp's a brute," Ginny says, "but that's just his way. The girls laugh about it all the time. He'll keep you working hard, but that's 'cause he's got high standards. Don't worry."

Mary opens her mouth to say something else, but then she nods, as though to herself. "Oh, Ginny. I'm gonna miss you something terrible, you know. It's all gonna change now, isn't it?"

Ginny reaches out and grabs Mary's palms, so small in the pure white gloves. There's so much she'd like to say, those things that feel inconsequential when you see somebody every day, too senti-mental for a couple modern girls trying to make it in this city. She'd tell Mary that these lonely days at the office, lost in the shadows of her dead-end advice column, would've been a drag without her. And while they'll still see each other after Mary joins the Follies, it will never, ever be the same.

Instead, she forces a smile and squeezes her friend's hands.

"Don't be silly. Nothing has to change at all. Actually, what are you doing tonight?"

Mary slips out of her grip, looking apologetic. "I have some plans with Mr.— Well, there's this Follies thing. Why?"

"The Eighty-Three is reopening. Thought we could go, for old times' sake."

"Yeah, I heard about that. I don't know." Mary gives an absent wave to a passing telephone girl, her eyes glossing over. "My fella says I shouldn't go there anymore. Not for a while, at least. Says it's dangerous for my reputation."

With the headache powder numbing the pain, Ginny can feel her anger hammering loud and clear in her head.

"Since when do you care about all that?"

"Come on, Ginny. We both know it's different if you're on stage. Nobody cares what happens to a *Photoplay* secretary, but it's a different story for a chorus girl at the Follies." She hesitates. "He says I should stick to the main nightclub circuit. The Radium Club, the Cotton Club when it opens again."

Ginny can feel her chest constricting. She can't tell if this is part of pep powder withdrawal or something deeper, an emotional wound she doesn't want to explore just yet. One thing is clear: Mary belongs to the Follies now, and she'll happily turn her back on Ginny and the rest of her *Photoplay* past for the bright lights of Broadway.

"Well, I'm going. Swing by if you find the time, all right? Nobody has to know."

Ginny's on her way out when Mary calls her back at the revolving doors, her soft voice rising plaintive in the empty hall.

"I'll do my best, Ginny. Really, I will—"

But then she's out on the street, drowning her own bitterness in the raw summer air, knowing full well that Mary will never show, and there's no way to turn back the clock.

CHAPTER THIRTEEN

"**I**f this is your idea of how an investigation is supposed to go, you definitely haven't been listening."

Ginny flings a solid grin across the bar and clinks her glass against her partner's empty hand. For all his talk of blending in, Jack is stubbornly opposed to drinking on the job. He watches her with unconcealed distaste as she throws back the violent blue liquid, Mary's bracelet sliding down the length of her arm.

"Do you even know what's in there?"

"Shot of vodka, shot of cordial. Some secret sauce they keep under lock in the cellar." She leans in, breathing fumes against his bare cheek. "Might be the blood of innocents, you know—good little boys who abstain from liquor—"

"So irresponsible," he mutters, keeping his eyes on their surroundings. He's done a good job of cleaning up, Jack. There's some bruising along the ridge of his nose, a fresh scar gashing his cheekbone, but with all the gore scrubbed out, it almost makes him look better. Gives a little edge to that accountant persona he wears like a badge of honor.

It's barely eight, but the joint is already jamming with bodies. The crowd is decidedly upper crust. Diamond stickpins the size of boiled eggs, tiaras dripping with more emeralds than leaves on a tree. Sure enough, the place has been upgraded since her last visit. That's the story for the seedier Harlem joints: as soon as they get big, the locals get pushed out by prohibitive entry fees, and the Park Avenue crowd comes flooding in.

"This place sure has changed," says Ginny. "If those guys left behind any clues when they kidnapped Josephine, I doubt they're still here."

Jack pierces the crowd with a probing look, and Ginny's struck by a sudden flash of affection. Something about last night's brush with death has shifted the air between them, and it's getting harder to remember why she thought they wouldn't be good together.

"They might've hiked the cover charge, but some things never change," Jack lowers his voice and points toward the stage, where Clive is shredding quick fingers against his guitar. "I don't see Billy, but his guitarist is playing with the band tonight. And with so many rich folks in one place, you can bet somebody will be dealing. I say we follow the drugs, and then we might end up finding our motive."

Something about his tone gives her pause. "We could spend the whole night chasing dealers and get nowhere. Besides, I still don't see any connection between our cases. You sure this isn't a personal thing?"

"What are you saying?"

"Come on, Jack." She heaves a sigh. "You don't drink, and I figure you don't get high, either. Not all drugs are lethal, that's just what they say to sell more papers. The heart attacks might still be caused by the heat—"

"I've got my reasons." Jack stiffens his shoulders, a sign that the conversation is over. "I've seen what some habits can do to you. Wreck your health, your whole damn life. Just keep an eye out, all right?"

Across the dance floor, Ginny notices a sharp group of folks striding through the crowd like they own the place. Caroline's precise brown bob zips through the air as she inspects the premises.

The writers approach with bravado rolling off their shoulders, talking a little too loud to carry their voices above the swell of the jazz on stage. Prescott slides over to the bar, looking dapper in a black silk dinner jacket, his hair pomaded in slick waves. He leans toward Ginny with an air of familiarity, but the glassy look in his eyes tells her he doesn't recognize her one bit.

"What's good here? I'm absolutely parched."

"Can't go wrong with the house special. It's got—"

Prescott interrupts her, pitching his voice loud above the din. "Paul, what's *good*?"

"I told you we should've stopped over at Chumley's to get the night started." Paul sniffs. "Warm, delicious whiskey or acid-green cocktail with a splash of moonshine? Of *course* you go for the latter—"

Caroline knocks right into Ginny, pushing her out of the way with a bony elbow. Her cool voice goes shrill as she waves an imperative hand in the air. "Hey, bartender, we don't have all night. Do you even know who I *am*—"

It's like a spectacular car crash; she can't look away. Prescott launches into petty bickering with Paul about who has the best connections in the city, the two of them pulling fat leather date-books from their pockets to compare notes. Caroline finally gets her drink and takes a heavy slurp, blue liquid dribbling down her chin, coloring the diamonds on her choker.

It takes all she's got to hold back a sudden burst of laughter. So many years spent in the shadow of this intimidating trio, putting everything on the line for one big dream of joining them someday. All for nothing, now that she's finally seen them up close, with no more room left for her own imagination to elevate them to legendary status.

Standing next to the writers in their gaudy jewels and silk suits, Jack looks like a tall, cool glass of water, and Ginny can't stop looking at him. Stepping closer, she extends an arm.

"What are you doing?"

"Come on. Dance with me, detective."

She doesn't expect him to take her up on it, can't be sure he even knows how to dance—but he takes her hand, and then they're in the middle of the dance floor, together.

It's one of those nights that puts you in a good kind of trance, where the music ebbs and swells to the beat of your heart. Ginny starts with a Charleston, knees and elbows knocking against the tightening flow of the crowd. Before she knows what he's doing, Jack pulls her close, leading her into a rapid foxtrot with her chin resting on his shoulder, their movements clearing a circle in the middle of the crowded dance floor. She can feel the soft fabric of his gray flannel suit, the sharp tang of pine cologne, the confident pressure of his palm against hers, raised into the air. The stage lights catch the green in his eyes. It feels like they're the only people in the room.

Something goes wrong halfway through the dance. It starts deep in her chest, her breath constricting in her lungs, sweat rolling down her face in fat beads. She breaks away from Jack and falls against the bar. Her entire body thrums with more than just her pulse. The edges of her vision blur into a hazy glow. She's never been so bone-tired after half a dance, and it feels all wrong.

"Water," she gasps to the bartender, pressing a hand to her chest. Her heart feels like a trapped sparrow, flapping its wings against her rib cage. The clear liquid flows down her throat in greedy gulps.

"Ginny," Jack is close behind, hovering just out of sight. "Are you okay?"

"It's fine." She squeezes her sides, breaths coming out all ragged. "Happens sometimes. I'll be better soon."

"You've got the shakes. Maybe you shouldn't drink so much, it can't be good for you—"

"It's not the damn drinks." Her voice comes out harsh. It usually takes more than a couple shots to knock her out, and she's never felt like this after a drink and a dance, not that Jack would get it. "You don't understand—"

"I'm just saying, you should be careful with bootleg. Nobody knows what's in there, and it's careless to drink anything on offer without checking—"

"Careless, right. That's me." The sweat keeps rolling down her face. "I like to drink, I like to dance, and that's who I am, all right? Sorry if I don't match your idea of the perfect woman, or whatever. Excuse me."

She knocks through the crowd, feeling Jack's stare burning against her back. The powder room greets her in a blare of bright lights, cushions in front of tall mirrors with marks of grease and lipstick across their surface. One of them is already occupied by a blonde woman in an extravagant blue men's suit.

Splash of water across her face, panting hard in front of the glass. Her cheeks have hollowed out, like she's been running for a long time. Ginny falls into one of the cushions, barely caring that she's not alone. Damn it. What's the deal?

"Looks like you're coming down into an ugly low," comes a familiar voice. Ginny jerks around. Of course. It's the blonde from Ace, Vivian Templeton. Her spicy perfume hangs in the air.

"I remember you."

"I'm not surprised. I get around enough to linger in the back of everybody's mind." She clicks her purse open, fishes a lipstick from its depths. "If you carry on like that, the night's only gonna get worse for you."

"What are you talking about?"

She spreads the deep orange hue across her mouth. "I've seen enough pep powder junkies to know it never ends well. Listen, kid," lips smacked together to even out the color, "off the record, because I'm feeling charitable tonight. Get off that stuff, soon as you can. That's if you care about the long-term. Living past thirty, that sort of thing."

Ginny looks down at her hands. Shaking fast enough to blur the rings into a kaleidoscopic mess.

"And what about the short-term, then? How do I get through the night?"

The woman gets up to leave. "Take another hit. But hand on heart, I say you'd better sleep it off instead."

Ginny blocks the exit. Another hit. The words pound through her body, singing sweet songs into her ear. One quick fix to get through the night. There's no way in hell she can call in sick, now that they're here. Right at the scene of the crime, with all the answers waiting around the corner.

"You got any on you?"

The woman gives her a hard look. Up close, Ginny notices the faint lines gathering in the corners of her eyes. The paint on her face is like a mask, and Ginny can't imagine what she looks like with the makeup off.

"I'm not supposed to do it like that." Quick look around the room, no one else there. "Don't you know how this works?"

Ginny blinks.

"Fine. Play it that way. It's ten clams for you tonight, because I don't approve."

Ginny fumbles through her purse, pulling her last ten-dollar bill from its depths. The cover charge was already enough to bankrupt her, and now she's left with hardly enough to last her to the end of the month, but it doesn't matter. The woman passes her a shiny lipstick tube and pushes out of the room with an air of being conned. Tripping over her own feet, Ginny burrows into the corner. Two clicks. A double dose this time. The powder on the table, her nose against the surface, breathing deep.

This kick comes headier than last night's. Like something solid, slamming into her forehead until she's almost flying across the room and out into the raucous ring of dancing feet. The night shimmers brighter, sequins studding constellations across their wearers' bodies.

But she makes a wrong turn, and suddenly she's in the dark. Whoosh of a curtain to her right, concrete hallways trailing behind her. She peels back the red velvet. There's the band, the backs of their heads collecting sweat in the harsh glow of the stage. A jolt of envy shudders down her spine. The drugs kick her back to age twelve, tucked into the curtains at the Cherryvale Town Hall, Dottie spinning in gossamer white on stage as the crowd erupts with applause. Her last show before the Denishawn scouts whisked her away. That's how it's always been, so many lonely nights spent in this same position, wondering why her sister is out in the light while she stays shrouded in shadows.

The powder sharpens her perception like a magnifying glass, offering feline vision in the shades of backstage grays. This is the spot, she can feel it deep in her body, the exact place she found herself the night Josephine was kidnapped. Ginny drops to her knees, patting down the floor. Nothing but dust and cigarette butts. She crawls farther, pawing around until her arm hits wood. Stacks of crates reach high to the ceiling, one of them still showing smears of her blood where she gripped the sides. Letters run along the side, gleaming yellow against a faint crack of light from the curtains.

She runs through the words a little too fast. It makes her wonder if she's seeing things.

Property of the Ziegfeld Follies.

If found, please return to the New Amsterdam Theater.

Her speeding heart picks up the pace. The leap from nameless Harlem speakeasy to Broadway stage sensation is a mighty big one. She'd write it off as coincidence, if only their missing star hadn't made the exact same leap a few months earlier.

Something creaks in the dark. Ginny freezes. A silhouette takes a tentative step toward her. No telling who it is, with those folds of heavy fabric billowing behind them when they move.

"Come any closer and I'll scream so loud you'll hear my voice in your ears until you're dead." She hopes they don't see her shaking. The figure pauses, head tilting to the side. Laughing? She can't tell.

"Be careful, little bird. All kinds of things can happen in the dark." It's a man's voice, one she knows all too well, the slippery slide of it. The tall man who issued that warning outside the New Am last night.

"You." Ginny stumbles to her feet, emboldened by the pep powder. Anger pierces through her fear, and she's suddenly wondering why the hell she can't catch a break from this guy, why he follows her wherever she goes. "Will you ever get tired of following me around?"

The man takes a few steps closer, walking with the controlled tension of a seasoned predator. "You should count your blessings. You're only alive because the Eagle likes to play with you. If it were up to me . . ." A sudden laugh crackles through the dark, its cold edge shivering all the way down her spine. "Well, I guess that doesn't matter, right? You'll be dead soon enough."

"That's ridiculous," Ginny stutters, taking a step back. "I'm not going anywhere, and I don't see why the Eagle would care about me at all."

"The Eagle is closer than you think." The man backs away, retreating into the shadows.

Whip of a cloak in the air, and he's gone.

Ginny runs out into the club, eyes darting for a sight of Jack. The dance floor is packed now, revelers brought to frenzy by the croon of a solo saxophone. She catches a glimpse of her coworkers, dancing in a tight ring with their chins in the air, breaking into grotesque laughter as they knock into one another. Jack is where she left him, staring wistfully into the crowd.

"We have to go," she gasps once in earshot. "Come on, Jack."

"What's the matter?"

"Please. It's— I went backstage, and he was there. I saw him. The guy from the theater." Her vision zips through the puzzled faces staring at her, too blurry to focus on anything. "The guy who tried to kill us both? Who took Josephine—"

He hooks an arm beneath her elbow, dragging her to the side before she can say any more. His fingers burn against her skin.

"Hey, not so rough."

"What the hell are you doing," he mutters. There's venom there, a controlled flame about to burst. "Revealing the investigation for anyone to hear—"

"No, I swear." She points behind the curtain. "Please trust me. I—He was right there. We need to follow him."

"You're drunk, Ginny." He leans closer. "And you've got something on your nose."

Ginny drags a finger against her face. It comes away caked with powder. Fuck.

"Trust me," she says once more, rubbing her face with one hand while pulling on his sleeve with the other. "He's here. We have to follow—"

Her heart squeezes tight, the air dissolving into black dust. If she didn't know any better, she'd say she was about to have a heart attack. The sharp pain knocks her over, falling against Jack for support.

She loses a few moments of consciousness after that. Then somebody's tapping her lightly on the face, pressing a cool glass into her fingers.

"Drink this," comes Jack's voice through the fog, and she obliges. "What did you take, Ginny?"

The water makes her feel a bit better. Sure, her heart is still an anxious rattle in her chest, but at least she can still stand. Taking a deep breath, she pulls away from Jack, thinking hard.

Even in her altered state, the pieces are falling into place, and she wonders how she never figured it out before. Jack was right all along. The heart attacks in Harlem. The drugs in the lipstick tubes. A fatal addiction for the uptown party scene, and she's willingly brought herself right into the thick of the action, consequences be damned.

Mazie is dealing pep powder at the New Amsterdam. Josephine went in for an audition, but something went wrong along the way. And now people are dying from heart attacks in Harlem. Dying from pep powder.

Still, something stops her from spilling the whole story to Jack, especially since it means admitting she was dumb enough to get hooked on the same drug that's been killing people all this time. Plenty of time for confessions later, once they get their guy.

"Backstage," she says, reaching for stability, but her voice is blurry. "We have to catch him first. I'll tell you everything later."

She pulls him by the hand, and he has to speed up to keep pace with her stumbling steps. The warmth from his touch climbs up her arms, spreading all over her body, and she twines her fingers harder with his. It might be the drugs or the drinks, but walking into the shadows with her partner's hand in hers is exactly what heaven must feel like, her heart glittering in the dark.

Jack pauses by the crates, leaning down to wipe away some dust.

"Looks like we got our Follies connection."

"Right, I was just looking at them when he came out of there." She points ahead. "Big guy in a cape. It was the leader, Jack. He was right here."

Jack rises to his full height, leaning against the wall as he looks in the direction of the man's getaway. Ginny can't stop staring. Even in the dark, she can make out the width of his shoulders, the sharp shadows of his cheekbones, and those eyes, like two traffic lights that always say go. He's so beautiful, and he doesn't seem to know it. Not like Charlie with his calculated gestures, every tilt of the head meant to catch the light in the most flattering way. She can't believe she never noticed that before.

Ginny takes a step toward him. The music is deafening here, all hard thrumming jazz with the band only a few curtains away, but her heart is pounding even louder.

"He must be gone by now," says Jack, his head still turned sideways, trying to see in the dark. "What are the odds that he's still here?"

She takes another step, reaching her hands toward him.

"Ginny?"

"You're so cool," she whispers, "how's that even possible?"

He's staring straight at her now, and she can feel his breath curling against her cheek as she curves her arms around her body, pressing into his soft gray suit. Even in her dancing shoes with the highest heels, she has to stand on her tiptoes to reach him. He takes a sharp breath as she runs a hand along the side of his face, and then she can feel his hands wrapping around her waist.

"You don't know what you're doing," he says, but he doesn't sound so sure. It's too late to stop, and Ginny pushes her fingers against the back of his head, bringing him close. Then she kisses him, and nothing, nothing else matters.

The world spins out of focus. For a few heavenly moments, she forgets everything. She can feel him getting into the kiss, the polite front dropping like a magician's hat as he pulls her closer, drawing her deeper. Fire shoots through her veins. God, she wants him right then and there, on top of the crates with her skirt hiked high, and it doesn't matter who sees. Just as long as he doesn't stop, those calloused fingers running down her neck, heating up her cold heart until it's pounding hard enough to burst out of her chest.

But then it's over as quickly as it started, and Jack's turning away, leaving her gasping for breath against the empty space left behind.

"Why did you stop?"

He shakes his head. She can't see his eyes, can't catch the meaning behind this sudden interruption.

"It's wrong," he says. "I shouldn't have let you do that. You're drunk, and God knows what else, and here I am, taking advantage— Even worse, we're partners, for Christ's sake—"

He's going deeper backstage, retracing the steps taken by the man in the cape. Ginny straightens her dress and catches up with him, every step on the cold concrete echoing through her head. It's beyond disappointment, the way things are going. She's never had a man turn her down like that, never had to beg for it. She can feel her cheeks heating up.

"I know my own mind," she says, reaching for his sleeve. "Drunk or not, I want this. I want you."

"Don't." He brushes her away. "It's not right."

"You like playing hard to get?" Her breath comes in sharp, painful gusts. "We can play it that way. Want to make me work for it?"

They've reached the end of the hall, where another curtain covers the entire wall, swaying lightly in some invisible breeze. Jack runs a hand against the velvet. It's lighter back here, and Ginny can see conflicting emotions flicking behind the surface of his eyes. Finally, he looks at her, the severe intensity of his gaze nearly knocking her out.

"What I want is irrelevant. This—" Jack looks down, takes a breath. "This can never happen. And if you had any sense of self-preservation, you'd agree."

It hurts more than anything before, his rejection. Like cold nails stuck straight into her heart. Somehow, it's even worse that he's trying to make it sound like it's not her fault. *It's not you, it's me.* Yeah, she's heard that one before.

Ginny leans against the curtain, trying to come up with a witty reply, but her mind goes blank. It's just her, the darkness, and the damn pep powder rattling through her brain.

Then she feels something solid behind the velvet. Ginny pulls the curtain aside, and there it is—a wide steel door, seamlessly set into the wall. She strikes her knuckles against the surface and holds her breath. Moments later, there's a clatter on the other end, and the door swings open, releasing a warm pool of light into the backstage hall.

Ginny's mouth falls open. It's like nothing she's ever seen before.

A voice, butter-thick with cordiality, welcomes them inside.

"Welcome to the Hall of Mirrors, monsieur, mademoiselle." A hand in a starched white glove beckons with a flourish. "Please make yourselves comfortable."

CHAPTER FOURTEEN

Chandeliers swing from a domed ceiling, painted dark gold and sky blue, sending millions of refracted crystals of light across the checkered floor. Mirrors cover every inch of the walls, reflecting several velvet tables, a sweeping bar heaped with polished glasses, and a raised platform where a band is playing an energetic jazz number. A mixed crowd wanders from table to table, flashing diamonds and dirty fingernails, the mighty brought low and the poor uplifted in equal measure. There's no telling the winners from the losers.

The host is dressed in a pink frock coat, white tights, dark shoes with shiny buckles, and a preposterous powdered wig in dissonance with the florid shade of his fleshy face.

Bowing slightly, he offers them foam-frothed golden drinks from a tray. Jack shakes his head, and the man moves on, weaving through the crowd in search of thirstier prospects.

"Free liquor?"

Ginny points to one of the poker tables, where a ragged group of guests are throwing back golden drinks like there's no tomorrow.

"Nothing's free." She turns and turns, crystal light beaming through her eyes. It feels even better with the sharp edge of pep powder bringing this splendor into focus, and it's enough to push Jack's rejection to the back of her mind, if only for a while. "So it's real. I wondered if this place existed."

"You've heard of it?"

"Oh, yeah. The Hall of Mirrors, where fortunes are reversed in style."

Judging by Jack's face, his feelings toward gambling far outstrip his distaste for liquor. He clears his throat, and Ginny can tell that he's trying to smooth the blow from their backstage encounter. Good. She's not about to make it any easier for him. "So, uh, do you see your guy anywhere?"

"Not yet." Ginny rolls forward on the balls of her feet. The pep powder hits harder in the light, and she has trouble staying still. "I'd know that face anywhere, and he's not here."

They walk across the floor, and their reflections follow.

"Funny idea, putting mirrors into a casino." Jack's shaking his head. "Someone has a twisted sense of humor."

"Upping the stakes. Maybe some of these people like a challenge."

"Right, like they stand any chance in the first place. The game is rigged from the start. Add liquor and mirrors into the mix, and I bet these guys fall like bowling pins."

A crack of glass on wood. Ginny twists her head toward the commotion.

The bartender is staring down a young Black woman in an orange dress, a polished glass smacked down on the bar in front of her. She pushes it away with defiance.

"What's your problem?"

"You're needed backstage," he says. "No talkin' before the show."

The woman gasps for air as she tries to counter the solid assertion in his gravelly voice.

"But Snow White is—"

"Gone with the dwarves, that she is. New orders. Now go."

The woman leaves the bar in a shiver of flaming sequins, disappearing behind a plain steel door at the far end of the room. The bartender flashes his eyes on Ginny and Jack. They turn away in a hurry.

"What's up with that?"

Snow White. Rose Red. The words stir a distant childhood memory, images of sitting up late with flashlights, Dottie twirling roses in her hair. It's a story of sisters, and if Ruby is Rose Red, then the other one must be Josephine.

"I'm going in." She glances over at Jack, who looks like he'd rather swallow nails than let her run off on her own again. "Listen, maybe you can talk to some of the guys here? See what they know. I'll be back in a second, I promise."

"These guys?" His sweeping hand takes in the tables, the cards, the sick faces of a couple gamblers too far gone to cut their losses. "I'm not sure, Ginny."

"Come on, this is our chance."

She leaves before he can stop her. The pep powder is wearing off, in a good way, her perception mellowing with her pulse slowing from ragtime to blues. Backstage, she meets an explosion of feathers and beads in a room the size of a utility closet, choked with sweat, perfume, and face powder. An army of girls are buzzing past each other, scrambling with last-minute costume fixes. Ginny shrugs behind a stack of boxes, piled high with pale tutu skirts and crowns bewitched with fake jewels.

The woman in orange is changing into a revealing two-piece number in the same bright shade, whispering to another Black woman with her back turned on Ginny. Although their costumes are identical, the similarities stop there. The first woman waves her hands in the air in nervous swoops, while her companion listens with a regal posture, squared to shoulder any crash of anxiety.

And then the second woman turns in a cascade of soft curls, her profile catching light from a dressing room mirror. Ginny swallows a gasp.

It's Ruby Hurston.

"You sure about that?" she's whispering to the girl. "Well, keep me posted. I need to know if he comes through here again."

When the showgirls rush out on stage, Ruby lingers behind, running a hand against an old dressing table, examining her fingers. A change has come over her since they last met. Her face is flushed with health, her movements calm and measured. Even that lurid number looks like it belongs on her. Ginny has a hard time trusting any woman who can pull off orange so fabulously.

There's a creak, the door swinging into the room, followed by the slow shuffle of a new pair of feet. Ruby turns on her heel, freezing with her chin in the air.

"Hello there, traitor," she says evenly. "Come here to gloat?"

The footsteps come closer, heavy and resonant in the tiny room. From her place behind the boxes, Ginny catches a pair of leather shoes polished to a gleam, a silver-black sax case hanging from a clenched fist.

"Not the welcome I was expecting."

It's a man's voice, silky smooth, slowed down to a careless drawl. Ginny remembers a different backstage area, gasping through dust and greasepaint as the crate swung open. As the man moves closer, her suspicions are confirmed. It's Billy Calloway, dressed to the nines in a dark suit that accentuates the broad swoop of his shoulders.

Ruby's teeth flash beneath crimson lips.

"That's the best you'll get, Billy. How much did they pay you to sell me out?"

The smile fades from his voice.

"C'mon, darling. You know that's not true." He takes a slow step forward, creaking across the rugged tiles. "Don't tell me you're doubting my loyalty, after everything I've done for you. For the cause."

"Forget the damn cause. Who else knew?"

"You were right there. You know it was an ambush—"

"Just tell me. The plan was airtight. It was all our people. No outsiders." Her breath is hot and heavy, daggers in her eyes. "Except you. And those kids you sent to my house. Don't ask me to trust you when you go behind my back like that."

The force of her attack barely dents his calm expression. Instead, he steps closer, pulling Ruby into his arms, resting his chin in her coiled curls.

"What's wrong with the kids?"

She doesn't return the embrace, but she doesn't push him away, either. "You know what I mean. I told you I wanted to keep this a secret, and now who knows how many people will find out—"

"Too late for that," says Billy. "The girl saw the whole thing, and they shot her for it. She was already running her own investigation, that's how she found me."

Ginny crouches lower behind the crate, hoping she won't give herself away.

"Her sister is—" Ruby lowers her voice and continues in a whisper, while Billy nods along. "But I don't know about the others. She might be playing the other side. You're a damn fool for trusting her, and I have half a mind to—"

"I *love* you," he says, like it's the simplest thing in the world. "Don't you remember?"

There's a sharp intake of breath, and she hesitates, looking up into his eyes. Then she rests her head against his chest. They stand like that for a solid minute, him holding her close in his arms, her breathing against his chest. Then she reaches up for a kiss, lips resting briefly against his, the kind of familiarity that comes from years of closeness.

So that's what this is. Ginny leans her forehead against the crate, trying to calm her breath. Billy Calloway, always so good with his words, so smooth with his gestures, a real crowd-pleaser with his sax. A good guy, by all accounts, and yet. Takes a certain kind of deceit to play both sisters at once, and with that single kiss, Ginny can feel the truth of Otto Sharp's words cutting through her mind.

Billy Calloway, falling for his girlfriend's sister while Josephine was busy making it big. Reaching for Josephine once more when she threatened to leave. Squeezing too tight when she tried to make her escape, and then—Ginny doesn't want to imagine what might've happened then.

Ruby pulls away, leaning against the table with her hands on her stomach. Tears sparkle beneath the hard edge in her eyes. Billy's shoulders go slack.

"You're hurt."

She shakes her head, turning away from him to face the mirror. "A flesh wound. One of them got me while I was leaving the club. Nothing I haven't handled before."

Breath whistles through his teeth. "You were *shot*? Why didn't you tell—"

She whirls around. "All the more reason to get those bastards before they can do any more damage. I wish I knew who betrayed me. It's like fighting shadows."

"I went back to search the theater last night." He paces back and forth, keeping his eyes down. "No luck. If they've taken her out of the city—"

"They wouldn't. I told you, location is crucial for their business. So we find the Eagle, get to his headquarters, and that's where he's keeping my sister. Plain and simple."

The Eagle is closer than you think. Ginny shivers against the crate, trying to banish the tall man's slippery voice from her memory. Looks like Ruby's been running her own investigation, and she might be a few steps ahead of them already.

Billy comes closer to Ruby, studying her face with gentle care. "Did you destroy the stash?"

"Didn't get the chance. But I moved it again." A quick look, colored with a hint of apology. "Sorry. I was running on edge and I had to be sure." Her eyes drop to the floor. "I let her down, Bill."

He clasps her palms in his, an action both tender and urgent at once.

"Your sister knew what she was doing when she put on that veil. Do you think she'll talk?"

Ruby shakes her head. "She knows what's at stake. We'll be fine. I just hope we can get to her before they wear her down. I don't know what she'll do under pressure."

A round of applause clatters through the club. Billy releases Ruby's hands.

"Keep it together, my darling. We'll find her, don't even doubt it, and then we can finally put everything behind us."

He leaves. The dancers tumble backstage for a change of clothing, orange to oyster white, and Ruby falls into place as though she never left them.

Ginny waits for the commotion to reach a peak, then slips out the metal door and back under the dancing lights of the mirrored hall. The world blurs as she tries to make sense of what she witnessed. Ruby's hiding some kind of stash as leverage against her sister's kidnapper. Billy's in on the deal. Drugs, betrayals, theaters—the words jumble in Ginny's mind like bits of a crossword puzzle, falling apart when she tries to fit them together.

One thing rings clear above everything else. Her sinister love triangle theory is looking more like a loud headline in a gossip rag than a real answer. Too many clues don't fit. Josephine is alive. Their prime suspects are leading the search. Her head aches with clues, and she wishes for a painkiller and a jug of pure water to get her off this painful high.

Ginny stops by the bar. A strange scene unfolds in front of her eyes, and for a minute she wonders if it's an unknown side effect of the powder, a hallucinatory product of her fevered mind. Weary guests from all around the room are shifting toward the center table, where two men sit behind fanned out sheaves of cards, the other players skidding to the sides with their chips surrendered.

Ginny's stomach plummets. One of the guys is Jack, gray suit hiking up as he studies the cards in his hand.

The other is Charlie.

She can't bring herself to look away. A mountain of chips teeters in the middle. Jack sits in proud solitude, while Charlie fumbles with a girl on his lap. His face is a drunken red, the buttons of his shirt undone. Still, his smile holds a ghost of that charm that brings both debutantes and their mothers to their knees.

"Quit playing it safe, Black Jack. I know better than to buy your act. C'mon, let's finish this like men, you all in or what?"

He shoves the rest of his chips into the middle of the table, planting a sloppy kiss on the girl's bright mouth as she wriggles with pleasure.

Ginny slips through the watching crowd for a closer look. It feels like a fever dream, a moving picture with the actors saying all the wrong lines.

"You never learn." Jack pushes his chips forward with a single hand. The crowd whoops with delight. "I can beat you in my sleep. Always could."

There has to be at least a hundred on the line. More than Jack can afford, from what she's seen so far. If she doesn't act soon, they'll both end up behind bars. The gambler and the junkie, what a story that will make.

"What the hell are you doing?" Ginny swings through the bodies, leans into Jack's ear. "Listen, there's some new things I have to tell you. It's important. Don't take the bet. Just fold and go, come on—"

Too late, she looks up at the face across the table, Charlie's smile twisting into something vicious.

"Well," he says slowly, running a hand along his girl's bare arm. "I certainly underestimated you, my dear. All this time, you've been ditching me for Black Jack Crawford?"

"Ginny, stay out of it," Jack hisses. "I'll meet you outside, just go—"

"We go way back, Jack and I do," Charlie says. "I thought I was lucky to catch him tonight. It's been so long since we played, and I've been dying for a rematch."

The urgency of the moment slips away. "You know each other?" She looks at Jack, but he doesn't meet her gaze.

"He's real bashful about it now, aren't you, Jacky boy? Wasn't always like that. A couple years back, he was the biggest gambler this side of the Hudson. Did me dirty, right before getting out of the game too. You see, Ginny, it's a mean game, poker. When the money runs out, you're liable to start betting things you shouldn't. Things that don't belong to you, not really."

On the table, Jack's fingers curl into fists.

"Remember Maribelle, Jack? God, was she the sweetest thing. This was before I was with your sister, Ginny. We were talking of getting married—yes, that's right. Except your boy here decided he had to have her."

"It wasn't like that. Ginny—"

"I was still green, and Black Jack had me exactly where he wanted. So I said yes. He won. He took her away from me." Charlie's eyes flash. Even the girl in his lap goes still. "It's all been downhill since then. I can see it in your eyes. Even a girl like you can see I've gone lower than a gentleman in my position ever should. Now you know who's to blame."

The air burns, white-hot electricity shooting above the table. Ginny feels the rage coming up inside, sharpened by the pep powder, compounded by months of bottled-up emotions. His confidence sizzles through the air, and the people in the crowd are already nodding along, turning their accusatory glances toward Jack. Charlie's always been convincing, and even Ginny might've believed him in the past. Lapped up every word like a good little pet. But something snaps inside her then, the pep powder crackling through the ache in her neck, her arms, her damn soul. That's how she knows the spell is finally broken. She won't fall for his tricks ever again.

She runs up and jumps onto the table, landing smack in the center of the piled chips. Murmurs erupt all around. One poor blue chip catches beneath her heel, and she stomps down with enough force to crush it to bits.

"I don't believe a word that's coming out of your mouth, Charlie Darby." The words sear her tongue like acid. "But even if my partner is the devil himself, he's still ten times the man you'll ever be."

A kick sends the chips flying into Charlie's face. Sensing trouble, the girl escapes, her little heels pattering a hurried getaway across the chessboard tiles. She whispers something to one of the men in the powdered wigs, and he disappears behind a steel door on the other end.

Charlie laces his fingers together and leans forward.

"Since our chips are out of the picture, I've got a deal for you, Jack." He flicks a look at his cards, then back at his opponent, skimming past Ginny like she's invisible. "You should know it well from our last game. Winner gets the girl."

Standing up there on the table, Ginny suddenly feels the color draining from her cheeks. It's like she's exposed, a showcase model raised above the audience for a better look. Whatever is going on here, there's no way in hell she's letting them go on.

She whirls around. Jack is barely moving a limb. He's doing the odds in his head, she can see that, and she hates to think that he might be considering the deal. He looks nothing like the man she knows, his face gone hard under the glare from the chandeliers, nostrils flaring with anger.

But then he stands up, flinging his cards in the air so they fall around him. One of them is an ace, she can see that much. He might've had a winning hand, but he's forfeiting.

"No deal. Come on, Ginny." An outstretched hand, quivering more than the audience can see. Ginny grabs it and hops off the table, the floor spinning in front of her eyes.

They're on their way to the door. It's over. But then there's a scrape and a shuffle, followed by the drunk drag of heavy footsteps behind them.

"You've lost your touch, Black Jack. I can see it, everyone can, you've gone soft like a little girl. Don't have the stomach anymore, do you?"

"Ignore him." Jack tightens his grip on Ginny's arm, but she jerks free.

"What the hell did you say?"

It burns through her even stronger, the rage. Charlie's leer is enough to set the entire damn joint on fire.

"Your guy lost his balls in the war, from the looks of it. Tell me, what does it feel like, Ginny? Like being with another woman?"

It pumps through her head in thick, hot bursts. The voices fade away. She can smell it on him. The whiskey, the cigars, the easy women. Only one thing left against a man who's pushed past all her limits.

She lunges against him, fists out. The first one gets him in the nose. Her rings scratch his face, gush of blood seeping out like sweat. He slams an elbow into her stomach, and she doubles over, rolling away from another blow, her shoulder screaming as she hits the ground. And then he's got her by the hair, pulling her across the floor, all that cold tile searing against her skin.

Jack's yelling something, trying to break them up, but it's like she's underwater. No sound comes through.

She twists and kicks Charlie in the knee, and he lets go of her hair, folding into the pain. She rises. The whole world spins around her, but Charlie's on the floor, blond hair fanned over his pink face. Ginny presses her heel against his shoulder, pinning him to the tile, enjoying the hiss that escapes through his lips.

"How does that feel, huh?" She can't stop it, itching for more, more, messing his face up real good to wipe away that dirty smile. But then a group of guys come over and lift him by the arms, dragging him away just as she prepares to strike.

As Jack pulls her away, she catches sight of Ruby, leaning against the bar with a curious expression on her face. They lock eyes, and the woman breaks into a smile that would put the brightest lights above Times Square to shame.

CHAPTER FIFTEEN

Jack is silent all the way to his car. He starts the engine without looking at Ginny, slamming his foot into the gas pedal with a sort of helpless resignation.

"None of that should've happened." His fingers are limp on the wheel, eyes glinting in the dark. "I shouldn't have lost control."

Ginny taps her fingers against the side of her head. There's blood all over. Slicking her cheek like a garish shade of rouge, filling her mouth with the taste of bitter metal. The charm on Mary's bracelet drips with blood, and she wipes it on her skirt, trying to get the crimson trapped between the points of the star. The scene in the Hall of Mirrors plays on repeat in her head, Jack looking like a stranger at that big card table, and then her fist coming down against Charlie's nose.

"You're too hard on yourself. I have you beat when it comes to losing control, don't you think?"

He curses under his breath. "It's all my fault. I put you in that position."

"No dice," she says. "It's been a long time coming, and you had nothing to do with it. Anyway, what's your deal with Charlie?"

"I don't—"

"Don't want to talk about it? Yeah, sure. Play it like that, only don't expect me to have your back next time somebody comes for you."

He jerks the wheel, skidding the car against the sidewalk. They're halfway up Broadway. Across the street is the New Amsterdam, jammed between two lesser buildings, twinkling golden green through the darkness.

"Want to know the truth? Fine." He heaves a breath, tapping his fingers against the dashboard. "I wasn't always a detective. Many years ago, before the war, I was another broke kid working the docks. I dropped out of high school. Didn't know a thing about the world, just knew I wanted more. After those long shifts in the dark, all I ever wanted was to be seen."

He runs his fingers down the steering wheel, and Ginny remembers those calouses, how they felt against her skin backstage at the Eighty-Three. She shivers despite the heat.

"You wanted power," she says, her voice cracking. He doesn't have to answer. She can see it all over his face, the truth of it.

"Before long, I took a bad turn. Started hanging around carpet joints all over Harlem, moving up from three-card monte with the back-alley drunks to the big leagues. I was damn good at poker, but not good enough to win against the house. That's how he got to me."

Ginny turns to stare at Jack. He takes a deep breath, like he's getting ready for a big jump into the dark unknown.

"It was this guy who ran a club called The Empire, later I learned he owned half of Harlem. He called me into his office. Said I had two options: pay him back in full, or start working for him. Said there was some heavy sugar in it for me if I played nice. So I said yes. From that point, he owned me."

Jack's shoulders slump forward under the weight of his memories. She wants to pull him close, wrap him tight against her body until the hurt goes away. But she knows it won't work.

"What happened?"

"It was good for a while. The boss would plant me in games against high rollers, throw some cards into my sleeves. I'd win almost every time. He gave me a cut of all the earnings, said I had a bright future ahead. I quit working the docks. Started drinking too much, putting stuff up my nose. Thought I had it under control, but of course I didn't. Most people had no idea, they thought I was moving up in the world—and I was, in a way. I might've become a fine crook by now, but it was never meant to be—because that was when I met Charlie."

There's movement across the street, a couple dark figures shuffling through the alley between the New Am and the building beside it. The lights of Broadway shine behind Jack's profile like a halo.

"It was only a matter of time until someone figured out the con, and it had to be Charlie. He didn't let on at first—pretended to be my friend, took me around town. I was a damn fool, thinking he saw something in me. Shiny guy like that, fresh out of Princeton. Should've known there was a catch."

"There's always a catch with Charlie," Ginny says, leaning back against the seat. "He said something about a girl. Maribelle."

The name makes Jack wince. He presses his lips together. "She was the only light in my whole damn life."

Ginny can't be sure yet, but it sounds like Charlie's engagement to Maribelle was nothing but another one of his lies.

"What happened?"

"Soon after he learned about my con, Charlie decided to take his revenge. He got me wasted, took away my trick cards, so I was losing against him over and over again until I owed him more than my entire life. Then he gave me the ultimatum. Give up my girl, and he'd forgive my debts. He wanted to bring me even lower. I couldn't believe anybody could be so heartless. I refused to do it. Things got ugly with Charlie, and in the end my boss had to pay up. Maribelle never spoke to me again. I decided I was done with that kind of life, done with sinking to rock bottom and bringing down the only person who mattered along with me."

Ginny can feel the anger rising inside her again, fingers tensing into fists. God, how she wishes she'd finished the job. Pounded that smug smile into a bloody mess.

"Your boss helped you out," she says. "So that was good, right?"

Jack laughs at that, a dry, humorless sound. "Not that simple. Charlie's dad had just been elected senator. The boss wanted to strike a deal with him. At that point, the war was past its peak, and he was getting whispers of Prohibition around the corner. The thing with Charlie weakened my boss's position. He had to make some serious concessions, and he never forgave me for that. Luckily, I was drafted around then, giving me enough time in France until it all blew over, but his boys still left me a souvenir to make sure I would never forget."

He unbuttons the sleeve of his shirt with fumbling fingers, then rolls it up to his elbow. A scar stretches up his arm, dangerously close to all the veins. Ginny runs her fingers down its length.

"Oh my—" She shakes her head, looks into his eyes. "Jack, I had no clue—"

"Yeah, that was the idea." He rolls his sleeve back down. "I've done everything I could to leave that life behind. I got clean. Stayed out of nightclubs, and God knows I'm not welcome in most of them anyway, even all these years later. And now it's my turn to fight back. I don't want kids getting hurt in this part of town ever again."

Something about his words strikes a familiar chord. She remembers the fervent rush in his voice when he asked Ruby about the Harlem heart attacks, that desperate departure from his cool private eye persona.

Jack keeps going, tapping his fingers against the wheel in a frustrated rhythm. "Can't believe I lost myself again. One look at Charlie, and I was gone. All those years—"

"The Harlem heart attacks are personal for you," Ginny says. "Why?"

He turns toward her and looks her in the eye. Really looks at her for the first time that night. Ginny's breath drains from her lungs, it's so sudden, so stunning.

"I thought I owed it to the world. Reparations for all the bad things I've done. It started because I suspected my old boss at first, thought he might've moved from liquor to drugs." Jack pushes the hair out of his face. "Except that's not his style. He's a crook, but he'd never risk his business on a drug with such an obvious body count. Reefer, coke, he's good with those. But I've done my research, and this one's different. You heard of something called pep powder?"

Pep powder. Ginny can still feel it rushing through her veins, crackling painfully inside her brain. She wonders how much powder it would take for her heart to knock out its last beat. Maybe it's not a question of quantity at all, but a spin of the wheel, dumb luck like everything else in her life so far.

She can see herself lying dead on the dance floor, surrounded by strangers.

That's where she'll end up if she keeps this going. Keeps hiding things from Jack. The only way out is to come clean, even if it's going to hurt like hell.

"I've heard of it, all right." She pulls the lipstick tube out of her purse and places it in his hand. "Tried it too. Got this one from Vivian Templeton in the powder room tonight."

"You've taken it before?" She can't see the expression on his face, but he's rolling the tube around his palm, examining it from all ends.

"Got my first dose from Mazie at the Follies last night." She gasps against the memory, suddenly remembering how sick Mazie's been looking lately, that fainting spell at Gloria's party. She should've seen the signs sooner. "Left me craving more, and then I took another hit, and—"

"That explains it. God, Ginny. You could've died."

I know, she wants to say, and somewhere deeper, she wonders why the thought isn't as frightening as it once was. She can see his eyes clouding over, and before he can give her another lecture, she says, "Look, I know it was stupid, okay? Reckless, impulsive—"

But he's looking at her bruises now, shaking his head with the saddest eyes in the world. "You were looking for something to stop the pain."

She can't face him. It's too powerful, the feel of his eyes all over, she doesn't like how close he's coming to reading her, cover to cover. Nobody's ever seen through her like that.

"No, I was just looking for a good time—"

"It's okay, you don't have to— I saw how you were with Charlie. I—" He tightens his grip around the lipstick. "I understand."

They sit in silence for a while, staring out into the distance. A couple cars flash past, taillights flaring. There's dirt and blood under her fingernails. She's thrown off-balance by Jack's sympathy. It would almost be better if he'd scream at her again, tell her off for being reckless. That, she can handle.

Then she remembers the scene in the Hall of Mirrors, and she turns to Jack fast as a flash.

"Listen, there's something you need to know. You were right. I think our investigations are connected after all."

She tells him everything. Ruby's stash and Billy's investigations and the random scraps of information she's managed to pull from the conversation. Jack is quiet through the entire monologue, his green eyes darkening in the dim.

"Ruby was moving a stash that night," he says slowly. "A stash of pep powder, I'm guessing. Billy had his eye on Josephine while she was singing. Then something went wrong. But who would want to kidnap her? Think it has something to do with the drugs?"

"I'm sure of it. The stash is the key. I'd say the kidnapper is mighty unhappy about getting their goods stolen. So, this Eagle fellow sends his guys to kidnap Josephine, but she refuses to talk. And then—" A sudden spark of inspiration hits her hard. "Say he learns about a couple detectives, asking around about Josephine. Say he wants to scare them off the case."

Jack squeezes the bridge of his nose between two fingers, wincing at the memory. "The guys outside the New Am."

"You kept saying something that night. I couldn't figure it out. Sounded like pain, but I think it was something else—"

"I know. It was paint," he says. "I wanted to tell you, but it slipped my mind later. Their shoes. They were covered in paint."

Of course. Ginny stares at the theater across the street, cupping her hands over her eyes. She remembers the wet boot print on Jack's suit, white paint mixing with the grime.

With the premiere only days away, there's still so much work to be done. So many decorations to be painted.

Stagehands. They were stagehands at the theater.

Ginny whips around to share the revelation with Jack, but he's pointing across the street, brow crinkling beneath the brim of his hat. She follows his pointed finger and nearly gasps at the scene unfolding on the other side.

Dark figures are darting through the alley beside the theater. Four of them are carrying a crate, shoulders sagging with the effort. Two glossy black cars are parked outside the theater, and the men place the crate into the backseat of the first one. When they return with a second crate, Ginny twists her fingers around Jack's wrist, leaving a bloody smudge on the edge of his sleeve.

"We have to follow them," she says. "Whatever's in those crates—"

"Might be the drugs," Jack says. "They could lead us right to their leader."

Then the front door of the theater swings open, spitting out a girl in dazzling white. She trips down the stairs and falls into a crumpled heap on the sidewalk, the voluminous tiers of her dress following like so many wilted petals.

Ginny's heart jumps into her throat. It's Dottie.

She waits for her to rise, to brush off the dust with a petulant air, but her sister only sits there, rubbing her shoulders against a chill that's not there. Two of the men come over and lift her with rugged familiarity, and she flings some kind of insult into their faces. They erupt in laughter, then return to their work.

Ginny opens the car door. "Look for a crate full of lipsticks."

"What are you—" Jack places a hand on her shoulder, but she twists away.

"I have to go. Follow those guys, all right? And call me with any news—"

"Ginny, wait," says Jack, but it's too late, she's already outside, slipping from car to trash can, trying to outrun her shadow across the street.

In the past, she would've jumped straight into the action. Pulled her sister away from these men, dealt with the consequences later. But working alongside Jack has taught her something. There's power in information. So, she tucks her hair into her cloche, bringing the collar of her jacket up to her chin as she pulls out a cigarette. Nobody ever suspects a lonely smoker. She leans against a streetlamp a few feet away, trying to calm the frantic ache in her heart.

She waits for screams, for protests. Instead, the conversation is restrained, dialed down to a cool simmer. Of course, she thinks, her fingers quivering around the cigarette. They're stagehands. Her sister knows them all. It might be nothing.

"You owe me," Dottie is saying, rocking back and forward on her heels. "You got what you wanted, now hand me the damn plates."

Her mild-mannered sister's voice rings through the air with a new edge, the softness nearly gone. Her words rush together like she's drunk. But that can't be true, Dottie's never gone past her one-drink limit in her entire life.

The man seems to consider her words for a while, then he releases a laugh that sends prickles of fear down Ginny's neck.

"Don't know what you're talking about."

"I know you've got them," says Dottie. Ginny can see her sister stepping closer to the man, prodding him in the shoulder. "We had a deal—"

The stagehand pushes her away, like she weighs nothing at all. "You must've misunderstood. Now run along before you get into any trouble, sweetheart."

Dottie stamps the pavement for a moment, her entire body tensed like a violin string. As the men get back to work, slamming the doors of their shiny cars, Dottie turns and leaves. She walks past Ginny with her eyes staring blindly ahead, mascara settling in pools of crushed black powder beneath her eyes, lipstick streaking down the sides of her mouth.

Ginny takes off after her sister, trying to ignore her shattered walk, the fine layer of dust staining the edges of her pure white dress. Many times, she's wished her sister would ease up, but not like this, never like this. She swings dangerously close to the road, lit up by the lights of Broadway like a broken music box ballerina. Ginny's heart twists as she looks into the faces of passersby, strangers noticing this odd, fractured quality. It's only a matter of time before someone takes advantage. A rowdy group of college boys with cigars between their teeth corner her in the middle of the pavement.

"What's a pretty thing like you doing all alone at night?" drawls the captor, a stocky blond guy in a shiny suit. His friends paw at Dottie's skirt, sending the white gauze tiers fluttering in the night.

Ginny steps out of the shadows, and the blond guy releases Dottie as soon as he sees her. She must look like hell, with all that blood caking her face. Not all of it her own, she thinks with a shiver.

"She's not alone." Ginny throws a hand around her sister. "Do you mind?"

Dottie's dress wins them a taxi on the first try, even though the driver does his best not to look Ginny in the face. They're home in record time, Dottie muttering about mirrors and premieres while Ginny tries to drag her sister up the stairs, into the elevator, and into the bathroom inside the empty apartment.

"I'm gonna be sick," Dottie mutters, sliding down the sink. "Why's it all gotta spin like—"

"How much did you drink?"

"Don't know. Don't care." Her face is gray, cheeks sunken in with a fresh sheen of sweat coating the surface. "I needed more because I couldn't do the garden number, Ginny. I was falling over and then I couldn't get up and it was too much and Sharp is a bad man, a truly despicable—"

"I know, honey." She runs a hand over Dottie's head, tucking a loose wave behind her ear. "Listen, if you gotta be sick, do it. Better get it out of your system before you—"

Dottie retches all over the toilet, her arms going blue with goosebumps. Even in this condition, her sister flushes with embarrassment, giving the metal string a quick tug to flush it all down.

"Excuse me."

"Feeling better?"

"A little."

"Take some of these, should help absorb whatever's still in your system." Ginny fills a glass with tap water, passes a couple black pills into her sister's hands. It's a well-worn routine she's perfected after years of late nights with too many toxins in her system. She owes a great deal to whoever came up with Requa's Charcoal Tablets.

"Where did you learn all this? You're like a nurse."

"Perks of living dangerously. Now, let's get you out of this old greasepaint and into bed, what do you say?"

She goes through all the motions. Fresh water splashed over Dottie's face, followed by Pond's cold cream rubbed off with a worn washcloth. Layers of tulle traded for a cotton nightgown. She tucks her into bed with a large glass of water and some more charcoal pills on the nightstand, wondering how their lives have turned upside down in only a week.

"I'm so tired."

"You've been working so hard, baby." Ginny kneels next to the bed, resting her head against the side. It's better in the dark. She's tired of meeting people's eyes, tired of everything. "I've seen you at rehearsals. You've got it all made. Don't you worry about it one bit."

"But it's my last premiere. It's the one I'll remember for the rest of my life. I *have* to be perfect."

Something in the way she says it gives Ginny pause.

"Why would you say that?"

"Once we're married, I have to stop dancing. So this is my very last time."

"Charlie told you this?"

The silk blend sheets crinkle as she nods. "He says I can't go putting the Darby name to shame like that. Up on a marquee like some vaudeville h-hooker." Her voice breaks against the last word. "I wish he'd understand, but it's different for him, I suppose. His father's a senator. Did you know his ancestors came up here on the *Mayflower*?"

"You don't say."

"You're so lucky, Ginny," Dottie says, sitting up with a sudden start. Must be the liquor still playing tricks, loosening her tongue. "You can do whatever you want and get away with it. Write your column, stay out dancing till morning. Whenever I try to let loose, I get hurt so bad, it's like my world is all shattered, and I just—"

"Don't marry him."

Dottie goes still in the dark.

"What are you—"

"Listen, Dot." Deep breaths, the hush of the room pushing down on her. "I did something bad. Real bad. But I want to be the one to tell you. So you hear it from me first, not him."

"Ginny, what are you talking about?"

She should probably slow down, pick out her words with care. Wait for her sister to sober up, that's what a good person would do. But the confession comes tumbling out before she can stop, and then it's too late to stem the flow.

"Charlie's not the man you think he is. He's a drunk and a gambler, and—and worse, he's cheating on you. I should know. That time at Gloria's party, he sought me out, Dot. I didn't come up to him, it was him first. And he took me into the guest room—"

There should be shouting up there on the bed. Tears, gasps, anything. Instead, only a deathly quiet.

"You slept with Charlie?"

Her voice sounds distant, like she's talking through a thick pane of warped glass.

"Yes, and I'm so—"

Dottie flicks a switch, and Ginny shies away from the light. In the dim, Dottie's eyes are dark, twin black holes that have lost all meaning.

"Get out."

Ginny staggers to her feet. "Listen, I never meant for it to happen. But I wanted you to know—"

"I want you out of the apartment tomorrow. Do you understand?"

Ginny nods, even as she can feel her heart dropping like a cold stone. "Of course. I— You will break up with him, won't you? Please promise me that—"

Dottie isn't looking at her anymore, her straight posture frozen at unnatural angles like a broken doll. Her voice flattens to a cold monotone. "You've got until the end of the day tomorrow. Now get out of my sight."

There's nothing else she can say. It's all over.

She can hear her own footsteps echoing through the apartment as she walks back to her room, wondering if she was right all along. There's no glory in honesty, and now she's dealt the final blow to something that was already half-broken.

She pulls an old bottle of gin from beneath her bed and drinks until the juniper numbs her to the world, and the night fades to nothing.

CHAPTER SIXTEEN

Although the gin dims her pep powder high by a fraction, she spends most of the night twisting in her sheets, aching in bed with raw eyes popping open to the first light of morning. Everything comes rushing back at once, last night's memories adding to the pain from the hangover. She's really done it this time. As she sits up in bed, Ginny tries to console herself with the thought of Dottie finally leaving Charlie, flinging that big rock in his face as he drops to his knees and begs for her forgiveness. The image cheers her up a bit, and with a half-hearted swig from the gin bottle, she gets to her feet.

There's a knock, and then the maid comes in with an envelope in her hands. "This came for you just now, miss. And there was a man who called late last night."

Damn. She remembers Jack's promise to call her with any news about the cars. She was supposed to wait for his call, but instead she drowned out the night with liquor and self-pity. Typical.

"Did he leave a message?"

"He left the number of his—" The maid hesitates. "His office, miss. The telephone operator says it's in a residential area in Harlem. Are you sure . . . ?"

"That's fine, thank you."

With the bottle still cradled in her arms, she opens the envelope, wondering if Dottie's decided to make their separation official in print. Inside, there's only a small piece of lined paper, jotted with a quick message in a careless hand.

Ginny—Sorry I couldn't see you last night. Meet me at the Eighty-Three so I can make it up to you? Mary

The words are all jumbled together, a few shades off from Mary's careful cursive, but she's been so busy with all that Follies business, it only makes sense that she'd be in a hurry. Ginny thinks of canceling, making up some excuse for later, but the gin makes her feel a little better, and she could definitely use a friend after everything that happened last night.

In the bathroom, she runs Mary's charm bracelet under the tap for a full minute, making sure to get rid of any rusty trace of blood. She left in a hurry yesterday, and she never gave Mary the proper send-off into her glamorous new life. Today, she'll make it up to her, she decides. Take her out to breakfast at the Waldorf-Astoria like she always wanted. They'll order extra champagne and flirt with all the foreign diplomats. With Dottie throwing her out of her life, she needs Mary more than ever before.

Half an hour later, she's standing outside the Eighty-Three. A knock on the heavy door yields only silence. No suspicious man in the grate, no grunt to go away. Ginny kicks at the door with her toe, and it swings inward with a menacing creak.

Nobody inside. Gray sunlight streams through the open door, alighting on broken shards of glass, trampled streamers quivering in the breeze, cigarettes stubbed by many dancing feet. The stage is empty, but a microphone stand remains, looking down in silent judgment.

"Mary?"

No answer. She repeats her name a few more times until it bounces off the walls, the echo of her voice lashing back at her from every angle.

The door to the powder room is open just a crack. She lingers on the threshold, one hand to the door, squeezing her eyes shut to delay the moment, even as she knows what she will find in there. Even when the smell hits her nostrils, the rotting chill of it, she still stays rooted to her place, head shaking against the inevitability of whatever's waiting on the other side.

Then she pushes on the door, and there's no going back.

The air is still. All the mirrors are shattered, as if someone took a series of angry swings with a baseball bat. Only one remains intact, and in front of it—Ginny falls against a wall, it can't be, it can't—Mary sits with her head against the table, shimmery white dress scattering beads on the floor. A mist of white powder coats the dressing table. Her arms reach forward as if to pull something out of the mirror, crimson nails chewed to the quick, wrists gone blue, blood clotted into her hair.

Ginny slides to the ground. Her knees buckle in front of her. She tries to scream, shout, anything—but her voice is suffocated deep in her lungs, and all she can do is stare off into the distance as the world around her blurs into darkness.

There's no telling how long she stays there, but eventually she must find the strength to call Jack's office from the pay phone outside, because he bursts through the door a while later, followed by a group of uniformed cops. Jack comes over to her side a couple times, putting a hand on her shoulder, saying something with an intent look on his face—but it's nothing to her, like they're worlds away and she just can't hear him.

The cops swarm into every corner of the club, occasionally flinging comments to one another in rough tones. The medical examiner comes in, telling them to be gentle as they sweep for prints, lifting her arms and dropping them back on the table. Ginny feels a small flash of gratitude toward this stranger, but mostly she only feels numb.

They turn her face toward Ginny for one terrible moment that seems to last a lifetime. Asking her to identify the body. It's her, sure enough. Mary's cornflower blue eyes stare lifelessly through elaborately beaded lashes, her mouth opened wide as if she was surprised by the shocking twist in the last moments of her life.

It feels like a play. None of it feels real. Actors going through the motions.

They keep butchering her last name. Ginny spells it out, yanking the policeman by the sleeve until he gets it right. G-l-i-s-z-i-n-s-z-k-y. Mary would've hated this. Her life ending like it probably started, with a bunch of strangers saying her name all wrong, the letters immortalized in a police file instead of up on a marquee where she belongs.

And Ginny knows it's all her fault.

The clues were right before her eyes, but she was busy chasing other things. Drawn toward the light. Getting wasted in clubs, pretending she was making progress, when the killer was always two steps ahead. There's no doubt about it: the white powder scattered over the table, the flashy showgirl costume. And Mary, in danger this entire time, even though she didn't know it. Not once did Ginny wonder about the Follies audition, so close to the premiere, and the off-season hire that had to be kept in strict secret. Instead, she'd only encouraged her to keep pushing, shooting for a dream that was never meant to be. If only she'd listened—

Why stop there? This whole investigation went haywire the moment she got involved. Every day, she's brought them within an inch of death, risking everything for her own misguided sense of justice. The lives of others were always in greater danger than her own, but she kept pushing for answers, oblivious to the damage she caused every step of the way.

Now, she can only think of that last time she saw Mary at *Photoplay*, the excitement burning in her eyes. Always there with a kind word and a slice of kolacz. The charm bracelet weighs heavy on Ginny's wrist. That's who she was, Mary. A giver. And all Ginny could do was take and take, until there was nothing left.

While Mary's body is loaded onto a stretcher, the cops stand around taking notes, nodding to each other with grave faces. Ginny leans in for a listen.

". . . another overdose. Girls like this are always getting into something. Liquor, drugs—"

"I wish somebody would tell 'em you don't live long like that—"

Ginny stumbles to her feet, prodding one of the officers in the back. He turns in surprise. It's one of the older guys, a fatherly type with a name tag that reads *H. Tallman.*

"You got it all wrong," she says, trying to give him the note, which has gone damp from her hands. "She sent me this note in the morning. It can't be an overdose if she was waiting for—"

He places an arm on her shoulder. It's not unkind, but Ginny takes a step back, bumping into the wall.

"Your friend made some mistakes, miss. Maybe she did send you something, but then she decided to get high while she waited." He squeezes his eyes shut. "A terrible tragedy, what's happening to young people these days."

"What about the blood?" Her voice rocks up and down an octave. "There's blood on her head. Somebody hit her—"

The officer gives her another pat on the back. His eyes light up, and he nods to somebody behind her.

"I'm sorry, miss, I have to go—"

They're getting it all wrong, and there's nothing she can do to stop them. They won't listen. They never do. Ginny throws her head against the wall. Shocks of pain shoot through her skull, last night's bruises lighting up across her face. Good. After all she's done, she deserves worse than that.

Jack appears at her side, wrapping his arm around her back.

"Ginny, I'm so sorry." He means it, but she can't look at him. It's too awful. She pulls out of his grasp.

"She didn't kill herself."

"I know." His whole posture seems to sag under the strain. "I don't think it was an overdose either. These guys are more dangerous than we first thought. I followed them last night. Both cars went uptown, but then they split up. The car I trailed took me straight back to the New Amsterdam. Looks like they knew they were being followed."

Ginny wipes her eyes with the heel of her hand. "It's all my fault, Jack. I could've saved her."

She shows him the note. His eyebrows shoot up, and he takes it away with enough force to rip the corner, his features clouding over.

"She sent this to you? When?"

"I don't know. The maid brought it in this morning. Maybe she wrote it a couple hours ago—"

Jack stares at the cursive letters with naked fear.

"Ginny, I heard what the cops were saying. Mary couldn't have sent this. She—" He looks up at her. "She's been dead since last night."

A sudden jolt pierces through the numbness. She can feel the pain building at the center of her forehead until her entire skull is burning. Mary died last night. She couldn't have sent the note.

"The killer sent this," she says quietly, then louder, "the Eagle. They know where to find me. Last night, one of his guys said the Eagle was somebody close to me, he knows I've been working the case—"

"And he won't stop until you quit." He folds the note into his hand, passes it to Ginny. Something's shifting in his face, the sadness hardening into a new expression. "You have to quit, Ginny. It's the only way."

"W-what?" She can't believe what he's saying. "Are you fucking kidding me?"

He clears his throat, shifts his weight. There's something impersonal in his stance, the cool gray suit hanging off his body like a department store rack, that black notebook looking so clinical under his arm. She was wrong to think they were ever a team. They're strangers.

His silence makes her break down again. "Is that your plan, then? Give up at the first sign of danger? Right, when the going gets tough, detective Jack Crawford gets the fuck out of here."

"You know that's not true. I—" He flicks a look at the cops, then back at her. "Please trust me on this, Ginny. I've taken enough cases to know when to stop. I got off with a beating, but now your friend's dead, and next thing you know—"

"What? They'll come for me?" Ginny slams a fist into the wall, unleashing a mist of loose plaster. "Not if I get to them first."

"Stop it." She's got him really riled up now, his voice the loudest she's ever heard, his cheeks burning red. "You're acting like a child. It's unreasonable, and if you stopped to think for even a moment, you'd know I was right. This kind of behavior will only get more people killed."

His words heat up the air between them. She wants to slap him for underestimating her like all the other men before him. She was wrong to ever think he was different, but it doesn't matter anymore. He can quit the case, put Mary out of mind like she's just another body, but Ginny can't forget so easily. She looks down at the star hanging from her wrist. It's high time she took matters into her own hands.

"We're done," she says. "You can go back to your safe bets, your cheating husbands, whatever—but I'm not giving up. I'll find out who did this to her, and I'll make him pay."

And before Jack can say anything else, before he can stop her, she leaves. The cops follow close behind, carrying Mary's body through the empty club on a stretcher, their faces blank as slabs of stone.

CHAPTER SEVENTEEN

It's only a short walk from the Eighty-Three to Grill King, and Ginny runs the entire way, the air ripping through her lungs so she has to grab the side of the booth when she gets there. The investigation is the only thing keeping her in town, and with Dottie's ultimatum, she has no choice but to keep pounding the pavement anyway. She doesn't know what she might find at Ace, but with the pep powder scattered around Mary's body and Vivian Templeton's many evasions, she seems like the next likely suspect.

Bertha is in her usual spot by the counter, the frown on her face deepening as she watches the sweat rolling down Ginny's face. She swipes her hands on her apron and comes closer, tapping cautious nails against her notepad.

"Table for one?"

"I prefer the kitchen."

Ginny tries to push past her, but the woman isn't as soft as she appears. The muscles on her arms feel like sailor's knots. "Kitchen's closed, and I don't see your invitation."

That damn card. She doesn't remember what happened to the ace of clubs, but after the past couple nights, it could be anywhere. Ginny leans forward, close enough to smell Bertha's skin, talcum powder mingling with deep-fried grease.

"I'm not in the mood for games, Bertha. Remember what I told you that night?" She jabs a finger into the woman's shoulder. "I'm a big fucking deal."

Bertha rocks back on her heels, licking the lipstick stains off her teeth. "You said you were a showgirl, but you look like a junkie running on empty. You're gonna have to try a lot harder than that to get past me, girl."

Ginny looks around the diner. She can see her disheveled state reflected in the stunned faces of the patrons. The deep circles under her eyes, the mad jag of her heartbeat against her chest—with the pep powder in her system and Mary's death weighing heavy on her conscience, she's never been lower. She never should've bought that double dose from Vivian Templeton.

But maybe that's something she can work with.

"You're damn right, Bertha. I'm here for my next fix, so you'd better tell Vivian I'm waiting."

The smile drops from the waitress's face. Moments later, she's leading her through the kitchen again, through the steel door and right into the empty dance floor.

The entire club is bathed in blue lights. Ginny feels like she's swimming underwater, fighting some invisible current as she runs through the empty space. She shakes down a young waiter, her voice cracking around Vivian's name, and he takes her to the back of the club with nervous glances tossed over the shoulder. Ginny knows she looks like she's gone off the rails. In a past life, she would've discreetly popped open a compact, touched up her rouge, practiced a couple smiles until she looked presentable again. But that was when the world still came in a million different colors, and she wanted to be one of them. Now, it's all fading to black. All that matters is Mary.

They reach a small dark room in the back. It looks like an office in a gangster flick: rickety cherry wood desk at one end, a plush red chair behind it, the stench of stale booze and smoke lingering in the walls.

Miss Templeton is smoking from her slim cigarette holder, her bright lips forming a perfect O when Ginny comes in.

"If I didn't know better, I'd say you had a thing for me," she says, uncrossing her legs. She's dressed in last night's clothes, simple slacks and a men's shirt unbuttoned halfway, a dark blue jacket hanging off the back of her chair.

Ginny slams two palms against the desk, but the woman barely reacts, instead turning her chin to take another tug on her long cigarette.

"You killed Mary Gliszinszky."

Vivian taps her cigarette into an ashtray. "I have no idea who you're talking about."

"Cut the act. You sold to me last night at the Eighty-Three, and somebody sold the same stuff to my friend—except now she's dead. You were there, you obviously pulled a night shift. What do you say about that?"

The woman raises a brow like they're swapping intriguing beauty secrets. "I'd say the same thing. Get off the pep as soon as you can. That stuff will drive you crazy if it doesn't kill you first. Come, now. Do I look like a killer to you, honey?"

Ginny once thought she knew what a killer looked like. She's no longer so sure. Vivian Templeton is throwing her off her game with her relaxed manner, those carefully arched brows like a society girl's, dressed in a college boy's finest suit. Her face is perfectly plastic, muscles shifting in careful increments whenever she deigns to change her expression. Ginny would call it a poker face, except Vivian looks like the kind of woman who never leaves a thing to chance.

"Just tell me if you sold to my friend." She gives her a description. Eyes: cornflower blue. Hair: short, bouncy curls clipped back. It's enough to unspool her completely, tears pricking her eyes. "I need to know."

Vivian stares at her for a moment, the smoke from her cigarette fogging up the room so her features fade to gray. She doesn't move a muscle, but after a while her cool expression thaws by a couple degrees.

"Listen, kid, I told you clients were confidential, but you seem so hung up on this girl." She rises from her chair and leans against the wall. "I never sold to her, if that's what you want to know. Barely knew the kid. She came into the club once with her fellow, had one glass of sherry and that was all. I never saw her again."

That sounds exactly like Mary. Getting high off her own ambitions, that's what she called it.

"Who was the guy?"

Vivian purses her lips into an impeccable bow shape. "That I can't tell you. But if you ask me, your friend was doomed the day she met him. Tough luck, getting attached to somebody who can hurt you."

Ginny grips the back of the chair, breathing hard. The room spins around her.

"She never told me his name," she says, more to herself than to anyone else. "She said he pulled some strings to get her a place in the Follies chorus line."

Something flashes behind those hard eyes. A spark of recognition.

"You know him, don't you?"

Vivian puffs out a smoke ring, letting it float to the ceiling. "Careful, kid. I know your type. Won't be long until you burn out, and for what?"

Ginny keeps her eyes on the desk, staring at the mess of objects scattered over the surface. Stacks of files that look like ledgers, a paperweight shaped like a miniature Venus de Milo, gold-tipped pens glinting in the faint light from the desk lamp. And right there in the middle of it all, a small black pistol with a mother-of-pearl handle. If she could reach the gun, maybe Vivian would be more eager to answer her questions. Ginny pretends to listen closely as the woman speaks with misted eyes, all the while inching closer to the weapon.

"I was like you, a long time ago. Thought I had to climb to the top with teeth and nails. Turns out you can get a lot higher if you look the other way. My advice, keep your head down—"

Ginny lashes her arm forward and grabs the gun. She points it into Vivian's face, trying to calm the tremor in her fingers. The woman only smiles, lifting her arms in mock surrender. "Please. You don't even know how to use that."

"Try me." Ginny grits her teeth and pulls back the hammer with a click. "You'd better talk."

"Then you'd better kill me." Vivian drops her smile. "I'm just a foot soldier, honey. You want to get even with your friend's killer, you gotta find the real boss of this operation."

"What are you saying?" Ginny can feel the sweat slicking her fingers, the cool metal slipping from her grip. She can't keep this going for long, and if Vivian calls for backup, the odds will quickly stack up against her.

"Think about it. Seen any other women selling drugs in your favorite haunts? You might've met some of my colleagues. Pretty girls. Approachable. Skip the back-alley bootlegger and get your kicks from a showgirl in the powder room. You get it?"

"Your boss hires women to sell pep powder. But what does that—" Ginny's heart pounds in her neck. Of course. "He's the guy you saw with Mary. She was seeing your boss. And when he promised to put her in the Follies, he asked for something in return, didn't he? Asked her to deal for him?"

"You're a sharp kid. You'll figure it out." Vivian's face shifts into a teeth-baring smile. "But you'd better be careful who you trust. Your friend didn't understand what it took to make it big, so she followed her schoolgirl dreams to the end, and look what that got her. Can't get ambitious without losing your innocence first, or you'll get burned right away."

Ginny's mind races through this new information. She can't tell if Vivian Templeton is lying, can't see all the angles yet. Once, she knew the right questions to ask, the best ways to find the truth beyond the lies. Not anymore. The frantic tangle of this case taunts her just out of reach. "You trusted him too, didn't you? Why else would you agree to work for him?"

This brings up an unexpected wave of laughter. "Oh, honey. You really think I'd hitch my future to some man?"

Vivian's arm shoots forward in one fluid motion, knocking Ginny's hand down. Ginny pulls the trigger at the last moment, but the gun clicks around empty space before dropping out of her hand. All this time, it wasn't even loaded. She steps away, trying to gauge Vivian's mood, but the woman's face has gone blank again.

"Why would you— It wasn't even—"

"Come get her, boys." Vivian swings a bell into the air, looking rather bored as she rings it. She lifts her cigarette and takes a long, delicious inhale. "Thought it might be fun to let our conversation go on for a while. Too bad you're not much fun for long, jazz baby."

"Listen," says Ginny. "I can see it's not all about the business for you. You could've kept all those secrets, but instead you decided to tell me. Deep down, you feel guilty about Mary's death, don't you?"

"That's ridiculous, honey." She puffs the smoke straight into Ginny's face. "I don't do guilt."

Footsteps clatter down the hall, and Ginny takes a deep breath. This is it. One last shot before she goes.

"Just give me something. One clue."

Two waiters in black and white enter the room, placing their gloved hands under Ginny's elbows and gently leading her away. The last thing she sees is Vivian's smile spreading around her cigarette, her rouged cheeks glowing bright in front of the desk lamp.

"You want answers? Go talk to one of my colleagues. You'll be surprised how many of us are hiding in plain sight—just follow the music."

CHAPTER EIGHTEEN

An hour later, Ginny is sitting on Ruby's doorstep, studying the scuffs in her patent shoes against the pavement.

The maid comes out a couple times, tutting with her hands digging into her sides, trying to get her to leave. "Miss Hurston is out on business," she says each time, "you'd better leave a message. What's the point in sitting around like that, miss? Don't you have somewhere else to be?"

Every time, Ginny shakes her head and goes back to staring into the distance.

It's not far from the truth. With Dottie kicking her out of the apartment, she doesn't have a home in this city anymore. By the time Dottie gets back from rehearsals, she'll have to pack her things and leave with what's left of last month's wages crumpled into her pocket. She hasn't come up with a plan, not yet, but there's no way she's going back to Kansas before she solves this damn case. She owes Mary that much.

So that's why she's sitting here, with the midday sun burning through the brim of her hat, heating up her body to a raw pink shade. It takes another hour of anxious contemplation until Ruby finally appears at the end of the yard. She strikes an impressive image from afar, with a deep violet dress hanging in a rectangle from her straight posture, but then she comes closer, and Ginny notices the tears streaking makeup down the sides of her face, the hard set of her lips against the world.

"What's wrong?" Ginny rises from her seat, dusting off her skirt. Ruby opens the door and beckons for Ginny to follow without a word.

Then they're in the parlor, Ruby taking her time getting settled, unpeeling gloves from her fingers, beating her hat back into shape. She still winces every time she's forced to bend around the waist, her hands going back to graze the place where the bullet hit, but it's no longer a stoic gesture. Everything about her posture reads defeat.

"You can tell me what happened." Ginny tries to meet the woman's eyes as she sorts through the pages on her end table. Ruby claps a hand to her mouth, holding back a scream. Then she gathers the pages into one big heap and presses them to her chest, hugging them like a loved one. A single tear rolls down the side of her face.

"They took Billy."

Ginny's heartbeat quickens. "What do you—"

"He's been arrested, Ginny. And now there's no way they're letting him go. If I knew this would happen—" She swipes beneath her lashes. "It's all over now, they've won."

She falls into an armchair with the stack of papers, folding her body against it, crinkling the violet fabric of her dress. Ginny tries to think of a way to comfort Ruby, but she's like a live wire. Reaching out would get her burned.

"You don't know that yet," she says. "What was the charge? They can't have anything on him, he's innocent. Right?"

Ruby rises from the armchair and starts pacing around the room, as though movement is the solution to her own lack of power. The maid pokes her head into the room, but Ruby waves her away.

"You don't understand. They found a brick in his sax case. It was covered in blood." Ruby slams a hand into an armchair, sending a cloud of fine dust into the sun-bleached air. "They're saying he killed someone. Some girl they found at the Eighty-Three. Just because he was there last night—"

"They think he killed Mary."

Ginny looks down and realizes she's squeezed the fabric of her skirt beyond recognition. She tries to smooth it back into shape, but it's no use. The wrinkles will stay.

"You knew her?"

Ginny nods. She's back to that numb feeling, distancing herself from the immediate scene, so it doesn't hurt, can't hurt as much. "She was my best friend. They said it was an overdose, but there was so much blood— I guess the cops decided it was murder after all."

A choked sound rips through Ruby's throat. "He was never supposed to get hurt. I should've stopped him before it was too late. First my sister, and now—"

Ginny comes over to where Ruby is standing and grabs her by the shoulders. The gesture makes her flinch, but she doesn't make any moves to escape.

"We're going to clear his name, Ruby. You hear me? I won't stop until I get the bastard who did this to Mary. The real killer.

Same goes for Josephine. Now will you tell me everything that happened?"

A few minutes later, they're sitting on the sofa with a tea tray between them, Ruby taking shaky sips of chamomile as she talks, stopping occasionally to catch her breath.

"He left his sax at the Eighty-Three. He's done this a couple times before, just leaves it in one of the empty crates backstage, comes back in the morning. Except this time, somebody saw him." She takes a deep breath. "They tipped off the cops. So Billy comes back, pulls the sax case from one of the crates, a place only he knows to check, and—"

"The cops arrest him?"

"Asked him to open the case. Sure thing, there it was—a red brick half-covered in somebody's blood. Never mind that Billy nearly passed out. He's always been like that about blood. Couldn't take the sight of it. Still, they carted him off to the station. When I came over to talk, they barely gave me a minute with him. His face was covered in bruises."

"They beat him up?"

"'Resisting arrest.'" Ruby makes mocking quotations in the air, her mouth twisting with distaste. "He won't make it in prison. He's not built for it."

Her anger sizzles through the air, but Ginny can see it's just Ruby's way of masking her fear, as her hands keep shifting, bright nails blurring against her lap.

"Listen. Did you get him a lawyer?"

Ruby lets out a hollow laugh. "Oh, sure. Let's take this to court, see what a jury of nice white folks will think of my man, when a Black sax player is already their worst nightmare. Add to that a white girl bricked to death in Harlem, and you might as well send him straight to the chair. No way, we need to think of something else."

Ginny curses herself under her breath. It's a damn naive suggestion. You can't play by the rules when the system is rigged. But something slips through Ruby's words, and Ginny gives her a long look.

"You called him your man."

"Excuse me?"

"You said, what a jury will think of *my man*." The silence stretches wide between them. Ruby looks down at her teacup, and Ginny can tell that she's weighing her odds, trying to figure out the right solution.

"Relax," says Ginny after a while, "I saw the two of you last night. You don't have to hide anymore."

"What are you talking about?"

"Backstage, at the Hall of Mirrors. I heard your entire conversation." She settles against the back of the sofa. "So you've been seeing your sister's boyfriend. It's not that big of a deal. I don't see why you tried so hard to hide it."

"Please." Ruby's voice is charged with venom. "Like you didn't think, at least for a minute, that I was responsible for Josie's kidnapping? Or worse, you thought it was Billy? Men get away with anything these days, but if you're a woman, you'd better be a saint, otherwise they'll burn you as a damn witch. Your partner would've condemned me for sure. Where is he, anyway?"

"He's—" Ginny hesitates. "He's off the case. It's just me."

They sit in silence a while longer. Ginny doesn't touch her tea. Ruby's words swirl through her mind. Ruby will lie to hide her own transgressions, because she knows how quickly a bad girl can be condemned. Who's to say she wouldn't lie for her sister's sake?

"You know, something's been on my mind for a while. Your sister auditioned for the Follies in May. Then she couldn't leave the house for a week, she was so upset. Billy told me that much."

"So?" Ruby watches the leaves swirling at the bottom of her teacup, like she hopes to read her future in their patterns.

"So I don't think it was just because of the show. Josephine sounds tough as nails. I think she was asked to do something else. Something that went against her deepest beliefs." Ginny raises her chin and looks intently at Ruby. "They asked her to sell pep powder in Harlem, didn't they?"

Ruby brings her teacup back to the tray. She takes her time, slowing down to align the cup with the edge. When she speaks, her voice is raw with emotion.

"She was devastated. Something died in her that night. I remember— I waited up for her, we were both so excited about the audition. Billy brought her home. She wouldn't look us in the eye. Locked herself in her room and didn't leave for days. I thought she was upset about the rejection, but it was so unlike her. But then she came out and—"

Ruby pushes the tray away and hugs her knees inward. The stack of pages rests beside her on the sofa, and occasionally she tears away to stare at it, like her own poetry might give her some answers.

"She didn't tell me everything then. I only figured it out a couple weeks ago, piece by piece. Josie was on a mission. When she refused to sell pep powder in Harlem, they told her they'd find somebody else. But then she started sabotaging the operation.

Intercepting shipments. Once, she replaced a full crate of pep powder with lipstick samples from Madam Walker's beauty supply. Still, the drugs kept coming. People started dying. She lost a pianist that way, real nice guy named Jimmy. They were closing in on Harlem all the same, and suddenly, Josie had a target on her back."

"Did she tell you who was running the operation?" Ginny leans forward. "Give you any names? Maybe the guys who auditioned her?"

Ruby rubs an exhausted palm against her temples. Her makeup is smudged beyond salvation, a dark spot streaking down the left side of her face. "All I know is they were people at the theater. She mentioned somebody she called the Eagle, but that doesn't tell you much."

Ginny remembers the conversation she overheard at the Hall of Mirrors. The coincidence of Billy performing at the clubs where the pep powder victims were found is starting to make a lot of sense. Jack had it all wrong. Billy was working with Josephine to keep the drug out of Harlem. "Billy was searching the theater. He thought they'd be keeping her there?"

"Made sense, since that's where they stored their shipments. But he never found a thing. I wanted to join the search, but he told me it wasn't safe—I look so much like Josie, you know. It's best if they don't know I'm on their trail. But now I don't know if that was right anymore. Billy's been arrested, and it's just me and the band left behind."

"It all comes down to one guy." Vivian said as much, when she was talking about Mary with the empty gun pointed at her. Ginny can't be sure anymore if she was being honest or just playing with her, but it's a start—and if the tall man was straight with her in the shadows, the Eagle is somebody close enough to know her name.

"My friend was seeing a guy who offered her a place in the chorus line, and I think he asked her to start selling to return the favor. But nobody can tell me who he is—"

"You know the girls, though." Ruby folds her arms. She seems to pull herself together right there, her open face shuttering closed to hide any trace of vulnerability. "Your sister's with the Follies, right? Why don't you ask Dottie?"

"That's not an option anymore." Ginny laces her fingers together. Mary's bracelet rattles down her wrist, the tiny star charm flipping over to their names. "She kicked me out. We're no longer on speaking terms."

"Wow. You must've messed up real bad." Ruby looks her up and down. Ginny doesn't like the judgment in her voice one bit. "What did you do?"

"I'd rather not talk about it."

"You should make up with Dottie, you know. She's a good person. If you made her angry, then I bet the reasons are solid, and you'd better apologize."

"Really?" Ginny rises from the sofa. She's sick of it all. Everybody giving her advice as if they know better. "What, like you know her?"

"We met." She gives a noncommittal shrug, and Ginny wants to slap the teacup out of her hand. "My sister signed a picture for her. I get feelings off people sometimes, I can tell what they're like. Her heart's in the right place, and that's damn rare. Not to mention that you never know how much time you've got with your sister. Better appreciate her while you—while you still can."

"Fine. I get it." Ginny sighs. Barely past noon, the day already hangs from her shoulders like a lead-weighted coat. If only it were as easy as Ruby makes it sound. The way things stand with Dottie, it will take more than a few apologies to mend the rift between them. "I can probably ask around anyway. Talk to some of the other girls at the Follies."

"Sure. You do that."

Something about the way she says it, that hard edge, makes Ginny wonder how much Ruby is actually telling her. All these lies, holding back all this information that would've helped them solve the case much faster. Sure, she didn't trust them at first. But now the case has taken a personal turn for Ginny. Surely Ruby can see that she won't stop until they catch the killer.

But then she understands. The suspicion turning her face inward. Ginny's connection with the Follies is an asset to the investigation—but also a huge risk, especially when there's no telling how many of the chorus girls are dealing for the Eagle. For all Ruby knows, Ginny might be in on the gig, swapping her own stash of pep powder for shiny coins in back alleys, lining her wardrobe with drug money like the other girls.

She can feel the disappointment twisting in her stomach, but then the thought leads her in a new direction. If the Follies girls are the key to this case, then Ginny knows exactly how to solve two problems at once.

Out in the blinding sun, she finds the first pay phone and dials the only number she knows by heart.

CHAPTER NINETEEN

Gloria meets her outside the apartment building, leaning against her car as her driver packs the trunk with bags from Macy's. She looks radiant in the sun, the ribbon from her wide-brimmed hat trailing down the back of her bright chiffon dress.

"Is that really everything, darling?" She follows Ginny's single suitcase with concern.

Ginny looks up at the sky. Twenty stories down, she still feels the heat of her sister's anger. Dottie made a point of locking herself in her room, keeping her answers to monosyllables passed through the maid. Ginny stubs out her smoke. She did her best. Dottie might hate her forever, but at least she knows the truth about Charlie now. At least she can escape him before it's too late.

"I don't know how to thank you, Glo. You're a lifesaver."

"It's the least I could do after— Oh, darling, you must be devastated. I'm so sorry." She bites her lip, denting the thick red lipstick. "You and Mary were close."

The charm bracelet slips down her wrist. Ginny flips the star round in her hands, staring at their names on the back until her vision blurs. She leans against Gloria's shoulder, trying to focus her attention on the driver stowing her suitcase. "She had so many dreams, Mary. Her whole life ahead of her. And now—"

Gloria wraps an arm around her, pulling her close. Her eyes crinkle with concern. "I wish I could turn back time for you. Mary deserved better, and so do you. What a terrible loss."

Ginny doesn't unleash her tears on the world, not then. Swiping under her lash line with the heel of her hand, she looks around her neighborhood for one last goodbye. She watches two paperboys fighting over a corner, their tiny ink-stained fingers tensing into fists. A man with an impressive mustache lifts his girlfriend off the ground to dodge the gray splatter of a puddle, her startled laugh filling the air. And then she notices a familiar figure in a dark gray suit, and her tears dry up in an instant.

"You've got to be kidding me."

Jack's out of breath when he reaches her, sticking a hand against a stitch in his side. "I came as soon as I could. Listen, Ginny— Wait, where are you going?"

"None of your business." She raises her head, squinting at him through the sun. "You made it clear you didn't want anything to do with me, or this case, anymore. So stay out of it, all right?"

"There's something you need to know," he says. "I went up to the station with Hector—I mean, Officer Tallman—"

"Of course you're friends with the cops." She pictures Billy Calloway, his face a mess because he resisted arrest for a crime he didn't commit. With every word, she can feel the distance between her and Jack widening. Maybe he's worse than a stranger. Maybe he's on the other side.

"That's not the point. Listen, Billy Calloway's been taken into custody, but Tallman says they were tipped off. They got the call right after they brought her body to the station. Kept the person on the line long enough to trace the call back to the New Am."

Ginny's heart skips over itself. Last night comes back in sharp flashes, the guys outside the theater, the sag of their arms as they carried those large crates outside. Large enough to fit a body.

If Mary died at the New Am, then Ginny's on the right track. All roads lead back to the Ziegfeld Follies.

Jack takes a ragged breath. "I think I know who made that call, Ginny. All this time, we've been trusting the wrong—"

Ginny cuts him off, taking a step back toward Gloria's car.

"The wrong people? Yeah, I bet *Hector* can tell you everything about the right people. You go on back to the station, Jack. Who knows? Maybe they'll even hire you. I hear they're big on violence, so I'm sure your past experience will be a bonus."

The comment rings through the air like a slap. She's gone too far this time. He steps away like he's been burned. Ginny climbs into Gloria's car, and then they're gone without a single backward glance.

Gloria gives her hand a tight squeeze.

"Is he giving you grief?" Lowered to a conspiratorial whisper, Gloria's voice still oozes with her warm magic. "I thought he might be trouble, first time I saw him. But then, the pretty ones always are."

"You can say that again." Ginny shuts her eyes. She's shaking all over. It takes all she's got not to look back at Jack's tall figure growing small in the distance.

Gloria taps her lightly on the elbow. "Come on, chin up, darling. I've got something that might brighten those sad eyes."

"A new identity and a one-way ticket out of town?"

Gloria pushes a hand into a bag at her feet and pulls out a small white mask, made to cover the right half of its wearer's face.

"For you," she breathes. "There's a card on the other side."

"Don't want to kill your enthusiasm, but if you think no one will recognize me with this on—"

"Oh, just look at the card, smart girl."

It's an invitation, with an address in Long Island and a starting time at nine o'clock tonight.

"I know you're probably exhausted, but I think this could be good for you. I'm hosting a masquerade, and since we're staying in Long Island anyway—"

"Wait, we aren't going to your apartment?"

"And now you're upset." Gloria taps her fingers against the surface of the mask. "I thought you wouldn't want to stay in the city, especially since the guest room at my apartment—well, it might bring up some bad memories, darling. And you did say you wanted to get your mind off everything, right?"

A party is the last thing she wants right now. After everything that happened with her sister, there's no way she can face the Follies girls. They'll know the score by tonight, they'll ask questions about Dottie's missing engagement ring, and Ginny will be cast aside for what she is—a homewrecker who should've known better. She should know, since the showgirls live by her own code of honor. *Be as bad as you want, just don't get caught.* And Ginny surrendered herself like the last sucker.

Still, there might be an advantage to her disgrace. Might open up some interesting conversations, and with all the clues leading back to the Follies, it might be good to throw them off-balance. Some girls might be more forthcoming about their own transgressions to somebody who has fallen even lower than them.

"And before I forget—here's another thing. For you."

It's a small bag filled with silver tissue paper, and as Ginny looks inside, she catches a flash of emerald. Her heart lurches at the memory. It's that same beaded green dress from the Follies dressing room, bright as a mermaid's tail against the gray afternoon.

"How did you— Don't you need this for the show?"

Gloria's eyes swim with unfathomable emotions, a flicker of a smile tugging at her lips. For the first time that day, Ginny can feel her body surging with warmth. With Mary's death, Jack's betrayal, and Dottie's cold scorn, it feels good to know there's at least one person in the world who's got her back.

"It's yours now. It always was." She pulls the dress out of the bag, presses it against Ginny's cheek. "You can wear it tonight. If only you could see yourself right now, my darling."

Ginny pushes the fabric into her skin, the luxurious material summoning mixed feelings of desire and fear. She hasn't worn an evening dress of her own in so long, her entire wardrobe filled with slightly altered hand-me-downs from Dottie, always chasing trends but coming up a few years short no matter how hard she tries. Still, the day weighs heavy on her shoulders, and she can't imagine herself dressed in such finery after everything that happened.

"I don't know, Glo. I'm not sure I'm ready to face the girls."

"That's the beauty—you won't have to. Everyone's wearing a mask, and besides, it'll be a different crowd. The kinds of people you won't see in the city. Theater types outside the Follies. Directors, producers. Actors." There's a twinkle in her eye as she leans close, whispering the name of a famous young heartthrob into Ginny's ear.

"He's coming?"

"He never misses my soirees. Who knows—tonight might be the best thing that happens to you. We'll go swimming and drink ourselves silly. Wipe those slates clean for good. What do you say?"

Ginny looks down at the bright green sequins. Gloria's Long Island mansion is infamous for parties that don't stop for days, rivers of gin and famous guests getting up to all kinds of mischief in the locked upstairs rooms. The masks might conceal the guests' identities, but they will also put them at ease, giving Ginny the perfect opportunity to question them. And with the showgirls mingling with the rich and famous, she knows they'll use the opportunity to dole out pep powder—and the Eagle might be watching close by.

Setting the mask against her face, she can see it's a perfect fit, the cool polished plaster sending shivers of excitement across her skin. "I'm in."

Gloria's house burns like a carnival. Lights pop from every window. Guests scatter across the gardens like so many jewels in brash violet, garnet, gold-flecked jade. One of them might have all the answers. The thought hums through Ginny's veins as she makes her way down the stairs from her room, enjoying the way the lights hit her emerald-green dress. It fits like a second skin, tight straps molded around her shoulders, cascading in loose folds down the back, exposing her spine to the summer breeze floating through the open windows. It's hard to stay focused on her plan when the night is so damn pleasant, right from the beginning.

A full-throated brass band fills the air with a constant thrumming melody, the kind of tune that carries your feet into dance despite anything else, and Ginny finds herself tapping along as she reaches the bottom of the steps. The slim Venetian mask curves to hug the crook of her neck. She stops at the foot of the stairs, fumbling to tighten the knot behind her head.

"Allow me," comes a cool British whisper. Gloved hands brush her neck. The ribbon twists against the slippery pomade holding her hair in place, and then the stranger ties it into a double knot.

When she turns, she sees a tall young man in a tailored black suit, the top half of his face covered in a silk band with slits for eyes. She recognizes him from the pages of *Photoplay*, an actor playing a supporting role in an upcoming picture called *The Pleasure Garden*, from a new director called Hitchcock.

His eyes are all over her, scanning the bare half of her face with open appreciation. "It's moments like these I most regret the masks-only policy."

"Lucky for you, the left side's my good one." Ginny runs a finger against her mask. It's cold as ivory. Over his shoulder, she catches a glimmer of ocher disappearing into the hallway, a flash of platinum hair like Gloria's, but she can't be sure. "It's not often I get to go to a masquerade."

"It's not so bad, is it? Most of the time, I like the anonymity. We don't want to give the reporters more than they deserve." He leans forward suddenly, his face looming close enough for Ginny to notice a constellation of freckles across his cheekbones. "You're not a reporter, are you?"

Ginny taps him on the nose. "Get me a drink and you might find out."

It's like a dream, layers peeling away as they move deeper into the house. They glide through shadows, passing shimmering groups of guests in twos and threes, barely visible in front of the dimmed-down wall sconces. Beaded curtains and sheaves of filmy gauze hang in each doorway, so passing between rooms forces her through a series of new sensory experiences.

Ginny's companion swipes two glasses of gin from a passing waiter. He swallows the contents of his glass in a single fluid motion.

"You're sure in a hurry."

A lock of dark hair tumbles across his forehead. He clinks an empty glass against hers.

"That's why we're all here, isn't it? No need to be shy, everyone's got something worth forgetting. Can you keep up?"

The jazz and the gin and the actor's hand on her back make her head spin. Ginny looks down at her reflection, distorted by the ripples in the glass. She inhales the juniper fumes, then swallows herself whole with her eyes shut.

She knows exactly what she would do next, if this were any other night. She'd dance on the platform in front of the band, tapping out a rowdy Charleston to the whooping cries of the crowd. There would be endless rounds of gin and jumping into the pool fully dressed, sinking to the bottom until somebody pulls her out, laughing through the sting of chlorine. She'd finish with her mask off in one of the upstairs bedrooms, straddling the British actor with her dress hiked high, numbing her memory of the night with booze and pleasure until it fades into the background like all the others.

But tonight is different. Tonight, she needs to stay sober.

So Ginny drops her empty glass on a passing waiter's tray and takes off to look for chorus girls.

She finds them by the pitch of their laughter, always a shade brighter than the rest, their dresses hanging in the same shape around their toned bodies. The girls are sitting on silk cushions in one of the upstairs rooms, taking turns smoking from a pipe of lemon hookah while their admirers look on from dark corners. All of them are wearing identical full-face masks painted with exaggerated bow lips and heavy lashes.

"Would you believe it?" comes Anita's smoky voice, inflected with awe, "And a last-minute reservation, at that. I never thought it was possible, but he's so madly in love with her, he always finds a way."

"And you know he's a gent, Charlie. Not like those other Wall Street types who curse like sailors even when they know you're in the room. Did you hear he got promoted to junior partner at Winthrop and Co? I could die of jealousy."

Ginny freezes by the door, wooden beads knocking against her face. The girls have just returned from rehearsals, which means they've spoken to Dottie. If the engagement had been called off, they would be the first to know.

They notice her watching, and Mazie rises from her cushion. "Is that you, Ginny? Can't see a thing through this damn mask—"

"You got me." Ginny joins the circle, grabbing the pipe for something to do with her hands. The hookah smoke tastes sweet in her mouth, but it coats her throat in a fine wax that makes her feel like she's suffocating. When she mentions this to the others, they collapse in inexplicable fits of laughter.

"So," Ginny says through a dry cough, grasping for normalcy through the fog. "Have you seen my sister around? I thought she'd be here—"

Their masked faces turn toward one another, and Ginny's glad she's decided against getting wasted tonight. The effect is terrifying in the dim, like identical showgirl clowns knocking around a dark room.

"Guess you haven't heard. Charlie's taking her out tonight." Anita drops her chin into her hands. "Chez Georges. Got a reservation and everything. We invited her to join us, but of course this party is too lowbrow for somebody like Dottie, now that she's gonna be a *Darby*."

Ginny can't believe it. She tries to picture Dottie, sitting across the table from Charlie, the red glow of the candles lighting him up like some romantic hero. And then it hits her. Of course she'll forgive him. Because it's the only way out of this situation that keeps her in the clear. If Charlie's blameless, then the wedding can go on, and nothing has to change in her perfect life.

No. She can't think about that anymore. There's only one thing that matters tonight, and that's finding Mary's killer. Taking another puff of smoke, Ginny forces a smile, hoping at least one half of her face looks genuine.

"Sounds just like her. Oh, well." She leans closer. "Hey, you didn't hear anything about a new girl joining the chorus line? Somebody named Mary?"

The girls nod in unison, their masks bobbing up and down.

Mazie is the first to share, bracelets clicking together as she shifts closer to Ginny. "There was a girl in the audience last night, watching our rehearsals. Didn't say anything about joining, but she looked real enthusiastic, so I brought her backstage. Tried on some costumes, the kind of thing I wished someone would've done for me, back when I was nobody."

The costume. Those pale beads scattered all around her. And Mazie, waiting behind the curtains to deliver a killer dose.

Swallowing around an angry lump in her throat, Ginny wraps her fingers around Mazie's elbow, rings digging into her pasty skin.

"Did she ask you for a pick-me-up?" The girl flinches away.

"I don't know what you—"

Ginny reaches over to whisper in her ear. "Mary's dead, Mazie. Soon they're gonna start looking for suspects, asking questions. You'd better tell me everything, or I'll go right to the station and give them your name."

"All right!" Her voice rises to a breathy screech. Beads of sweat roll down her neck. "Let's get out of here."

Ginny follows her out of the room. They pass a row of bedrooms with half-open doors, some of them already occupied by half-dressed couples, others roaring with drunk laughter. She thinks she catches Gloria in one of them, curving the telephone cord around her wrist, her voice muffled against the receiver, but it's hard to tell in the darkness.

They trip down the stairs together, where the band is slowing down into a moody blues ballad. Two girls in matching gold dresses are dancing on the platform, swatting the air with feathered fans in hypnotic rhythm. They change places so often that Ginny can no longer tell them apart. It's as though one golden girl has duplicated herself so she can dance with her own reflection, laughing at the suckers in the audience who fail to see through the trick.

When they settle at an empty table on the back veranda, Ginny repeats her question.

"I don't know what to tell you, Gin." With a sigh, Mazie begins to fumble with the strings of her mask. The bones in her wrists are sharp as blades. "The boss said he wanted me to interview her. See if she was a good fit for the job. But we ended up having so much fun with the costumes that I lost track of time. She was such a doll. I tried to make a move, but she made it clear she wasn't into girls. And then I had to get back to rehearsals, so that was it."

"You left her in the dressing room? Alone?"

The mask comes off in her hands, and Mazie fans it against her damp face. "Just for a while. We were rehearsing the garden number one last time. When we came back to change, she was gone. I figured she'd gone home or something."

"Did she take anything? Pep powder?"

"I offered, but she didn't want any. Said she was high on life. I thought that was kind of stupid, but she was a sweet girl." Mazie's face scrunches slightly. "I'm sorry she's dead, Gin. Really am. But you can't save everyone. Sooner or later, you make your choices, and then you have to live with them."

"Like you chose to start dealing for the Eagle." Ginny watches her closely, but Mazie doesn't flinch. She's smiling without her eyes. "Did he approach you during your audition?"

"Something like that." She scans the veranda for a while. An anxious jolt passes across her face as she notices somebody in the distance, and she fumbles to replace the mask. "I gotta go. You take care of yourself, all right?"

Then she's gone, leaving Ginny alone at a table of untouched food. The showgirls might be chatty, but she can see how she's underestimated her challenge. None of them will reveal the Eagle's identity. She'll have to find out on her own.

Gloria cuts through the empty veranda, her burnished ocher dress shimmering like a mirage. She's the only one without a mask. When she notices Ginny, her face spreads into a smile that dimples her rouged cheeks.

"I'm afraid I haven't been a very good hostess. I couldn't find you all night, and now you're all alone, probably bored out of your mind."

"You're not wearing a mask." Ginny watches her taking a seat, crossing her ankles beneath the table.

"That wouldn't be fair to my guests, would it? I give them their privacy, but I'd never dream of hiding from them. Besides," she leans closer and lowers her voice to a thrilling whisper, "how else can I show off my new rouge?"

She turns from side to side, dangling the diamonds in her ears. Gloria is the kind of woman who looks more like herself with a painted face, as if the makeup brings out some hidden depths that are invisible when she's barefaced.

"What's with the long face, darling? Aren't you having fun?"

Ginny pulls a slim sandwich from a nearby plate, picking apart the crust. She can't tell if she's hungry or not, but it gives her something to do while she lies.

"It's a swell time, Glo. I was just talking to some of the girls upstairs."

"How exciting." Gloria inclines her head, releasing a platinum wave that flicks out at the edge in a sharp crest. "Let me guess, were they still raving about Dottie's romantic night out at Chez Georges?"

"You've heard?"

"Couldn't shut up about it during rehearsals. That bastard doesn't deserve the easy break he's getting after what he's done."

"Isn't that just men in general? Give them a lick of attention, and suddenly they're acting like they own you. And why wouldn't they, when they have all the damn power, and nobody ever fights back?"

Ginny bites into the sandwich, cream cheese oozing out the edges. She thinks of Charlie, and the idea of another drink no longer feels that crazy. No bright-frocked waiters out here, only tables set with delicacies and a few stray couples holding hands, locking eyes across the candles.

"It doesn't have to be like that. There's more than one kind of power in the world."

Ginny lights up and offers a smoke to Gloria, who declines. "Sounds a lot like giving up and taking it. I've heard it before. Talk of feminine wiles and charming them into doing your bidding. A load of bull, if you ask me."

She puffs a stream of smoke into the night, lost in thought. A line of drunken guests form a conga line in the distance, tottering into the garden maze with masks unlacing as they go. Gloria's face is cut sharp as a precious stone, her sobriety startling against this rowdy backdrop. She's staring at Ginny with a probing intensity that almost makes her want to look away.

"You don't strike me as the kind of girl who takes it lying down."

Ginny falters. "Well, I guess not. I do what I want, but that doesn't mean—"

"So what's in your way?"

Men, Ginny thinks, but that's not entirely true. Charlie played her like a sucker, but he was only expressing his true nature. She should've known better. All those wild nights have taught her nothing about being a woman in this rotten world. Sure, she might know never to leave her drink alone, to pretend there's somebody waiting for her just around the corner, somebody who will care if she goes missing. She's learned to tell good danger from the deadly kind, but she thought Charlie was an exception to all her rules. Charlie felt like home. That's something she'll never get back.

She thought she might find a home in Jack. It was barely a glimmer in the dark at the Eighty-Three, but she felt it. Despite his troubled past, Jack is solid. And with her world turned upside down overnight, with nothing as it seems anymore, she could use somebody solid in her life. Somebody to help untangle her messes before they consume her.

She doesn't even want to think about how badly she's botched the investigation, following a trail of distracting clues and losing the one thing she should've kept close.

Always skimming the surface, never getting past the smoke and mirrors.

Gloria wraps a hand over hers, warm against the evening chill. There's something profound about the gesture, like she's read Ginny's mind and she understands it all, feels it down to her core. Ginny twines her fingers through Gloria's, enjoying the feel of her many rings digging into the skin of her palm.

"Chin up, kid. Half the people in the world are stumbling over their own feet because they don't know what they're looking for. But you've got fire. You're almost there. Once you find what you need, you're golden."

She starts to say something else, but they're no longer alone. A mixed crowd pours out of the house, bringing the stale smells of smoke and liquor into the courtyard.

Gloria launches into a stream of happy chatter, and her audience picks up the thread, laughing in all the right places as they dig into their meals. A man in a sun-shaped mask takes a seat at Gloria's side. His laugh, brisk and humorless, reveals rows of blocky white teeth. It takes her a moment, but then Ginny recognizes Otto Sharp, Follies stage manager.

Aside from the occasional laugh, he keeps quiet. It looks like something's bothering him. Face turning side-to-side, eyes darting, flinging away a sleeve to check his wristwatch every few minutes.

Gloria takes note after a while, resting her fingers on his twitching arm.

"Is everything peachy, darling?"

He jerks away. It's a small movement, but Ginny is close enough to see the raw tension in his muscles as he shakes her off.

"It's getting late. I think I'd best be going, and I told you from the start that I disapproved of this—this *charade*—"

"Now, don't be like that." Gloria snaps her fingers for a waiter. "It's nice to unwind sometimes, isn't it? This strain can kill you if you're not careful. We'll get you something to drink, how about that?"

"I said it's late." He pulls away from the table, shaking the cutlery with a tinny clatter as he rises. "You'll get your beauty sleep if you know what's good for you. Big day ahead."

"I've got it covered," she snaps.

He lifts a finger, opening his mouth with force, but then he drops his arm at the defiance in Gloria's face. Leaning close, he lowers his voice into her ear.

"You might think you're the prima in this theater, but you won't be on top forever. They love you today, but watch how fast they'll put a knife in your back when you're not looking."

Whipping his napkin onto the table, he returns to the house, leaving his warning burning through the mild summer air.

CHAPTER TWENTY

For a moment, Gloria seems thrown off-balance. She follows Otto's retreating figure with her eyes, a strange look glossing over her features. But then a cool smile replaces the previous moment's distress, and it's like nothing happened.

"You must think I'm some sort of hypocrite," she says. "Talking about empowerment one moment, letting some man walk all over me in the next."

"Of course not. He sounded harsh back there."

"He's a perfectionist." Gloria rubs her lower lash line with a pinky, swiping away the ghost of a tear. "If he had his way, we'd be waking up with a glass of lemon water and going to bed before sundown, with a prayer and a kiss for mama. Good little girls throwing their legs in the air on command."

That explains Dottie's anxieties, her usual intensity dialed up a notch for the stage manager. The outburst gives Ginny another idea, something that's been scraping at the back of her mind since she saw her sister stumbling out of the New Am, drunk.

"He's been putting a lot of pressure on all of you lately," she says slowly, "hasn't he? Rehearsing after hours, expecting perfection on every try. I know Dottie's been running herself ragged."

Gloria waves it away. "Those are the rules of the game, darling. The girls all know what they were in for, and there's no compromising if you're shooting for greatness. Otherwise they might as well settle with some nice guy in the suburbs and forget all about their dreams."

"So less than perfect is nothing?"

"Not if you want it all." The light falls on Gloria's beaded lashes, casting long shadows down her cheeks. She looks Ginny straight in the eye, and there's something else under the surface, her hard gaze swimming with secrets. Like she's on the verge of spilling over, but she stops herself in time for a commotion at the front of the house.

Tires screech against the driveway, followed by the hurried slam of a car door. A late guest? Ginny peers into the dark, but only the flash of taillights shines in front of the house. Gloria stiffens at the intrusion. Ginny notices the hard set of her jaw, and then comes the voice, and she knows why.

"Where are you hiding my husband, you bitch?"

It comes in a scratchy wail, ratcheting up a nervous octave before plunging low into the last word. The owner of the voice doesn't take long to announce her presence. Stumbling out of the growth with her dress flapping open at the chest, turban unraveling around her hairline, Zita looks like hell. Lipstick smeared, fingers clenched into fists.

Gloria rises to meet her, hanging on to her composure with a polite smile pasted on her face.

"What a pleasant surprise. Come join us at the table, we're just getting started with the roast, grab a chair and—"

Zita spits at her feet. Her anger brings out the Texas in her voice, the rounded accent slipping off like an old coat.

"I'm done tired of your games. I know he's here, tell him he'd better come out now. I'm not moving an inch until he does."

Gloria takes a cautious step toward her, steel slipping through the honeyed tones of her voice.

"Easy now, darling. I don't know who you've been talking to, but I doubt you'll find Otto here."

"Don't you 'darling' me." Zita's eyes rove through the crowd. The masks must be driving her mad. "I know he's here, and I bet that little slut is with him." She cups her hands to her mouth, looks up at the building. "Otto! Otto, get down here!"

Whatever is going on in that marriage, Ginny realizes she might have a chance to spare Gloria the scene that's coming—and get a moment alone with the stage manager.

"Hey, Zee." The air around Zita is undercut with vodka and honey. Up close, Ginny can see the red webbing in her round eyes, the smear of lipstick at the edges of her mouth.

Zita adjusts her turban, like she's suddenly conscious of the many curious eyes watching.

"Ginny? What are you doing in this brothel? Oh," she rocks forward, slipping into a stage whisper, "I get it. You're working with *him*."

"What's that?"

A rough laugh escapes her mouth, and she claps a gloved hand over her lips. "Jack Craw-ford, my private guy. I mean, private eye. Same difference, you catch my meaning? Except he dropped me, Ginny. Was it all for you?"

Something shifts in Ginny's perception, a glimmer of truth in Zita's jumbled words. "You were his client?"

"Until today. He was so close to finding the tramp who stole my husband. But then he just quit. Didn't take the money or anything." Zita sighs. "Such a waste of potential. Say, you *sure* the two of you aren't together? He's *so* dreamy—"

"Never mind that. You need help finding your husband?"

Zita narrows her eyes. "You've seen Otto around?"

"Sure. He wouldn't shut up about how much he missed his wife. Kept saying you were the prettiest girl in the Follies, and he couldn't wait until he got home."

It can't be further from the truth, but it works a charm. Zita stumbles to the side, her face relaxing into a sad smile.

"The bastard's got a smooth way with words."

"Want me to get him for you?"

"Yeah." She rubs her nose with the heel of her hand, sighing deep. "Gosh, I'm tired."

Stepping back into the house feels like a dive into the underworld. The party is in its final throes, the band banging out some desperate brassy number as the few remaining couples breathe into each other's necks on the dance floor. Zita's words keep slamming around her mind, their meaning sending shivers down her neck. She hired Jack to track down her husband's mistress, and he came straight to the *Photoplay* front desk.

Mary. Of course it was Mary.

Something made him drop the case today. She doesn't want to think about what that might mean, Jack turning down cash for what? Some sense of decency, a moment of silence for Mary?

Maybe it was something else, but she can't say for sure, can't figure out what he was thinking.

If Otto Sharp was Mary's mystery man, then he might also be her killer. He might be the Eagle, *closer than you think.* The thought makes her shiver as she knocks through several beaded rooms, pushing past wasted strangers in gaudy costumes. She dreads the moment of discovery, half expecting to find him shouting his head off at some other starlet for breaking the rules, but the search comes to an end much sooner. There he is, in the corner of what used to be a parlor, leaning against the makeshift bar and staring into the distance.

She slows her steps, taking in his tense posture, the hard set of his jaw beneath the sun-shaped mask. This is a man who has it all. A flashy wife on his arm, a young mistress on the side, entry to all the best joints in town at the drop of a name. But standing in the corner with an empty glass in his hand, he looks like a man who's lost everything, a man who's resigned himself to a lifetime of disappointments ahead.

Grabbing two big drinks from a nearby tray, Ginny comes over to him, trying her best to fake confidence even though her hands keep shaking.

"Hello there, Mr. Sharp." She offers him a glass, but he pushes it away without looking.

"You again. Here for another interview?" He digs his elbows in the bar. "I've told you everything, now would you leave me—"

"You seem tense. Guilty conscience?" Ginny takes a sip. It's whiskey mixed with something sweet, the sugar sticking to the roof of her mouth. "You should've been nicer to Gloria out there. If she quits the Follies, you'll be left with nothing."

He barks out a laugh, shaking his head. "Gloria isn't going anywhere. What else?"

"Your wife's here. She knows everything."

He turns to face her. Through the slits in the mask, she sees his blue eyes narrowing.

"What are you talking about?"

"Mary Gliszinszky. The girl you promised to turn into a star. The girl you *killed*. No, don't deny it—" Ginny slaps away his palm as he raises it to stop her, mouth dropping open in surprise. Her heart pounds heavy in her head, but still she presses onward. "I saw the two of you that night at the Eighty-Three. She thought she had it made, but that was never the plan, was it? You were just playing along, waiting for the right moment to get her involved in your operation. Maybe she turned you down. Guess she knew too much, so you got rid of her in the end."

She keeps her eyes level with his the entire time, her voice running in an angry hiss against his golden mask. After a while, his hand goes slack under hers, and she can tell she's hit a nerve.

"You should get your facts straight before you start accusing people." He rubs a hand over his chin. "I was seeing Mary, sure. That much is true. But I . . . I had no idea she was dead. When did this happen?"

It's hard to tell with the mask, but it doesn't look like he's lying. Ginny leans back against the bar, trying to figure out where she went wrong.

"Last night," she says. "You brought her to see the girls rehearsing at the New Am. What happened there?"

Otto puffs out a breath and picks up the drink she brought him.

"I don't know, honestly. I was too busy directing the girls. Mazie took her backstage to try on some costumes, and that was it. I waited for her after rehearsals were over, but she never showed. The girls said she left. I thought she was angry with me." He takes a sip of his drink, shaking his head in disappointment. "Guess you never know when your luck will turn, huh?"

"But it's not really about luck, is it?"

"What do you—"

"You sought her out. A girl with big ambitions like that, you knew you could use her for your own benefit. When you asked her to sell pep powder, did you make it sound like a dream? I bet you did. Just like you did with Mazie before that, and Vivian Templeton—"

"Lies." He slams the glass down on the bar, loud enough to turn the heads of several tired revelers beside them. "Vicious rumors, that's all that is. Not a surprise, coming from a *Photoplay* writer. Now you write this down—I'm not responsible for the bad choices these girls make on their own time. If Mary took a wrong turn, got carried away with the nose candy, that's not my problem. You got it? Your friend was a junkie in the making, and she couldn't take the heat—"

Ginny slaps him across the mask. It's not strong enough to make a serious impact, but he shuts his eyes for one painful moment, then opens them again, bloodshot.

"You're wrong," she breathes, feeling her angry heart speeding up. "Mary was good. She'd never—"

"You're gonna regret that someday," he mutters, and turns away, clattering through the beaded door and out of sight. He's lying. She leans against the bar, trying to think. There has to be someone who knows what happened that night, someone who can confirm that Mr. Sharp went into that dressing room—but then, she doesn't know who to trust anymore. Ginny lowers her forehead to the bar and tries to untangle her thoughts, but all she gets is one hell of a headache.

After a while, the band goes quiet. Conversations dissolve into whispers, then nothing at all. The time on her wristwatch inches closer to two in the morning. Nothing good ever happens at this time. Ginny's about to get up and find her way back to the guest bedroom when she realizes she's not alone in this corner of the parlor.

Gloria swings her long legs over the bar, flinging a smile her way. "Thought I'd find you here."

"Am I so easy to read?" Ginny rubs her eyes. Gloria rattles under the bar, pulling out bottles with a professional swing of her wrist, throwing big chunks of ice into a polished shaker. The musicians are packing up their instruments and leaving the room. All the other guests are long gone.

"Oh, no," says Gloria. "I just figured anyone would want a stiff drink after dealing with Otto for more than a minute. He came out, you know. Took Zita home like a gent, so thanks for that."

She mixes two or three kinds of liquor and shakes them with a brisk motion, her diamond bracelets clattering together. Then she pours the silvery green liquid into two slim-stemmed glasses.

"Otto told me a strange story." Ginny runs her thumb along the star charm on her bracelet. It's become an obsession, dragging her fingers across the metal as if it's her way of telling Mary she hasn't forgotten. "Something about last night's rehearsal."

Gloria garnishes the glasses with sprigs of mint, then steps back to admire her work. "What about it?"

"Did he go into the dressing room at any point during the night?"

"Not sure I remember. I left long before the others, I was absolutely exhausted. He did seem especially nervous that night, but who knows what's going through that man's mind, anyway." Gloria pushes one of the glasses toward Ginny. "Cheers, darling."

"I shouldn't," says Ginny, pressing her forehead against the cool glass. "This headache—"

"Come on," Gloria clinks her glass against Ginny's, a light challenge simmering in her eyes. "Indulge me. I haven't had a chance to mix my own drinks for too long, and I want to make sure I've still got it."

The drinks take her back to last night at the Eighty-Three, and she thinks of Jack. Not the disapproving curve of his lips when she passed out from the pep powder. But the way he looked at her in the car on the way back. Those green eyes miles deep, revealing all the multitudes inside him for one pure, painful moment. He didn't ask her to stop. He just told her he understood, in more ways than one.

You were looking for something to stop the pain.

If Jack were here, he'd tell her to take it easy on the liquor. But Jack has made it clear that he's no longer on her side. If she wants to get to the bottom of this case, get her life back to where she needs it, she'd better forget about him and start thinking for herself.

Ginny shuts her eyes and throws back the shimmering liquid, which flows cool and smooth down her throat. She tastes the sharp tang of gin and limes cushioned by the froth of egg whites and sugar. Gloria grabs her by the hand and looks right into her eyes.

"Well?"

"It's heaven, Glo." She rises from the bar, feeling the room swirling around her. At least her thoughts are no longer all tangled. Everything is beautiful. All her pain is gone. "What's in this?"

Gloria catches her as she starts to tip over, placing a warm hand against her bare spine. She's saying something, her passion fruit mouth opening and closing, but Ginny can barely hear a thing. Gloria's voice is dripping into her ear like melted gold, and she can only lean into the warm comfort of her shoulder.

And then they're upstairs, laughing over nothing, Ginny spinning out of orbit with her green dress like mermaid scales. Gloria leads her into a bedroom, and it's like a scene from *The Sheik*, all peach silk and filmy curtains blowing into the night, the boudoir table glinting with many glass bottles, necklaces tangled together, seed pearls and rubies and Gloria so close, leading her to the chair in front of the mirror, her whisper-soft touch trailing like kisses.

"You don't need this anymore," and Gloria unfastens the mask, exposing the right side of Ginny's face to the breeze. Ginny rakes her fingers across the table, pulling a lipstick at random, opening it to a shock of deep crimson.

"So beautiful," she says, her speech slurring. "Can I—"

But Gloria is already taking it from her, spreading the color all over her lips with a finger. Just a breath away. Up close, Ginny can make out the shadow of a birthmark splashed across Gloria's chin, barely visible under the heavy greasepaint. Moonlight cuts across her face and lights those hard eyes with pale fire. She comes closer still, kneeling before Ginny with the sweet lime fumes of her breath heavy on her face.

"Do you have any idea how incredible you are?" she whispers, her fingers tracing the contours of Ginny's mouth. "I've never met anybody like you, Ginny Dugan. You're brighter than this whole damn town. I just— I wish—"

Ginny's heart pounds through her entire body. She can't stop staring at Gloria. The power in her taut arm muscles, the shimmer of her burnished ocher dress, a single platinum curl falling slick across her forehead.

She reaches forward to brush it away, and touching her feels electric.

"What're you talking about," she says, her speech slurring. "When I've spent all my life trying to be more like you. Gloria, I—"

But her voice cracks, and there's no point in saying anything else, because Gloria leans in and presses her lips against hers. She's soft at first, but then she brings her strong arms around Ginny, pulling her down from the chair so they're pressed to each other, heartbeat to heartbeat.

When she pulls away, her lips are stained that same shade of red, and she smiles as she turns Ginny to face the mirror. "Look, we match."

Ginny's never felt so dizzy. Her face is numb. She no longer remembers how she got here, how she ended up with her fingers running down Gloria's neck, their legs tangled together on the floor. All she knows is the heat building between her hips, spreading through her entire body until all she can do is turn away from the reflection and fall into another deep kiss, sweet and rough and desperate all at once.

The night dissolves into a series of disjointed scenes, Ginny slipping in and out of consciousness. One moment, they're tumbling together on the shag carpet, the long strands matching the color of Gloria's hair, one of her diamond earrings getting lost in this sea of white. Then darkness, and they're on the bed, Gloria whispering soothing words against her cheek, running through the tangles in her hair with the softest bristled brush.

The drinks and the sweet perfume soon send her into a heavy sleep, filled with ghostly dancing girls always trying to escape the hot glare of a spotlight. She only resurfaces a few times, when Gloria shifts in bed, pressing lips to her ear for a low whisper that sounds an awful lot like *love*, but the words dissolve in her sleep until she can no longer tell the difference between dreams and reality.

CHAPTER TWENTY-ONE

In the cab the next morning, she can't stop thinking about Gloria. Her breath still whistles in Ginny's ears, the curve of her body stretching in bed, moonlit hair fanned out against the dewy sheets. Whenever she tries to bring her thoughts back to the case, to Otto Sharp as the Eagle and all those other sinister characters spinning their dirty webs behind closed doors, all she can picture is Gloria kneeling beside the boudoir table, rubbing red into Ginny's lips, lighting the whole damn place on fire.

She feels a slight tug in her chest at leaving Gloria in bed alone like a stranger. But she felt so out of place when she first woke up, cotton-headed and disoriented, she was out the door before she knew what she was doing. It was the right call in the end, she decides. That dreamy, fractured quality of their night together can't be replicated in the harsh light of day. Besides, she needs some distance to process everything that happened.

She passes through the entrance to the building in a daze, barely registering the doorman's quizzical look at her running mascara, the elevator boy pointedly averting his eyes from her bare back. She didn't expect to be back here, but hearing the showgirls going on about Dottie and Charlie gave her some ideas she can't shake. One, Dottie didn't tell them the full story about Ginny's betrayal, which means there's still a chance she'll forgive her. And two, there's no way in hell Ginny will watch her sister go through with the wedding after everything that happened. The least she deserves is one last conversation. One last chance to make things right.

A still quiet fills the apartment, the air tasting stale on Ginny's tongue. Must be too early for anyone to be up, just her luck. She flings her shoes off by the door and makes her way over to her old bedroom, running her arms over all the parts of her body still echoing with Gloria's touch. With every hour away from Gloria's big house, the reality of that night dims, dreams blending with her memories until she begins to doubt everything.

It was her first time sleeping with a woman, and she doesn't know what it means. It might've meant anything. A bit of fun between girlfriends—or a faltering step into new territory with Gloria's elegant fingers twined with hers for years to come. She wonders if this was new for Gloria, but despite her confident movements the night before, she had never mentioned previous dalliances with women. There were only ever men in her life, from the tragic death of her first husband when she was seventeen to the pharmacy tycoon who gave her that ringing last name and a place in the Follies chorus line. They were divorced years ago, back when it was still scandalous, and Gloria's been in no hurry to remarry. She'd always say that men are for money, and why bother getting shackled again if she has everything she ever wanted? But women, on the other hand. She never said a thing about women.

Ginny stares at her reflection. The world has shifted around her overnight, and yet she looks exactly the same. To be held by a woman, she thinks, running circles around her arms. To be held by Gloria. Every moment in her presence like a slice of decadent chocolate cake savored under the covers, like stars in your eyes against a camera flash. The satisfaction of a delicious secret. The painful pleasure of being seen for the first time.

There's nothing soothing and domestic about her feelings for Gloria, but she's so much more. Hoping for her affection fills Ginny with an infinite longing, wondering if she should dare taunt the universe with a dream so big. Instead, she strips out of her dress, trying to snap back to reality as the pale sun filters through the curtains.

When her fingers hit her wristwatch, she notices it's later than she thought. Long past eleven. There goes her reputation at *Photoplay*. And then she remembers that she soon won't have a job to go back to, her living arrangements up in the air with Dottie's banishment and the strange new shift in her relationship with Gloria. And she might not have any friends left in this city, not if Gloria feels differently about last night. She doesn't want to think of what she'll have to do then.

Ginny changes into a day dress and rubs off her makeup. Then, before she can talk herself out of it, she rushes through the hall and gives Dottie's door a solid knock. She doesn't start practice at the Follies until much later, and she should definitely be awake by now. When nobody answers, Ginny pushes on the door, clearing her throat—but it's all for nothing, because the room is empty.

The place is a mess. Tangled sheets, dresses pulled from hangers, and discarded receipts litter the bed, as though some emergency shook Dottie awake at night, forcing her to pack in a hurry. But all her favorite pieces are still in the room, and when Ginny checks the bathroom, her toothbrush still rests in its glass. She sinks into the chair by the vanity and drops her chin in her hands, trying to think.

In more than two years of living together in the city, Dottie's never done a single spontaneous thing. It's not like they shared everything in their lives, but she'd always check in, her schedule marked down in a leather datebook that never left her side. Ginny can't imagine a single thing that would convince her to leave town just days away from the premiere, especially if she thought it was her last chance to shine on stage before her marriage.

Ginny drops to her knees, trying to find something, anything that would give her a clue. She goes through the clothes, running her fingers through the fabric. Then the wardrobe catches her eye. She remembers that morning not too long ago, with Dottie in the middle of the floor, her journal flipped open in front of her. All her belongings scattered around her. She should've stopped to think about it right then. Something was off. Dottie's never that messy.

It takes a few tugs to get the wardrobe to budge, the wood scraping scars into the floor. Dottie's secret cubby is right behind it, latched tightly shut this time. Ginny picks the lock with a hairpin until it snaps open. Then she sees everything.

There's the usual stash of old journals, but there's something else too. A heavy trunk fills the entire space. She opens it. The trunk is filled to the brim with shiny lipsticks. There must be hundreds in here, different shades marked on every tube, peony to raspberry to vampy crimson. Ginny plucks a tube at random and presses the button. A mist of white powder comes out the other end. She tries a few more, but each one yields the same result.

Dottie's hooked on pep powder.

No, it's worse. Dottie's selling.

Ginny rakes her fingers through the trunk, trying to find an explanation that fits what she knows about her sister. It feels like a dream, her mind at a distance from the scene, observing the loaded trunk from the moldings in the ceiling. At the bottom, her hand scrapes against something else, a piece of card paper stuck to the side. She pulls out a sepia photograph of a half-naked woman, her shoulder slipping out of a decadent fur stole, big diamonds gleaming around her neck, her lids lowered with a slightly dopey come-hither look beneath the lashes. Her makeup is heavy enough to distort her features into something anonymous, a beautiful doll from any man's fantasy, but Ginny would recognize that face anywhere.

It's Dottie.

This doesn't make any sense. It's like she's woken up in some alternative reality, her nightmares taking shape in broad daylight. For any other woman, an artful nude might be a gift. Ginny's even thought of taking some of her own. A shot at immortality in print if she can't get the real thing, her body frozen in time at its best. Dottie's different. She's spent years trying to get her figure to the brink of perfection, crafting it into a finely tuned instrument for dancing, and still she can always find some new weakness to attack. Every curve is a reason for merciless scrutiny, for a week of cabbage soup smells settling in the wallpaper. Her body is a constantly shifting creation, and there's no way in hell she'd let somebody pin her down in time with a photograph, not when there's always room for improvement.

Feeling the ground slipping beneath her feet, Ginny runs out into the hall and dials the New Amsterdam. After going through several annoyed stagehands, she reaches Mazie, who assures her that rehearsals have already started, but Dottie's nowhere to be seen.

"Are you sure?" Ginny can feel her heart banging on her ribs, her breath going shallow. "Maybe she mixed up the times—"

"Nah," says Mazie, chewing gum into the receiver. "She said she'd be here, but she's not. Guess that means Mr. Sharp will give me her number, can you imagine? I've always wanted to do a fan dance."

Ginny leans against the wall. Josephine, Mary, and now Dottie. All of them connected to the Follies. All of them missing or dead. The odds aren't looking good at all.

Mazie blows out a gum bubble. "I gotta go—oh, here's Gloria—"

Ginny presses her eyes shut. When Gloria's smooth voice slips through the line, every syllable thrums through her skin, summoning memories from last night.

"You were in a hurry to leave."

"Sorry about that, Glo. I just— Something's happened—" She looks down at the photo in her hands, trying to keep her breath steady on the line. "Have you heard anything about the Follies girls taking nude photos?"

"Oh, darling, you're bad." Gloria's voice is like many beads rolling inside a jewelry box. "If you wanted a memento from me, all you had to do was ask."

"I'm serious. Something happened to Dottie, and I— Well, I really need answers."

"I'm not sure what you want to hear. Everyone knows about those Johnston prints, of course. For mine, I was wearing this marvelous peacock headdress—so heavy my neck ached for weeks! I'll show you next time we meet, something tells me you might like it."

Ginny feels her pulse slowing. Maybe that's what this is, that photo burning against her palm. An artistic shot from a famous photographer, nothing more. But the look in Dottie's eyes throws her off. Filled with a deep sadness thrown off-balance, like something far beyond repair.

The muffled laughter on the other end gets louder. There's a softer note in Gloria's voice when she speaks again.

"What's wrong, darling?"

"You saw Dottie at last night's rehearsals, right?"

"Of course. She was in high spirits all night, said she was looking forward to her date with Charlie. Sounded like she couldn't wait."

Ginny drops the receiver. Of course. It's the first rule in the book. When a woman goes missing, you have to talk to the person who saw her last, and it sure looks like Charlie's got some explaining to do.

She expects to reach him on the first try when she calls up his office, but the secretary at Winthrop and Co seems intent on making life difficult for her.

"Charles Darby, did you say? Could you spell it out for me?"

Ginny complies, but still, there's nothing. "Is he in his office today?"

The secretary lets out a heavy breath. "You must have the wrong number. Mr. Darby was fired three months ago. I'm sorry."

Ginny can feel her fingers going numb around the receiver. She thanks the secretary and drops the phone, trying to think. Charlie brought up his big-time job any chance he got, but now it sounds like he's been lying this entire time.

When she calls his home number, a man who doesn't sound like any kind of butler picks up the phone, flinging a chain of curse words into her ear when she mentions Charlie's name.

"I bet he's at that club of his again," he says, sniffing into the receiver. "Spending all his cash impressing his college pals. You see that no-good bastard, tell him he'd better pay his rent this week, or I'm changing the locks. You tell him—"

Soon, she's at the restaurant at the Princeton Club. The maître d' keeps his eyes politely averted from her bruised face, but still he leads her into a dark corner of the room, where Charlie sits alone with his back to everybody. The place is almost empty at this hour, dark walnut tables gleaming with fresh white tablecloths, amber lights muted to a soft glow. Ginny drops into a chair across from him, but her words die on her tongue as she takes in the view.

The bravado is gone from his posture, shoulders sloping forward, one arm entirely encased in a plaster cast. He tries to stand when she joins him, but the effort colors his cheeks bright red, matching the tone of the deep scratches all over his face, one eye almost sealed shut with a swelling bruise. The entire right side of his head is covered in bandages, those golden locks gone dishwater sallow.

Ginny grabs the edge of the table, trying to make sense of what she's seeing. The night at the Hall of Mirrors comes back in jagged flashes, her fist against the side of Charlie's head, her foot digging into his shoulder. She can't remember if she ever stopped.

A single thought swirls madly through her mind.

Did I do this?

In that moment, she misses Jack with an intensity that makes her heart hurt. All she wants is to see his face, hear his voice, let him tell her everything's fine. That she's more than the sum total of her mistakes. That she's not a monster.

"I see you've come to gloat," he says, his hoarse voice still grasping for the upper hand. "Well? Are you happy with your work?"

"I don't know what you're talking about. I— This isn't my fault—"

"Sure. Like you don't remember." He puffs out a breath, then takes a small sip. No food on his plate, just an inch of scotch in the glass. "Serves me right for always going for the crazy ones. Great sex, but everything else—"

"Quiet." Ginny tries to even out her breath, but it's useless, the situation keeps slipping away from her. "I don't know what kind of trouble you got yourself into, and I honestly don't care. I'm here to talk about Dottie. What have you done with her?"

Charlie shifts in his seat. "Relax. I don't want anything to do with your sister, or any other members of your crazy family. I'm done."

He tries to raise his arms in surrender, but the cast prevents him from completing the gesture, and he only winces across the table as the waiter comes by to take Ginny's order of water and nothing else.

"You were with her last night, and now she's gone. Knowing the kind of guy you are, I wouldn't put it past you to have some part in her disappearance. You'd better tell me everything."

His laughter is dry and unpleasant, and he wipes a tear from the corner of an eye with his good hand. One of the only other people in the restaurant, a studious guy in round glasses, looks up from his work with obvious distaste.

"Oh, that's rich," says Charlie, slapping his leg with an open palm. "You think I'm the bad guy? Maybe you should take a closer look at your sister."

"What are you—"

"We might've been engaged, but I was definitely not the only man in her life. Oh, I probably didn't even make it to her top three, can you imagine that?" His eyes mist over with humorous tears, but his lips are a tight line. "All those late-night rehearsals, when the other showgirls were long gone? Except our Dottie was never alone. I bet she never told you about that big party she went to last week. Had to pick her up at four in the morning. Hopped up on who knows what, half-naked with her makeup messed up. Wouldn't tell me what the hell happened, so you know she got around that night. Must be why she got to do the fan dance. She earned it."

"You're lying." Ginny feels the heat creeping up her face, and she brings a fist down onto the table. The spectacled man shakes his head and snaps his book shut, but she doesn't bother with apologies. "I know all about you now, Charlie Darby. Dottie's just a meal ticket to you, isn't she? You've lost your job, sold your apartment, but you can't stop gambling it all away. You think the worst of people because of your own sick mind."

His good arm whips across the table, latching on to her wrist. Despite the injuries, his grip is still almost as powerful as it was before, and she can feel the pain burning a ring around her arm.

"If you're so smart, why the hell are you talking to me, anyway? Something tells me I'm your only hope for finding Dottie, so you'd better play nicely, or I won't tell you a thing."

"I bet you have nothing to tell," she all but spits into his face. "Probably spent last night at the bottom of a bottle—"

"Shut it," he says. His breath is getting heavier, eyes narrowed against her insults, and she knows her ruse is working. Charlie needs a kick to get going, and the only way she'll get him to spill is by getting him real angry. "We went to dinner, all right? Chez Georges. You can ask any of the waiters, you'll see my story checks out. Except she got a call halfway through the meal, and she left before I could order dessert. Didn't say where she was going, but I have a pretty good idea."

"I bet this is where your theory about Dottie's many men comes in."

"That's right, and it's not a damn theory. Otto Sharp only had to say the word, and she went running after him."

"What time was this?"

"We had reservations for nine, after her rehearsals. We barely got through our first course. You do the math."

That can't be right. Otto spent the entire evening at Gloria's party. He left with his wife after midnight. Something doesn't add up here, but she can't think of any reasons for Charlie to lie, not when he's so angry with her sister.

Dottie's nude picture burns through her beaded purse, but Ginny doesn't dare share it with Charlie. Still she remembers something he said to her a few short days ago, that feels like an eternity away after everything that's happened.

"You told me the Follies girls took pictures on the side." She pulls in a breath. This isn't going to be easy. "Nude pictures. You know, the night we—"

"Sure." He smiles at the memory, his grip loosening around her wrist. "What a night."

"Why would they agree to it?" When the whole world watches them on stage in rapt attention, when the Follies unlock every door in town.

"That's only the tip of the iceberg." He laughs into empty space, shaking his head. "You really are just a kid after all, aren't you? The dancing is a showcase. If you're a man of a certain social standing, you can have your pick of the chorus line. Of course, there are always options for smaller budgets. Some guys like to watch."

It sounds like a load of nonsense. Some guy's wet dream, knocking the Follies girls offstage like tarnished gold idols. "What's that supposed to mean?"

The waiter returns to their table, a cut glass carafe sloshing with water on his tray. Through the clear water poured into her glass, Ginny watches Charlie's face, the self-satisfied smirk growing deeper.

"I think I've given you enough to work with, don't you?" He flicks his eyes into the restaurant, where a group of slick college boys are making a fuss at the door. When they notice his stare, he waves with his good arm. Despite the injury, it looks like Charlie will emerge unscathed, continuing his act until he's flush with money again, one way or another.

Ginny rises, leaving the water untouched on the table. She doesn't hang around to say goodbye.

Outside, she leans against the wall and lights up a smoke, trying to make sense of everything.

She sorts through the things in her purse. Silver lighter, half-finished tube of Kissproof lipstick, Dottie's picture folded into the inside compartment so she doesn't have to look at it every time she needs a smoke. But then her fingers slip over something else. Another picture at the bottom of the purse. It's the sepia print from Ruby's wall, the one with the girls smiling up at the camera, oblivious of their shared tragedy waiting around the corner.

They look so close here. Arms swung over each other's shoulders. Josephine leaning her head on Ruby's shoulder, her eyes half-shut against the sun. Ginny stares at the girls until her vision blurs, the whole weight of her failures crashing over her.

She's let them down, both of them. These strong, beautiful women, daring to defy the dark powers that try to control them. The shame is so powerful she could curl up and die.

But then something catches her eye. It's faint at first, a speck against the photo, but it's still there when she swipes at the surface with her thumb. A mole at the edge of Ruby's left eyebrow. Yesterday's memories stir in her mind, a streak of makeup in the wrong place, a woman with a face that's so similar to Ruby's, but not quite. Not exactly.

She chokes out a laugh, pressing a hand against her mouth. There it is. Their missing link.

CHAPTER TWENTY-TWO

S oon, Ginny is outside the Hurston residence yet again, leaning
against the mailbox. Her neck aches from twisting left and right,
trying to spot Jack's figure in the street. He's late. That's not like him at
all. She pulls another cigarette out of her purse and sticks it between
her lips, trying to light it with shaky hands. He won't come. She can't
blame him for that. Last time they met, she said some real ugly things,
and he'd have every right to cross her out of his life forever.

Still, he picked up the phone when she called. Didn't say much,
his silences crackling down the line as Ginny stumbled over her
words, trying to tell him everything she's discovered. In the end,
when she invited him over to Ruby's place, he stretched out that
silence even longer until she couldn't take the wait anymore, cold
sweat trickling down her face. She asked him again, and he said
yes. That should stand for something.

Ginny drops the lighter to the ground.

She bends to pick it up, but there's a shuffle of approaching steps.
Some guy lifts the lighter between his fingers and passes it to her.
When she looks up, she's face to face with Jack.

"You're a mess." He's giving her a slight smile, but his eyes are serious. She returns the unlit cigarette to her purse.

"Tell me about it." She licks her lips, which suddenly have gone dry. "Trying to clean up, though."

Jack doesn't say anything. He's going to make this damn difficult for her, and she can't blame him.

"I heard you dropped Zita. That must've hurt."

"I couldn't keep working the case when I found out Mary was involved. Didn't seem right."

"But what about the money?"

"Screw the money." He crosses his arms. His entire posture is guarded, waiting. Like he's not sure if he can trust her anymore. "Why am I here, Ginny? First you say we're done, and the next day you call me—"

"You don't have to like me anymore." She tries to look him in the eye, but there's too much there, so she drops her gaze to the pavement. "Not that you ever *had* to, but— Look, I know you care about this case as much as I do. Let's say we forget about our differences until we catch the bastard."

"You seem to be doing fine on your own. It's not like you *need* me." He tilts his head, shading his eyes with his hat brim. "After all, I'm just some crook—"

"All right! I get it," she says. "You want me to say it? I'll say it. I need you, detective Jack Crawford. I need you *bad*." Ginny steps forward so she's barely a foot away from him. The pine and Ivory soap smells fill her nostrils, and she could almost laugh with relief at the comfort of being close to him again. He's so solid and true, he makes Gloria feel like a peach-scented mirage. "Can we try this whole thing again?"

A charged moment passes. He looks like he's not sure if he wants to kiss her or walk away. Finally, he cracks a smile, and she knows everything is forgiven, even if he might never forget.

"That depends. What have you got for me?"

She goes over everything she shared on the phone in greater detail, stumbling over her words, feeling a cold block of ice melting inside her when she gets to the part about her sister. She slumps against the mailbox, and soon Jack's wrapping an arm behind her shoulders, his face darkening at the news.

"Those bastards. You think whoever took your sister is the same person who kidnapped Josephine?"

Ginny nods, swallowing around a lump in her throat. "That's right. She's been using, and maybe selling. I—I don't know how much longer she's got, but I think I know where they're holding her."

When she tells him what she's figured out, his eyes light up. He looks at her like she's given him a winning lottery number.

The weary maid at the Hurston residence seems less pleased to see them this time. She shifts her weight to her right hip, looking them up and down like they've got bad news written all over.

"I'm afraid Miss Ruby is absent."

"I'm sure she is." Ginny steps up with a blithe smile. "Take us to the lady of the house, why don't you?"

A shadow passes over the maid's face. She opens her mouth with a fresh retort on her tongue, but then she shakes her head and beckons them inside.

In the parlor, Ruby is arranged on the divan once again, looking like she never moved since their previous meeting in this house. Only a fresh layer of makeup and a different set of earrings, five-pointed sapphires edged in white crystals, show any sign of a life beyond this room.

She straightens when they enter, pushing up against the back of the divan. Ginny squares herself in front of the woman.

"You're not who you say you are."

Ruby folds her hands above the blanket.

"What is that, some kind of riddle?"

But there's a calculating glint in her eyes, a challenge, a dare. Like she's been waiting for someone to put her to the test all this time. Well, here comes the bombshell.

"You're Josephine Hurston."

For an instant, the woman freezes, shoulders stiffening at the name. The entire room is still enough to hear the whistle of the teakettle in the other room, the maid humming a jazz tune in a deep voice in the kitchen.

Then she smiles, wide and bright, just like that night at the Eighty-Three.

"What gave me away?"

Ginny feels the tight string in her chest relaxing. She pulls the photo from her purse.

"It was the mole."

"The mole?"

"You were crying when I came to see you yesterday. The mole came off. I didn't pay attention to it before today, but I looked at the picture, and— Well, Ruby's the one with the mole. I remembered Josephine's ill-fitting clothes the night of her disappearance. If that costume was tailor-made for her, it didn't make any sense."

The smell of chamomile fills the room as the maid places the tray on the table between them.

"And then came the Hall of Mirrors," she continues. "At that point, I still thought you were Ruby. I heard your conversation with Billy. I saw you together. At first, I thought this was some love triangle. But the way you were together—something about that theory didn't stick."

"I was worried sick by then." Josephine brushes a strand of hair out of her eyes, bangles clacking down her arm. "I was sure someone had betrayed us, and of course I lashed out at Billy. And now they've captured him, and I've still got nothing. Nobody else knows the truth. Now I wonder if I've been too careful, and I should've told you everything from the start. What else have you got?"

Ginny presses her lips together. "You were the one who auditioned for the Follies. That seemed personal, the way you talked about it. Ruby took your place that night at the Eighty-Three, because you wanted to move the stash you stole from the Eagle. But something went wrong."

"I'm glad you've figured it out. Time is running out."

"And you're still missing a sister," says Jack. "That part is true? Ruby's gone?"

"I suppose I might as well come clean about everything."

Josephine tucks her feet beneath her. Light filters through the room, illuminating her face for the first time. Shadows gather beneath her bright eyes, the whisper of a frown line emerging around her painted mouth. The wait, the act, all of it has taken its toll on her, and she looks almost relieved for the chance to reveal the truth at last.

"I was singing for years, and then suddenly I was famous. Couldn't walk a block in this neighborhood without getting stopped by someone who saw my face on a poster, asking for autographs, asking questions. Like they owned part of me just because they saw me up on that stage. So I started performing in a veil. Life became quieter after that, and I thought I had it all under control—but that didn't last long.

"I was a regular singer at the Cotton Club when he came up to me. Tall guy in a well-made suit, giving me his card for an audition for the Follies. Face covered with scars, but a real nice smile. It was a trap, and I was a fool to fall for it: no one wanted a Black woman on the stage of the New Am. Instead, the Eagle offered me a deal. Drugs in lipstick tubes. A hefty cut for every tube I sell in Harlem. They thought I'd snap up that opportunity." Josephine's face clouds over. "They came to the wrong woman."

"You turned them down. I'm guessing that didn't go well."

"They hired Vivian Templeton instead. She didn't share my concerns." Josephine curses under her breath, then takes a sudden swallow of her tea. "I've been destroying their shipments since May. This last one was supposed to be the final blow. A huge crate of lipsticks. I was moving it the night they took Ruby. You know we thought the stage was the safest place for her that night? But then the lights went out and the bodies came tumbling. Somebody shot me. You couldn't see a thing, and they took her right there—in the middle of a song. And it's been so long, I haven't heard a thing, which means either she's not saying anything—"

Or she's dead. The unsaid possibility lingers in the air like dark smoke.

"You think they haven't figured it out by now?"

She shakes her head. "Ruby didn't know anything. But in any case, she could always keep a secret."

"Where did you take the stash?"

Josephine hesitates. "I've moved it again. I can't tell you my partner's name, but she helped me hide it where they won't think to look."

Josephine falls against the back of the divan, her eyes hot with anger.

"She was supposed to make it big, Ruby. Her poem got accepted for publication for this new magazine, *The New Yorker,* did I tell you that? I'm sick of pretending to be her, keeping up the conversation with the guys at the magazine—all this time, wondering if that will be the last poem she ever writes."

Jack places his hand over Josephine's. "We'll do everything we can, Miss Hurston. But, please, may I ask—why haven't you gone to the police? With the dangers involved—"

Josephine whips her hand away like she's been burned.

"The police? Are you kidding? The Eagle's got the cops in his pocket. It would be like surrendering. How else do you think they got the case wrapped up so quickly? The brick at the Eighty-Three, how do you think that got into Billy's sax case?"

"But I know there are good cops out there. Surely—"

"No such thing as a good cop. Know what? I hope you never have to live in a city where it's just you against the world." A sudden spark flits through her fiery brown eyes. "I'm sick and tired of hiding, and I say we'd better catch the bastard before anybody else gets hurt."

"Too late for that. They took my sister."

Josephine knocks over her teacup. The liquid splashes over her bare knee, but she doesn't even move, and only Jack's handkerchief makes her snap out of her shock.

"They took Dottie?" Josephine's face crumples. "But . . . That can't be right. . . ."

The stale air in the room grows heavy. Ginny can barely breathe. "If you know something, you'd better tell me now, or I swear—"

"I— Dottie was my last hope. Nobody knew we were working together. Only Billy, but he wouldn't talk. He'd never—"

Ginny remembers the signed photo of Josephine, the disarray on the floor. She should've looked closely that morning. Maybe this never would have happened.

"She helped you move the stash."

Josephine nods. "Said she had a special hiding spot where nobody would think to check. The plan was airtight."

A sound stuck somewhere between a laugh and a gasp forms in her throat. Every time she thinks she knows the score, the world goes upside down on her. Of course Dottie was never a drug dealer. She was the opposite, but Ginny was so quick to jump on any theory that would knock her sister off her perfect throne. Always judging her by her own twisted standards. What a mess.

"But I don't understand. Why would she do it? The Follies were her world."

"That was true for a while. She turned me down when I first offered, after signing that picture. But then something happened to her. It was last Wednesday, the night of the kidnapping—a coincidence, but it makes you wonder. . . . There was some kind of party, she was vague on the details. They drugged her. Took pictures. She was dead worried about her fiancé finding out, so she wanted to destroy the negative plates, but those boys always wanted more. Blackmailed her with them. Said they'd send out pictures to all her friends and family if she didn't take more of them. It got out of control."

Ginny's vision blurs out of focus. It didn't sound real when Charlie told her, but there's no denying the truth in Josephine's words. Dottie, alone at a party with Otto Sharp. It had to be him. She remembers her hushed conversation with him in the corner at Gloria's party the next day, that blank look in her eyes as she watched him leave. Talking about paying her dues on the rooftop for his Midnight Frolic. Dottie hasn't been herself for days, and Ginny never even noticed. She must've felt so alone.

And despite the crushing weight of her secrets, she didn't feel safe enough to share them with Ginny. She came all the way across town to see Josephine before she knocked on her bedroom door.

"Did she say who it was? That took the pictures?"

"She doesn't remember the night. She thinks the stagehands were somehow involved, since they're the ones who've been taunting her since then. Anyway, we were going to hit them where it hurt. Destroy the drugs, then get them to surrender the negatives. It was a solid plan, but— Well, you see what happened."

Ginny thinks of her sister, shivering in the corner of some dark room while a group of men in bandanas close in on all ends. She must be terrified. There's no telling how long she's got and what they might do to her, but something tells Ginny she's still alive. She can see that same look on Josephine's face, not knowing, but choosing to believe that her sister's still alive somewhere. Still waiting to be saved.

She remembers Charlie, sitting across the table at the Princeton Club, bragging about the dirty secrets he's dug up about the Follies. The nude pictures. The secret club for wealthy patrons. The revelations tie together into one big knot in her mind, and suddenly she knows exactly what to do. There's still one room they haven't searched in the theater, despite Billy's best efforts.

"I think I know where they're keeping our sisters, but we'll have to work together, and fast. As a team. You in?"

Josephine rises from her seat, barely wincing from the bullet wound still healing in her stomach. There's an energy about her, crackling from her coiled curls to her tight fists, not a trace of hesitation. Jack takes a sharp breath by Ginny's side, and she knows he can feel it too. Josephine's a powerful woman to have on your side.

Ginny and Jack get to their feet. As she looks at the other two people beside her, Ginny reads the same expression on their faces, eyes weighed with sadness, lips curving down in hard determination. They've all lost someone, but there's still a chance to make things right, and Ginny can see at last that she was wrong to tackle the case alone.

Ginny shoots an arm into the center, taut fingers stretched out into a star, just like the charm hanging from Mary's bracelet. "Let's get him."

Josephine and Jack stack their palms over hers. The weight of the moment swells and sizzles between them. On their own, the three of them don't stand a chance against the Eagle. But together, they just might have a shot at bringing him down—and at saving both Ruby and Dottie from meeting the same end as Mary.

CHAPTER TWENTY-THREE

T he New Amsterdam is already swinging with activity when
they arrive that night. Valets scramble to park shiny cars, welcoming guests dripping minks and diamonds. It's a full house
tonight, the cream of New York society getting ready for a night
of easy laughter, followed by the dark pleasures of the Midnight
Frolic on the roof. None of them spare a glance for the alley by the
theater, where two dusty cars are skidding to a halt.

Ginny lifts a hand in Josephine's direction, who nods from her
car as she turns to Clive. She's got some guys from the band with
her for backup, but Ginny knows their best hope is that none of
them have to actually fight. With only three guys including Clive,
their calloused fingers more familiar with strings and keys than
the heavy weight of a gun, they won't stand a chance if they're
forced to fight the stagehands. But that's just another shaky point
of their tenuous plan that they've decided to skip over and hope
for the best.

Jack's knee knocks against hers in the front seat of her Buick.
She soaks up the sight of him like there's no tomorrow.

"Jack. I've been thinking—"

The theater is already jumping with music, the warm-up bars of the band welcoming the audience inside, but looking deep into Jack's eyes, it feels like a blanket of silence is wrapped around them both. Soft and comforting and just right, for once.

Jack turns toward her, his jawline swooping through the darkness in a single perfect arc. Eyes locked with hers, he runs a hand down the side of her face. His touch sends shivers down her neck, warmth building beneath her skin until she's on fire again, except this time, it's so much better than that desperate backstage kiss at the Eighty-Three.

This time, it's more than lust. It's understanding. Like he doesn't need the light to see her.

But then she looks back at the theater, and all she can think about is Gloria. Peaches and vanilla and the glow of her attention hot like stage lights all over her body. She's probably already in her dressing room, walking through heavy clouds of perfume, a soft powder puff kissing her cheeks, her signature crimson lipstick spreading smooth across her lush mouth. Ginny thinks of sneaking into her dressing room, clapping her palms over her eyes and asking her to guess. Gloria would see her coming in the mirror, but she'd act surprised all the same. And then maybe she'd kiss her again. They'd share that same crimson lipstick, and Ginny would finally know where she stands. She'd know their night together was no mirage. That Gloria's real. That what they have is real.

Josephine taps the front window. "Come on, it's showtime."

Jack gives her hand one last squeeze, his fingers lingering reluctantly as she pulls away.

"If anything happens—" Fear crackles through his whisper.

"It's going to be okay, don't worry—"

"No. Listen, Ginny—" He pulls her close, each word lingering against the skin of her neck. "Ginny, promise me you'll get the hell out of there as soon as Dottie and Ruby are safe. Promise me that."

She gives him a quick nod, and then they're outside, slipping into the alley with their chins tucked in their collars. The backstage exit is choked with caterers, stagehands, and musicians rushing back and forth, and the three of them pass unnoticed as they're caught up in the crowd.

The backstage hallways feel different. Every corner is suffocated by heavy shadows. The thick walls consume every sound, so it only takes a few steps to drown out the outside noise, leaving nothing but the sound of their breaths shuddering through the stale air.

A sudden wave of applause rushes through the hall, and they flatten against the wall, chests heaving. As a door on the far end slams shut, Ginny lets out a breath.

Jack breaks away by the door to the dressing room. The brim of his hat shades his eyes, so Ginny can't see what he's thinking.

"I'll be right outside," he whispers. "Hurry."

Ginny opens the door to the dressing room just a fraction. The coast is clear. Josephine follows her inside with her hands on her hips, taking in the opulence with her mouth in a hard line.

"What a world," Josephine says under her breath. "To think I actually believed all this could be mine. Of course they'd never give it to me."

"Trust me." Ginny walks up to the mirror and starts patting it down from ceiling to floor, looking for ridges. "When all this is over, you'll be glad you never joined."

The mirror appears seamless from all angles, polished to a smooth gleam like a lake of pure melted silver. Nothing to catch her fingers on, not a single sharp edge to hook her theory onto. Her idea seemed so obvious when she presented it to Jack and Josephine, all the facts falling into a neat line, but under the bright lights of the Follies dressing room, Ginny's no longer too sure.

Applause rumbles in the audience, and Ginny freezes as the stage door swings open. Josephine's fingers tremble against the glass. But it's only Mazie, rubbing a sheen of sweat from her round forehead, already shrugging out of a feathered costume. Her face brightens when she sees Ginny.

"You here to cover the premiere?" she says, then throws an obvious wink her way. "Or maybe looking for another pick-me-up? Oh—who's your friend?"

Ginny swallows around a dry lump in her throat. "This is—"

"Ruby," says Josephine, raising her voice half an octave. The transformation is uncanny. "Poetry editor at the *Harlem Herald*. Miss Dugan invited me along on a tour. Nothing like a premiere to inspire the poetic temperament."

"Huh." Mazie pulls on a white bodysuit tight enough to cut all circulation off her legs. "I'm doing the fan dance after all, Ginny. Sorry about your sister."

Ginny steps back toward the mirror, nodding along automatically to calm her jagged nerves. She knocks into a gilded chest of drawers, and Mazie's features freeze for a moment. Fear flashes across her bland face.

After a charged moment, she relaxes and brushes off a stray sequin, but her fingers are still shaking.

"Where's Mr. Sharp?" Ginny says. "I'd love to interview him later."

A bell chimes in the distance, and Mazie straightens her costume with a final tug. She pulls a set of large white fans from a dressing table. "He's hanging around stage left, on the other side, so he can give us directions. That's my cue—see you later—"

As soon as Mazie's back onstage, Ginny drops to her knees beside the chest of drawers. She'll never forget her mother's fuss over the original Chippendale commode in the parlor, followed by weeks of stormy silence after a dinner guest pointed out the uneven side seams that exposed it as a fake. This gilded chest might be a flashy piece, but the wood is cheaply grained, and the gold might as well be fast-dry paint, given how unevenly it's been applied to the surface.

She gives the chest an experimental tug. It's heavy, and only with Josephine's assistance does she manage to get it away from the mirror, with a fresh splinter in her thumb and sweat trickling down her neck.

There's a square hole cut into the carpet beneath the chest, exposing a tiny metal lever. Josephine runs her fingers down the surface.

Ginny grabs the lever and pulls down hard. A small panel pops out of the mirror, a door opening into the dressing room.

Ginny fumbles with her silver lighter and beckons for Josephine to follow. Not a single sound, but she can sense another presence. She squints through the darkness, her eyes slowly adjusting to the dim. The room stinks like a public bathroom in a train station.

"Hello?"

Wood scrapes on tile. Ginny leans her head through the door. The presence seems to grow stronger. Someone is breathing in the dark. She leans her entire body into the space, feet still hesitant on the carpet outside, the lighter flame too small to reach all the corners of the room.

"Dottie?"

A muffled sound echoes through the space. Josephine pushes into the room. She lets out a gasp that strains through her entire body like she's been wounded.

Ginny follows with the lighter, the flame quivering in her out-stretched hand. It's smaller than she expected, a cement-plated cave strewn with cigarette butts and candy wrappers, a dirty bucket pushed against the wall. A young woman sits in the corner, wide-eyed with horror, her wrists and ankles bound with rope. Her skin is drawn tightly around a bony face, dried streaks of tears running through an old layer of makeup. She's still dressed in a thin stage costume, silver scales worn through from friction against the floor. She looks like an exhausted, emaciated version of Josephine, but the likeness is striking despite the differences. Ginny feels a tug in the pit of her stomach as she notices the bruises up and down her arms, with most of them concentrated where she's tried to pull free of the restrictive rope bindings.

Josephine drops to her knees beside the woman and starts working on the gag around her mouth. Ginny joins, fumbling to untie the rope around her wrists with one hand. But with the lighter in her other hand, she can't stop looking around the room, can't stop searching for somebody she knows isn't there.

When the gag comes undone, Ruby takes a deep, rasping breath.

"Oh my god, Josie." Fresh tears trickle down the sides of her face. She can't stop shaking. "Oh my god. I thought—"

"I know, honey." Josephine unties the rope around her wrists and wraps her sister into a hug. "It's okay. You're safe."

"Listen, was there another girl in here?" The lighter shakes between Ginny's fingers. Maybe they moved her, and she's still somewhere near. Maybe there's still hope.

"Just me, all by my lonesome." Ruby leans down to help Josephine with the rope around her ankles. There's more applause in the distance, the band belting out a few rousing notes. "We have to hurry. This place is never empty for long. Soon, they'll be back, and we'll have no chance of escaping."

Ginny turns, expecting to find another concrete wall. Instead, the entire dressing room is in front of them, bright as day, only slightly tinted by the dark glass wall. She brings the lighter close to the mirror.

"This is crazy." She traces a rack of costumes with her fingertips.

"It's a transparent mirror." Ruby's voice is hollow. "Can't see into this room from the other side, but you can see everything happening in the dressing room. Everything."

Ginny presses her forehead against the mirror. *Transparent mirror.* The words stir familiar memories, snippets from Jack's detective manuals, fragments from old spy books she read under the covers with a flashlight. Some new scientific development, that's what they called it, with great applications in law enforcement. Sure looks like the Follies are ahead of the pack in the innovation department.

Whoever installed this mirror was dead set on keeping it secret. She trails a hand across the caulking between the top ridge of the glass and the cement ceiling. It couldn't have been here for long. Even the paint is fresh, slightly damp on her hand, coming away in little flecks of gray.

Charlie's words echo through her head, twisting her stomach into a tight knot.

Some guys like to watch.

Oh, she gets it now. Takes a sick mind to come up with something like this, but it doesn't take a genius to figure it out. For a small price, men can get their fill of the Follies girls through the glass. Smoking their cigars and staring at those taut young bodies slipping in and out of sequins and feathers. Every inch of their flesh exposed to the light, while these men remain in the shadows, their identities safely concealed. Then they go back to their wives, and no one's the wiser. They can get away with it all. This mirror's just another mask.

Josephine is guiding her sister out of the darkness with Ruby's arm hanging over her shoulder. Ginny follows with her knuckles clenched around the lighter. The golden dressing room flushes red before her eyes. None of the noise from the audience reaches her anymore. The room presses down from all corners, every gilded surface taunting her with its hidden darkness.

And Dottie's still missing. Locked away in a room like this one or worse, and there's nothing Ginny can do about it. Her eyes rove over the objects in the dressing room, hovering on the metal rack hung with shimmering stage costumes.

"We have to go." Josephine's at the door with Ruby, twisting her neck backward toward Ginny. The urgency in her voice has taken a different quality now that she's found her sister. Ginny's actions are no longer paramount to the plan. It's all about getting Ruby to safety. "I'll take her to the guys, and then we can—"

"You go on. I've got unfinished business here."

The sisters disappear out the door, their footsteps echoing through the hall before they're swallowed entirely by the distance. One by one, Ginny pulls the costumes from the rack, hardly bothering to keep them intact. She saves Gloria's costume, dropping it on a nearby chair, but she is merciless with the others. She rips the sleeve on a short tulle dress covered in paste rubies. A sequined violet two-piece turns dusty beneath her feet. Violent sounds rattle through her brain, and she thinks she hears a commotion in the hall, but then returns to her work, scattering every last costume until the rack gleams bare in front of her eyes.

When all the costumes are lying in a heap on the floor, Ginny swivels the rack toward the mirror like a battering ram and runs forward with it, tightening her lips against the scream building in her chest.

Metal hits glass, sending spiderweb fractures across the surface of the mirror. It's not enough. The mirror still holds. Ginny grits her teeth and runs back again, this time putting her weight into it, adding the sharp heel of her shoe against the glass.

The mirror shatters down the middle, shards of glass flying in all directions. Ginny slams a fist against the point of fracture, breathing hard. There's blood all over her hands now. It doesn't matter. She keeps pounding until she can see straight into the hidden space, ignoring the pain in her arm. With the bright dressing room lights pooling into the space behind the mirror, there's no more hiding the dark secrets of this theater. If she lives to see the end of this day, she'll make damn sure this part of the business will go down forever.

Ginny leans against the wall, trying hard to think. Her head keeps spinning. The sounds of the audience come back into focus. Footsteps rush toward the dressing room, and soon she's surrounded by showgirls in matching bodysuits, their eyes going as wide as their heavy lashes will allow.

Gloria is the only one who comes close, grabbing Ginny around the shoulders, staining the tips of her pale gloves with her blood.

"Darling—what's going on?"

Ginny points toward the mirror. "They've been spying on the girls. All this time. It was a transparent mirror, Glo. They had men paying big bucks for a flash of skin from the Follies girls, and nobody, *nobody* knew—"

Murmurs rise in the ranks, anxious eyes flicking from the fracture in the mirror to the blood on Ginny's hands. A sudden wave of exhaustion crashes over her. She'd like to shut her eyes against the whole night, watch it fade away like another bad day. But something keeps her alert, a truth emerging from the rubble.

Mr. Sharp had to know about the mirror. When Mary came into the dressing room that night, she must've heard Ruby's muffled screams. Without any pep powder to dull her senses, she might've even discovered the true purpose of the mirror. Then Sharp came back to find her. Came back and made sure she'd never talk again.

Otto Sharp is still out in the open. She can't leave until she brings him to justice.

"Listen here." Ginny stumbles to her feet, shaking off Gloria's grip. "Your stage manager's been up to no good, and tonight, we're going to catch him."

One of the girls lets out a dramatic sigh. "We're in the middle of a *premiere*. Can't it wait—"

"Don't be a little fool," Gloria snaps, and the girl shuts her mouth at once. "This is serious. What do you want us to do, Ginny?"

Make him pay. Ginny pictures herself pummeling Otto Sharp's smug face into oblivion, until all his snappy orders die on his tongue. Finding out where he's keeping her sister, and then silencing him forever for all he's done. She can taste the bloody satisfaction, the iron in her veins jangling with excitement at the prospect of this sweet revenge.

But then she thinks of Jack, those last words he said to her before they parted.

Ginny, promise me you'll get the hell out of there as soon as Ruby and Dottie are safe. Promise me that.

Dottie is far from safe. He can't argue with that. And she won't be, not until Ginny gets the information she needs out of Sharp. After that, Jack can call the cops, set up a proper investigation, whatever.

Ginny bends over and rips a piece of shimmery rayon from one of the fallen costumes. With every nerve humming anxiously through her body, she turns to the showgirls, trying to think of a plan as she wraps the fabric around her bloody hand. But then the door to the dressing room swings open, and Josephine comes back alone, looking like she's seen a ghost.

"What's wrong? Is Ruby okay?"

"Ruby's with the band. It's not that." She grabs the doorframe for support, ignoring the curious eyes of the showgirls. "Jack was supposed to wait by the door, right?"

Ginny backs up against the wall, feeling her pulse rattling to infinity again. And then Josephine lifts something in the air. When Ginny looks close, she recognizes a familiar black leather notebook.

"This is all that's left."

CHAPTER TWENTY-FOUR

When the bell rings, the girls leave the dressing room for another number. Ginny follows with her heart in her throat. She looks beyond the heavy red curtain, trying to catch a glimpse of Otto on the other side of the stage, but he's gone. So is Jack. Ginny can imagine exactly what that means, and it's not looking good at all.

The only showgirl hanging back is Gloria. She's changed into her next costume, but still she lingers by the door. She keeps looking from Ginny to Josephine, picking at the silk petals of a lily attached to her skirt.

"So you think Sharp is behind this?"

Ginny's filled her in, but as much as she'd like to spend some time with Gloria, she can't waste any more of it on small talk. "Aren't you supposed to be on stage?"

"I'm not in this one, remember." With one final tug, Gloria rips the lily off her skirt and twists it between her fingers.

The girls launch into the garden number, bringing waves of polite laughter from the crowd.

"Where could they have gone?" says Josephine. "I could bring backup—"

"No time for that. Gloria, what's on the other side of the curtain? Stage left?" Past the dazzling stage lights, she can just catch somebody moving around in the shadows, and it looks like he's wearing a familiar tailored blue suit.

Wherever Otto Sharp is going, she's going to be right behind him.

"Oh." Gloria drops the lily to the ground, the silk petals going limp. "Only one thing over there. The roof."

"I'm going in." Ginny turns on her heel and starts running, making her way through dark backstage hallways. She catches Josephine in her side vision, and the sound of heels on tile tells her Gloria is close behind, even though the exertion is cutting her even breath into short, jagged bursts.

"What are you—"

"I'm not—leaving you—"

At the end of the hall, a spiral staircase offers a shortcut to the roof. The trap door is open. Ginny begins to climb, slipping along the dark iron rungs, glimpsing sharp flashes of Gloria and Josephine beneath her as the moonlight strikes their faces. It's quiet up there. Carefully, she pokes her head above the opening, turning left and right.

The rooftop is primed for the after-party. A special glass bridge hangs above a dozen white tables, with blue and gold balloons swaying in the summer breeze. Ginny shivers. Sure looks like a party that will never happen.

She uses her arms to hoist herself out of the gap. Again, that eerie silence. She's certain the guys have run up here, but now she can't hear a soul.

And when she does, her blood runs cold against the summer heat.

"Welcome to Ziegfeld's Midnight Frolic, little bird."

The man with the scar is right behind her, flanked by two others, bandanas slipping down to their chins. Ginny trips backward. She can see everything now. Jack is on the glass bridge above her, two stagehands holding him by the arms, tipping him slightly over the edge so his tie dips into the night. On the far end of the roof, Otto Sharp stands with his arms open wide in welcome, evening jacket flapping behind him like a pair of dark wings.

Ginny looks through the opening, meeting Gloria's questioning gaze with numb silence.

"What's wrong?"

Ginny shakes her head. "Gloria, don't—"

A sharp jab between her shoulder blades, and Ginny drops to her knees on the ground. She rolls away from another attack, but she's not the target. The tall man grabs Gloria around the middle and hauls her away. She keeps kicking at the ground as he drags her toward Otto, but she only dislodges a few orange petals from her costume and loses a shoe in the process.

Josephine comes out of the opening, but another guy wraps his arms around her. Although she aims an elbow at his ribs, he only smiles, muttering something about catching the best prize.

"Hey, boss, this the sister?"

Otto gives him a withering look. The man goes quiet, pointing his gun at Josephine's head with perverse enjoyment.

They don't waste any muscle on Ginny, but they don't have to. Outnumbered and outsmarted, damn it. The wind picks up at this altitude, whipping at her sleeves and bringing angry tears to her eyes. Best-case scenario, Jack called for reinforcements in time, but the deflated look on his face tells her she'd better stop believing in miracles.

She remembers what Dottie said about this dreadful Midnight Frolic. An after-party for the guests with the deepest pockets, in a discreet location high above the crowds. Nobody will hear them until it's too late. This is the end.

Screams from the bridge above, Jack dipped over the edge.

"You better tell us what you know," one of the stagehands says, "or else we'll see if gravity agrees with you. Right, boss?"

Otto wraps a familiar arm around Gloria. The edges of his lips twist upward in a face like a rubber mask. "That's the plan. But now that the ladies are here, we might have a better shot with Miss Dugan."

Ginny's heart leaps into her throat. "Show's over, Sharp. We know everything. You're never getting away—"

"Show's over when I say it is." He tightens his grip around Gloria. "I'm the stage manager, honey. And I say it's too soon to drop the curtain."

"He doesn't know anything." She doesn't dare look up at Jack. Stumbling to her feet, Ginny grasps for what little power she has left. "It's me you want. It's my investigation."

"He might serve his purpose yet." Otto snaps his fingers. Jack lets out a string of curses as the stagehands dip him lower, so he's almost parallel to the ground.

"Stop! Stop it," Ginny takes a step toward Otto. "I said, he doesn't know—"

"Black Jack Crawford. That's one person I didn't expect to find on the side of the law. I guess stranger things have happened. . . . No, I don't think he's the one. Gloria, on the other hand . . ."

He swings her beyond the edge of the roof. Ginny runs forward, nearly tripping over her feet, heart pounding in her throat—but then he brings her back, laughing his head off like it's the world's best joke.

"There's my answer. You two have something special going, don't you?"

Gloria struggles against his grip. "Cut the charade, Otto. This girl means nothing to me." There's a vicious note ringing in her voice, a hardness in her eyes.

Ginny's thoughts race circles in her mind. She looks at Jack, struggling against his captors as they bring him back up on the bridge, and she wonders what he would do in her position. Jack is the ace with diplomacy, not her. He'd know what to say to get Otto away from the edge, stalling long enough for help to arrive—or for any other destabilizing event to shift the power back into their hands. Before she can say anything, Josephine speaks up.

"We both know this is between you and me, Sharp. Let these people go." Even with her arms pinned behind her back, her dark dress torn and dusty, Josephine keeps her head high.

"You've had your chance. Now I want to hear Miss Dugan's story." Otto tightens his grip around Gloria. "You ready to answer my questions now?"

"Where's my sister?" says Ginny.

Otto's smile falters by an inch. "Your—Dottie?"

Ginny rubs a sleeve against her eyes, steadying herself. "I know you kidnapped her. Just tell me if she's alive, damn it. That's all I—"

"Now, listen here." A trace of the old stage manager is back, all snappy commands and ego. "I was as upset as you were when she skipped out so close to the show. That girl is no longer any concern of mine—"

"You're lying." Ginny takes a shaky step toward the ledge. The stagehands tighten their grip on their guns, but Otto flicks them a signal with his eyes. Not yet. Ginny remembers the story about the party, the drugs, and the pictures that followed. He's complicit, she knows it, and yet he's lying straight to her face. Rage simmers in the pit of her stomach. "You had her taking *your* drugs, posing for *your* damn sponsors—"

"Quiet." The wind whips Otto's jacket behind him. There's a displeased twist to his features, a storm settling over his eyes. "Your sister's her own woman. And here I thought you were a threat to the operation—never should've wasted all that muscle trying to keep you quiet."

Ginny bites down on her tongue. She'd expected a triumphant confession, something that would give her ground to condemn Otto Sharp once and for all. But if he was flippant about Mary's death, this time is different. He sounds genuinely clueless. She can't connect the dots anymore, the dark night swirling into a mad blur before her eyes.

Otto Sharp is the Eagle. That's all there is, she'd swear to it. But if he didn't kidnap her sister, then she's all out of ideas.

Josephine takes advantage of the silence. "You're gonna get yours, Otto Sharp."

"And you should be careful what you say, Miss Hurston." He tilts his head at a rakish angle, savoring her simmering rage. "Still, I'm glad you could join us. Reunited with your sister at last—"

"You're done." She whips a stray curl out of her face, and even in this doomed moment, Ginny can't help but admire her fierce beauty. "My sister's safe now, Mr. Sharp. You'll never find the stolen stash, and I'll make sure you never go back to my neighborhood again. Understand?"

Otto nods to the man holding Josephine, and he clicks the hammer on his gun. Ginny takes an instinctive step in her direction. Josephine, Gloria, Jack. She's torn three ways. It's like a nightmare, every decision turning fatal, none of her choices giving her a happy ending.

"Let's try this again. Tell us where you're holding the drugs, and we'll let you go." His cruel mouth twists, and it's obvious to everyone that he won't deliver. Josephine spits in his direction.

"Go ahead. Pull the trigger. But then the secret dies with me." Josephine smiles. "And my friends will just keep on interfering with your business. You can't kill all of us, Mr. Sharp. Especially not the ones hiding in plain sight."

"Bitch." He clenches his arm tighter around Gloria. Her eyes go wide. "You should've just stayed out of my way."

"You're not even curious?" Josephine inclines her chin, mock flirtatious. "Girls in your chorus line. Good girls, bad girls. You'll never know which ones will keep betraying you, over and over again."

Otto shoots a sign to Josephine's captor, and he rams his gun hard against Josephine's head.

"Wait a minute." Ginny takes a step toward Sharp. She tries to keep her voice casual, keep it cool. "Guess I was confused. Let's start over. Since I got it all wrong, what do you say we part ways and forget about this nasty business?"

Otto barks out a laugh, his mean eyes narrowing. "You really think I can let you leave after all this?"

"Then what are you waiting for?" Ginny moves toward him until she's only steps away from him and Gloria. Close enough to reach forward and pull her friend away from the edge, but she wouldn't dare any sudden movements, not yet. "You could've killed me a dozen times since I came up here. No, there's still something you need from me, and I know exactly what it is."

His grip seems to loosen around Gloria's body, but it might just be a trick of the light.

"I want this over," she says, trying to steady the tremble in her voice. "I know where the stash is hidden."

"What?"

"You didn't figure it out?"

Josephine lets out a stream of curses, looking at Ginny with betrayal and anger mingling. Jack shuts his eyes. She hopes she's making the right decision, for all their sakes.

Gloria's breath grows choppier by the moment. *Hold on a little longer*, Ginny wants to say, but instead she struggles to keep that insolent smile on her face.

"Here's the deal. I'll tell you where to find the stash, so long as you let my friends leave unharmed."

This bold request sends a ripple of laughter across the rooftop.

"You're brave, I can give you that, kid. But if you think for one minute I'll let all of you leave on a damn promise, you're mistaken."

"I'll stay," she says. "For insurance. Like you said, I'm the one you wanted."

"No!" Jack's muffled cry rings down from above.

The guy holding on to Josephine lets out a sudden painful howl. "She bit me, boss!"

"You're a disgrace," Otto hisses. "Can't handle a little girl—"

It happens in a flash. A struggle, and then Josephine elbows her captor in the ribs, pulling the gun out of his grip. The tall man lunges toward her, but without pausing for breath, she raises her right hand and fires a shot that hits him square in the kneecaps. He doubles over with pain, pressing both palms against the blood gushing from his leg.

"This has been going on for too long." Josephine trains the gun on Otto. "You're coming with me. Ginny, would you—"

She wants to bring him into the station. Ginny can see it in her eyes, in her stance. Josephine wouldn't shoot to kill, not when that means Billy's name won't be cleared. That's her mistake. It's a mistake, because everybody else can see it too.

Otto hides behind Gloria. Her makeup has rubbed off below the jaw, and it looks like she's breaking out in hives, a dark splotch blooming where the greasepaint is gone.

"Josephine, wait," says Ginny. "Gloria."

"I'll bring her down with me if I have to," says Otto.

"She's just a showgirl. She's harmless. You don't have to do this, Otto. Please let her—"

Otto wavers on the edge. He seems to find Ginny's words ridiculously funny.

"A harmless showgirl? Oh, I've been in the business long enough to know none of these girls are harmless, least of all Gloria. You really want to know what happened to your secretary friend?"

Ginny's breath catches in her throat.

"Mary?"

"That's right," says Otto. "Her killer is closer than you think—"

In a split second, his hand loosens around Gloria, and she drops to the ground like a rag doll. Ginny throws herself at his legs.

Gloria rolls toward the edge, almost unconscious. In a moment, she'll fall right over.

Ginny catches her by the arms, pulling her back to safety, legs flailing back and forth. Then Gloria strikes Otto in the ankle with her sparkling heel.

At first he waves his arms in the air, eyes wide with some unrecognizable emotion. Then gravity gets the best of him, and he flies off the rooftop with a final flap of his dark suit. His body dissolves in the flashing traffic lights below, landing in the middle of Broadway with a dull thud.

The tall man rises to his feet. Blood gushes from his knee, but he doesn't seem to care anymore. For once, his smile is gone. He looks from the space where Otto once stood to Gloria, who is panting on the ground, trying to prop herself up on her elbows.

Time halts for a moment. Ginny notices everything in slow motion. The determined set of the man's jaw, the tensing arm muscles, the gun whipping out of its holster and pointing directly at Gloria.

"Don't shoot her! Don't—"

Ginny jumps in front of Gloria.

The bullet rings through the air. She trips and falls flat on her back, her skull slamming against the concrete.

The last thing she sees is a string of gold balloons rippling through the night, not a single star in the sky above Broadway. Then her eyes fall shut, and there's only darkness to keep her company.

CHAPTER TWENTY-FIVE

There's no telling how much time goes by after that.

There are flashes of consciousness, brisk hands lifting and moving her body like a doll. Whispers and shouts, cool fingers against her forehead, and once, the mosquito prick of a needle under her elbow. It's smooth sailing after that, drifting away through moonlit dreams. Always running somewhere, while the clouds converge above her head, the dream space lit by nothing but a single yellow streetlamp.

And then she's awake. All at once, like a drowned woman resuscitated on the shore, gasping shallow breaths as she shoots up in a bed that's not her own. A quick assessment answers most of her questions: cold light strips flicker above her head, white sheets turned down on crisp edges, muted mutter following the roll of a cart down the hall. Heady smell of menthol and laudanum, and the clean scrubbed smile of the middle-aged nurse in the corner.

"Nice to meet you properly, Miss Dugan. I'm Nurse Louise, and I'll be taking care of you until you're fit as a fiddle again, what do you say?"

Ginny drops back to the pillow, a pang shooting through her head, and everything comes flooding back, the tangled events of the previous weeks unspooling her all over again.

"How long have I been out?" Ginny tries for pleasant, because that's what you do when a sweet Midwestern nurse tries to make nice with you, but it comes out in a humorless grunt.

"They brought you in last night, and now it's just past the lunch hour. Sure looked like you needed the sleep, honey."

Stitches crisscross over her right hand where it bled from the mirror. Ginny runs her hands down her stomach, searching for a bullet wound. She can't find anything, but the heavy meds turning her brain to cotton are a clear sign of damage.

"Is it . . . bad?"

The nurse gives her another smile, the kind you offer to people who are dumber than you but don't know any better. Ginny wonders just how bad she looks, given the circumstances. The back of her head feels swollen to twice its regular size.

"Now don't you worry about that, honey. You're here to get your rest. The doctor will be in for some tests soon, he'll tell you all about your next steps."

"Look, Louise." Ginny swallows hard around a lump in her throat. Dottie's still missing, and Ginny is in no fit state to go after her, but she has to try. Even through the meds clouding her brain, she can't give up just yet. "I need to know what happened. I know there were gunshots. Would you be a doll and fill me in?"

There she is, a glimmer of the woman she was before. Stringing together full sentences, that's the least she can hope for, no matter how bad it got last night.

The nurse sighs. "The bullet missed you. The doctor stitched up that hand of yours, and you hit your head real bad, so that'll hurt for a bit, but no concussion. Looks like you've been shot before, poor dear, but even so, you'll be back on the dance floor in a month or so. Isn't that swell?"

She waits for Ginny to give her something, some show of excitement for all the rugs to be cut in the future, so she offers up a weak smile. Her dry lips crack from the strain.

The nurse isn't saying anything about the others. On purpose, Ginny knows it. You don't hide good news from a hospital patient.

"What about my friend?"

She's not sure if she means Jack or Gloria.

The nurse throws a quick nod into the hall to someone Ginny can't see.

"There's good and bad news, honey. But since you seem to be feeling better—well, I'll just leave it to the pro, shall I?"

Ginny's heart leaps up in her chest as she cranes her neck to see who it might be. And then Jack walks into the room, looking exhausted in last night's suit. He gets to her side in a single motion, dropping into the visitor's chair with concern crackling through his features.

"You were out for so long," his words rush together, "they didn't let me see you—"

"It's okay." She reaches for his hand. He presses his fingers into her palm, the callouses reassuring against her skin. "I'm fine. What happened to the others?"

He offers up a quick nod, leaning closer. Ginny can almost taste the burnt coffee on his breath.

"Cops rounded everybody up, soon after you passed out. Somebody must've called them after Otto's body fell to the ground. They got almost everyone. Josephine's fine, I drove her back home after a night at the station, and I came here soon as I could—"

Ginny rises on her pillows. "And Gloria?"

Jack averts his eyes. "Maybe you should get some rest—"

"Jack." Her voice rises. "Tell me."

"I don't want to hurt you."

He means it. Those green eyes crinkling at the corners, his mouth stretched into one long, melancholy line. She can't handle this now, this careful man playing it soft with her feelings but only making it worse.

"You're not getting off that easy. Come on, spit it out, you're killing me here—"

"She ran away, Ginny. Left the scene of the crime without a second glance."

So she's alive. The taut string in her chest loosens a bit, but she feels a sudden twinge at the idea of Gloria running away and leaving her behind.

"She just killed a guy to save us all. Of course she'd run." Ginny swipes a hand through the mess on her head. Typical Jack, blowing everything out of proportion. "It's not like you stuck around for the cops to cuff you—"

"Ginny, I know it's a lot to take in. Maybe it was wrong of me to tell you like this—" He searches for the right words for a moment, waving his arms through the air. "I've done some investigating. She's covered her tracks well, but I still found the trail. Everything points to her. All the clues. She was behind the entire operation."

Ginny lets out a laugh. It's a ridiculous idea. The kind of thing that might fly on stage at the New Amsterdam, glorified girls emerging in matching striped costumes, robber masks sliding from their pretty eyes. Gloria in the center like the Bobbed Haired Bandit, twirling diamond-studded handcuffs on her wrists, the crowd going wild for an encore.

"You're funny, Jack. Thanks for coming round to cheer me up."

"You heard what she said, Ginny. I hate to break it to you, but—well, did you ever think she might've been using you?"

This girl means nothing to me.

She remembers those words, all right. Like a knife to the fucking heart. But they were all out of their minds last night, saying anything to get off that roof in one piece. Even Ginny played into Otto's game when she offered up the location of the stash, but she doesn't see Josephine complaining now. Lose a battle to win the war. They were all doing their best.

"That was part of the plan. We've all said some things we didn't mean—"

Jack's next words wipe the smile clean off her face.

"Your sister's still missing. Think about that. If Otto didn't kidnap her, who did?"

Ginny swings her legs off the bed, pushing Jack to the side. There's a throbbing ache in her head despite the painkillers. He's jealous, that's what it is. He must've seen the way she looked at Gloria last night, how she jumped to take that bullet. Even now, staring up at him in broad daylight, she can't be sure that she would've done the same for him. That he would've done it for her.

But Gloria did. She pushed Otto off the roof and saved them all. Of course she left the scene of the crime, she's no sucker. And yet Ginny knows that she never would've left town without saying goodbye.

She gets dressed in last night's clothes behind the screen in the corner. Jack keeps talking to her, trying to get her back into bed, but she ignores him. Then she slips out of the room before anyone has a chance to stop her.

The concierge in Gloria's apartment building fixes Ginny with a penetrating look.

"And you said your name was . . . ?"

"Dugan. Ginny Dugan." She's seen the guy dozens of times, but never sober. He's a thin, reedy fellow with a mustache that overwhelms his pointed face, giving him the look of a man in an ill-fitting disguise. With the painkillers numbing her entire head, she can't be sure of her expression, but the suspicion in his eyes tells her she looks like a dubious character at best. "C'mon, you've seen me around, haven't you?"

"I really couldn't say." He looks down at his guest book.

Although her first impulse is to make a mad dash for the elevator, hurling curses, she swallows the anger and forces a sweet smile. She'll play the flapper darling for him, and maybe he'll buy her act. "Glo said I could crash anytime I liked." She pulls out a cigarette and lights it for show, making him flinch against the smoke. "Last night was a wild ride, darling. Let a girl get her beauty sleep and I'll tell you all about it."

He drops his eyes to the guest book again, turning a delicate shade of pink around the collar. After a while, he gives her a quick nod. "You're on the list."

Gloria never mentioned any kind of list. The concierge always rang her home phone to get her guests approved. But there's no time to think it over as the concierge tilts his head toward the elevator, so Ginny climbs into the gilded cage and crosses her fingers for smooth sailing.

When she arrives on the top floor, it's hard not to remember the last time she stepped through these polished doors, the elevator swinging shut like the lid of a coffin. The apartment is the same as Ginny remembers, except scrubbed clean with an extra degree of care. The smell of lemon disinfectant is masked by the heavy aroma of vanilla and peaches. Gloria's signature scent. An alligator leather suitcase stands by the door. No maids come out to greet her, but Ginny knows better than to announce her presence.

She creeps down the hall, the oil portraits staring down in judgment. The door to the guest room stands slightly ajar, a faint medicinal aroma wafting through the crack. Inside, the dust covers are off all the furniture, the hunting scene towering over the golden bed, and there, with her hair spilling over the pillows, lies Dottie.

Seconds drag like hours. Ginny feels her entire body going slack as she falls against the bed, trying to make sense of the scene unfolding in front of her.

Jack was right. Otto Sharp was never the Eagle.

It was always Gloria.

The bedside table is stacked with mottled glass bottles, medical labels peeling in faded print. There's a jar of Veronal powder that's been recently touched, the lid screwed half off, most of the grains gone from the container with only a small residue on the bottom. No telling how much she's given Dottie. Ginny presses an ear to her sister's chest just to check the heartbeat. She's still breathing. Tears trickle down numb cheeks and into the silk sheets as Ginny brings her arms around Dottie's body, relief flooding her mind until all that's left is the powdered rose smell of her sister's perfume.

"What . . ." Dottie stirs in her sleep, eyelashes fluttering over her cheeks. "Gin . . . What's happened?"

"Come on. Let's get you out of here."

"Need to get ready." Dottie groans, twisting against the sheets. "Showtime."

Ginny doesn't have the heart to tell Dottie she's missed her own premiere. That news can wait till later. She swings her sister's arm over her shoulder and tries to heave her out of bed. Dottie keeps muttering, tugging on Ginny's sleeve with limp fingers, slumping against her ear with fervent whispers.

"The trunk behind the wardrobe." She struggles to keep her eyes open. "Ginny, she doesn't know."

There's a commotion on the other end of the hall, and Ginny stiffens, listening, waiting.

Gloria appears in the open doorway.

She's transformed overnight, the makeup rubbed off, her costume swapped for a sober skirt suit. The flame of a pale brown birthmark licks her chin. Her platinum hair is tucked into a dove gray cloche. She doesn't seem in the least surprised to see Ginny.

"I knew you'd find her in the end. Well done, darling."

The room grows hot around Ginny. Her rage is dulled by the meds, but it's still there, kindling deep in the pit of her stomach until she can't look at Gloria for fear of lashing out.

"You."

"Now, no need for hysterics. I'm not here to stop you." Gloria tilts her head sideways, taking in the view. "Just thought I'd say goodbye in person. Make sure we didn't part on bad terms."

"Bad terms?" Ginny rises to her feet, trying to ignore the pain poking through the painkiller haze. *"Bad fucking terms?* You murdered my friend, Gloria. Kidnapped my sister, nearly had my partner killed—not to mention the whole case with Josephine and half of Harlem dying from heart attacks. And for what—all so you could get rich?"

"You make me sound like a real villain." Gloria examines her nails for a moment, then flicks her eyes toward Ginny. "If that's the case, why haven't you called the cops yet?"

"I have." Ginny swallows. "They'll be here any minute."

"We both know that's not true, but it can be. Phone's right there. Do it."

She's right. There's an ivory telephone mounted into the wall a few steps away. She could make the call in seconds.

Dottie slumps against her shoulder. Ginny tightens her grip around her sister and brings her upright, staggering under the weight. Gloria might deserve the chair for what she's done, but Ginny's first priority is getting Dottie to a hospital—and playing mind games will only make her lose time.

Gloria lets out a low whistle. "Thought so. You might play with the boys in law enforcement, but you'll never be one of them. You've got too much fire in you, but if you learn to see all the angles, learn which ones to play, then I see a bright future for you yet. Really, we're more alike than you might think."

Ginny takes a step forward, heaving Dottie along with her. The strain sends sweat running down her neck.

"I'm nothing like you. Now you'd better step aside."

Gloria obliges, twisting her body sideways as Ginny brings her sister across the threshold, limping down the hall toward the exit. It's almost like old times, Gloria's easy posture against the doorframe, her eyes lingering on Ginny's a second too long. No anger, no resistance. It's difficult to reconcile this cool young woman with the cruel killer she's been all this time. Even knowing the full truth, Ginny can't stop thinking of the taste of Gloria's lips that night in Long Island, can't help longing to return to that feeling.

Gloria seems to sense this, because her clear voice follows Ginny through the hall. "So you really feel nothing for me now?"

"How can I," Ginny's voice comes out choked as she whirls around to face her, "now that I know what you've done? You were right when you said you didn't care a thing for me, Gloria. Not if you'd do this to my sister. My own *sister*—"

"I needed protection!" The perfect front slips just a fraction, and she leans against the wall. "You were getting too close to the truth. I had to stall you for a few more days, to set everything in motion for the premiere. It tore me apart to do it. I tried to distract you at first, you know—thought that actor might do the trick. Remember him?"

The guy with the British accent, appearing out of thin air as soon as Ginny came out of her room that night. She remembers, all right.

"But then you kept asking questions. It looked like you suspected Sharp, but I had to be sure. So I called your sister, and I've kept her here since then. But Dottie was never in any danger. Worst case, she got the best beauty sleep of her life—and trust me, she needed it."

Ginny slams a palm against the elevator button. A small hope rises at the back of her mind, as Dottie's words resurface through the haze. Maybe she's right, and Gloria doesn't know about the stash. If this is all pure coincidence, then there's still time to destroy the drugs for good.

Dottie's eyes are open at last, but her face remains blank as a wall, those perfect features undistorted by a single emotion.

"Am I supposed to say thank you?" says Ginny.

"Not for that. But I—" Gloria steps closer, and Ginny recoils against the elevator. "I've done my best. Made sure Charlie would never bother you again. That counts for something, doesn't it?"

Charlie. The bandaged head, the scars rucking up the side of his face. Well, that's one sin off her conscience.

"You're talking about settling the score? Fine." Ginny shifts to accommodate Dottie's weight. "Why don't you hand over the negatives to Dottie's pictures, and then we're even."

Gloria's eyes go wide. She adjusts her hat, straightens her suit. She seems torn between concealment and confession.

"I would if I could. That was—" She hesitates. "That was Otto's deal, Ginny. I had nothing to do with it. He had his transparent mirror, his rich patrons, his side business with the nudes. I only had the powder, and now the last of that's gone—"

There's something she's holding back, but it's buried too deep for Ginny to retrieve. She turns away.

"You can tell all that to the cops. I'm done believing you, Gloria. It's over."

The elevator clicks open. Ginny leads her sister inside, but Gloria jams a heel against the open door, forcing the elevator boy to look up in surprise.

"You won't turn me in, Ginny." Gloria's breath is labored now, a glimmer of sincerity underneath the artifice. "I'm leaving town, and you'll make sure the case dies, won't you? Promise you won't come after me?"

Her face is so open in that moment, vulnerable as a child's. Ginny drinks in the sight of her, those diamond eyes flashing in the weak morning light, lips painted a perfect crimson, the same shade they'd shared that delirious night. A face she won't forget anytime soon.

In another life, she'd bring her close into a deep kiss and mold her body against the gray linen. She'd squeeze her hand and promise to never let go. They'd dye each other's hair, spend the night on a Pullman sleeper on a fast track out of town. Start a new life somewhere out west, where past histories are shrugged off like old clothes, discarded into the depths of the Pacific.

A week ago, she might've said yes to everything. But that good-time kid is dead, and there's no going back.

So she kicks Gloria's heel out of the elevator door and flashes her a big, sad smile.

"You know I can't promise you that."

The doors swing shut, and they plummet down in that golden cage, leaving Gloria alone in her tower high above the park.

CHAPTER TWENTY-SIX

O n Sunday, Ginny's sitting on the floor of her sister's bedroom with the door locked from the inside. Dottie's in bed reading through the same letter over and over again, her lips forming soundless syllables, lashes moving up and down with the text. Ginny braids the strands of the carpet, studies her chipped nail polish, stares out the window, where the sun is setting in violent orange. She's not supposed to say a word until Dottie's finished, but the tension in the room builds until she can't take it any longer.

"Well?"

Dottie shakes her head, looks up from the letter. Although the Veronal is long out of her system, occasionally an absent expression crosses her face, like she's still splitting her time between reality and dreamland. She's been better since they destroyed the stash last night. Joining hands with Ruby and Josephine as they flung the trunk into the river, then watched the water swallowing it whole as it sunk to the bottom. Josephine whispering about Billy's upcoming release from the station, his name as good as cleared by a confession from the stagehands. Hector Tallman pulled some kind of game on them, shaking down each guy separately until they spilled the whole story, pointing fingers at Otto Sharp as the head of the operation. Not a word about Gloria. Ginny knows she shouldn't be surprised at this point.

Now, Dottie's expression is oddly empty as she beckons for Ginny to join her in bed.

There are two piles on her quilted coverlet, with the ivory-handled letter opener and brown paper wrapping cast off to her bedside table. The first is a long, rambling letter written in Charlie Darby's sloping cursive. The second is a stack of glass plate negatives.

"It doesn't make any sense," says Dottie. "These came in the same package. No date. No return address. Do you think some-body's messing with me?"

Ginny holds up one of the plates to the waning light. It's an exact copy of Dottie's nude shot in stark black and white, the shadows deeper and more sinister. She goes through a few others, which show the same scene from different angles, Dottie tilting her chin left and right, her expression strangely lopsided. Without the soft-ened glamour of the prints, Dottie looks absolutely lifeless.

Dottie still hasn't told her the whole story about that night. She mentioned drinks with Otto Sharp and some of the girls, then waking up hours later in a stranger's bed to the sound of stage-hands laughing in the next room. They showed her the pictures. She called Charlie to pick her up. That's all she's shared so far, and Ginny knows better than to press for more. Some memories are better off tucked away in the dark until you can face them without flinching. They resurface again and again, and each time you might be gutted all over again, but eventually it gets better. Eventually, you can move on. Until then, Ginny will stand by her sister's side and try to be the kind of woman who deserves her trust.

She returns the plate to its pile, wipes her hands on the coverlet. She has a sudden, intense urge to take a shower.

"What does the letter say?"

Dottie covers her eyes. "Charlie's back in Kansas."

"What?"

"I don't know what to make of it. He starts by saying he's had some sort of crisis, that he doesn't want to live in this city anymore. That we shouldn't get married. I can understand that, maybe he had a change of heart, but then he writes such awful things—" Dottie turns the letter over to the other side, points to a line. Tears brim in the corners of her eyes, but she swipes them away with an angry palm. "Here, he says he's slept with at least a dozen women since we got engaged. That he can remember! How is that even possible?"

Ginny scans the rest of the letter, trying to make sense of everything. She's not surprised by the numbers, but the honesty is off-putting, oddly out of character for Charlie. His entire identity hinges on keeping the dirt concealed, every gesture carefully calculated to charm. He can lose his job and his apartment, get stuck with a year's worth of gambling debts, fuck around town as much as he likes, but when it comes to Dottie, he would always clean up like a gent. Give her a smile, a kiss, a sweet word to send her heart fluttering.

Of course, now Ginny knows why. With his finances in shambles, he needed somebody to pull him out of his debts, slap some respectability onto the Darby name while she's at it. Dottie stands to inherit most of the family money in the long run, and her trust fund unlocks as soon as she's married. Charlie would be in the clear.

This letter kills any chance of that. It's self-sabotage. Then she remembers Gloria's words. Maybe this is what she meant when she said Charlie would never bother them again. And with the plates in the same package, it looks like she's trying to say sorry the only way she can.

Dottie keeps listing off Charlie's many crimes on her fingers, her eyes widening with hurt and surprise.

"—gambling, Ginny. He says it's an addiction. Not to mention all the drinking— I never thought he was a drunk, did you? He didn't look like one. Always so careful— Even that night at Gloria's, remember how he wouldn't drive until he got sober? Oh, Ginny. I should've believed you when you told me about him. All this time, I let him play me for a fool. How could I let him do this to me?"

They've done a lot of talking these past few days. Ginny's walked her through the whole sordid affair, but Dottie still struggles to reconcile her version of Charlie with the truth. After everything she's been through, a part of her still clings to the idea of her dashing, gentlemanly fiancé, the man who would've shielded her from the darkness she's had to endure. This letter might help, but it'll be a while before she can fully accept the truth. Ginny wraps her sister in a hug, like they're kids again, and Dottie's crying over some other boy who doesn't deserve her.

"I'm so sorry, Dot." She doesn't say it's true. Doesn't say he deserves all the hell he gets for his transgressions. Doesn't tell her she can do much better than that bastard anyway. Instead, she just rocks her side to side, breathing in the heady scent of her sister's rose perfume and wishing for a future where they can both get some shot at happiness, without all the pain that comes along with it.

Monday morning after the release of the new issue is a special kind of calm: the office half-empty, the writers nursing hangovers from the weekend's shindigs, fresh issues winking from every desk. Light streams into Mr. Quirk's office in long rectangles through the blinds, landing on Ginny's arms like tiger stripes as she listens to his big pitch.

The latest *New York Tattle* is opened to the first page on the desk in front of him, Ginny's crooked high school yearbook smile beaming beneath a headline that reads *Society Scandal: Dugan Heiress Caught in Broadway Shootout*. Ginny's already read the piece to Dottie over breakfast, raising her voice to dramatic heights while her sister giggled behind a slim slice of toast. If she's being honest, the content of the article didn't matter now that she could hear her sister's laugh again. That laugh had hitched when some of the visiting showgirls dropped Charlie's name into a conversation by accident, staring at Dottie's bare ring finger. But then she'd just shrug, and the conversation would move on.

The *Tattle* version of Ginny is your typical modern girl elevated to scandalous proportions: apparently, she snuck backstage to surprise the chorus girls with a bottle of bootleg, only to be summoned to the roof by a group of roughnecks who threatened to fling her into the sky if she refused to give up her supplier. There's plenty of witty dialogue (including a placement of Kissproof lipstick she never endorsed; they must've found it in her bag), but not a single lick of truth.

Mr. Quirk keeps shaking his head at the magazine, as though his disapproval is enough to wipe the story out of existence.

"I wanted you to know that I got in touch with the editor as soon as I saw that scandalous piece in his magazine. It's a disgrace, if you ask me, the drivel that passes for journalism these days!"

"If only those other editors had your eye for morals, sir."

Ginny swings her legs beneath the desk as her boss nods in fervent conviction. Quirk isn't half as shocked as he might pretend. The man thrives on scandal. She can bet his telephone's been ringing off the hook since the story was published, and the healthy flush on his face betrays his excitement.

"Exactly, Ginny. Thank you. Not many people share my moral views while also producing high-quality work, and you seem to bring together these two elements with quite a bit of style."

He fumbles through the words this time, busying himself with a sheaf of papers on his desk. It's funny to hear him say these things about her, because the woman he's describing doesn't exist.

She never did, not even when her fingers went raw against the keys into the late hours as night fell outside the newsroom windows. She was never much of a writer. Too jittery in her chair, pulled in so many directions, compelled to explore the great outside, follow a pair of fashionable pumps, anything, anything—

As for morals, she never cared much for those either.

Still, she no longer sees any reason to upset the old man.

"Thank you, Mr. Quirk. It means a lot."

And it does, she supposes. To some other girl, this conversation is a road paved with pure gold.

"I've read through that article you submitted." He clears his throat. "Some things would need changing. You get so close to these girls, it's almost uncomfortable. What was it about that one showgirl? Mazie?"

"She's lonely. Desperate for approval, so she grasps for any piece of gossip she can get and treats it like currency." And she sells pep powder like it's her calling, that smile never dipping a single degree.

"It's too intimate. It makes our readers feel guilty, like they should be helping this young woman, even though they're unable. Then there was that piece about the Italian girl that I'd ask you to cut out. We don't like any nudity in our magazine."

Right, too many descriptions of healthy female bodies might kill sales on all those diet pills. Should've seen that one coming.

"And my final comment. I was excited about your review of Gloria Gardner, although—well, in light of recent events, we might have to tone this down to avoid any controversy. But there was one metaphor I didn't quite understand. When she's standing with the lilies in her hands—"

"Lady Liberty on fire."

"That's awfully un-American. What might you mean by that?"

Ginny turns her eyes toward the window. The cops stormed Gloria's apartment soon after she called them from the hospital, watching nurses taking Dottie's vitals, her sister trying for polite conversation despite her condition. The place was empty. It's been almost a week, but they haven't caught her yet. She's out there somewhere, and Ginny still doesn't know how to feel about it.

"What might you mean by that, Ginny?" he repeats.

That she blasted through this city's underworld and left it in flames. That she brought together the most refined delights and the lowest depths of depravity and packaged them as a dream. That nothing will ever be the same.

"I don't quite recall, Mr. Quirk." She smiles. "Just some silly thing."

"Good, good." He dashes the line with obvious relief. "Other than that, I thought it was an insightful piece. It shows great promise. And based on your first article published in the magazine, I can say I look forward to seeing how you progress. As a staff writer with *Photoplay* magazine, effective immediately."

Shoulders straightened at that last phrase, he gives her a respectful nod. Waiting. For excitement or gratitude, she can't really tell, but what follows doesn't satisfy him one bit.

"Afraid you'll have to make that my last article for the magazine, Mr. Quirk. First and last, eh? It's got a ring to it."

His posture stiffens, and he searches the office with narrowed eyes, as though trying to locate the reason for her sudden change of heart.

"But Ginny, isn't this what you wanted?" He flips through the pages. "Perhaps I underestimated you when you first came in—but now I can see you've had it all this time."

Ginny rises, the chair creaking against the floor. She feels weightless, and it's not just the afterglow of those heavy pain-killers she's been taking since they checked her out of the hospital. The sensation pulls at her like a helium-filled balloon attached to the top of her head, until she can swear that her feet will lift off the ground, and she will float right out the window.

Freedom. That's what it is, right there.

"Don't you worry about me, Mr. Quirk." On impulse, she steps forward and grabs his hand for a firm shake. "I've learned a lot here, but I'm ready to move on. Take care, now."

At the door, she hears the heavy movement of his body as he rises, leaning forward on his desk.

"Is it *The Times*? *The Enquirer*?" Her silence seems to dial up the intensity of his frustration. "Don't tell me *New York Tattle* got you! I can—"

"Sure," she calls. "Something like that."

Since it's her last day, she makes sure to take her sweet time in the newsroom. There's a dreamy quality to the place, dust floating in gold flecks of sun, the clean look of freshly laundered clothes, manicures renewed over the weekend, click of nails on keys, heels on floorboards. The neat rhythm that brings every issue into existence, each person an inevitable cog inside the big machine.

The celebrity machine puts up a dramatic front, but underneath it's a business like any other. Maybe that was her problem from the start. Dumping the contents of her drawer into a cardboard box, Ginny remembers Gloria's final words. You have to see the angles, know which ones to play. That's how you win, she said.

Two years of her life, crammed into a tiny box. None of it is worth salvaging: not the discarded drafts of old advice columns, not the scribbled notes or the bits of candy wrappers.

With the box under her arm, more out of some sense of ceremony than any practical purpose, she makes the rounds. Checking in with Betty in the accounting department, dipping into the chattering booth to see the telephone girls. Stopping by each writer's desk to wish them well. She catches the famed trio of staff writers at their desks, looking slightly hungover with their eyes shaded against the light.

Prescott Folmsbee steps in front of her, running a hand through his dark waves.

"Heard you were leaving."

Ginny hoists her box under the other arm. She's never exchanged more than a handful of words with these people, and yet here they are, scrunching up their faces in identical distress.

"You heard right."

"Well, um," he stares down at his feet, past the shocking indigo scarf on his neck. She wonders if he's going to apologize for that night at the Eighty-Three, but then he looks back up, a dazzling smile replacing the frown. "Congrats on getting out of this hellhole. Who got you in the end? *The Times*?"

"It won't be *The Times*," Paul mutters, adjusting his glasses. Caroline muffles a laugh behind a dainty palm. Looking at the three of them, swapping ridiculous jokes like children, Ginny wonders why she ever thought this was a dream worth chasing. She's got nothing in common with these people, their snide jabs, their superficial judgments of everyone they ever meet.

So she hikes a shoulder and turns to leave.

"Don't worry," she calls over her shoulder. "It's not the kind of place you'd like to be."

There's a new girl at the front desk now, a tiny thing in an apple-green dress. Ginny presses a finger against Mary's bracelet as she passes, saying a silent goodbye to all their good times here. She wonders if that was as good as it would get. The two of them, always caught up in their upward climb, reaching for the stars when they had everything they needed in their grasp.

The new girl chases Ginny down the steps, breaking through her reverie.

"Ginny Dugan?"

She fumbles in her pockets, then returns to the desk, rummaging through the drawers before emerging with a small green envelope.

"This came for you in the morning. Marked urgent. It doesn't say who sent it."

As Ginny walks out the door, the old thrum of her heart picks up, and she rips through the letter as soon as she rounds the corner.

It's typed, without a name at the bottom. Without a return address. Because she knows who sent it, of course. She knows it all.

> Dear Ginny—
>
> I hope you got my package.
>
> So many things I should've told you, and nothing that could've changed the way it all played out.
>
> Next time we meet, I'll be somebody else. You might say I'm far from home, but I've never had a home to speak of, so it suits me just fine.
>
> Just know this: beyond all the lies, it was real. We were real.
>
> You're in my thoughts forever, darling.
>
> Until we meet again.

That's all there is. She flips the letter over several times, trying to find something, anything. A clue. It makes her angry, the brevity of it, the irresponsible stroke against the keys.

She pictures Gloria out west for some reason, sunglasses wrapped around her head, a cocktail resting by her side as she types out this message. The carefree glisten of those jeweled eyes. Returning to the beach after posting it, putting the events out of her head like last month's magazine.

It's crazy, how easily she's riled up by this message. Part of her wants to march over to the station, smack the letter on Officer Tallman's desk. Tell him everything she knows about the fallen star. Lead the hunt, track her down, and make her answer for everything. For Mary.

And then there's the other part that can't stop thinking about her laugh.

But it's different this time. Like a fist curling inside her, a new energy rising through her body until her hands are shaking around the pale green letter. And then she's on the streetcar, watching the *Photoplay* office grow small as the vehicle jangles uptown, back to Harlem.

She enters their new office, slamming the door behind her. It's a shabby place in a brownstone just off Lenox, with letters peeling off the front door and neighbors that talk too loudly. But the money from Josephine's case will hold them over for a year's rent at least, and there's a bedroom in the back that's good enough for Ginny.

She wonders if Jack's thinking what she's thinking. Awfully convenient to have a spare bedroom on the premises. Who knows what might happen one of these late nights in the office. Jack never talks about it, and he makes sure to leave promptly at the end of the day with a formal goodbye. But still. Who knows.

"It's official." Jack points to a badge on her desk, a freshly laminated card with her name on it.

Ginny Dugan, Private Investigator.

She throws him a smile and comes over to where he's sitting, slamming the telegram onto his desk.

"I think we've already given her enough of a head start. What do you say?"

"I say we'd better get moving."

A sharp ray of sun pierces through the small windows, catching the room on fire for one sudden, divine moment. The small reading lamps glow emerald. Jack's profile is silhouetted in sharp shadows, dust motes floating behind him like so many flakes of snow. Ginny wonders if this is the glamour she's been seeking all this time. The quiet kind, tucked away from prying eyes in rickety brownstones, flashing in Jack's green eyes when he's listening to her, really listening, above the din of the traffic and the shouts of the street vendors.

This was always the plan; she knows it now. Even as she watched her sister from behind the velvet curtains in Cherryvale, somewhere deep inside she knew her place was in the shadows. So she'll keep on fighting, for people like Mary, chasing impossible dreams against all odds. Like Dottie, facing off against her attackers with a dancer's steely grace. And Josephine, standing up for what's right even when the world is all wrong.

Today's victory might be a line in the sand, waiting to be swept away by the next wave of darkness tomorrow, but when that happens, Ginny will be ready.

It's not the kind of work that will bring her glory, but it was never glory she needed, not really.

Jack was right. You can't bring down all the evil in the world.

But Ginny will be damned if she doesn't try.

ACKNOWLEDGEMENTS

E ndless thanks to my editor, Luisa Smith, and the incredible team at Mysterious Press for guiding this story out of the shadows. To my agent, Chris Bucci—thank you for fighting the good fight and believing in these words from day one. Layne Fargo and Halley Sutton, my Pitch Wars mentors, you saw the spark before anyone else and kept me going when I almost gave up. To my writing friends—too many to name, but special thanks to Lyz Mancini, Sara Hashem, and Diba Bijari—for your sharp insights, patience in reading through countless drafts, and unwavering support. To my Toronto friends—thanks for listening to my endless rants and keeping me sane. To my family for being the best support system, with a special shoutout to my mom, for raising me on a steady diet of Agatha Christie and true crime. You're the reason I consume and now produce so many words. And finally, to you, reader—thanks for taking a chance on these pages. I'll catch you in the next one.

ABOUT THE AUTHOR

Olesya Lyuzna is a Toronto writer with one fatal flaw: she can't resist a good mystery. When she's away from her typewriter, you'll find her hosting Pre-Code movie nights and scouring the archives for unsolved crimes. Find her on Instagram at @olesyaisonline.